D0605415

TWIN ROCKS

Center Point
Large Print

Also by Wayne D. Overholser and available from Center Point Large Print:

Gunlock

**This Large Print Book carries the
Seal of Approval of N.A.V.H.**

TWIN ROCKS

A Western Duo

WAYNE D. OVERHOLSER

CENTER POINT LARGE PRINT
THORNDIKE, MAINE

This Center Point Large Print edition is published
in the year 2014 in conjunction with
Golden West Literary Agency.

"Trouble in Gold Plume" first appeared under the title
"Six-Gun Fiesta" in *Action Stories* (Fall, 47). Copyright ©
1947 by Fiction House, Inc. Copyright © renewed 1975 by
Wayne D. Overholser. Copyright © 2005 by the Estate of
Wayne D. Overholser for restored material.

An earlier version of "Twin Rocks" first appeared under
the title "Hunter's Moon" by Dan J. Stevens in a double
paperback book from Ace Publishing. Copyright © 1973 by
Wayne D. Overholser. Copyright © 2005 by the Estate of
Wayne D. Overholser for restored material.

The text of this Large Print edition is unabridged.
In other aspects, this book may vary from the original edition.
Printed in the United States of America on permanent paper.
Set in 16-point Times New Roman type.

ISBN: 978-1-62899-199-4

Library of Congress Cataloging-in-Publication Data

Overholser, Wayne D., 1906–1996.
[Trouble at Gold Plume]
Twin rocks : a western duo / Wayne D. Overholser.
pages cm
Summary: "Two western stories about men who ride into town with the
odds stacked against them, but determined to right wrongs"—Provided
by publisher.
ISBN 978-1-62899-199-4 (library binding : alk. paper)
1. Western stories. 2. Large type books.
   I. Overholser, Wayne D., 1906–1996. Twin rocks. II. Title.
PS3529.V33T76 2014
813′.54—dc23

2014019474

Table of Contents

TROUBLE AT GOLD PLUME

I

It had been a long chase and so far a futile one, but Jim Harrigan had every reason to believe that the end was in sight. He pulled up his gaunted roan saddler atop Star Mountain Pass, his gaze sweeping the new mining camp of Gold Plume that lay below him, squeezed thin by high granite cliffs hugging the creek. Somewhere in that scattering of frame buildings, log cabins, and tents would be Rush Kane, the man Jim had trailed across the Continental Divide from Dodge City.

Answers to Jim's questions in Pueblo told him Kane had been there less than a week before. Rush Kane, gambler, was not one who could easily be mistaken for another. He had crossed Marshal Pass, paused in Gunnison, and gone on to Ouray. Gradually Jim had closed the gap, and now, if his calculations were right, Kane had ridden into Gold Plume last night.

The promise of winter was in the thin air here on the pass, and Jim did not pause long. He turned his roan down the twisting trail that lay like a looped ribbon against the mountainside, passed a slow-moving line of burros carrying coal to the mining camp, and came into the aspens, aflame now with the gold and orange of fall. But the beauty of this wild land held no lure at that moment for Jim

Harrigan was thinking of the job that lay before him, and of his own chances that were, at best, slim. Gold Plume was Duke Madden's town, and Madden would give Kane the help he needed.

Then he was down, the trail cutting across an open park toward the camp. Log ranch buildings lay hard against the cliff, and below him a line of haystacks bulked high along the creek. Jim was surprised because the ranch had been hidden from the trail by overhanging rock, but he was more surprised by the drama that was being enacted here. A girl stood facing a half circle of mounted men, a Winchester in her hands, her voice crisp as she said: "The answer's no, Burke."

"You're smart, ma'am," a familiar voice was saying, "smart enough to see the butter on your bread."

"We'll hold the hay," the girl said firmly.

"You'd better take Madden's offer," the man pressed. "Ten dollars a ton is better'n winding up with nothing."

"Dad said you were bad enough to steal anything!" the girl cried.

"He was a little hard on us." The man laughed softly. "We wouldn't steal the hay. We'd just borrow it. No use packing it in when we've got some right under our nose."

"Still playing the old game, ain't you, Boomer?" Jim asked.

The man wheeled, hands dipping for gun butts,

and falling away when the girl said flatly: "I'll kill the first man who draws his iron."

A careful alertness came into Boomer Burke's face. He was a wide man with squeezed features that made him look as if the top of his head had been hammered down toward his feet, leaving his chin where it was. Licking his lips, he turned his gaze back to the girl. "You can put your rifle down, ma'am. Jim Harrigan don't need a woman's help."

Jim leaned forward, hands resting before him, a loose lank man who belonged in the saddle. The dark leather-brown of his cheeks and his sun-bleached blue eyes were evidence that he had spent most of his waking hours where the sun and the wind could touch him. He laughed silently now, a kind of mirth that jarred Boomer Burke and made him shift uneasily in his saddle.

"I've met up with Boomer before," Jim said contemptuously. "He won't pull a gun on me. Not when I'm facing him."

Jim's tongue was a knife ripping skin from Burke's body. His men looked at him as if expecting swift and violent action, but the cool courage that it took to face Jim Harrigan wasn't in him. He said mildly: "I don't see your badge, Jim."

"I'm a private citizen, Boomer."

"Then what in hell are you doing here?"

"Looking at the scenery."

Burke's shrill laugh was a strange sound coming from such a bulky-bodied man. "You've got plenty to see around here." He rubbed a pimply nose. "Harrigan, you wouldn't cross the street to see the purtiest sunset this side of hell. Now what are you doing here?"

"I hear Gold Plume's got five thousand men who've showed up in the last six months. Wouldn't be surprising if another rode in."

"That ain't it, neither." Burke wagged his great head. "You wouldn't know a chunk of gold ore if you saw one. Me and Duke get our fun relieving the other fellow of his *dinero*. You get yours playing bloodhound. Who are you after?"

"Maybe you. Maybe Duke." Jim shrugged. "Still working for Duke, are you?"

"Sure. It's Duke's town." Burke motioned to the girl. "Only some don't know it."

"But Duke's got ways of persuading folks. Even pretty girls."

"That's right." Burke's grin was a wicked tightening of lips against yellow teeth. "If you're after me or Duke, you've got a chore."

Jim built a smoke, his mind making a quick study of this development. Rush Kane had worked for Madden in the Montana gold camps when Jim thought Kane was a square shooter. Now Burke would take word to Madden that Jim Harrigan was in camp and Kane would hear. He'd guess why Jim had come, and he'd ride on, or Madden would ride him out until the sign was right for Jim's removal.

12

"Might be quite a chore at that." Jim thumbed a match into flame and held it to his cigarette. He flipped the charred stick away, his eyes blue slits. "You tell Duke, Boomer. I'll be looking him up pretty soon."

It was a plain raw challenge, and there wasn't an ounce of bluff in Jim Harrigan. Burke, knowing that, said: "I'll tell him. Belle, you'd better think over what I said." He wheeled his horse toward town, gray dust boiling behind him, his men lining out along the trail.

"I'm Jim Harrigan." Jim raised his hat. "Didn't look like they were shoving you around any, but I couldn't keep my nose out of it."

She held out a brown firm hand that was swallowed by his big one. "I'm Belle Calvert. I'm afraid I was in for more shoving around than you figured. It's a good thing for me you stuck your nose into it."

She was small and slim and straight with black hair and black eyes and a determined chin. To Jim Harrigan, with the long ride and lonely campfires behind him, she made a lovely and distracting picture, the fulfillment of an old and cherished dream.

"I'm glad I was some help," he said.

She tried to smile, and he saw she was close to crying. "I guess you're a rip-roarer from Bitter Creek the way Burke rode off."

"I shave with a Bowie knife and I cut my teeth

13

on a stick of Giant powder." He winked. "What was the ruckus about, ma'am?"

"Duke Madden wants my hay for any song he decides to sing," she said sourly. "Six months ago Rocking C was one of the biggest spreads in the San Juan. Then they made the strike and miners came in like locusts. They've stolen our beef, killed my father, and I can't pay enough to keep hands."

"I've got an idea the tune Duke would sing," Jim said dryly.

"Get down and rest your saddle," Belle invited. "You won't find a bed in town, and you'll be lucky to get a meal."

"Thanks, but I guess I'd better mosey on." He lifted his reins. "If you have any more trouble with Madden or Burke, let me know."

"I will," she promised. "If you can't find accommodations in town, come back."

"Thanks," he said again, and, raising his hat to her, rode away.

It was after noon when Jim rode into Gold Plume. Sunlight was sharp upon the town, and the air, caught between the high cliffs, was still and hot and gray with the dust that was constantly being churned into motion by burros and men. The dirty turbulent creek ran with swift abandon along the east cliff, and between it and the west wall lay the town, two long lines of buildings and tents threaded by the dusty street.

Gold Plume made no pretensions of dignity or permanence. There was no brick, no stone, no paint. It was a town of pine box houses and tents and rectangles of four planks claiming a building site, a circus with 100 side shows. Stores and offices with canvas tops. Log foundations. Houses with Leadville fronts. Plank walks or dusty paths piled with lumber. Canned goods. Kegs of beer. Here in Gold Plume 1,000 men preyed upon another 1,000 who blasted gold from a stubborn earth. Tinhorns. Tinseled women, flaunting themselves and their merchandise. Barkers chanting their persuasive spiel: "Come in, gentlemen, to the Domino where the games are square and the girls are beautiful!" This was Gold Plume, wild and tough and bawdy. This was Gold Plume, Duke Madden's town.

Jim racked his horse and, ducking around a pile of lumber, stepped into a canvas-topped restaurant. Every stool along the pine counter was occupied, and Jim took his place at the end of the line of waiting miners, long experience in boom towns having built a patience that was not natural in him. Outside, a couple of riders were pushing a dozen small steers through the burros and horses, cursing and being cursed. Jim, looking out, saw with some surprise that the steers carried the Rocking C brand.

The line moved up and presently Jim had a stool. "Steak, fried potatoes, and coffee," he said.

As he ate, he thought about Belle Calvert's steers. Two-year-olds, he judged. With the amount of hay he had seen below the Rocking C ranch house, it struck him that it was a fool thing to be selling the steers now. Another six months would put weight on them, but the girl had impressed him as one who knew her business.

Jim had a slab of peach pie. He ate slowly, savoring the sweetness, the long trail and hot days giving him an appetite for it. When he was done, he made way for a miner, and asked: "How much?"

"Five dollars," the aproned man said.

Scowl lines marked Jim's forehead. "Ain't that a mite high?"

"Good meal, wasn't it?"

"Hell, yes, but five dollars . . ."

"You making trouble?"

"I'll pay, and get my next meal somewhere else." Jim slammed the money on the counter. "You're a damned thief, mister."

A miner elbowed Jim's ribs. "Shut up, friend."

The restaurant man scooped up the money. "Go somewhere else and be damned. I don't want your business. I've got plenty."

Jim went out into the sunlight, temper knotting his nerves. This, he guessed, would be Duke Madden's work. It surprised him because Madden had never been more than a sharp operator of gambling schemes.

"You pay high prices for everything in this

camp." The miner who had elbowed Jim in the restaurant stood beside him. "If you squawk too loud, you're likely to come up in the creek with a slug in your head."

"Madden?"

"Him and Boomer Burke and their wolf pack," the miner said bitterly. "They're squeezing the camp dry. Ain't enough gold on the creek to pay the kind of prices they ask."

"Madden's a gambler. What's he got to do with the price of a meal?"

"He's organized the businessmen. Every new man who comes in has to satisfy Madden or he don't get started."

"And if they don't stick with the price agreement, they'll get a slug in the back?"

"That's right." The miner pinned gray eyes on Jim. "You knew Madden?"

Jim nodded. "In Montana. He won't last long here."

"Looks plumb permanent now. The only way to beat him is with a vigilante organization, but we haven't got a man who can run one."

Jim told himself that Duke Madden was the problem of the men who had their stakes here, that it was nothing to him one way or another. He said—"You'll find your man when you get tired enough of Madden."—and turned away.

"Hold on." The miner fell into step with Jim and held out his hand. "I'm Ira Raeder. Got the

Blue Bonnet Mine up the gulch that ought to make me rich and won't as long as Duke Madden calls the turn."

Jim shook Raeder's hand and gave him his name. He liked the man. Raeder's grip was firm and his eyes had a way of meeting Jim's squarely.

"It'll catch up with Madden," Jim said.

"Not until it's too late for the rest of us. Harrigan, you look tough enough to do this job. Say the word and I'll get a dozen miners together tonight that we can trust. We'll have to know more about you, but I think you'll do. I don't often go wrong on a man."

Jim shook his head. "I'm no miner, and this camp don't make any difference to me. When I do the job I came here to do, I'll drift."

"We'll pay you," Raeder urged.

"No, thanks."

They walked in silence for a time, Jim's eyes raking the street for Rush Kane, Raeder eyeing Jim as if cudgeling his mind for something that would win the tall man over. As they came to the log butcher shop crowding the plank walk, Jim saw the Rocking C steers held in a pole corral along the creek. The two riders who had delivered the beef were inside, one a tiny bowlegged man with frosty green eyes and a deep-lined face, the other a club-footed cowboy who was backing away from the counter and trying to pull the little rider with him.

"Another Madden job," Raeder breathed. "The little gent is Half Pint Ord, the other one Limpy Sanders. Ord came into this country with Sam Calvert ten years ago."

The butcher behind the bar was one of the biggest men Jim had ever seen, tall and heavy-boned and meaty. He was laughing now, great head thrown back, little red-flecked eyes almost lidded shut. He motioned to a pile of gold eagles. "Take it and drift, Ord. That's the price Madden says to pay, and, by hell, that's what we will pay."

Ord shook free of Sander's grip. "You offered Belle a hundred dollars a head. Now you're trying to pay half of that."

"Madden cut the price," the butcher said blandly.

"Come on," Sanders begged, pulling at Ord again.

"You're as big a thief as Madden!" Ord bellowed.

"Thief am I?" the butcher rumbled, and moved ponderously around the pine counter like a heavy locomotive going into a hard pull. "I don't take that off nobody, including runts and cripples."

"Stand pat!" Ord called, and grabbed his gun.

The butcher moved with surprising speed for a man of his size. His right hand smashed downward across Ord's frail wrist as his left hand clubbed him on the side of the head. The little cowboy went down into a still, twisted pile.

The temper that had been in Jim Harrigan since he had clashed with Boomer Burke broke now. Forgetting that this was none of his business, he stepped into the butcher shop, gun palmed.

"That'll be enough, mister," Jim said flatly.

The butcher had started toward Limpy Sanders who was backed against the wall. Now he came to a flat-footed stop. He put his gaze on Jim, rage staining his face and slowly spreading to the back of his neck. "Why are you horning in?" he demanded.

"Makes you no never mind why I'm in. If you've killed that cowhand, I'll see you hang. If you made a deal for one hundred dollars a head, you'll keep it."

"You're wrong, friend." Crooked snags of teeth showed in a wicked grin. "Mebbe you don't know that Duke Madden sets the prices and we pay 'em. If you've got an argument, go over to the Domino."

"You owe twelve hundred." Jim nodded at Sanders. "That right?"

"That's it."

"Pay him." Jim motioned to the butcher.

"Go to hell," the giant bellowed.

"I'll give you ten seconds. Got a watch, Raeder?"

"You bet I have," Raeder said exultantly.

"Start timing," Jim said coldly. "If you haven't showed that *dinero* when the time's up, you'll have a hole in your guts."

The butcher rumbled a defiant oath, gaze leaping from Raeder to Jim and back. Then he broke, bravado seeping out of him like wheat pouring from a cut sack. He counted out another $600 and handed it to Sanders.

"Give him the other stack," Jim ordered.

Still cursing, the man obeyed. Ord was sitting up now, rubbing his head.

"Help him on his horse." Jim nodded at Sanders. When the Rocking C men had gone, he slid his gun into leather. "If you want a fair draw . . ."

"Not me," the butcher snarled, "and you'll wish to hell you'd kept your nose clean."

"He's got a bad habit of making them kind of mistakes, Si," Boomer Burke said from the street. "I just wondered how long it would take you to kick up a fracas, Jim, and damned if you didn't fool me. You done it sooner than I figgered."

Slowly Jim made his turn. Burke stood in the doorway, a gun in his hand, malicious enjoyment showing on his wide face.

"I'm pretty fast, Boomer," Jim said.

"Not fast enough to make a play good," Burke said. "Duke wants to see you. Come on."

II

Duke Madden's Domino was a long hall with a carved mahogany bar running along one side, keno tables, roulette wheels, and other gambling games in a large back room. Here was Gold Plume's one bit of glamour. Chandeliers glittered overhead. Painted women filtered through the crowd. A piano against the wall separating the gambling room from the saloon was making a faintly musical racket under the fingers of a stooped, chalk-faced man.

Burke had holstered his gun. He said: "I've got a Derringer in my pocket that makes a hell of a hole in a man's back, Jim. Don't make a wrong move."

"I like my back the way it is," Jim murmured.

"Left," Burke ordered. "Up the stairs."

Duke Madden was doing all right, Jim saw, and it puzzled him. Madden had been one of the small fry in the Montana camps where Jim had known him, but there was no doubt about him being top rooster here. Even now in what should be the slack time of day the Domino was crowded.

Jim climbed the stairs to the balcony. A row of doors ran along the wall, none of them numbered. Burke said: "First one, Jim."

Turning the knob, Jim pushed the door open and

moved swiftly through it, fingers brushing gun butt. He hadn't known how he'd be received. Then his hand dropped. Duke Madden was sitting behind a roll-top desk, a sly smile twisting his thin lips.

"No rough stuff, Jim." The gambler pointed toward a leather couch. "This is just a friendly visit."

"A hell of a way to invite a man in for a visit," Jim growled.

Burke heeled the door shut. "I'd better get his iron, Duke. It was a damned fool notion letting him keep it."

"He don't want to die bad enough to make a draw." He laid his gaze on Jim's face. "Boomer tells me you've resigned."

"That's right."

Twisting his swivel chair, Madden took a cigar from the box on his desk and bit off the end. He held his silence for a moment, taking his time lighting the cigar. Jim, seated on the couch, saw that Madden hadn't changed except that his run of luck had given him an opportunity to satisfy his desire for comfort. The office was expensively furnished for a camp like Gold Plume where everything had to be packed in. The desk was mahogany, the leather covering of the couch black and of good quality. There were a number of chairs in the room, a small safe set against yonder wall, and some pictures of nude, round-figured women hanging on both sides of the door. Madden's suit was of costly black broadcloth, his white shirt silk. The diamond in the ring on his right hand was large and brilliant. He was a shrewd and elegant man, this Duke Madden, with a saber-sharp nose overlooking a carefully trimmed mustache. His obsidian-black eyes indexed his tough and unforgiving character, and now they showed a worry that was nagging him.

"Boomer and me know you didn't come to Gold Plume to look at scenery," he said finally. "I doubt like hell that you're after either of us. You dragged us back across the Bitter Roots and made us stand trial in Helena for a killing we didn't do. When we beat that charge, you were done with us."

"I know." Jim crossed his legs, smiling now as if he saw humor that escaped both Madden and Burke. "I don't see that it's any of your business why I'm here."

"Everything in Gold Plume is my business." Madden leaned forward. "I'm riding a grizzly, and you might be the huckleberry who's aiming to stick a burr under my saddle."

"I didn't have a notion about bothering you till you put this gun dog on my tail," Jim said sourly. "I don't like that."

"I don't give a damn whether you like it or not." Madden tongued his cigar to the other side of his mouth. "I'm going to find out why you're here. I've got too good a thing to lose. I was in Durango when I heard about this strike. There weren't fifty men in the camp when me and Boomer showed up. We sunk every nickel we had into this place and kept putting our profits back. This winter we'll clean up."

"My reason for coming has got nothing to do with you," Jim said.

"I wouldn't lay a bet on that." Madden took his cigar out of his mouth. "First, you sided the Calvert girl against Boomer. Then you butted into a deal between Si Taylor and the Rocking C boys. What does that sound like?"

"I ain't one to stand still while a bunch of men push a girl around," Jim said testily, "or beat up a runt Ord's size. Now what are you going to do about it?"

"Boomer says to give you a chunk of lead where it'll hurt." Madden pulled on his cigar, found that it had gone out, and re-lighted it. "I'm not sure. As far as I'm concerned, we're dealing from a new deck."

"Fair enough." Jim rose and paced to the window. He looked down at the shifting crowd in the street. "I'm kind of curious about your scheme for cleaning up, Duke. Looks like you're milking your cow dry."

"She'll be dry by the time I'm done," Madden said with arrogant confidence. "Most of the boys in camp have money. There'll be more by spring

25

because we've had some good strikes. With the monopoly I've got, I'll be in a position to tote the *dinero* out myself when the pass is open in the spring. That's why I can't let you go around tripping me up."

Jim shrugged. "Seems to be your cow. Guess I'll mosey. I don't figure on being here long, so I won't bother your milking none."

"A couple of boys in the next room have got their sixes lined on your belly, Jim," Madden said coldly. "You go out of that door before I tell you to, and you won't be eating no more."

Anger crowded Jim then. That was the reason for Madden's letting him keep his Colt. His gaze swept the wall, but he could not locate the guns. They were hidden behind the red-figured wallpaper, he guessed, with tiny eyeholes too small to be seen from where he stood.

"You must like my company," Jim murmured.

"I like it well enough to keep you till I know why you're here."

"You've made money in Gold Plume, Duke. Maybe I can."

"That's no reason for a bloodhound like you. I doubt like hell that you ever resigned your marshal's job."

"Ever hear of a marshal getting rich?" Jim asked.

"Never did," Madden admitted.

"I don't want this kind of money." Jim made a

sweeping gesture toward the main floor. "But I get damned tired of risking my neck for the kind of *dinero* Uncle Sam pays."

"So you came here on a job that'll pay more," Madden said with satisfaction. "You just put a gun to your head when you said that. Raeder hire you?"

"I didn't say so." Jim saw he'd made a mistake. Perhaps a fatal one. "I came here on a personal chore."

"You were talking to Raeder," Madden charged.

"He was in the restaurant when I ate dinner."

"He's been trying to organize some vigilantes," Madden pressed. "You're the kind of a man he needs to boss the outfit. I won't stand for that."

"You're wasting time," Burke said impatiently. "I've had something to give this yahoo ever since he fetched us back from Idaho."

"Boomer wants your hide," Madden said softly. "Know any reason why he shouldn't have it?"

Jim could smell death now, there on the other side of the wallpaper, and it was in Duke Madden's hands whether it came snarling through with a roar and tongue of flame.

"Boomer is a pretty fair trigger boy, Duke," Jim said as if he felt he was in no real danger, "but he doesn't have your brains."

"Shut up, Boomer." Madden grinned as he tossed his cigar butt into a spittoon. "What are you getting at, Jim?"

27

"It's always a mistake to kill a man when you don't have to. You don't have to kill me."

"Hell, I would be a fool to let you walk out of here and start working for the vigilantes."

"I didn't make this ride for that." This was it. Either Madden believed the truth, or Jim Harrigan was a dead man. "I trailed Rush Kane here from Dodge City to kill him. When that's done, I'm drifting."

"Of all the damned hogwash!" Burke bellowed.

"Shut up, Boomer. You've got a brain like a canary." Madden reached for another cigar, a thoughtful expression on his face. "What do you want Rush for?"

"He married my sister. I guess you know what happened in Dodge City. That's why I resigned my job. I couldn't do this chore as long as I was toting my badge."

"You believe that yarn?" Burke demanded.

"He's talking straight." The sly smile was on Madden's thin lips again. "I guess we're in position to do each other a good turn, Jim. I'd like to have Rush out of the way, and I'd just as soon play it your way as have one of my boys beef him."

"Say, you're talking sense now," Burke said. "Let Harrigan get Kane."

"You always were a hell of a checker player, Boomer, because you never could see more than one move ahead." Madden chuckled. "All right,

Jim. You can have Rush any time you want him. You'll find him at the Rocking C."

Watching the gambler, Jim couldn't tell what was going on behind those black eyes. "I don't get this," he said. "Rush used to work for you. I figured he was heading for Gold Plume to deal for you again."

"Rush Kane will never deal for me again," Madden said feelingly. "You go ahead and do your chore. Then get to hell out of camp."

Jim moved to the door and opened it. He turned then, eyes searching the gambler's bland face. He asked: "Why would Rush head for the Rocking C?"

The cat-like cruelty that was a part of Duke Madden was mirrored now in the widening of his smile. "Natural place for him to go, I guess. He's Belle Calvert's brother, and with her behind him he may be a little hard to handle."

Pushing his way across the crowded street to his horse, Jim found himself thinking about what Madden had said. It was unbelievable. Jim had seen Belle but a few minutes, but those minutes had been long enough to convince him that she was everything that was fine and decent. It was impossible for her to have a brother like Rush Kane, but it must be true, or Duke Madden, suspecting what he did, would not have let him leave the Domino alive.

Jim mounted, and turned his roan into the

southbound flow of traffic, hardly conscious of his surroundings. He would kill Rush Kane, but he could not think past that moment, could not think of what Belle Calvert would do or what she would think, and suddenly it seemed important that Belle think well of him. Duke Madden had told him more than he had intended. Reading between the lines, he guessed that Madden had pulled off too many killings. Public opinion was something to be feared even in a mining camp like Gold Plume. He was afraid of Ira Raeder, and he was afraid to make a bold move against Belle Calvert.

As far as Madden was concerned, Jim's arrival was a gift from heaven. It would result in Kane's death, and it would keep Jim from staying to side Belle if he wanted to. That was the way the gambler had figured it, and Jim cursed him for his shrewdness.

Before Jim was out of the traffic, a mounted man spurred a horse into the street ahead of him, almost running a miner down, and took the south road in a gallop. Jim gave it little attention at the moment. He rode slowly, his thoughts sour company.

Hate did not come naturally to Jim Harrigan, but it had been a corroding bitterness in him from the moment he had learned what had happened to his sister in Dodge City. Only the death of Rush Kane would purge that bitterness. Yet, when he thought about it, he saw Belle Calvert, her black eyes and black hair, the sweet set of her mouth, and he knew he would hate himself from the moment Rush Kane went down before his gun.

He had almost reached the Rocking C when he met the man he had seen leaving town just ahead of him. Still he thought little about it, for his own problem was gripping his mind and leaving room for nothing else. Ahead of him was Rush Kane, and Rush Kane had to die.

Half Pint Ord was pulling gear off his horse when Jim rode in. He called: "Howdy, mister! Say, you sure did us a favor in town. I didn't get a chance to thank you then."

Ord came across the yard in a fast, rolling pace, a grin creasing his wrinkled face. He held out his hand, and Jim, stepping down, took it.

"Glad to do it, friend."

"You're a marked man now," the little cowboy said soberly. "Nobody bucks Duke Madden, and lives to sing about it."

"I ain't much of a songbird, anyhow," Jim said.

"Come on in. I told Belle about it, and she was sure tickled. That six hundred dollars looked plumb big to her."

Jim fell into step with Ord, resenting the cowboy's friendly manner. For an instant he didn't know why, and then he did know, and he hated himself as he had known he would. He was entering Belle Calvert's house under the guise of friendship. She'd welcome him and she'd thank him, and then he'd kill her brother. No man, he thought with inward heat, could be lower than that.

Opening the door, Ord stepped aside. "Here's the man who took chips in our ruckus, Belle."

"I've met Mister Harrigan. Come in and close the door. If you make a move for your gun, I'll kill you."

Jim blinked for a moment in the gloom of the house. Then his eyes focused clearly on her, and he felt himself shriveling like a fly before a blast of flame. She was standing against the far wall, her Winchester held on the ready. He had never seen so much contempt on a human face.

"Have you gone loco, Belle?" Ord exploded.

"Loco enough to kill him," she said grimly. "Take his iron."

"Look, Belle. This is the man who pulled his cutter on Taylor. If . . ."

"He had me fooled, too. I said to take his iron."

Swearing feelingly, Ord obeyed. "It'll be a long cold day before he does you a good turn again. What's the matter?"

"He came out here to kill Rush," the girl said bitterly. "If Madden hadn't sent a man to warn us, he'd have done it."

"I'll be damned." Ord faced Jim. "That right?"

"That's right," Jim admitted.

He knew now why the man had left town ahead of him. More than that, he saw the real depth of

32

Madden's scheming. The gambler had still been suspicious of his relationship with Ira Raeder, and he'd rigged the play this way, hoping to get rid of two men he wanted removed and still keep his hands clean.

Hate was in the room, hate and scorn that Belle and Half Pint Ord had for him, as intangible as smoke and as real. Resentment rose in him then. "Maybe I look like a skunk, but I don't smell like one," he said hotly. "Rush Kane needs to die. If I'd caught him on the street, I'd have killed him the same as I would any sidewinder."

"Give him his gun," Belle said in sudden decision.

"Now you *are* loco!" Ord shouted. "Rush can't . . ."

"Give it to him."

Reluctantly Ord obeyed and drew his own six. "Just one funny move, mister, and I'll forget what you done in town."

Belle motioned toward the stairs. "Rush is up there."

III

Jim went ahead of the girl, not understanding this. Nor did he understand why Rush, if he had been warned, hadn't met him in front of the house with his gun in leather ready to smoke it out.

33

"The room on your right," Belle said. "I want to see if you're any part of a man."

Jim stopped in the doorway, surprise holding him there. Rush Kane was in bed, a bandage around his head, his face as white as the pillow on which he lay. Pale lips pulled tight in a grin when he saw who it was. He said—"Long time no see, Jim."—and held out his hand.

"He's not here to shake your hand," Belle said in quiet fury. "He's here to kill you."

Kane's arm dropped, pleasure washing out of his face. "I guess you've got something wrong."

Jim stepped in the doorway, surprise making him suddenly weak and foolish. He had known Rush Kane as a tall, vigorous man, filled high with the love of life, a strong man and an honest gambler. Finding him this way was something that had never entered his mind.

"You can put down your Winchester, ma'am," Jim said heavily. "What's between me and Rush will wait till he's on his feet."

"What's this all about?" Kane asked.

Jim came to stand at the head of the bed. "You knew what I thought of Ann," he said dully. "I respected you when you married her, but I reckon I had you pegged wrong. Ann wrote that your luck had run out. When I got there, I found you'd killed her."

Kane flinched as if he'd been struck. "If that's

34

what you believe, then go ahead and do what you came to do."

"Isn't that what happened?" Jim demanded roughly.

"No. If I never had another decent thing in me, my love for Ann was decent and fine and beautiful. I'd have killed myself before I'd have knowingly let anything happen to her."

"Sure, you didn't hold the gun." Jim gestured impatiently. "But you got into a ruckus and killed a man. Then you hightailed to your room, thinking that with Ann there they'd let you alone, but they came after you and Ann was shot. In my book that says you killed her."

Kane closed his eyes. "Go ahead, Jim, if it's what you believe."

Jim stared at the still, white face of this man he had planned to kill, and for the first time doubt rose in him. "I'll listen to your yarn, Rush," he said at last.

"Go to hell," Kane whispered. "You wouldn't believe anything I said."

"I'll tell you what happened!" Belle cried, crossing the room to face Jim. "An honest gambler didn't have a chance in Dodge City. Not with the sharpers he was playing with. He lost everything he had, and then he got my letter telling him Dad had been killed and that Duke Madden was here. I asked him to come and help. He didn't have any money to bring Ann, and he couldn't leave her there, so he tried to use the same tricks that had been used against him."

"I'm not a very good gambler, Jim," Kane whispered. "I wasn't smart enough to catch them, and I wasn't smooth enough to keep them from catching me. One man pulled his gun, and I got him. I thought that ended it, but they followed me to the room. When they yelled to come out, Ann tried to make me stay inside. They shot through the door, and she got hit."

"You rode off," Jim accused bitterly. "You didn't have the guts to stay and bury her."

"Ann was dead, and I couldn't help her then." Kane motioned to Belle. "She needed me. I killed the two men who shot Ann, and rode out of town. I couldn't have done anything more." He opened his eyes and looked at Jim, self-condemnation on his face. "I've never been worth a damn. Dad said that when I left here. I should have been shot when I married Ann. Now go ahead and get it over with."

Rush Kane's eyes closed as if the effort of keeping them open was too much for him. There was silence; the metallic beating of the clock on the bureau was the only sound in the room. Some of the long pent-up hatred drained out of Jim Harrigan then. They might have lied to him back in Dodge City, friends of the men Kane had killed. Yet, staring down at this man who seemed close to death, Jim couldn't bring himself to say he believed him.

"I wouldn't kill you when you're lying here like this," Jim said finally and with some anger. "You know that. I've got some thinking to do."

Kane looked at him then. "I was hoping you'd take the job I fizzled at. The man who needs killing is Duke Madden."

"That's why Rush is this way," Belle cried. "When I told him all that had happened, he went to see Madden. He told him he'd get proof that Madden had killed Dad. They dry-gulched him on his way back."

"A fool way to go at it," Jim said.

"I've been crazy ever since I lost Ann," Kane muttered.

Belle motioned toward the door. "That's enough talk."

When they were downstairs, Jim said thoughtfully: "Madden told me where I'd find Rush. Then he sent word out here I was coming, figuring that maybe we'd both get plugged, but I can't figure out why with Rush shot up like this."

"Madden doesn't know how bad Rush is. I asked the doctor not to tell."

"What are his chances?"

Belle gestured wearily. "Doc wouldn't say." She hesitated, glancing at Ord and then back to Jim. "What are you going to do while you wait for Rush to get well so you can kill him?"

Jim paced across the room to stare out of the

window. Sunlight had fled from the cañon floor, and evening shadows were thickening into dusk. The knifing sharpness of her words curried his nerves raw. Without turning, he said: "I don't know."

"Madden will kill you if you go back to town," she pressed.

"It might work the other way. Mebbe I'll kill Madden."

"That's what Dad thought. He got ten thousand dollars for the town site and some cattle. Then he was robbed. He accused Madden, and the next morning we found his body between here and Gold Plume."

Jim turned then. "I'm sorry."

"Dad should have known," she said miserably, "that one man can't touch Madden. You ought to know it, too."

"Your dad was a rancher. I've been a lawman. That makes a difference when you buck a tough like Duke Madden."

"Not enough difference."

Ord had slipped out through the kitchen. From where he stood at the window, Jim couldn't see Belle's face clearly, but he felt that she was watching him, weighing him, perhaps hoping that he was a different man than she now judged him to be.

"It's an old game with me," he said. "When you fight a man who has the grip Madden has, you don't go at it the direct way. You whittle him down first."

"Then you are going to fight Madden?"

He felt the tension that was in her, the expectancy. He sensed again, as he had the first time he had seen her, that here in Belle Calvert were the qualities he had dreamed of finding in a woman. He had never had time to look for them before, and he had always thought that a lawman, risking his life as he did, had no right to ask a woman to be his wife. That was behind him. His life was his own now, to live as he saw it, to take what he wanted. Here she was, and she might have loved him if a perverse fate had not dealt him the hand it had. Now she could only hate him.

"I guess I don't have much choice," he said at last. "I ain't in the habit of running when a man rigs up a play like Madden did today."

"I have your word you won't harm Rush now?"

"Yes."

"I hope you'll stay for supper, Mister Harrigan. I know how Duke Madden can be licked."

Jim sat on the front steps, smoking, while the last bit of daylight left the cañon and heat fled with the light and a chill wind swept down from the peaks above him. He tried to bring his mind to focus on Rush Kane, to form a sane judgment, but could not. His thoughts were turbulent whirlpools, always sweeping back to Duke Madden.

The desire for vengeance that had been a driving force in him these last days had subsided until it was a mere spark beside a roaring flame, this need for smashing Duke Madden.

Jim had no idea how Belle meant to fight Madden, but he made his own plans, and he was still thinking about them when she called him to supper. Half Pint Ord and the crippled rider, Limpy Sanders, ate with them. Jim had liked Ord from the moment he'd seen him make his stand against the butcher, and at the same time had instinctively distrusted Sanders. He was a sullen man, keeping his face lowered over his plate while he ate.

When they had finished eating, Jim asked: "What's your plan for whipping Madden?"

"With food," she said. "It's that simple. We sold our last steers today to get money to buy another herd and drive them into the valley before the pass is blocked. Winter shuts us in unless you want to go out on snowshoes and risk the slides. Most of the miners won't do that, so by spring they'll have to pay what Madden and his organization asks for food."

"And you'll control the only supply of meat that Madden doesn't."

She nodded. "We've got plenty of hay to winter two hundred head. We can buy cattle cheap in Utah, and by doing our own slaughtering we can undersell Madden's butchers, and still make a profit."

"Even at Utah prices, twelve hundred dollars won't buy many steers."

"We've made other sales," she said quickly. "Not for as good a price as you wangled out of Taylor, but enough to buy two hundred head."

It would work if Belle Calvert had enough men to hold her cattle until the day when winter privations and Madden's greed forced Gold Plume to come to her. Jim knew that because he'd been in snowbound mining camps, and he'd seen the fantastic prices that the threat of starvation forced people to pay. But he knew, too, that long before that day Madden would act in a drastic and unpredictable manner.

Jim shot a glance at Sanders, but he still couldn't see the man's eyes because his head was bowed over pipe and tobacco pouch. He said: "It's late in the year to make a drive like that."

"I know," Belle said, "but some falls the snow comes late. We'd have to gamble on that."

Jim rose. "I've got a better notion. Want to ride to town with me, Ord?"

"Sure." The little cowboy came to his feet. "Gonna make a call on Madden?"

Sanders's head had snapped up. He sat motionlessly, his filled pipe and tobacco pouch held in front of him, interest lines deep around his brittle, glass-sharp eyes.

"I was hoping you'd go to Utah with the boys,"

41

Belle said, disappointment honing an edge to her voice.

"If you're dealt two hands, you play the best one first. Come on, Ord."

Jim waited until they were in the saddle before he asked: "How long has Sanders been with you?"

"He rode in just after Sam was killed. All the old hands but me had drawed their time to take a crack at the mines. Limpy asked for a job, and Belle was glad to have him. He's a good hand, Harrigan."

"You trust him?"

Ord hesitated as if choosing his words carefully. "Sometimes when you don't have a sharp blade handy, you have to use a dull one. Or maybe one that ain't tempered right and snaps off in your hand. Might even fly up in your face. Can't tell till you try it."

The old rider's implication was plain enough. As far as he was concerned, Limpy Sanders could be trusted—about as far as Jim Harrigan could.

"You know Ira Raeder?"

"You bet. A top hand gent, Ira is, and a good friend of Belle's. He liked her dad. Prospected all through the San Juan before he made the strike here. Stayed at the Rocking C whenever he came through."

"He's the man I want to see. Know where his cabin is?"

"Right up the gulch."

42

●●●

Gold Plume was simmering when they rode through; within the hour it would be boiling. Traffic ebbed and flowed along the plank walk; men elbowed and rammed their way from one saloon to the other, finally coming to Madden's Domino. Flares threw a leaping, lurid light across the street, and barkers intoned their persuasive chants into the laughter and curses and ribald song that rose from the crowd.

"Spend their days in the bowels of the earth," Ord said sourly, "and their nights in hell making Duke Madden rich."

The business block fell behind, and they were threading their way through the miners' shacks and tents when Ord said: "Here it is."

There was no light in it. Disappointment knifed through Jim. "He ain't there."

"That's damned funny," Ord said thoughtfully. "Ira ain't one to go sashaying around at night."

"Maybe he's out visiting someone," Jim suggested.

"Maybe. Reckon it'd be all right to go in and wait a spell."

They dismounted in front of Raeder's cabin. Jim laid a hand on Ord's arm. "Wait," he said softly.

"What's up?"

"I had a notion I saw a man's face at the window. Too dark to be sure."

"Wouldn't be Raeder. He ain't the kind who sits in the dark and looks out at folks who ride up."

"Something's wrong, Ord. You get a feeling about things like this when you pack a star for a while."

"Hell, let's go see."

"And get some round windows in our skulls."

They held their position beside the horses, listening and hearing nothing but the business block. It was dark, no moon shining between the high cliffs and only a narrow patch of black sky set with a few stars. Miners' cabins on up the creek held lighted windows, pinpoints piercing the thick night.

"Black as the inside of a bull's gut," Ord said. "You couldn't see no face."

Jim didn't argue. It might be only the work of overly tight nerves, but he'd learned years ago that careless men didn't live long at this game. He said loudly: "Guess Ira ain't here." Then he whispered: "Take the horses up the creek. Stay there till you hear me holler or hear some shooting."

Ord grumbled a curse and obeyed. Jim dropped flat and bellied toward the cabin. Before the sound of hoofs had died, he plucked his gun, and jerked the door open with his left hand.

He called—"Hello, Raeder!"—and dived for the window.

The response was instant, and not the kind of greeting that would come from Ira Raeder. Jim reached the window as the gunman inside blasted his third shot through the doorway. Jim fired from where he stood, targeting the spot where the gun flash ribboned out. He put three more bullets into the room, firing low and spreading them two feet apart. Moving back to the door, he waited there while he heard the man die.

"All right, Harrigan?" Ord asked, coming back with the horses.

Miners were pouring out of their cabins and running toward Raeder's place, filling the air with shouted questions. Still Jim waited until half a dozen men had gathered. Then he struck a match and went in. Lighting a lamp that he found on a pine table, he heard Ord cry out. He turned, and saw Ira Raeder lying on his back in the corner, a gaping knife wound in his abdomen. Another man lay against the far wall, a bullet hole in his chest. Both were dead.

"It's Grizzly Brashada," a miner said bitterly.

"Madden's man?" Jim asked.

Puzzled, they stared at him for a long moment before one asked: "How did you know, stranger?"

"I know Madden. You'll have killings like this as long as he rods the camp. Come on, Ord."

Duke Madden had said he had too good a thing to lose. He might have added that he'd go to any length to hold it. Riding back to the Rocking C,

Jim thought bitterly he should have foreseen this and countered Madden's move. Madden was still convinced that Raeder had sent for Jim to run the vigilantes, and he'd decided to snuff out that danger permanently.

"Another five minutes and we'd have saved Raeder's life," Jim said with regret. "He propositioned me today to help organize some vigilantes, and I turned him down. Then I changed my mind after I talked to Belle. That's why I wanted to see him tonight."

"There ain't anybody else in this camp who could pick out the right men," Ord grunted. "I mean nobody who could get 'em to follow him like Ira could."

"I guess we'll play our other hand. I'll go to Utah with you, Ord."

IV

They ate breakfast by lamplight that morning. When they were done, Belle handed a heavy money belt to Ord. "You'll carry that, Half Pint. Top Zachary Rule's herd, and make the best deal with him you can." She brought her gaze to Jim. "You'll give the orders. Travel as fast as you can, even if you take all their fat off. We'll put it back after you get here, but you may not get here at all if you don't beat the snow."

46

"Damned fool thing to be taking orders from this yahoo when he came here gunning for your brother," Sanders said sullenly.

"Perhaps it is," Belle said. "There's one way to find out."

"How do you know he ever handled cattle?" Sanders pressed.

"Have you, Jim?" she asked.

It was the first time she had called him by his first name. He grinned. "A little."

"Rush has told me a good deal about Jim Harrigan, Limpy." Belle pinned her gaze on Jim's face. "You see, he worships you. Perhaps because you're Ann's brother, or perhaps because of you yourself."

He was yet to be tested. Again Jim sensed that Belle hoped he was the man she had first taken him to be. He said now: "The herd will come through."

"I still don't like it," Sanders said doggedly.

"You can draw your time."

"Let it go." Sanders turned to the door. "I was thinking about you."

Jim lingered until Sanders and Ord were gone. Then he asked: "I thought I heard a man ride in after I went to bed."

"It was Limpy. He went into town for a drink." She caught his arm. "Why, Jim?"

"Just curious." He stood at the door a moment, filling his mind with the picture of her. Then he

47

left, certain that the threat of treachery would ride with them to Utah.

They were atop Star Mountain Pass before the sun showed a complete circle above the east wall, the cañon bottom still dark with shifting purple shadows. A chill wind knifed them when they reined up to blow their horses, and Jim pulled his collar around his neck. There had been no word spoken since they had stepped into saddles. Now Jim put his gaze directly upon Sanders's dark saturnine face.

"You ain't fooling me, Limpy. If you've got a notion about playing Madden's game, you'd better pull out now while you can still ride."

"You two would play hell trailing two hundred head from Utah," Sanders sneered. "I ain't playing Madden's game no how."

"I like to let a man know where he stands. The first trick you pull that looks off-color will get you a slug in the brisket."

"Save your lead, Harrigan."

"Let's ride." Jim turned his roan down the west slope, having one look across the great vastness of sage and piñon and cedars to the sky-reaching La Sal Mountains that sprawled across the Utah/Colorado line. Then the fast-dropping trail brought them into the spruce, and the distance was blotted out.

Ord took the lead because it was an old trail to him, paying no attention to Sanders's grumbling that it "sure as hell ain't no rack track." They came down into the flame-tinted aspens and scrub oak, reached the San Miguel that rushed toward a distant sea through red-flecked cañon walls, and made camp that night beside its singing waters.

They were in the saddle again by dawn, angling up the south wall, and rode westward across a sagebrush plain, slashed by innumerable cañons into a series of sweeping downgrades and steep uplifts. Southward, Lone Cone stood gracefully sharp against a cloudless sky.

It was a raw wild land holding a primitive challenge, and on another day Jim Harrigan would have thrilled to it, but now the need for haste was a never-ceasing prod. They reached the Río Dolores—River of Sorrows, named by the Spaniards a century before—and went on across the south slope of La Sal Mountain into the weird red-rock country of eastern Utah.

Beyond Moab they came to Songbird Creek and the Bridlebit Ranch. Here Half Pint Ord dickered with Zachary Rule. "I want good steers," he said. "The top of your herd. We aim to push hell out of 'em until we get 'em across Star Mountain into Gold Plume."

Zachary Rule, who ran a good Mormon outfit by strict Mormon standards, lifted his gaze to a cerulean sky. "Mebbe you'll get 'em across before snow flies. Mebbe." And the way he said it told Jim he didn't have the faintest hope they would.

It took a day to cut out the steers Ord selected, a precious day that could not be picked up on the trail. Here, beside the red waters of Songbird Creek hemmed in by red walls fringed with needles and spires and strange figures resembling ancient gargoyles that grinned down from lofty perches, riders twisted and wheeled their mounts, working out the cattle Ord wanted. Dust rose over the bawling, shifting mass, and hung there in the still air like a red, sun-bright blanket.

They were on the move at dawn, north, and then east, letting the cattle run their fractiousness out. Back across La Sal Mountain, Ord riding point, and on to the Río Dolores. The cattle slowed with that first burst of energy gone. Then they had to be pushed. No time to feed. Cover as many miles as they could between sunup and sundown. That was the only goal. Through scrub brush. Broken country. Through the cedars. Black stands of piñon. Holding them at night in a box cañon, if they could find one, logs and brush dragged across the mouth. In saddles by dawn. Pushing. Always pushing while days fled and the nights grew colder and the chances of winning this gamble grew less with each passing hour. Always Jim Harrigan slept with a sixth sense alive, for the danger of Limpy Sanders's treachery was a live and constant thing.

But Jim had no fault to find with Sanders's work. He was in the saddle as many hours as the others, and he had stopped his grumbling. They reached the San Miguel and then it rained. Jim, looking eastward to the mountain pass, saw the shifting ominous clouds, and knew that it had snowed.

Still they pushed. Hoofs sucked in the mud. The river ran high and murky. The sky cleared and it grew cold and Jim, lifting his eyes again, saw the white hoods that fitted the mountains like new mantles. Then they were at the foot of Star Mountain. If their luck held, they'd drive into a Rocking C pasture by another sundown.

"We're licked," Sanders growled that night as they hunkered beside the fire, the wind a bitter cutting blast as it rushed down from the snow peaks.

Jim stared at him in surprise. "What's the matter with you, Sanders? We ain't licked by a hell of a long way. Tomorrow we'll shove 'em over the hump."

Sanders rose, eyes turning from Jim to Ord and back, the firelight a shifting scarlet on his stubble-black face. "You think we're not licked. Hell, man." He motioned toward the herd held in a box cañon behind him. "They ain't et a mouthful since we left Utah. Ganted up till there ain't nothing but hide and bone, neither. Now you think you can push them critters through the snow." He shook his head. "I'm done."

Jim and Ord were on their feet, as tired and

tight-nerved as Sanders. Clothes ragged. Stubble long on gaunt faces. Covered with the dust and grime of these days on the trail. Wanting nothing so much as sleep and more sleep. But neither had complained. Luck had been better than they had expected.

Jim, watching Sanders closely now, wondered about this sudden rebellion. Ord had guessed the snow would not be more than six or eight inches. Unless it was a good deal deeper, there would be no great trouble on the pass. It was strange that Sanders hadn't quit back along the trail instead of waiting until they were within a day's drive of Gold Plume, and Jim thought he could guess the reason. This would be as good a place as any for Madden to steal the herd, a great deal safer than after it had reached the Rocking C.

Sanders did not move. He had made a statement, and now stood motionlessly, sullen eyes meeting Jim's as if waiting to see what action his words would provoke.

It was Ord who broke the silence. "Them steers ain't as bad off as you're letting on, Limpy, and neither are we. Hell, we ain't been on the trail long. It just ain't sense for you to quit."

"I figgered we'd beat the snow," Sanders grunted.

"All right," Jim said in sudden decision. "Ride and keep going. Don't let me catch up with you."

"I'll wait till morning." Sanders began backing away from the fire.

"You're getting out now." Jim motioned toward Sanders's horse. "Go on, drift."

Sanders pulled at an ear, belligerence seeping out of him. "Reckon I'll stay. We might get through. No use throwing a good job away."

"If you're staying," Jim warned, "don't ride out during the night."

Jim made his bed close to the cliff, wondering about Sanders and seeing little logic in his actions. The treachery he had expected had not materialized. Weariness and the nearness to trail's end had relaxed his vigilance. Now his nerves were tight as a fiddle string again. He moved his bed farther along the cliff when he heard Sanders snore, and dropped into a light sleep.

Jim was never sure what woke him. It might have been a stirring of the cattle. A strange movement in the brush. A splash in the river. He sat up, senses alert, silently drawing his gun. Overhead a round moon laid a platinum shine upon the water, and the aspens, stripped now of most of their leaves, ranged up the mountainside like countless ghosts on the march, the wind whispering through them.

Then he caught the sound of movement upstream, and called: "Who is it?"

A ribbon of flame leaped at him and a bullet snapped past. His answering fire was quick and accurate. Limpy Sanders came up on tiptoes and reeled away from the shadowed cañon wall to sprawl out fully, his head almost falling into the hot ashes of the fire.

Jim moved position quickly, keeping the cliff to his back. More guns opened up, Ord's on the other side of the fire, and at least three men in front of him. Lead chipped the rock behind Ord and screamed away into the night. Jim dropped to his knees, holding his fire, and mentally cursed Ord for giving away his position.

It was an old game to Jim Harrigan, and one that he understood well. Experience had taught him not to waste a bullet. Ord's gun, too, had gone silent. Confident that their raking fire had done its work, the three left the cover of the boulders near the river and came toward the cliff. In that instant Jim's gun became a leaping, living thing, foot-long tongues of flame lashing from its muzzle, its thunder rolling waves of sound beating against his ears.

One man jackknifed at the knees and went down. Another threw a wild, hurried shot at Jim and took a slug in the chest. The third made a run for it along the edge of the river. Jim fired at him and missed. It was Ord who drove two bullets into him, caused him to break stride, stumble, and topple into the swift-running river.

"You all right, Ord?" Jim called.

"Got a nick in my left arm's all. I figgered they got you after you downed Limpy."

Jim walked to where Sanders lay and rolled him over. "Dead," he said, and pulled him away from the fire. He glanced at his watch. "Be sunup in an hour or so. We'd better get breakfast and start 'em moving."

"I reckon." Ord stared at Sanders's face, sullen in death as it had been in life. "What in hell was biting that coyote?"

"He went to town the night Raeder was killed. I'm guessing he saw Madden and told him what Belle was figgering on. Chances are they rigged this then, aiming to salivate us and take the herd."

"What was his idea for trying to quit?"

Jim shrugged. "Hard to tell. Maybe he aimed to worry us. Or maybe he wanted to ride off and meet these *hombres* up on the pass. Then he got boogery and changed his mind. Not much bottom. Never is in men who hire out to double-cross somebody."

Dawn was breaking across a bright cold sky when they cleared the mouth of the box cañon and started the herd. It was steady pushing, the snow at first a thin sprinkle like stingy frosting on a cake. Gradually deepening, it slowed but didn't stop them. They topped the pass shortly after noon, and came out of the snow. It was dusk when they reached the valley floor and shoved the herd into a pasture behind the Rocking C buildings.

Belle had steaks sizzling when they came into the house. She stood at the stove, staring at their bearded faces as if she found it hard to recognize them, a tight worry in her face Jim had not seen before, her shoulders drooping a little as if some pride had gone from her.

"You've got your steers," Jim told her, "and I don't reckon it'll take many days to put some taller on 'em."

"Where's Limpy?"

Jim told her while she forked the steaks onto a platter. Then he asked: "How's Rush?"

She faced him now, lips trembling as she fought to control her emotions. When she did speak, it was a whisper that barely reached him. "I don't know. He went to town yesterday, and hasn't come back."

V

Jim ate hungrily and went to bed. Bone-weary, he gave little thought to what Belle had said. He slept like a dead man, and woke to look upon a white world. They had beaten the snow by hours.

Ord was finishing breakfast when Jim came into the kitchen. "Some lazy devils can sleep all day," he said amiably, "but I've got cattle to feed."

Jim grinned and rubbed a hand across his

whiskery face. "Sure, I slept all day. Must be almost daylight now." He pulled a chair up to the table. "You'd have to put snowshoes on them critters to get 'em over the hump now."

"Lucky all the way." Ord rose and moved to the door. "If you ain't above it, Harrigan, you can come out and give me a hand."

"I ain't above it, but I got another job that needs doing first. Bringing the beef in ain't much good if we don't fix Madden. I wish Raeder was alive."

"There's talk that you killed him," Belle said.

Her words jolted breath from him. He stared at her blankly.

Ord, still standing at the door, cursed softly. "There's no sense in that, Belle. Jim didn't even go inside the cabin till there was five or six of us there with him."

"I'm just telling you what I heard." Belle set a plate of food in front of Jim. "There was some pretty wild talk the day you left, most of it against Madden. Then the story got started that he'd sent Brashada to ask Raeder to see him, and, while Brashada was there, Jim came in, shot Brashada and knifed Raeder. One of the miners said he saw you step out of the cabin and wait until the rest came."

"That sure is a bucket of hogwash!" Ord exploded.

"It's the talk," Belle said soberly. "You can't go into town, Jim. Madden's men will lynch you."

Ord grinned crookedly. Before he went out, he said: "You'll find another pitchfork in the barn, Jim."

Jim ate slowly, thinking about this and knowing that no matter how illogical it was, Madden, with enough free whiskey and enough talk in the right places, could make this accusation stick. If Jim was found dangling from a rope some cold morning, no one would connect Madden with it.

Belle filled Jim's coffee cup, and poured another for herself. "What are you going to do about Rush?" she asked, coming back to the table.

"I ain't had much time to think about it," Jim answered evasively.

She stirred her coffee, misery-filled eyes on him. "Rush wasn't as badly hurt as the doctor thought. He'd been up a couple of days when we heard this talk about your killing Raeder. Rush couldn't stand it. He said this wasn't your fight in the first place, and he wasn't going to sit around and wait for you to come back to a rope."

"That's why he went to town?" Jim asked, thinking that Rush might have had another reason for leaving.

She nodded. "I don't suppose he's alive now."

It was a funny hand fate had dealt Jim Harrigan. He lowered his eyes thinking of the one compelling urge that had driven him to Colorado after he had looked at his sister's grave in Dodge City and heard the story of her death. Yet now the urge was gone. Hate had been a lever burning high in him, and then breaking.

He knew what Ann would tell him if she were here: that he wasn't God, that revenge was not for human hands. Besides, she loved Rush Kane, and what woman would do less for the man she loved than she had tried to do for Rush?

"I'll find out why he ain't back," he said at last.

"And if he's alive, you'll kill him," she said tonelessly.

Jim built a cigarette, his chair canted back against the wall, his mind reaching into his memory to the day when Ann had come to him in Helena and told him she was leaving with Rush. Jim had told her she was crazy to follow him, that she should stay in Helena where she had her home.

"You've never been in love," Ann had said simply. "When you are, you'll know what it means to be with the one you love, to work for that person, and maybe die for him."

She had done exactly that, and he knew she would have no regrets. Whatever blame could be laid upon Rush Kane, killing him would not bring Ann back. He saw himself in a new light, saw the corrosive effect of the hate that had been sucking at him through these weeks.

"I guess me and Rush won't have any trouble," he said.

"Jim." Belle leaned forward, elbows on the

table. "You came here to kill Rush and instead you risked your life going after my cattle. Why?"

He couldn't tell her. She wouldn't believe it. Or if she did, her answer to his question would be no. She couldn't love a man who had come so close to killing her brother. So he said lightly: "Madden shoved me around. Now I'm going to do the shoving. See if you can find some paper and a pen and ink."

When she brought them, he pushed the paper to her. "Put this down, will you? Nobody can read what I write."

For half an hour he paced the floor, smoking steadily, having her write and scratch out and rewrite until she had what he wanted. Then he read it through again.

How long will you accept one man's rule?

How long will you pay high prices for everything you buy in Gold Plume?

How long will you allow gamblers to set the prices you pay?

Rocking C has beef to sell at a fair price, but it will not have it long unless Duke Madden is licked.

Rocking C asks the help of every honest man in Gold Plume in this fight.

"It'll do," Jim murmured.

"You aren't going into town, Jim?"

"Sure." He slid into his coat. "If you listen, you'll hear Madden cuss when he reads this."

She caught his arm. "You can still get over the pass if you start now."

"I never leave a job half done." He took hold of her and pulled her against him. He saw how near she was to breaking, and yet he knew she would not break. There was a strength in her that Rush lacked. If she had been Rush, she would have stayed and died in Dodge City. It was that proud courage that had held her here after her father had been killed, had made her fight against odds that no gambler would take.

"But it isn't your job!" she cried.

"It is now." Then he forced himself to ask a question that had been in his mind all the way to Utah and back. "Would it make any difference to you if I got killed?"

She tore free and walked away. She stood for a moment facing the stove, her back to him. There was no sound but her breathing and ticking of the clock on the shelf above the table. Then, without turning, she said: "I am in debt too much to you now."

He went out and strode through the shifting white curtain of snow to the barn. He should not have asked the question. He could not expect her to love him. He saddled and, mounting, took the road to Gold Plume, a bitterness in him that he had never felt before. Now he had a chance to live his own life, and he had found the woman who would give meaning to that life, but his hatred had killed whatever chance there had been of earning her love. And hope died then in Jim Harrigan.

Jim settled down into his coat collar, hearing the high scream of the wind, watching snowflakes whip around him in dizzy horizontal flight. Winter had come a month ahead of time. A spell of good weather might take the snow off in the cañon bottom, but it would stay in the pass. He wondered in grim relief what it was like up there now in that treeless open space that looked out upon the world.

He rode slowly when he reached town, remembering he had seen a log cabin that served as a newspaper office. Even by hugging the path that twisted along the creek side of the street, he found it hard to see the buildings, for snow was a white curtain drawn across his vision. Then, finding the cabin, he left his horse on the sheltered side, and waded through the snow to the door. He opened it, stamped snow from his boots, and slid in.

The interior of the cabin was warm and strong with the smell of ink and paper. A man sat huddled on a stool at the composing bench, straining forward to catch all of the thin light that he could. He turned when he heard the door and said—"Good morning."—in a nasal twang that marked him as an Easterner. "I mean it's a hell of a morning, isn't it?"

"It is for a fact." Jim laid his paper on the bench. "I'd like a hundred of those run off. I'll wait."

The editor read it and lifted pale blue eyes to Jim. "I can't do it. I'd be dead before night."

He was an old man from whom age and defeat had sucked away the desire for battle, but he still nursed a small pride that made him hate himself for his cowardice. His trousers were baggy and patched; his shirt collar showed careful stitching where he had whipped down the frayed threads. He had not shaved for several days, and his white stubble made a faint fringe along his cheeks and chin. The smell of cheap whiskey and chewed tobacco made a stench about him, and Jim thought sourly that he would be a poor ally at best.

"Likely I'll be in the same fix," Jim said, "but I'm risking my neck to fight the rotten deal you've got in Gold Plume. What kind of a newspaperman are you who won't do the same?"

The editor slid off the stool, lips pulling into a determined line. "The Gold Plume *Eagle* stands for justice and fair play, my friend."

"How much have you got in Gold Plume?"

The skinny shoulders sagged, and the editor turned to the window. "The snow covers a lot of filth," he murmured, "but it doesn't change it. The filth's still there. I'm too old to be a hero."

"You'll be a hero or a dead coward." Jim drew his gun and thumbed back the hammer. "Start in."

The editor wheeled when he heard the gun

coming to cock. He stared at Jim's grim stubble-dark face, and fear laid hold of him. "All right," he whispered and, climbing back on the stool, began to work. Presently he reached for a sheet of paper and rolled it across the type. "Have a look at your suicide invitation," he said and, lifting the sheet, handed it to Jim.

Jim scanned it. "Run 'em off," he said laconically and, pulling a stool up to the stove, sat down. *Suicide invitation?* Well, maybe the editor was right, and it didn't make a hell of a lot of difference. His thoughts turned to Rush Kane, and he wondered where the gambler had gone. He'd run from Dodge City, and he'd likely run again.

"There you are," the editor said at length, stacking the papers on a table.

"How much?"

"Nothing." The old man chewed his lower lip. "Except the privilege of helping you. There was a time when I'd hold to a belief through hell and high water. Then I made the mistake of running, and I've been running ever since. It's kind of good to think of myself as a man again."

"No need of you getting into trouble," Jim said roughly.

"The name's Fred Webb." The old man held out a claw-like hand. "You're Jim Harrigan, aren't you?"

"How did you know?" Jim asked in surprise.

"Heard a lot about you since Ira Raeder was

killed." He sliced bacon and put it on the stove. "I thought you'd be the only one with enough courage to do what you're doing."

There was more strength in this man than Jim had thought. He said: "I didn't kill Raeder."

"Didn't suppose so." Webb filled his coffee pot from a bucket and put it on the stove. "I knew Grizzly Brashada. I felt his fists the second week I was in Gold Plume after I'd printed something Madden didn't like." He grinned wryly. "What are your plans, son?"

"I aim to pass these out. After the miners read 'em, I've got a hunch Madden will get spooked and make a mistake."

Webb stood at the stove thoughtfully scratching a cheek. "The lid's off the minute you show your face on the street. If you're bound to die, lick Madden first."

"What are you getting at?"

"Don't pass those papers out yourself, or you'll die before you start. I'll get the kid who sells my *Eagle*. Madden won't catch on."

Jim nodded. "All right. Get him."

"Watch the coffee and bacon." Webb pulled into his coat and went out.

Discontent grew in Jim Harrigan while he waited. It was time for action, and waiting was against his nature, but he knew the old man was right. He paced the length of the office, smoking constantly. When he'd carried a badge, he had all the agencies of the law on his side. Now he was alone except for a girl, an old cowhand, and a broken-down editor who had been aroused enough to grasp again for a departed self-respect.

And Rush Kane. Or was he an ally? Jim couldn't guess. A year ago he'd have said yes. Now Kane was unpredictable. Jim had known more than one man of promise to lack color when the final assay was made. It was even possible that Kane had gone over to Madden to escape Jim's gun.

Webb came in with a wizened, leggy boy who read the top paper, and threw Jim a broken-toothed grin. "I took a beating from Boomer Burke. It's time somebody had the guts to fight 'em."

"Pass a few of those out in the small saloons," Jim said, "and then try the Domino. Get back in an hour, and there'll be five dollars for you."

"I don't want five dollars." The boy scooped up a stack of the papers, and moved to the door. "All I want is to see you pitch some lead at Madden and Burke."

"You may get another beating if Burke gets his hands on you."

The boy grinned again. "That'll be all right if you crack a few caps."

"Let's eat," the editor said when the boy had gone.

Jim glanced at his watch. "I'll give him an hour," he said worriedly.

New hope burned high in him now. The old

66

editor and the boy had taken the beatings and done nothing, but the moment somebody came along who wasn't afraid to fight, they had accepted their responsibility. There must be hundreds like them scattered in the Domino and the other saloons, in the mines, in the cabins and tents.

It was an hour that held 1,000 minutes for Jim Harrigan. He ate and paced the floor, came back to the table for another cup of coffee, and paced the floor. He worried his watch in and out of his pocket, and, when the hour was up, he reached for his coat.

"The kid should've been back. I'm gonna kick the lid off."

"Wait a minute." Webb gnawed off a chew of plug, tongued it into his cheek, and picked up a double-barreled shotgun from a back corner. "I'll go along. I never killed a man, Harrigan, but I can."

"When I came in this morning . . ."

"I wasn't any part of a man. I was something they should have buried the day Grizzly Brashada beat me up. Kind of funny, isn't it?" He spit into a can. "You gave me back what Brashada stole."

Jim Harrigan's grin was a quick break across his dark face. The last doubt was gone. He had to win. There were hundreds in Gold Plume like Fred Webb, like the wizened, broken-toothed kid who hadn't come back.

VI

It had stopped snowing, but the wind screaming down from the high cliffs had a slashing cut to it. It broomed the snow from the street and threw it in ragged white columns against the fronts of tents and buildings, or carried it through the open spaces and piled it high against yonder cliff, leaving the street a gaping, frozen streak threading the camp. Jim held his hands in his pockets, keeping them warm against the moment when a fast draw meant victory against Duke Madden, or death for Jim Harrigan.

"Keep 'em off my back," Jim said when they reached the Domino. "I'll do the rest."

They pushed open the saloon door, a rush of wind sweeping in with them. Jim shut it, his right hand close to gun butt as his eyes scanned the packed crowd. Boomer Burke was bellied against the bar halfway along it. Duke Madden was in his shirt sleeves, his back to the door as he watched the keno game in the gambling room.

Silence spread across the saloon like a high wave spills water over a flat beach. Boomer Burke whispered—"Harrigan."—as if the word were a curse, and the whisper ran into the silence.

Slowly Duke Madden made his turn, saw who it was, and tongued his long cigar to the other side of his mouth, his inscrutable eyes giving no hint of the feelings that were in him.

Even the chalk-faced man stopped playing the piano and turned on his bench to watch Jim. There was no sound but the girl's voice at the roulette wheel: "Seventeen and black." It, too, died as Jim climbed to the bar top.

He had seen some of the papers on the floor that the boy had delivered, he knew the seed had been planted, and he understood the silence that his entrance had brought to the big room.

"Where's the kid I sent here, Madden?" Jim demanded.

Madden shoved long white fingers into his waistband as he said carelessly: "How the hell would I know?"

Hard on Madden's words a floor man in the corner by the piano went for his gun. It was a mistake, a fatal one, and he died without firing a shot. Head thrown back, he took a wobbly step, and then his control gave way and he fell like a tent with its ropes slashed in a single stroke.

Jim swung his smoking gun to Madden. "Get the kid," he said, "or I'll drill you between the eyes."

"He's around somewhere." Madden motioned to a floor man. "See if you can find him, Pete."

Madden was playing this in his usual shrewd way so that no blame would come to him. Nor could he be held for what his employees did. The floor man who'd made his try. The barkeep who sidled back along the mahogany and was carefully lifting his shotgun when Webb pulled one trigger. The blast nearly took the barkeep's head off.

"I've got another barrel," the editor croaked. "Anybody want it?"

No one did. Silence came again as the echoes of the shotgun's roar died. Then Madden nodded at the boy who was being pushed through a door in the back.

"Here's your kid, Harrigan," Madden said coolly. "Now get out and let the boys get on with their drinking."

"I've got something to say first," Jim said. "Mebbe some of 'em didn't see the papers the kid passed out."

Light from the overhead lamps made a bright shine on the uplifted faces: gamblers' white ones, the paint and rouge on the percentage girls, miners' beards, the bronzed faces of packers. Here was a cross section of Gold Plume, tough and licentious, but holding a spark of decency and a flame of resentment against Duke Madden.

"If you can handle yourself on snowshoes," Jim said, "you don't have to worry. There's plenty of grub on the other side of Star Mountain. If you're staying here all winter, you'd better start worrying because you'll be busted by spring. Either in here or paying Madden's prices. With five thousand people stuck in Gold Plume for a winter that's starting early, you don't have to be smart to see how it'll be by spring."

"That sheet the kid passed out said Rocking C had some beef." It was the big butcher, Taylor, who had tried to crook Half Pint Ord that first day Jim was in camp. "That's a lie because I bought the last Rocking C steer."

"We brought a herd in from Utah. Come out and see 'em. If they're stolen, you'll know who done it and why. In the end it'll be our beef that decides whether Madden busts you with his prices."

"You're piling it on," Madden said in his mild tone. "You reckon the boys will believe the coyote who killed Ira Raeder?"

"The coyote who killed Ira Raeder was your man, Grizzly Brashada," Jim shouted angrily, "and I killed him! Who's the *hombre* who claims he saw me come out of the cabin?"

"He ain't here!" Burke shouted.

"The hell he ain't!" a man in the gambling room cried. "Here he is, Harrigan. Mink Drusy."

Drusy was a little man who was being shoved into the saloon from the gambling room against his will. Raising bloodshot eyes, he cried: "Don't shoot me, Harrigan!"

"But you'd have hung me with your lying story!" Jim raged. "Tell the boys how you could see me in the dark that night!"

"I couldn't!" Drusy shrieked. "I lied!"

"Why?"

Drusy tried to duck behind Madden. Somebody hit him and drove him back into the saloon. He shot a glance at Burke and licked dry lips. "Burke made me."

Jim grinned. He'd planted more seed and he'd have a good crop. It was here in the faces of these men.

"Get back to your drinking, boys!" Jim called. "Don't send anybody after me, Madden, or I'll shoot their ears off."

Jim motioned for Webb and the boy to leave. Then he jumped down from the bar and backed through the door, cocked gun held hip high. Slamming the door shut, he slapped a bullet through it that sang over the heads of those inside.

"Go with Webb," Jim ordered the boy. "Webb, stay inside and keep your door locked. This'll boil up fast now."

Jim raced along the street to his horse and, swinging up, quit town at a fast pace, hoofs ringing on the frozen ground. There was no pursuit. Madden's move would come later. Under cover of darkness.

Stabling his horse, Jim went into the house to find Ord and Belle waiting beside the stove for the coffee to boil.

"What kind of a dido have you been up to now?" Ord asked.

Jim told them, and added: "The minute we

72

shoved that herd over the pass, we put a bee inside Madden's pants and took a reef on his belt. We'll hear from him tonight."

"But you don't know what he'll do," Belle said.

"Burn our stacks," Ord suggested.

"He ain't the one to destroy anything he thinks he can get later on." Jim took the cup Belle handed him. "He'll try to get me and Ord, thinking he can make a deal then."

"I won't deal with him on any terms," Belle said.

"Then you'll get the same dose. Any place in town you can go?"

"I'm staying here."

The way Belle said it told Jim there was nothing he could say that would change her mind. He finished the coffee and set the cup on the table, feeling admiration for this girl.

"I didn't see anything of Rush," Jim said. "We'll find out tonight."

He expected her to flare up, to say he had been the one who had driven Rush from this house. But meeting his hungry searching gaze, she said simply: "We can't help Rush if Madden kills us."

"He won't," Jim said sharply. "We'll be ready for him. Fetch all the guns and ammunition you've got. Pile it on the table. Ord and me will nail up the windows. We can hold off an army for a month."

"Dad made shutters for the windows," Belle told him. "They're upstairs."

Ord had moved to the window. Now he said: "Looks like Madden's coming, Jim."

Swearing, Jim wheeled to the window. A line of horsemen, dark against the snow, were coming from town. A dozen, Jim saw, and he cursed himself for letting Madden outguess him.

"It isn't Madden's bunch," Belle said with certainty. "Those are the men Raeder would have picked for his vigilantes."

Breath came out of Jim in a long relieved sigh. "Then it's what I've been playing for. Come on, Ord."

Jim and Ord were waiting in front of the house when the riders pulled up. "We're here to do what Ira Raeder would have done if he was still alive," the leader said. "We're ashamed that a stranger had to start the job we should have done."

"I'm glad to see you," Jim said soberly. "I was beginning to think we'd bitten off too big a bite."

The spokesman looked past the corrals to where the cattle stood huddled against the cliff. "Those steers are the only food in Gold Plume Madden don't control. Our job is to protect them and you folks. How do you want us to do it?"

"Two men to stand guard," Jim said quickly. "Madden might try to burn the stacks or steal the herd. The rest of you split the breeze getting here if you hear any shooting."

"Jones. Cartwright." The leader nodded at two of his men. "Take it till midnight. We'll send two more out then." He brought his gaze to Jim. "We've got to draw or drag now after what you done today. The camp's buzzing. The boys are talking like you was Paul Revere himself. Now reckon we'd better get back. We've got fifty men to organize."

Jim watched them go, feeling the tug of doubt. A dozen men like these would be stronger than fifty uncertain ones.

"You boys stay in the barn," Jim told the two who had been left. "I'll bring your supper out. If Madden tackles the house, you light out for help."

They were hectic hours until dark, checking guns and ammunition, seeing that there was ample food and water in the house, and putting shutters into place that Sam Calvert had prepared years ago against a possible Ute attack.

It was dark when Belle called supper. Jim took food to the men in the barn and, coming back, ate with Belle and Ord.

"Madden's licked," Jim said jubilantly. "What we needed was somebody to think there was a chance of licking Madden and start organizing."

Jim's feeling was contagious. "Sure," Ord said, "we'll give 'em hell."

And for the first time since he had come back from Utah, Jim saw real hope in Belle's eyes.

"I've been sorry I ever brought you into this, Jim," she said, "because I couldn't see anything but death for us. It was just that I was too stubborn to quit. Dad had so many dreams. . . ."

"*Belle!*"

It was a high cry, shrill and demanding, from somewhere back of the house. The wind had increased; there was the scream of it around the eaves that was as horrible as a banshee's wail, but this was different. It was human, yet it seemed to be something else, coming as it did with the screech of the wind.

"*Belle!*"

It came again. Closer now. Just outside the door. They sat at the table paralyzed, heads turned to catch the sound.

Then Belle whispered: "It's Rush."

Jim knew what was in her mind. If Rush was dead, this was not a human cry. But Rush wasn't dead if he could make a sound like that. With that thought, Jim knew what it was, but he was too late. Belle was out of her chair and raising the bar that held the back door.

"Wait, Belle!" Jim shouted, but there was no stopping her.

She flung the door open. Jim palmed his gun, but he was too late. They piled in, Duke Madden in front, Belle gripped tightly before him, the muzzle of his .45 shoved hard against her ribs.

"Drop your iron, Harrigan," Madden said with-

76

out feeling. "Boomer was right. We should have got you when you first hit town."

Jim let his gun go. Ord, caught flat-footed, made no try for his Colt. Burke was there. The big butcher, Si Taylor. Others Jim had never seen. And back of them, a bloody bandage around his face, stood Rush Kane.

Fury rolled through Jim. "You sniveling yellow pup!" he raged. "You knew Belle would open the door when you yelled like that."

"Pretty smart, wasn't it?" Madden glowed. "Maybe a little smarter than you were when you pulled off that job you did this afternoon." He jerked a thumb at Burke. "Look around, Boomer. Some of that vigilante bunch might be inside." He grinned at Jim. "We got the two boys in the barn."

A moment before Jim had been completely confident. Now there was no hope at all. He stood there, stooped a little, his mind on the gun at his feet.

"Even the yellow bellies in this camp won't stand for you shooting a woman," Ord said hotly.

Madden's smile was quick and wicked. "No shooting, runt, but any house can have a fire, especially on a cold night."

Jim saw that it would work as perfectly as Madden had thought. They'd be slugged, and left in a burning house with no proof that Madden had been there. There would only be the ashes, and the bones of those who had died.

Burke and the others came back into the kitchen. "Empty," he said.

"Got the coal oil, Si?" Madden asked.

"Right here," the butcher said.

"Lay your gun barrel across their heads, Boomer," Madden ordered, his voice held to a casual tone. "Put Harrigan's iron in his holster. It'll look better to find their guns beside their bodies. Better put them in bed, too. Somebody might wonder why they were burned to death in the kitchen."

Rush Kane was a forgotten man, a man who had lost his right to merit others' respect. Only his eyes seemed alive in that mass of bandages, eyes of a madman who can be pilloried no more. Taylor passed in front of him, and in one quick motion Rush swept the butcher's gun from holster and, wheeling, fired at close range over Belle's head. The bullet caught Madden above the left eye.

The kitchen was an inferno then, and Rush Kane's body broke under half a dozen bullets. Jim dropped to his knees and, gripping his gun, tilted it upward and drove a slug into Boomer Burke's wide chest. Ord's thundering .45 brought Taylor down in a sweeping fall.

Lead beat at Jim. There was the numbing pain of it along his ribs and his left thigh, the warmth of spreading blood. He propped himself on one arm, still firing until his hammer dropped on an empty. The door crashed open.

Jim heard, as if from a great distance, the pound of running feet. He came flat, trying to crawl toward a gun that lay in front of him, but he never reached it. For in that moment all sight and sound died for Jim Harrigan.

Jim was in bed when he came to. He felt the house rock as a blast of wind struck, heard the low moan. Then he was aware of the lighted lamp on the bureau, of Belle sitting beside him.

"Rush?"

"Dead," she told him. "He must have gone to town after Madden, and they got the drop on him. I suppose they held him prisoner until they needed him. His face was slashed to pieces with a knife. That must have been how they got him to call out like he did."

Maybe it was good guessing. Maybe bad. He wasn't sure what Belle really thought, for she said: "Rush was always a weak one, and he never got along with Dad. That was why he left and took another name. But Dad would have been proud of him tonight."

"He died a brave man," Jim said.

"He'd have liked to hear you say that. It's given to some to be strong just like it's given some to be weak. He thought so much of you because you were strong, and I think it was why he loved Ann."

"Ord?"

"He's gone for a doctor."

He closed his eyes then. The shadow of Rush Kane was no longer between them. There were many hills along his back trail. Lonely hills. He had ridden with a badge on his shirt and a gun on his hip. He had been cursed and hated and feared. Never, in all those years, had he done anything for the love of a woman.

He opened his eyes and looked at Belle, and she must have seen what was there, for she bent and kissed him. He knew, then, that the last hill was behind him.

TWIN ROCKS

I

Morgan Dill rode into Twin Rocks with the full moon a bright arc along the eastern horizon. The evening light was very thin, the flaming sky above the western hills the only reminder of the nearly spent day. Morgan was tired and dirty, his buckskin gelding was dusty and sweat-gummed from the long hours on the road. They had left Steamboat Springs at sunup. It seemed a long time ago.

The banker, Dick Lamar, had sent for Morgan and told him to stay on the side streets, but Morgan with arrogant perversity ignored Lamar's advice and rode down the middle of Main Street. He glanced at the Runyan house as he passed it, thinking briefly of Molly. At one time he had been very much in love with her and had expected to marry her. She had worn his ring for two years, and then had given it back without an adequate explanation.

For a moment the old bitterness rushed back into him, then it was gone. He had left town three years ago right after they had broken up because he couldn't stand living in the same town Molly did, seeing her and knowing he had lost her, but somewhere along the line he had been able to detach himself from his memories. Now he could think of her without pain.

Molly had lived in that house all of her life with her mother and her sister Jean. Her father had died soon after Jean was born and Mrs. Runyan had raised the girls and had succeeded in thoroughly spoiling Molly. Now, looking back, he decided that he had been lucky he hadn't married her. Still, he wondered what had happened to her. Maybe she had married someone else and had several children by now.

He stopped at a water trough near the corner and dismounted. He drank from the pipe, sloshed water over his stubble-covered face, and let his horse drink. He stood at the end of the trough, looking along the street that had not changed in the three years he had been gone.

Suddenly he noticed that Johnny Bedlow, the barber, had just left his shop, stopped to lock his front door, and now was hurrying along the street toward Morgan. For just a moment Morgan thought about turning his back as Johnny passed. Chances were that in the thin light the barber wouldn't recognize him, then he thought, to hell with it.

Lamar's reason for his staying off Main Street wasn't good enough. All he had said was that Morgan's sister Celia was ready to make a deal for his half of the Rafter D, the Dill ranch that had been inherited by them when their father had died four years ago, and that, if Buck Armand, Morgan's brother-in-law, saw him, there would be trouble.

Johnny Bedlow had been one of Morgan's best friends and the last man in town he would turn his back on. He stepped from the street to the boardwalk, saying: "Howdy, Johnny. Long time no see." He held out his hand, but Johnny didn't take it. He simply stopped and stared as if he were seeing a ghost, then he wheeled and ran back up the street without saying a word.

"Well I'll be damned!" Morgan said aloud, staring at Johnny's back until he disappeared around the corner at the far end of the block.

He mounted and, wheeling his horse, rode along the side of the Mercantile that was on the corner. He turned into the alley behind it, thinking there was no use to worry about Johnny Bedlow, but he couldn't get what had happened out of his mind. Of all the friends he'd had in Twin Rocks, he had been sure Johnny was one he could bank on, the one who would be glad to see him and give him the warmest welcome.

Morgan had never had a real enemy in his life unless it was Buck Armand. Maybe Dick Lamar, too, who used to fawn over Molly for the two years she had been engaged to Morgan. On the other hand, he'd had a number of good friends such as Johnny Bedlow and the deputy sheriff, Tully Bean.

There were many who were in between, folks who said the Dill boy never would grow up. Not bad, they said, but a hell-raiser. He'd ride into town with the Rafter D crew, shooting at the sky and yelling his head off and sending chickens squawking as they scurried off the street and making dogs dodge horses' hoofs as they ran to safety with their tails between their legs.

Part of this was just letting off steam. The rest of it was plain Dill arrogance that Morgan had inherited from his father, old Abe Dill, commonly known as Lucifer Dill. The crew, including Buck Armand, the foreman, shared Abe's arrogance. So did Morgan's sister Celia.

Morgan reined and dismounted a few feet from the back door of the bank. He grinned as he thought about Celia. Nature had sure made one hell of a mistake in deciding her sex. She should have been born a boy. She had been cut from the same pattern old Abe had and had been his favorite child. Morgan had fought with her from the day he learned to walk, but she had held her own until he was almost grown. He wondered if she lost her temper with her husband the way she used to with him.

He turned to the back door of the bank and was reaching for the knob when he heard a woman call: "Morgan! Morgan Dill!"

He wheeled away from the door, not recognizing the woman in the thin light until she had almost reached him, and then he thought it was Molly. He opened his mouth to call her by name, wanting to appear casual about meeting her, but his mouth was dry and he couldn't say anything.

Then he was glad he hadn't said anything. He realized it wasn't Molly at all, but her sister. She had changed so much he found it hard to believe it was Jean. He remembered her as a skinny schoolgirl with pigtails down her back and a wide-eyed admiration for him every time he called on Molly. Now she was a woman and a pretty one at that.

He was even more surprised at the way she greeted him. She threw her arms around him and hugged him, and then she kissed him. It wasn't an ordinary, run-of-the-mill kiss, either, but the passionate kiss of a woman who loved a man and hadn't seen him for a long time. He was too surprised to comment.

She finally drew back, whispering: "Oh, Morgan, I was afraid I was too late. I'm such a coward. I knew I had to come, but I kept putting it off, and then hated myself because I waited so long."

"So long for what?" he demanded. "And how did you know I would be here?"

"I was afraid I'd be too late to keep you from going into the bank," she whispered. "Get on your horse and ride out of town. Don't see Dick Lamar. Don't ride out to the Rafter D, either."

He shook his head. "I don't know what you're talking about, but I ain't leaving town until I've seen Lamar. He wrote to me saying that Celia wanted to settle up for my half of the Rafter D.

I don't want any part of the spread because I couldn't get along with Buck Armand, so I'll take what cash I can get and mosey on."

She gripped his arms. "You listen to me, Morgan. You've been gone for three years. As far as I know, you haven't heard from anyone in the county. Even Dick wouldn't have known where you were if you hadn't got into that fight in Steamboat Springs and got thrown into jail. He wouldn't have known where to write if he hadn't seen it in the newspaper."

"You're right on one thing," he said. "I ain't heard from nobody in this burg since I left, except Lamar. But I don't see . . ."

"Everything's changed since you left," she said. "If you stay here, you'll be killed. Or you'll kill someone and they'll hang you. I can't tell you about it now because I don't want Dick to know I'm here. If you'll come to the house, I'll tell you . . . and then you'll have to leave town."

"I won't leave town until I've seen Lamar," he said stubbornly.

"Did he tell you what kind of a deal Celia will give you?" she asked.

"No, but my half of the Rafter D ought to be worth twenty-five thousand dollars," he said. "Maybe more, but I'll take less just to get some cash, and then I'll stay away from here the rest of my life."

"You're a fool," she said, exasperated. "You

never could savvy a man like Dick Lamar. He's a liar and a cheat and a thief. I can't prove those things, but I *know* he's all of them. Stay away from him, Morgan. You don't know how to handle a slimy crook like that."

"I never figured he was much man, but I can't believe he's that bad. I'll take what Celia will give me and then I'll sashay out of town . . . which same will make you happy, I guess."

Her grip on his arms tightened. "Morgan, did you know that Dick was trying to take Molly away from you all the time you were engaged to her?"

"Well, yes, I figured that was what . . ."

"And did you know he was the cause of Molly's giving your ring back and that they're married now?"

The news jolted the breath out of him. He said after a long silence: "No, I didn't know that."

"Come to the house with me, Morgan," she said. "My mother's dead and I live alone. You'll be safe. I'll take care of you and hide you and I'll tell you a few things you need to know."

"I'll come after I see Lamar," he said, and turned to the door.

She stamped her foot. "Oh, you are a stubborn man. You always were. You haven't changed one bit. I'm going to get the sheriff. He's the only one who might keep Dick Lamar honest, but I'm not so sure he can."

She whirled away, and ran down the alley. He stared at her back until she disappeared in the twilight. For just a moment he wondered if he should have done what she said, then he shrugged. He could think of some men he ought to be afraid of, but Dick Lamar was not one of them.

He opened the door and walked along the hall past the door of Lamar's private office and went on into the bank. Then he found himself looking into the muzzle of Dick Lamar's gun.

The banker said: "Welcome back, sucker."

II

Sheriff Ed Smith climbed the stairs to Judge Alcorn's office above the bank. He was uneasy, and short-tempered because of it. The uneasiness stemmed from the fact that he didn't know what was going to happen, but he was dead sure that *something* was going to happen—something bad.

Plant enough whirlwind seed and sooner or later someone was going to reap it. There had been plenty of whirlwind seed planted in Twin Rocks basin, and Ed figured he was the most likely candidate to do the reaping.

The judge's door was open and Ed went in without knocking. Sam Colter, the hotel owner, and Baldy Miles, who ran the Mercantile, were already there. They were the town fathers who, along with Judge Alcorn, had run things as long as Ed could remember. That is, the three men had run things in accordance with the way old Abe Dill had wanted them run, and as long as Abe had been alive the relationship had worked very well. Now, with Buck Armand running the Rafter D, everything was different.

The men in the room nodded and said, "Howdy." The judge motioned to a chair and pushed a box of cigars at Ed. The three men were old; Ed Smith was of the following generation. He had a wife he loved and three children in whom he took inordinate pride. Because of them, he did not have the slightest desire to get himself killed.

No one said anything for a moment as Ed took a cigar and bit off the end. He fumbled in a vest pocket for a match, thinking that this situation reminded him of the saying about wars: the old men started them and the young men fought them. He didn't consider himself a young man at thirty-five, but he was still the right age to do the fighting and the dying. The other men weren't.

When Ed had his cigar going, the judge said: "I asked you men to come here to talk things over because I see some problems developing I'd like to get solved before they blow up in our faces."

"In case you're talking about the Rafter D," Baldy Miles said, "they owe me over two thousand dollars for supplies. Asking 'em for it is like spitting into a hard wind. I'd like to cut 'em off, but I'm afraid to. Buck Armand is the meanest bastard I ever seen."

Sam Colter laughed softly. "And we used to think old Abe was a mean one. At least you knew how you stood with him, but you never know how you stand with Armand or what he'll do."

"He wants something for nothing all the time," Miles grumbled. "That's one thing you always know about him."

"And he's pretty damned sure we're gonna give it to him," Colter added.

"So far you have," Ed said.

Miles and Colter got red in the face. Ed told himself he shouldn't have said it, but the truth was he couldn't stand up against the Rafter D by himself and he'd never had any help from the Twin Rocks businessmen. If Miles and Colter got sore about what he'd just said, he'd tell them a few of the facts of life.

They didn't say anything, but it was plain they hadn't liked what he'd said. They stared at the floor a while as the alarm clock on the judge's desk ticked off the seconds, then Alcorn said: "I've given in to Armand, too, Ed. I ain't proud of it, but I've done it, and I figure you have, too. You're afraid to arrest a Rafter D man. If you did arrest one of 'em, I'd be afraid to sentence him. Now it's got clean out of hand. Either we do what we know damned well we should have done a long time ago or we resign and let somebody else enforce the law and handle the court."

"If you two resign," Miles said, "the rest of us might as well walk out of the basin and let Buck Armand have everything."

"I reckon you're saying the same thing the judge just said." Ed nodded at Miles. "I agree. It's time we all took a stand."

He paused, thinking again of his wife and children. He guessed he hadn't thought of much else the last few days. For a moment he wished he hadn't said what he had, then he saw the pleasure that washed across the judge's wrinkled face and he was glad he had said it, after all.

"Then we'll hang and rattle," the judge said. "There's two things that pushed me into calling this gab session. One is Armand's proposition to all the small ranchers that they've got to throw in with the Rafter D this fall when he drives to the railroad. On the face of it I guess it looks good. It'll save money and work all around, but Armand made it a have-to deal. I don't like that."

"You figure Armand will make some money for himself out of it?" Ed asked.

"I dunno," Alcorn admitted, "but it ain't like him to make an offer like that if he ain't feathering his own nest."

"He can overcharge the small fry for handling their stock," Ed said thoughtfully.

"He might grab the cars for his Rafter D steers and let the rest of 'em whistle," Miles said. "Seems like there's always a shortage of cars."

"Why, hell, he may just come right out and steal 'em," Colter said. "He's too big for his britches. He figures he's big enough to make it stick."

"All right, there you are," the judge said. "It's my guess he'll do one or maybe all of those things. The second item that worries me is more important because it can happen any day, while the roundup is two months off. What will happen if Morgan Dill rides into the basin?"

"Nobody knows where he is," Miles said, surprised.

"It don't make no difference where he is," the judge said. "I've got a hunch he'll be riding in any day. You see, old Abe always favored Celia as I reckon everybody knows, so his will put everything in her hands until Morgan was twenty-five. Well, his birthday is two days from right now."

"Armand will kill him," Ed muttered.

No one said anything for several seconds. They sat considering what Ed had just said. Finally Miles nodded his head. "He might at that. He's a killer. I don't figure Celia can stop him."

"I've been thinking along that same line," Alcorn said, "only it struck me that Armand might figure out a way to lure Morgan back into the basin just so he can kill him. Maybe there's no

94

hurry for him to murder Morgan because the spread would all go to Celia if Morgan's dead. It's just that it would be a little neater and easier to handle if it happens before Morgan's birthday. At least, that's the way it seems to me."

"He always hated Morg," Ed said. "I saw a few cases of it when Abe was alive and Armand was rodding the Rafter D. It's my opinion that the will leaving control of the spread to Celia had more to do with Morg leaving the basin than Molly Runyan giving him his ring back."

"I wouldn't be surprised," Alcorn said.

"I don't savvy this," Colter said. "Morgan Dill's got to look out for his own hide. Why are *we* concerned about it?"

"Because I have always liked Morgan," Ed said sharply. "I don't want to see him murdered if I can help it."

"There's another thing, too, Ed," Alcorn said. "I always figured Morgan was wild, but that was just the kid in him. He'll grow up, and, when he does, he'll be a good man. If *he* was running the Rafter D, we wouldn't have no trouble. On the other hand, if he's killed and we can prove Armand did it, which I figure we can unless Armand's smarter'n I think he is, and Ed goes out to arrest him, there'll be all hell to pay."

"Yeah," Ed said, feeling sick as he thought about it. "I might just shoot myself before I rode out there with Tully. The two of us would get shot, so we might as well save ourselves the ride."

"I still don't see what you're driving at, Judge," Colter said.

"It's time I laid it out," Alcorn said. "How much does the Rafter D owe you?"

"About two hundred and fifty for rooms and meals and drinks," Colter said.

"The way I see it," Alcorn said, "Armand never intends to pay it any more than he intends to pay Baldy. It boils down to a matter of extortion, with Buck Armand's thinking he's got everybody buffaloed to the place where he can keep getting everything free. Now I want you two"—he nodded at Colter and Miles—"to notify Armand that you'll sue if they don't pay immediately. I'll ride out to the Rafter D and deliver our message. If there's trouble, I'll be the one to get it."

"I'll ride with you," Ed said.

He wondered what his wife would say when he told her what he'd volunteered to do. Playing safe had become a habit, and he wasn't proud of his record any more than the judge was proud of his. Better not tell Mary what he was going to do, he thought. Not till he got back, if he did.

"I'll write that letter first thing in the morning," Miles said.

Colter nodded. "So will I. I ain't sure it's a smart thing to do, but I guess we've all reached the place where we don't like ourselves much. It's like we've been saying. We've got to take a stand."

"One more thing," Alcorn said. "I ain't sure it's got anything to do with Armand or not, or with Morgan. I'm thinking about Dick Lamar. If the gossip about his gambling is true, the bank may be in bad shape. I'd hate to think what will happen to the basin if the bank has to close its doors."

Ed rose and dropped his cigar butt into the spittoon. "Why don't you ask Dick about it?"

"I have," Alcorn said, "but he denies doing any more gambling than any of us do. He claims the bank's as solid as the Twin Rocks themselves."

"There's talk about it not being solid," Colter said. "We hear it in the hotel bar. It's got to the place where all it'll take is for someone to yell . . . 'Fire' . . . and we'll have a run on the bank."

"I have been thinking," Alcorn said, "that, if you two could get your money out of the Rafter D, and if we can borrow enough in Grand Junction, which I think we can, we'd do well to make Lamar an offer. I think he'd be glad to sell."

"We'd never raise that kind of money," Colter said, "though I've got to admit that we need a solid bank in Twin Rocks."

"This ain't none of my concern," Ed said, "so I'll get along home. Mary's been expecting me for an hour."

As he turned toward the door, the thought occurred to him that the whole conversation had been a waste of time. It was a matter of locking the barn after the horse was stolen. They should have stopped Buck Armand as soon as he started throwing his weight around right after old Abe Dill died. Now it was probably too late, and all he and the judge would do, if they rode out to the Rafter D, would be to get themselves killed.

He stopped halfway to the door. Someone was pounding up the stairs from the street. A moment later Johnny Bedlow rushed into the room, out of breath. It took him a while to get his breath again, then he blurted: "Morgan Dill's in town. I just seen him." He swallowed and hurried on: "Buck Armand and a couple of his tough hands were in the shop getting their hair cut the other day. Armand got to talking about how ornery Morg always was to Celia. He said if Morg ever showed up in town, he'd kill him."

Ed wheeled to look at the judge, who was staring blankly at Johnny Bedlow. For several seconds there was absolute silence except for the hammering of the alarm clock. Then Alcorn said heavily: "He was just paving the way. What he'll really kill Morgan for is to keep him from claiming his half of the Rafter D."

"You've got to do something, Ed," Bedlow said. "Morg was my friend. That stinking bastard of a Buck Armand will do just what he says."

"If Morg will stay out of town . . . ," Ed began.

"But he ain't gonna do no such thing," Bedlow broke in. "You know that. He ain't the kind to run from nobody."

"Where'd you see him?" Ed asked.

"He was watering his horse in front of the Mercantile," Bedlow answered. "He said howdy and wanted to shake hands. All I could think of was Armand saying he'd kill him. I knew it wouldn't do no good to tell Morg to go hide, so I went to the courthouse to find you, and Tully told me you was here."

Again there was silence except for the alarm clock. Slowly Ed turned from Johnny Bedlow to face the judge. He asked: "How do you keep a man from being murdered?"

"You wait," Alcorn said. "You can't arrest a man just for what he says he's going to do."

"Yeah," Ed said gloomily, "and that'll do Morg a hell of a lot of good, won't it . . . arresting Armand after he's killed Morg?"

III

For a long moment Morgan stood staring at the banker, not moving a muscle. This was incredible. It simply made no sense. Dick Lamar had sent for him and then met him with a gun in his hand! Allowing for the fact that he had never liked Lamar and Lamar had never liked him, it still made no sense.

"What's the matter with you?" Morgan demanded. "And why am I a sucker? You wrote me that Celia was ready to make me an offer. You asked me to come to see you, and I did. What's the gun for?"

Lamar rose, the gun still lined on Morgan's chest. "The gun is to make sure you do what I tell you to," Lamar said. "You're a sucker for believing you'd get a good deal from Celia. I'm looking out for her interest, not yours."

Lamar motioned to a sheet of paper on the desk. Beside it was a pen and a bottle of ink. A canvas sack with the words, **Twin Rocks State Bank**, was there, too.

"I've got a right to know your intentions," Morgan said. "Do you intend to kill me?"

"Buck Armand would prefer it that way," Lamar said, "but I'm not one to take chances. I might have a hard time convincing the sheriff I had killed you in self-defense, so I don't intend to if I can help it, but I will if you don't do exactly what I tell you. I'm reasonably sure I could make it stick by telling Ed Smith you were holding me up and aiming to clean out the safe, but there is a slim chance he wouldn't believe me, so I'd rather play it safe."

Morgan's hands fisted at his sides and opened and closed again. With the exception of Buck Armand, he had never seen a man he could hate as wholeheartedly as he could hate Dick Lamar. He told himself he should have listened to Jean. He had thought he had nothing to fear from Lamar, but he'd been dead wrong.

"All right, Lamar," Morgan said. "You got me here promising that Celia was ready to make a deal for my share of the Rafter D. I don't want any part of the outfit. I want my money and I'll go out to Oregon and buy a spread."

"Good," Lamar said. "Very good. That's what Celia wants, too. Now on the desk you'll find an agreement. Sign it. Beside it is a sack of money that Celia left for me to give to you. Sign the agreement and take the money. It's that simple."

"Then why do you need the gun?"

"I was afraid you'd have second thoughts about giving up your right to half of the property," Lamar said. "I don't aim to let you change your mind. Buck and Celia have worked hard on the Rafter D after your pa died. They have no intention of giving up half of it to you."

Something was wrong, but at the moment Morgan couldn't see what it was. He could understand about Celia and her husband wanting to keep the spread they were living on, and he could also understand Buck Armand not wanting him around for the simple reason that they had never got along and there was no reason to think, with Morgan three years older than when he had left the basin, that they would get along any better now.

He stepped up to the desk and picked up the paper. The statement was short and to the point:

I, Morgan Dill, being of sound mind, and understanding what I am signing, of my own free will do surrender any rights I have to the Rafter D in favor of my sister Celia. In exchange I acknowledge the receipt of one thousand dollars ($1,000.00) in cash.

Signature:_____.

Witness: *Richard Lamar.*

So that was it. For $1,000 he'd give up his half of the Rafter D, which was worth at least $25,000. He stepped back, and shook his head.

"So, that's the deal Celia is offering," he said. "You crooked son-of-a-bitch. You called me here to offer me . . ."

"Don't call me names, you idiot," Lamar said angrily. "It won't do you any good. Celia wants this settled before you're twenty-five. It'll be less trouble this way. We didn't have to give you anything, but we thought it would be better to let you have a thousand dollars. Now sign the paper and take your money and git."

Morgan didn't move. He studied Lamar, thinking that the man had not changed in looks or habits. He had the same narrow, sharp-featured face and thin-lipped mouth, the same muddy brown eyes that never seemed to hold any expression and certainly did not reflect the smile that came so readily to his lips. He was smiling now as if certain Morgan would do exactly what he told him to do.

"I think I'll go see Celia," Morgan said. "This deal with you smells like there's something mighty rotten around here. I don't know whether it's you or the deal I smell, but I guess Celia can tell me."

The ready smile faded. Lamar's face turned red. He said: "I guess I didn't make myself clear. You don't have any choice. You'll sign or I'll kill you and swear you were robbing me. The safe door is open in case you didn't notice. There are a few gold pieces on the floor that I'll say you dropped when you ran. I'll tell Ed Smith you threw a gun on me and made me unlock the safe, then you grabbed all the money you could handle and left. Or started to, but I got hold of my gun in time to kill you before you left the bank."

Lamar's face was cold and utterly devoid of feeling. Morgan had never heard of the banker killing anybody, but he was sure he was capable of it. Morgan was as sure of that as he had ever been sure of anything. He probably could make it stick, too. Ed Smith was a good sheriff, and he'd have his suspicions, but he couldn't prove that Lamar had murdered Morgan Dill. He'd have to believe Lamar's story.

Still Morgan hesitated, telling himself he would have signed the paper if Celia had offered any kind of reasonable deal. He had not expected

$25,000, but he had expected a hell of a lot more than $1,000.

"Maybe you've never pegged me for a killer," Lamar said. "I don't want to be, but I'm in one hell of a tight squeeze. Killing you will get me out of it. I don't have any choice, Dill. Now make up your mind because I won't wait any longer." He thumbed back the hammer. "Now."

Death was there in Dick Lamar's face, and Morgan could believe the man was as desperate as he said. Morgan took a long breath, deciding it was better to take the money and sign his name than to be murdered. He'd see Celia before he left the basin. As much as they had disliked each other, he had never known her to be as greedy and unfair as this.

He stepped up to the desk, pulled the cork from the bottle of ink, and signed his name on the paper after the word Signature. He dropped the pen and picked up the canvas sack. "Now am I free to go?"

"You're free and you're going fast," Lamar said. "I'll give you thirty seconds to fork your horse and ride, and then I'm running to the back and I'll shoot at you. If you're riding fast, I'll miss, but if you hang around hoping to get a chance to pull your gun, I'll kill you."

He would do it. Morgan sensed that he was as close to death at that moment as he had ever been in his life. He wheeled and ran out of the room and along the hall. When he reached the alley door, he glanced back. Lamar was walking toward him, the cocked gun still in his hand. Morgan knew that if he had made a move for his gun as he was running down the hall, he'd have been a dead man by now.

He lunged through the door, wanting only to get away. Once he was out of range of Lamar's gun, he could start thinking about what he could do, but right now the only smart thing to do was to get out of Twin Rocks. He swung into the saddle and, digging in the steel, rocketed down the alley. He heard two shots, the bullets kicking up dirt ahead of him and to one side, then he heard Lamar yelling: "Help! The bank's been robbed. Help!"

Morgan was out of town before he fully comprehended what had happened. Lamar was going to claim he had robbed the bank. Why? There could be only one reason. Lamar had robbed his own bank and he had to have a patsy. Morgan Dill was it.

He started to pull his horse to a stop, thinking he'd go back and face Ed Smith and his deputy, Tully Bean, and tell them exactly what had happened. But he didn't. He kept on out of town, thinking that neither the sheriff nor his deputy would believe him.

He'd been out of town for three years, and he'd had a reputation as a hell-raiser when he had lived in Twin Rocks. Lamar had been here all the time; he was a banker, a solid citizen. Hell, no, there wasn't a chance he'd be believed. If he claimed he'd returned to sign a paper and receive $1,000 for his part of the Rafter D, they'd figure he was lying.

When the town was a mile behind him, he paused on the bank of Twin Rocks Creek and stepped out of the saddle. As he let his horse drink, he remembered what Jean Runyan had said. She was right. He just didn't savvy a slick schemer like Dick Lamar who dealt off the bottom of the deck. Morgan was used to having everything in the open. As for Lamar's having robbed his own bank—well, it had just never occurred to him that the man would do it.

Actually Lamar wasn't just robbing himself. He was also robbing his depositors. Morgan didn't know what was behind it or what the squeeze was Lamar had mentioned, but he'd have to close the bank. Maybe he'd go to men like Judge Alcorn and Sam Colter and the rest of the businessmen in Twin Rocks and ask them to raise enough capital to start another bank. He'd come out of it smelling like a rose and Morgan would go to prison, if they caught him.

Morgan wiped a hand across his sweaty face. He couldn't see much sense in doing anything but getting out of the basin. If he had any chance to clear himself, he'd go back and fight it out. Then the thought came to him that he hadn't had time to think it out, that he had been surprised and shocked by what had happened. He was sore, too, right down to his boot heels for being taken by Lamar the way he had.

He jammed the canvas sack into one of his saddlebags. Flattening out on the rocks beside the creek, he took a long drink, but the water failed to drown the butterflies in his stomach. He was a hunted man. He had no one to turn to except Jean Runyan, and he guessed there wasn't much she could do for him now.

No use to wait here. Ed Smith and Tully Bean and maybe a posse would be along soon, so he'd better make tracks. Somewhere up in the high peaks to the north he could hole up for a while until his horse was rested. Sooner or later hunger would drive him on over to the other side to find food.

He had a Winchester in the boot and plenty of shells for it, and his revolver. He knew this country. He'd hunted all over it when he was in his teens and early twenties with Johnny Bedlow and Tully Bean. He stepped into the saddle, thinking the next few days would be interesting. Johnny and Tully knew the country as well as he did, and they'd be after him.

He rode north, glancing at the great orange moon that seemed to be floating above the eastern hills like a giant balloon. For just a moment a memory pang shot through him. He had sat on the bank of Twin Rock Creek many a summer evening with Molly's head on his lap and watched the moon come up just as it was coming up now. Then he muttered to hell with it. She belonged to Dick Lamar. He guessed it served both of them right. They were made for each other.

It was not until then that Morgan realized a fork of this road took him right past the Rafter D, the same road he had traveled hundreds of times coming into town and going home. He told himself he'd see Celia, then he gave it up. He certainly didn't want to see Buck Armand. There would only be trouble, if he did, but maybe Armand wouldn't be home. He spent most of his time during the summer in the cow camps to the north. If Morgan could catch Celia and talk to her, he'd soon know whether the $1,000 he'd been given was what she aimed to pay for his share of the ranch, or whether it was Dick Lamar's notion to cheat him.

He wasn't even sure that blaming him for robbing the bank was Celia's idea. It didn't seem like her way of doing things any more than chiseling him out of his part of the ranch for $1,000 had seemed like her. She'd probably changed in three years, but not that much. Maybe, if Celia had cash at the ranch, she'd add something to the $1,000. She usually kept a good deal of money there, partly to pay the crew. It was worth a try, he decided. If he was leaving the basin for good, he'd better have all the money he could get his hands on or he wouldn't have enough to invest when he reached Oregon.

A short time later he turned right on the road that led up the long hill to the Rafter D buildings. He wondered if he would have to kill his brother-in-law if he was home. He'd be doing Celia a favor if he did, and, after being married to Buck Armand as long as she had, the chances were she'd agree with him.

IV

The men in Judge Alcorn's office heard two shots from somewhere below them. For a moment no one was sure where they came from, then Alcorn shouted: "The bank! Lamar's down there. He told me he'd be working late tonight."

Ed Smith was the first through the door and down the stairs, Johnny Bedlow a step behind. When Ed reached the street, Dick Lamar charged out of the bank, yelling: "The bank's been robbed!"

Ed stopped, staring at Lamar in the finger of lamplight that fell past him through the street door of the bank. Bedlow stopped beside him, the three older men reaching the street a moment later. Someone was pounding down the alley, but still Ed stood motionlessly, staring at the banker.

"What's the matter with you, Sheriff?" Lamar

shouted. "The safe was just cleaned out. You heard him riding away. Why aren't you chasing him?"

Under any other set of circumstances that was exactly what he would have done, but he was remembering the conversation about Lamar in Judge Alcorn's office. He had despised the man as long as he had known him. Lamar always reminded him of the garter snakes he had played with as a boy, squirming and twisting and a little too slick. Now, watching Lamar's flushed, narrow face, Ed asked himself why the banker couldn't get his work done in the daytime. Why was he working this late when he had never done it before?

"Who was it?" the judge asked.

After what Johnny Bedlow had said about seeing Morgan Dill in town, Ed figured he knew who Lamar would name. He guessed that Johnny and the rest would think the same thing. Now, still watching Lamar closely, he thought the banker was more squirmy than ever. He looked as guilty as hell, then Ed told himself his imagination was working overtime. He liked Morgan Dill and he detested Dick Lamar. After serving ten years as a lawman, he was still making personal judgments, and that could get him into a pile of trouble.

Lamar took a long time answering. He looked at Ed, then at the judge, the corners of his mouth working nervously. Finally he said: "Morgan Dill."

Ed went past Lamar into the bank, Johnny Bedlow following. The door of the safe was open and this seemed queer, too. Lamar should have shut and locked it long before this. Ed guessed that Morgan Dill, if it had been Morgan, had been in too big a hurry to pick up the money he had dropped.

Lamar was there, then. His face was pale and the pulse in his forehead was pounding as if it were about to break through. He was scared, Ed saw, but if it had really happened, he had a right to be scared.

"Tell us about it," the judge said.

"It won't do any good," Lamar said in a high-pitched voice. "The sheriff just stands there, staring at me. A lot of folks are sure mistaken about him. They say he's a good sheriff."

"Go ahead and tell me what happened," Alcorn said. "Don't pay any attention to the sheriff."

Lamar swallowed. "I was sitting there at my desk. I'd had a busy day and I hadn't found time to clean everything up. I was almost done when young Dill walked in from the alley. He threw a gun on me and said he was taking all the cash I had. He did, too, except for what he spilled." The banker pointed to the coins on the floor, then jabbed a forefinger at Alcorn. "I thought he was going to kill me. He threatened to."

"How much did he get?" Alcorn asked.

"I don't know for sure," Lamar answered. "It'd

be around ten thousand. I always keep that much cash on hand in case of an emergency of some kind."

Ed turned to the door, jerking his head at Alcorn. He said in a low tone: "Come on outside, Judge."

Tears began running down Lamar's cheeks. "Damn you, Smith!" he screamed in a shrill tone. "The longer you wait, the farther away he's getting. Aren't you even going to try to catch him?"

Ed stalked out of the bank, not answering. He waited on the sidewalk. When the judge joined him, he was irritated by Ed's behavior and showed it. Alcorn said: "I never saw you act this way, Ed. What's the matter with you?"

"A lot," Ed said. "A whole lot. This stinks to high heaven, Judge. Morgan Dill never robbed the bank."

Alcorn scowled and pulled at a tip of his white mustache. He asked: "How'd you figure that out?"

"Several things point that way," Ed said, "though I probably wouldn't have thought of it if we hadn't been talking about Lamar in your office."

"All right," Alcorn said. "What are they?"

"In the first place," Ed answered, "I can't see Morgan Dill robbing a bank, any bank, least of all coming home and robbing this one. In the second place, Lamar didn't have a busy day. I was in the bank twice and I walked past it several times and I never seen anyone in there except Lamar. In the

112

third place, I knew Morgan Dill pretty well when he lived here, and I've talked to Tully about him. Tully and him and Johnny Bedlow used to run around together. He's not a man to threaten anybody, and then walk off and not do anything."

Alcorn was still pulling at his mustache and staring thoughtfully at Ed. "I've been thinking some of the same things, but regardless of our suspicions the fact remains that Morgan was here and somebody was riding hell-for-leather getting out of town just now. That might have been Morgan. I want you to bring him in."

"He'll be a hard man to take," Ed said sourly. "It ain't that I'm afraid to tackle a hard man. I've done it plenty of times, but I figure Morg's not guilty, and I also figure he won't know I think that. I don't like the notion of killing or getting killed by an innocent man while the guilty one is sitting here grinning from ear to ear."

Alcorn nodded. "I know how you feel, but I need to talk to Morgan. About the Rafter D, for one thing. I also want to know his side of the story Lamar tells. It's a mighty funny business. I reckon the same idea occurred to you that I had. Lamar may have been stealing gradual-like, all this time, and, when he got down to cases, he figured out a way to get Morgan in here so he'd be blamed."

"That's about the size of it," Ed agreed, "but I sure can't see why Morg would show up here in the bank. Remember that Lamar married Molly

Runyan, and, if a man was ever in love, Morg was in love with Molly."

"Which might be the reason he robbed Lamar's bank," Alcorn said. "Just to get even."

"Hell, he didn't do it," Ed said doggedly. "I figure Lamar must have put some kind of bait that fetched him to Twin Rocks, though I can't make a guess what it was."

"Well, go bring him in," Alcorn said. "We'll see."

Ed hesitated, not liking any part of it. He said: "I'll never find him. He knows the high country like the palm of his hand, and that's where he's headed."

"You've got to try," Alcorn said impatiently. "With Lamar swearing Morgan done it, you've got to go after him or Lamar's long tongue will brand you from one side of the basin to the other."

"All right," Ed said, "but I'm going home and get something to eat first. I'll take Tully along, Johnny Bedlow, too."

Ed waited until Johnny Bedlow came out of the bank with Sam Colter, Baldy Miles remaining behind to talk to Lamar. Ed said: "Johnny, I want you to go with me and Tully. You know Morgan's habits as well as Tully does. Likewise, you know the country north of here."

Johnny shook his head. He said uneasily: "I don't want to go after Morg. I might have to shoot him and I always figured he was my friend."

"Damn it," Ed said harshly, "I don't want to go, neither. You go get Tully. Pick up a quick meal, both of you. I'll meet you with the horses at the jail in half an hour."

He wheeled and walked away, hoping they wouldn't catch up with Morgan Dill. He'd rather stay here in Twin Rocks and keep an eye on Dick Lamar, but Judge Alcorn had said to bring Morgan in. The smart thing was at least to pretend to do what the judge said.

V

Celia Armand sat staring through the window of her kitchen in the Rafter D ranch house. The moon was a full, round circle above the eastern hills and for one short moment she was aware of the beauty of it. She even imagined she could see a face in it, reminding her of a Halloween jack-o'-lantern.

She shrugged and, getting up from the table, walked to the stove and picked up the coffee pot. She filled her cup, and set the pot back on the stove. She had little time to think of any kind of beauty. Her life was filled with hard work and making money and scheming how to make more money, and fighting with her husband.

She often wondered why she had married Buck. She knew what he was before they were married.

Her father had made him foreman a long time ago, but she didn't think old Abe had ever realized how completely ruthless Buck Armand was. She didn't know to this day whether her father had been killed by an accident or whether Buck had murdered him.

Old Abe and Buck had been hauling poles down from one of the peaks to the north and Abe's team had run away with him. He was thrown off the load of poles, his head had hit a rock, and Buck said he was dead by the time he got to him. Maybe it had been that way, but Buck could have hit the old man on the head with a rock and laid him on top of the load of poles and egged the team into running away. The body could have been thrown off the wagon and smashed up just the way it was whether it had been an accident or murder.

Celia knew one thing. Buck Armand was capable of murder. There were times when he looked at her speculatively, as if trying to think of some way to kill her so it would look as if it, too, had been an accident. That was the only way he could ever own the Rafter D. She was thirty years old, she was strong and healthy, and the odds were that she would outlive him.

She sipped her coffee, mentally admitting why she had married Buck. She had discovered a long time ago that she would never find a husband who loved her or who would marry her for what she was. No, any man would marry her because she owned half of the Rafter D; and, someday, if she were lucky, she might own all of it.

She was aware that she was hard to get along with. She was fat and ugly, with an upper lip that held more of a mustache than some men could raise. The answer was plain enough. She married Buck because she needed a man who would run the ranch the way she wanted it run. She had thought, too, that she could manage him. Well, she had been wrong about that. Dead wrong.

She had been just as ugly as a child as she was a woman. Her mother had been slender and frail and very pretty. Morgan, who had been a handsome child, had been her mother's favorite, so Celia had done everything she could to show her father that she loved *him,* and it had worked. After her mother died, she kept on proving to old Abe how much she loved him, although there had been times when she'd hated herself for being a hypocrite. But she had managed well, helping raise Morgan and doing the housework and always playing up to her father in such a manner that he let her have her way and usually asked her for advice on important matters.

As long as she lived, she would not forget that bitter afternoon when she had sat between Morgan and Buck in Judge Alcorn's office and heard the will being read. She had worked so hard to discredit Morgan with their father, playing up his recklessness and telling old Abe that Morgan would never grow up and be capable of running the Rafter D. It hadn't worked in the long run. She had supposed that Morgan would be cut out of the will, maybe getting "one dollar and various considerations" or something like that, with everything else coming to her. But the will had been plain enough. She got half and Morgan was to get half of the ranch when he was twenty-five. One thing saved Celia from going to pieces. She was given the operation of the ranch until Morgan's twenty-fifth birthday. It had been lucky for her that Morgan had quarreled with Molly Runyan and left the country.

Now the time had passed. In two days Morgan would be twenty-five, but neither she nor Buck had the slightest intention of letting him have any part of the ranch. He was coming back, and she wasn't sure yet it had been a smart scheme. Maybe it would backfire. Smart schemes did sometimes. The fear had been growing in her that, once Morgan was out of the way, Buck might find a method of getting rid of her and making it look like an accident.

She hated Morgan. It wasn't just that her mother used to make so much of the boy, then look at her with distaste and say: "You'd better marry the first man who asks you. You're a girl who'll never have much choice." No, it was more than that. Somehow Morgan seemed to have inherited all the good things. He was handsome, he was popular, and he always enjoyed himself whether it was a dance with the girls hanging all over him, or a 4th of July bucking contest which he usually won. It hadn't been fair, she told herself bitterly. She finally had found a husband, but she hated him, too.

Still, hating Morgan was not enough to make her want him murdered. It was what Buck aimed to do, if he had a chance. That was going too far. It was enough to buy him out for a small amount and get him to leave the basin.

She didn't know Buck was standing in the doorway watching her until she rose to get another cup of coffee. He stood, spraddle-legged, his pale blue eyes fixed on her, a faint smile on his meaty lips.

"How long have you been standing there?" she asked as she poured the coffee.

"Quite a while," he said. "You were a long ways off."

"A long ways," she agreed. "I was thinking. Don't kill Morgan."

"Who said anything about killing him?" Armand asked blandly. "I've said all the time I'll just beat hell out of him and put him on his horse and tell him to git."

"You don't have to say anything about it," she said wearily. "I know you better than you know yourself. As long as Morg's alive, you'll be worried about him coming back."

119

Armand's face turned red. "Well, I'd have a right to, wouldn't I? I don't aim to live the rest of my life worrying about him hiding on some rim or behind a tree and plugging me as soon as I get close enough."

"Don't do it," she said. "I'm warning you. The ranch is mine and it'll stay mine, but we don't have to murder my brother to get it." She paused, sensing the anger that was in him, and then she added: "I made a new will and left it with Judge Alcorn. It says you inherit nothing from me if I die by any kind of accident."

His face turned redder. "You think I'm going to kill you?"

"If you knew a sure way to do it and get away scot free, you would," she said. "A man gets used to murder, Buck. One, and then two, and finally three. That's what it would take to make a ranch worth fifty thousand dollars all yours. You were working a few years ago for thirty a month and beans. It wouldn't be bad, would it, Buck?"

"If you're thinking that of me," he said harshly, "you must have the same notion about getting rid of me."

"Why should I get rid of you?" She shook her head. "No, I need you to run the outfit. You don't need me. It's that simple. I'm warning you again. Beat Morgan all you want to, but don't kill him, or I'll go to Ed Smith."

He made a step toward her, his head tipped

120

forward on his bull neck, his great hands fisted at his sides. He stopped, breathing hard, then he said: "No use arguing about it. What I do with Morg depends on what he does. Maybe I won't have to kill him. Maybe the posse will do it for me."

"Or maybe he won't even stop here," Celia said. "I hope he don't."

"He'll stop, all right," Armand said with cold certainty. "He's got a thousand dollars in his pocket and he knows that, if he's satisfied and leaves with that, he'll never get any more."

"I wish I'd never agreed to your scheme in the first place," she said.

"Don't be a fool," he said harshly. "We don't have nothing to worry about. Dick Lamar is the one who's got his neck in a loop. Smith is no fool. The chances are he'll see through that fake hold-up and Lamar will wind up in the Canon City pen for about twenty years."

"You think Lamar will come out here tonight for that thousand he's giving Morgan?" Celia asked.

"Plus the extra four thousand he was to get from us for framing Morgan." Armand gave her a wicked grin. "Oh, he'll be here, all right, but if he pushes too hard, he'll get a dose of lead poisoning. All we have to say is that Lamar was trying to hold us responsible for what your outlaw brother done."

One murder led to another, she thought again. Now, staring at Armand's dark face, she told herself there wasn't any doubt about her father's death. It had not been an accident; it had been murder.

She opened her mouth to accuse him of old Abe's murder, but before she could say a word, he jerked his head at her. "He's coming," he said. "At least somebody's coming, and I'm guessing it's him."

She rose and followed him outside. She was glad she hadn't mentioned her father's death. She couldn't prove anything. All she would have done would be to hasten her own death.

VI

The Rafter D buildings lay at the end of the road that forked off from the county road that led into the high country to the north. Morgan had a strange feeling when he saw the familiar buildings in front of him. He had come home. It was a feeling he had never expected to have about the Rafter D.

Morgan pulled up beside the corral gate and sat his saddle, staring at the sprawling barn and outbuildings, and then at the two-story house farther up the slope. All of the buildings loomed up, tall and dark in the bright moonlight. Nothing about them had changed since he'd been a boy and had played in the mow of the barn and around the corrals, and yet in reality everything had changed.

A tall man left the bunkhouse and strode toward him, but Morgan didn't recognize him until he was less than ten feet away, then he saw it was Slim Turner, a cowhand who was about Morgan's age and had worked here since he was a kid.

"Howdy, Morgan," Turner said. "I didn't recognize you till I got up close."

"Howdy, Slim," Morgan said in a careful tone.

He had no idea how the cowboy would react to his presence. He had always liked the man and had every reason to think Slim liked him, but this was a different situation than it had been when both were riding for the Rafter D.

After a short pause, Morgan asked: "You the only one here?"

"Just me and the boss and Missus Armand," Turner answered. "I guess everybody's been looking for you to show up with your birthday only a day or so away."

Something had happened in the last few seconds as he looked at this place he had once called home. His boyhood had been happy enough as long as his mother was alive. Maybe she had spoiled him as much as old Abe and Celia had claimed. One thing was sure. After his mother died, he had not been spoiled by anybody.

Now it struck him with sharp intensity that half of this spread was rightfully his. He had made up his mind to accept anything he could get from Celia and get to hell out of the basin, but for some reason he reversed himself, knowing he would not do anything of the sort. They would have to work out some kind of arrangement with him, or divide the ranch. If they tried to hold him to the paper he had signed in the bank, he'd tell them he'd had no choice with Dick Lamar's gun on him.

Slim Turner had come close to his buckskin and stood looking up into his face as if trying to determine what was in Morgan's mind. He said: "Was I you, I'd hightail out of here. Everybody knows that half of the outfit belongs to you, but owning it legal-like and getting possession are two different things. Nobody except the boss knows what he's going to do, but I figure I'd better warn you that he . . . ."

"Well! So the bad penny returns!" Buck Armand boomed. "Celia and me thought it would happen about now."

Morgan stepped to the ground. He had not seen Armand and Celia move out of the shadows around the house and cross the yard to him. He wondered if Armand had heard what Slim Turner was saying.

"Howdy, Buck." Morgan nodded at Celia who stood behind her husband, as fat and broad-hipped as ever. He had often wondered if her disposition was due to her physical ugliness. He added—"Howdy, Celia."—and waited.

Slim Turner moved away from him. Morgan stepped forward, watching Armand, who stood with his hands on his hips, a squat, burly man who could kill with his fists. He was like a bulldog, Morgan thought, too stubborn to back up from a position he once had taken.

Celia did not return Morgan's greeting. He was unable to see her face clearly enough in the moonlight to make out what she was thinking and feeling. Suddenly she burst out: "Damn it, Morgan, why did you have to come back?"

Funny how a man changes direction, Morgan thought. A few minutes ago he would have said he had come back to sell his interest in the Rafter D for any reasonable amount she would give him, that he wanted more than the $1,000 he'd received from Lamar. Now, even though he had not forgotten that a posse would soon be after him and he had intended to hightail it into the mountains, he knew he would do no such thing. He'd duck the posse and get back to town and he'd make Dick Lamar give back to him the agreement he'd signed, or make Lamar tell the sheriff the truth.

"I guess it's no secret why I came back, Sis," he said. "I always thought sisters kissed a brother when he'd been gone for three years."

"I haven't kissed you since you were a baby," Celia snapped. "You never wanted no kiss from me before, so I don't figure you want it now any more than I want to give you one. Now, why did you come back? If you think I'm going to give you more than five thousand for your share of the Rafter D . . ."

"Five thousand? All I got was one." Morgan shrugged. "Anyhow, I changed my mind. I want my half of the Rafter D, not the money. What's more, I want an accounting of what's happened since I left, and a check for the half of the profit that's mine. After that, we'll decide whether we split down the middle, or if we can work it together. Personally I don't figure I could work anything with Buck."

"That's right," Armand said. "You couldn't work anything with me and we ain't aiming to give up half of the ranch. It's a good spread the way it is. Cut it in two and you'd have two hardscrabble outfits with neither one of us making a living on it. It won't do, boy."

Fury soared through Morgan. Armand was older than he was, but that did not give him the right to call him "boy" in that condescending tone. Morgan clenched his fists and thought of all the years he'd worked as a cowhand and had taken the dirty end of the stick.

"I own half of this spread," Morgan said. "I aim to get it."

"I tell you what we'll do," Armand said. "We'll give you another dollar for your share of the layout." He threw a silver dollar at Morgan that fell into the dust in front of him. "Now git on your horse and ride out of the basin."

"You heard the will read," Morgan said. "I aim to get my half if I have to go to the sheriff and Judge Alcorn to get it."

"Won't do you no good," Armand said. "You're the same damned punk kid you always were. You'll never change. You ride off and let us run the outfit and work our tails off, then you come back as big as life and claim your half. Well, sir, you won't get it."

He was bound to make a fight out of it, Morgan thought. It was more than trouble; it would be the kind of fight that would maim a man or kill him. He saw it in the challenging way Armand faced him. He heard it in the man's overbearing tone of voice.

Armand was wearing a gun. For a moment Morgan considered telling him to draw, that they might just as well settle their quarrel for good. Morgan didn't. He hoped it wouldn't come to that. He wasn't afraid of Armand's fists or his gun, and he wanted Armand to know it.

"If that's the way you're gonna perform, I'll get back to town and find the sheriff," Morgan said. "I'll see the judge, too. There must be some law in this basin that ain't Rafter D law."

"You ain't going anywhere," Armand said. "I've wanted to teach you a lesson for a long time. I might as well do it now. When I get done, you'll wish you'd picked up your dollar and vamoosed."

He started toward Morgan, his big head tipped forward, his hands fisted in front of him. For just a short instant of time Morgan wondered if he had made a mistake. He had seen Armand fight; he had seen him smash more than one Rafter D hand who had been insubordinate or had done some-thing so stupid that it had cost the ranch money. Armand fought in bull-like rushes, willing to take the hardest punch a man could give him in order that he could land one of his bone-smashing blows. Once he had his opponent down, he would give him the toe of his boot. More than one cow-puncher had been so crippled he had never been able to ride for a living again.

This wouldn't happen to him, Morgan told himself. He said: "Take off your gun belt, Buck."

Morgan unbuckled his gun belt and, turning, draped it across his saddle. Armand paused, scowling as if surprised, then he shrugged, jerked off his gun belt, and tossed it toward the barn. He came on again, his hands fisted. This time he hurried as if wanting to get the fight over with.

VII

Ed Smith had not walked ten steps after he left Judge Alcorn and Johnny Bedlow in front of the bank until he heard a woman call: "Sheriff! I want to see you, Sheriff."

He turned, irritated as he wondered what else had gone wrong tonight. Then he saw it was Jean Runyan and the irritation left him. She was a very pretty girl, decent and even-tempered, and as different from her sister Molly as two girls could be. He was often irritated with Molly, but never with Jean.

"Come ahead and see me," Ed said when she reached him. "I'm not hard to see."

"You were tonight," she said. "I've been all over town looking for you." She paused for breath, and added: "I couldn't find Tully, either."

"I left Tully in the courthouse," he said. "He must have gone home for supper. The judge called me over to his office for a palaver. What's wrong?"

Instead of answering his question, she asked: "What was the shooting about?"

He was silent a moment, wondering how much she knew about what happened. She was Dick Lamar's sister-in-law, but it was doubtful he would have told her what he was up to, if he was up to something. Finally he said: "Dick claims that Morgan Dill robbed the bank this evening and he shot at him."

"He's a stinking liar!" she cried. "Morgan didn't do anything of the kind. I saw him in the alley before he went into the bank. I told him not to go, that he didn't know how to handle a slippery crook like Dick Lamar."

"What makes you say Dick's a crook," Ed asked, "and why did Morgan go into the bank?"

"Doesn't everybody know Dick's a slippery crook?" she snapped. "I thought it was public knowledge."

"Maybe it is, at that," Ed admitted, "though I've never had any proof that he was. Now why did Morgan go into the bank?"

"I don't know," she said. "He told me Celia was going to buy his part of the Rafter D, but there's more to it than that. All I know for sure is that Dick sent for him. He read in the paper about Morgan's being in that fight in Steamboat Springs and getting jailed, so he wrote him to come to Twin Rocks."

"How did you happen to see him in the alley?"

"I knew he was coming," she said. "I don't really know much about it. I just overheard enough talk between Dick and Molly to know he'd sent for Morgan. It's some kind of a trap. It would be like Dick to rob his own bank and have Morgan on hand as a scapegoat."

That was exactly the way Ed had sized up the

situation. He considered going back to the bank and asking Lamar why he had sent for Morgan, but it wouldn't do any good. Lamar would have some excuse, like saying Celia had authorized him to buy Morgan out. He was smart enough to have foreseen the question, and he'd have a ready answer.

"I've got to bring Morgan in," Ed said, "just to clear the record, since Dick's yelling about him doing it."

"You can't." Jean gripped both his arms. "Listen to me, Sheriff. Morgan is an independent kind of man. He won't let you put him in jail for something he didn't do. You know that. You'd feel the same way."

"I reckon I would," Ed answered, "but as sheriff I don't have no choice. At least I've got to try to bring him in, but I hope he's ten miles north of here by the time I start after him. Now you go on home. I'll let you know if anything happens."

She leaned forward to study his face in the moonlight. Apparently she believed him. She said—"All right, Ed."—and turned away.

He stood watching her until she disappeared down the street. He guessed that women were never very rational when it came to men. Jean must have seen a great deal of Morgan when he was engaged to Molly, but she had been a child then. Now she was a woman and there was no mistaking her feeling for Morgan Dill. Molly would have done better to have married Morgan than Dick Lamar, but it would have been worse for Morgan. Molly and Lamar seemed to have brought out the worst in each other. It was no secret that they fought like two alley cats.

Shrugging, Ed turned and went on toward his house, thinking that Molly's and Lamar's domestic problems were none of his business, but Morgan Dill's problems were. He guessed that made Jean's problems his, too. Well, one thing was sure. He'd take his time getting to the jail and starting out with Tully Bean and Johnny Bedlow.

He had always taken pride in being a good lawman; he had never held back when it came to risking his life going after a wanted man. Neither had Tully Bean, but this was a different proposition. Still, Judge Alcorn could make or break a man in Twin Rocks basin, and he'd said loudly and clearly to bring Morgan in.

Alcorn had a point, all right, with Dick Lamar accusing Morgan of the robbery. Ed didn't have the slightest doubt about Morgan's innocence or Lamar's guilt, particularly now that he knew Lamar had sent for Morgan. If he brought Morgan in and had his story about what had happened, he might be able to break Lamar down and get the truth out of him. Still, bringing a man like Morgan in was more than Ed could face. He couldn't shoot Morgan, if it came to that, but Morgan could sure as hell shoot him and he probably would.

When he reached the house, he found his wife and children finishing supper. He had a boy of six and two girls, four and three. When they saw him, they jumped down from their chairs and piled all over him, hugging and kissing him and getting grape jelly on his face.

His wife pulled the children off him and ordered them outside to play a few minutes before going to bed. When they were out of the house, she faced Ed, her hands on her hips, her lips drawn tightly against her teeth as they always were when she was angry.

"Well, Mister Sheriff," she said through tight lips, "you promised you would get home early. We held supper until it was practically spoiled. The children were so hungry I had to let them eat. Now it's cold for you."

He sensed that she was close to tears. He went to her and hugged her, then he said: "I'm sorry, Mary. I didn't have any way to let you know. The judge called me into his office along with Sam Colter and Baldy Miles, and, while we were there, the bank was robbed. Lamar claimed Morgan Dill did it. Now I've got to go after Morgan and I sure don't want to do it."

"I'm sorry, Ed," she said contritely. "I should have known it was something important. Sit down. I'll pour your coffee. At least it's still hot."

He pumped a basin of water and washed, then sat down at the table and began to eat. For a moment Mary stood watching him as if disgusted with herself for what she had said to him, then she shook her head.

"Something's wrong, isn't there?" she asked. "You don't think Morgan did it?"

"That's right," he said. "I wouldn't go, except that Alcorn said to bring him in. He ain't my boss, but if I want to get reëlected, I'd better do what he says."

"Is it so important to get reëlected?" she asked.

"Yes, it is," he said. "I knew how important it was as soon as I got home. A wife and three kids to feed! I can't go back to punching cows and that's all I know except packing a star."

"There must be other ways of making a living," she said. "Don't do anything you think is wrong just because you want to hold your job to feed us."

He kept on eating, not saying anything. Talk was cheap, he thought bitterly. He had seen more than one family starved into leaving the basin. The men weren't lazy. There simply were no jobs that paid a man enough to keep a family, not unless you had a little money of your own to invest in a business, and even then you couldn't be sure how it would work out.

No, he wasn't going to back out of what Judge Alcorn would say was his duty. The sheriff's salary was not great but they made out and even had a small savings account. He thought about Dick Lamar, who had inherited the bank from his

134

father and had never done a day's work in his life. Lamar could be a crook and get away with it, but not Ed Smith.

He rose, when he finished, thinking that all he could do if he did catch up with Morgan was to play it safe and easy. That might be a little difficult because Morgan would be as dangerous as a treed cougar.

"I don't understand about the Dill boy," Mary said. "He's been gone a long time, hasn't he?"

Ed nodded. "Just got into town tonight, I guess. I don't know what did happen at the bank. All we have is Lamar's story."

"But Morgan Dill was always a troublemaker, wasn't he?"

"No, not really a troublemaker," Ed said. "Just reckless. Always up to some orneriness, him and Tully and Johnny Bedlow. Tully's straightened out and I guess everybody likes Johnny. I figure Morgan would do the same if we give him enough time." He kissed Mary, then said: "Go on to bed. I don't know when I'll be back." He heard the children screaming in play from the front of the house, and added: "I'll go out through the back. Just tell them I had some work to do tonight."

He stopped in the back doorway and turned and looked at his wife. He was tempted to go back and kiss her again. She was younger than he was by five years, still slim and attractive of body after bearing his three children. He loved her more than he could ever tell her, and sometimes just the thought of getting killed and leaving her with nothing but the house and a few dollars in savings was more than he could stand. It was at times like that when he seriously considered not running for office again, but he knew more broken-down hungry cowpunchers who couldn't work—than he did dead sheriffs.

Quickly he turned and strode across the yard to the barn. He saddled his black gelding, and rode to the livery stable. He had taken more than the half hour he had told Johnny Bedlow to wait. Maybe Johnny had got tired and had gone home. Tully Bean would be waiting at the jail regardless of what Johnny did. He'd raise hell about going after Morgan, but he'd do it.

Ed saddled Tully's horse while the hostler saddled a livery animal for Johnny, then Ed left the stable leading the three horses. Tully and Johnny were waiting at the jail and both were cranky.

"I was just fixing to leave," Johnny said sullenly.

Tully said: "This is the damnedest thing I ever heard. Old Morg wouldn't rob no bank. If you ask me, it was that slick-tongued Dick Lamar who robbed his own bank and blamed it on Morg."

"We've thought of that," Ed said. "It's one reason we're going after Morgan. We need to hear his story about what happened."

He didn't tell them how near he had come to not

going after Morgan. One thought did give him a little comfort. Maybe Morgan didn't know he was being accused of bank robbery and wasn't really running. Perhaps they would find Morgan somewhere to the north, camped along the creek, and they could sit down and talk about it, and he'd come back to town and tell Judge Alcorn and the others. Then he could arrest Dick Lamar and get the truth out of him and release Morgan.

Ed grinned as he mounted and reined his black into the street, Johnny and Tully falling in behind him. He knew he was thinking plain hogwash, and he wondered how far a man's imagination would take him if he let it go.

A moment later the town was behind them, their shadows dark against the grass in the bright moonlight. They crossed the bridge spanning Twin Rocks Creek, the horses' hoofs striking the planks with pistol-like sharpness.

Ed stared north toward the sharp, granite peaks that raked the sky. He couldn't see them now because they were too far away to be seen in the moonlight, but he had been over the range and he knew how hard it was to get to the other side. There were passes, all right, but they were tough and steep. Morgan could make it, though. He knew the country and he wouldn't forget how it was in the three years he had been gone. It would be sheer hell to chase him over the range. Ed could think of many places up there where

Morgan could hole up and cut all three of them down before they could find any protection.

As he thought about it, he told himself Morgan Dill wouldn't do that, and knew at once he could not make such a judgment. There was—and Ed had learned this lesson well—no way to tell what a man would do when he was pressed hard enough.

"What do you think he'll do, Tully?" Ed asked.

"He'll keep going," the deputy answered, "but I'm damned if I know which pass he'll take."

"Johnny?"

"Same here," Johnny Bedlow said. "He'll keep going, all right, but there's at least three passes he could use to go over the range and we've got no way of telling which one he'll take. I ain't sure we can follow his tracks, either, once he gets above timberline."

"Or what he'll do if we're right on his tail," Tully said. "I keep thinking about something, Ed. We don't know how much he's changed in three years. I've changed plenty since Morg left the basin. So has Johnny. Well, we don't know how much Morg's changed or in what direction. He may be a curly wolf by now for all we know."

"I've been thinking the same thing," Johnny said grimly. "He ain't gonna be the same happy-go-lucky, hell-raising kid we used to ride with. He's got plenty to be bitter about, with Molly throwing him over and Celia and Armand treating him the way they have."

What they were saying, Ed thought, without quite putting it into words was that the Morgan Dill they had known three years ago would not, or maybe could not have held the bank up, but the Morgan Dill who had returned might. Certainly he had not come back just for a visit with old friends. Ed sighed. As he thought about the rugged passes that were ahead of them, he told himself there was but a very slim chance they could follow Morgan's trail over the top. He was thankful for that.

VIII

Buck Armand charged at Morgan with the tough confidence of a man who had never been beaten in his life. Morgan did not back away; he saw Armand start his blow below his waistline and saw the big fist swing up straight for his head, a pile-driving blow that would have knocked him cold if it had landed. Morgan tipped his head to one side just enough so that Armand's fist barely missed. The momentum of his charge carried Armand on past Morgan who sledged him on the cheek as he went by, a wicked blow that would have knocked a lesser man down, but all it did to Armand was to drive a grunt out of him.

The big man wheeled ponderously and rushed again, this time with his arms spread. If he succeeded in catching Morgan in his powerful grip, Morgan knew that his ribs would be crushed. Again he waited, timing his move to the exact second, then he raised a knee. Armand was coming in, bent over, hoping to catch Morgan around the waist. Instead, Morgan's knee smashed him under his chin, snapping his teeth together in an audible *click*. He hit the ground and lay there for a moment before he reared up, shook his head, and struggled to his feet.

This time the Rafter D man came at Morgan more carefully, his fists cocked in front of his face. Morgan was taller by a good six inches and so had the advantage of a longer reach. He drove a straight right into Armand's face before Armand was close enough to hit him. The blow smashed Armand's nose and brought a rush of blood. Morgan whipped a left through to Armand's face before the big man could recover, working on the principle that the best defense is a slashing offense. This time he smashed Armand's lips against his teeth, bruising and cutting both of them.

Morgan knew he had hurt Armand, hurt him enough to make him more cautious, perhaps had hurt him enough to take some of the brutal power out of his blows. Now Morgan elected to stand and fight, weaving and ducking and taking more blows on his forearms than he did on his face or body. All the time he was using his right and occasionally his left to batter Armand's already bloody face.

Morgan was getting hit, but the blows lacked the knockout power that had been in the first ones. Morgan worked on his eyes, on his nose again, and then in a careless moment let Armand catch him with a roundhouse right to the jaw. He staggered back, the world tilting and turning in front of him. He had not thought Armand had that much strength left, a mistake that came close to beating him.

Now Morgan back-pedaled, making a circle as he held Armand off and looping blows until his head cleared. In spite of his longer reach, now and then Armand got a punch through to Morgan's body that hurt and it became an effort to breathe. Armand was clumsy and slow, but still there was enough power in his blows to hurt when he landed one.

Armand was almost out on his feet and fighting more from instinct than conscious direction, but Morgan was plagued by the nagging feeling that he wasn't going to last. It was like fighting a bear that kept coming and was always dangerous as long as he was on his feet. Morgan knew, then, he had to make the kill, that if he kept on this way, he was bound to lose in the end because of the superior animal strength that was in Buck Armand. He backed up, feinting with his left, and

Armand took the bait, thinking Morgan was finished.

Once more the big man lunged at Morgan, a great fist swinging out in a roundhouse blow. Morgan ducked and drove in, and now Armand was wide open. Morgan caught him flush on the jaw with a wicked, turning fist that connected with the impact of a slamming club. It rocked Armand's head. For a moment he struggled to stay on his feet; he tried by the sheer power of will to drive another blow at Morgan's body, but his legs would not hold him, and he spilled forward on his face.

Armand was still conscious. His hands began searching on the ground for the gun he had dropped. As far as Morgan knew, the man had never been knocked off his feet before. He had no stomach for more, but there was little doubt about what he would do if he found his gun.

When Morgan realized what was in Armand's numbed mind, he wheeled to his horse and yanked at the holstered gun. He had it half out of leather when the sky fell on him. He went down at the side of his horse, the gun dropping back into the holster.

Morgan came to with a whacking headache. He lay on his back, staring at the sky. The moon was still up there, a fact that vaguely comforted him. He was wet. As he wiped his face and sucked air into his lungs, a man said: " 'Bout time you was coming around."

Morgan didn't recognize the voice for a few seconds, then he realized it was Slim Turner who had spoken to him. Apparently the cowboy had brought him around by throwing a bucket of water on him.

Morgan sat up slowly and put a hand to his head. He asked: "What hit me?"

"Missus Armand slugged you," Turner said. "She picked up a piece of limb or something. I guess she figured you was gonna drill Buck. You'd be worse off than you are if you'd shot him. He was trying to find his gun, and I guess he would have if I hadn't tossed it clean back to the corner of the barn. Come on and get on your horse. When Armand comes out of the house, he'll have a gun. Git moving. I've helped you all I can. Armand will kill me if he finds out I've helped you this much."

Morgan got to his feet and staggered to his horse. He grabbed the saddle horn, his head hammering as if a dozen devils were using it for a drum. He stood there a moment, his eyes shut until the worst of the headache passed, then he pulled his gun belt off the saddle and buckled it around him. He raised a foot to the stirrup, and with a great effort swung into the saddle.

He rode toward the creek. Every step the horse took sent a slashing pain up through his head.

He bent forward, hanging onto the horn and swaying in the saddle. He knew he couldn't ride, but he didn't dare stay in the open where Buck Armand could find him. One thing was as certain as death and taxes. As soon as Armand could sit his saddle, he'd start looking for Morgan.

It wasn't just that Buck Armand had been beaten for the first time in his life. It was more than that. He had built a reputation in the basin as a fighting man and now it was shattered; he had been humiliated before one of his cowhands and in front of his wife. He would never rest until he had repaid Morgan by killing him.

Morgan crossed the road and went on to the creek. He stepped down, again holding to the horn until most of the dizziness passed, then he led his buckskin through the willows to the bank. He let the reins drag and, kneeling, sloshed water onto his face. In time the headache would pass and he could defend himself, but he wasn't sure how much time he had.

He sat there, trying to arrange his thoughts, but he felt drained out as if every muscle in his body had been bruised and hammered until it ached like a throbbing tooth. It wasn't just the blow on the head that Celia had given him. Armand had hurt him more than he had realized. It was always that way in a fistfight. More blows were landed than a man was aware of at the time.

Presently his head cleared and he found that he

could think. First, he'd remind Judge Alcorn of his claim to half the Rafter D and tell how he had been treated. He wasn't sure what had changed his mind, but he was very sure he was not pulling out and leaving all of the ranch in Celia's and Armand's hands. If they had been reasonable, he might have reversed himself again and sold his share of the ranch, but Armand had intended to kill him or maim him for life.

Then he remembered hearing Lamar yelling bank robbery. They would be hunting him, too— Smith and a posse. He wondered if they had ridden past while he was fighting with Buck Armand.

Again he realized how much he needed time to rest and regain his strength. The only place he could do that would be back in town in Jean Runyon's house. He remembered, too, that she had promised to tell him some things he needed to know.

Suddenly it came to him he was not thinking straight. He was putting things in the wrong order. Before he looked up Judge Alcorn and talked about his half of the ranch, he'd better clear himself of the bank robbery. The only way he could do that was to get hold of Dick Lamar. When he did, Lamar would tell the truth or he would be a dead man.

Morgan rose and turned to his horse, then he froze. Horses were coming upstream. It might be Ed Smith and his posse. Morgan couldn't risk being arrested and taken to jail now, not until he had beaten the truth out of Lamar. When it came right down to it, he wasn't going to jail at any time. He had been locked up only once in his life. He'd go crazy if he were jailed even for a few hours. That one time had been enough.

A few minutes later the riders came into sight. He had guessed right. The lead man was the sheriff. *Funny,* Morgan thought, *only three men after him. Not much of a posse.* When they were closer, he saw that the other two were Tully Bean and Johnny Bedlow.

He watched them rein up in the fork of the road. For a time they talked, but he was too far away to hear what they were saying. Tully Bean was motioning toward the mountains to the north, then he stepped out of the saddle and began studying the road.

Morgan drew his gun and waited. It was enough to make a man laugh, he told himself. Smith had picked the two men who knew him better than anybody else in the basin, the two men who had been his best friends.

Suddenly Tully got up off his knees and straightened as he turned to Smith. He said: "I can't make it out, Ed. You know, he could be hiding right under our noses."

Morgan lined his gun on Tully's chest, wondering if he could bring himself to shoot either

Tully Bean or Johnny Bedlow if they decided to root him out. The three of them had raised a lot of hell together, then he reminded himself they were hunting him, hunting by that damned full moon overhead. If they found him, they'd shoot him for resisting arrest. Or, if he surrendered, they'd take him to jail. His lips squeezed together into a hard, bitter line. He knew then he could and would shoot either one or both if it came to that. He was not going to jail.

IX

Ed Smith rolled a cigarette, looking down at Tully Bean in the moonlight. He thought he knew what Tully was trying to tell him, that fresh hoof prints in the road indicated Morgan Dill was hiding in the willows. There was a good chance that he had his gun lined on one of them right now. Again the thought came to Ed that there was no way of knowing how much Morgan had changed in the three years he had been gone, but he had been a tough hand when he had lived in the basin. The chances were he had not softened any during these three years. Morgan Dill was not the kind of man who could stand being locked up in a jail. Tully Bean had said this about him more than once. He was like a wild animal that was penned up; he'd get sick and die. If that was

147

true, and Ed had a hunch Tully knew what he was talking about, Morgan would shoot it out with anyone who tried to take him to jail.

Ed fired his cigarette and flipped the charred match away. He said, trying to keep his tone casual: "Get back on your horse, Tully. We'll take a sashay up to the Rafter D. Morgan might have taken a notion to see his sister."

"Sure," Tully said as if relieved. "That's just about what he done."

Tully mounted, and Ed led the way up the Rafter D road. A moment later Tully moved up beside Ed. He said: "He was down there in the willows, all right. I could feel my skin crawling. If you'd said we were gonna hunt for him, he'd have let go and some of us would have got hurt. It would have been like shooting fish in a barrel with the moon as bright as it is."

"Yeah, we'd have got hurt permanent-like," Johnny Bedlow added grimly. "It'd been you or me, Tully, or both. Morg never was one to forgive a friend who turned on him."

"That's the way I was figuring," Tully agreed.

"Who knows what to do in a case like this?" Ed asked. "I sure don't. I'm still not sure he robbed the bank. Or if he did do it, I'd like to know why and just what did happen."

"Maybe we should have hollered at him," Johnny said. "If he was close enough to shoot us, he was close enough to holler at."

"No, he wouldn't have answered," Ed said, "unless he done it with a bullet." He paused, remembering how positive Tully was that Morgan was hiding along the creek, and the thought occurred to him that his deputy might have lied to give Morgan more time to get away. He asked: "What made you think he was down there, Tully?"

"I don't know that he was," Tully answered, "but it was pretty plain that somebody had ridden up the Rafter D road and then had come back and gone across the county road into the willows. Now, if he was headed out of the country like we figured, he was, he'd have turned north there at the forks. Or gone back to town if he figured he still had business there."

"I don't see much sense in hiding in the willows," Johnny said. "Might have been somebody else who made them tracks."

"Sure, sure," Tully said irritably. "I told you I didn't know for sure, but who else has been riding around this time of night? Damn it, I know Morg. He'd plug us before he'd go to jail. I can tell you I didn't feel downright comfortable a while ago."

A moment later they rode into the yard of the Rafter D. Ed saw there were lights in the back of the house, then he heard Tully say softly: "Over yonder, Ed. In the corral."

He looked to his left. A man was saddling a horse, but he couldn't see who it was even in the moonlight. He swung left just as the man led his horse out of the corral and closed the gate. He saw then that the man was Slim Turner.

"Where you headed, Slim?" Ed asked as he reined up.

Turner stepped into the saddle, then sat there, staring at Ed. Tully rode forward on one side, Johnny Bedlow on the other, so that Turner was boxed in unless he wanted to bull his way through. If he had any such thought, he changed his mind when Ed dropped his hand to the butt of his gun. He said softly: "I won't ask you again, Slim."

"I'm going to Indian Springs if it's any of your damned business," Turner said sullenly.

"You seen Morgan Dill?"

"Yeah, I seen him."

"Where?"

"Here."

"Was he here very long?"

"No."

"How long?"

"How the hell do I know?" Turner snapped, exasperated. "I didn't time him."

Something was wrong, Ed thought. Whatever it was must be important or Turner wouldn't be acting this way. Normally he was a friendly and talkative man.

"Maybe you'd better come to town with us," Ed said. "I always find that a man talks better in jail or sitting in my office than he does when he's outside forking his horse."

"You can't do that," Turner said hotly. "The boss is sending me on an errand. He'll have my hide if I don't get it done."

"I'll have your hide if you don't talk, so take your choice," Ed said. "Now let's have it. What happened when Morgan showed up?"

Turner hesitated, his gaze turning to Tully, then Johnny Bedlow. Apparently he decided there was no way out unless he talked, so he blurted: "We all knowed he was coming or guessed he was, seeing as half the Rafter D belongs to him, or will in a couple of days. That's why Armand's been keeping me here. Tonight Morgan rode in and got into a fight with Armand. He gave the boss a pretty good whipping and took a lot of punishment himself. After he knocked the boss down, Missus Armand knocked him cold with a club. He came around when I threw some water on him. He got back on his horse with a little help from me and rode off. I don't know where to, though."

So that was it, Ed thought. He had been hurt, hurt enough so that he didn't feel like riding. He had plenty of reason to hide out in the willows. Ed asked: "Why is Armand sending you to Indian Springs?"

"To get the crew," Turner said, meeting Ed's gaze with the arrogance that was typical of a Rafter D hand. "It figured that Morgan went back to town to get you and to tell the judge about what happened out here. The main thing is he took a whipping and he ain't aiming to let it go."

Fury swept through Ed. He said: "Didn't it ever occur to Armand that he's not the law in the basin?"

Tully snickered. "You ever hear of a notion like that coming into Buck Armand's head?"

"I didn't give the order," Turner said sullenly. "I just work for the Rafter D. You want some answers, go talk to Buck."

"All right, I will," Ed said, "but you tell the rest of the crew that I'll throw the whole outfit into jail if they try to stop the law from being enforced or to take the law into their own hands." As Turner started to ride away, Ed added: "You might remember that there's a good chance you'll be working for Morgan Dill when this is settled."

"No," Turner said, "he'll be a dead man. I've got nothing against Morgan. I wish he'd get out of the basin and stay out. Nobody stands up to Armand and his wife and wins, and you know it."

Then Turner spurred his horse around Tully and rode downslope as if anxious to get away from Ed and his questions.

"Well," Tully said thoughtfully, "he's got a point. Now the time's come."

"What time?" Ed demanded.

"The time to see if Slim's right. Who does

run the basin? Is it the sheriff's office or the Rafter D?"

Tully had needled Ed about this before and his question didn't help settle his anger now. Ed said: "Come on. Let's go see what Buck Armand's got to say. Might be we'll have to cut the Rafter D down to size and tonight's as good a time as any."

X

Morgan waited until Ed Smith and his men were well up the Rafter D road before he holstered his gun. He led his horse back to the road, stood motionlessly for a time beside the animal, one hand clutching the saddle horn, then his head cleared and he mounted, and rode slowly toward town.

When he reached the business block, he turned off Main Street and followed an alley to the back of the Runyan house. His head still ached, but he felt better than when he had left the willows. He turned his buckskin into the barn, tied him in a stall, and loosened the cinch, then stepped back into the alley.

He glanced at the sky and judged the time to be midnight or later. For a moment he thought about Dick Lamar and wondered if the banker would stay in town or pull out. If he were smart, he'd stay and bull it through, but Morgan figured him

153

for a coward, and he doubted that the man had enough guts to stay after what had happened. Either way, Morgan knew he wasn't up to facing the man, and it would be stupid to tackle him until he was ready. He had maybe four hours until dawn and he'd better use some of that time to rest. Jean would see that he had a chance to sleep and probably eat supper. She was still up. At least there was a light in the house.

Quickly he crossed the yard to the back door, stepped up on the porch, and knocked. He heard footsteps cross the kitchen, then the door opened and Jean stood there, holding a lamp in her hand. She said: "I thought it would be you, Morgan. Come in."

He stepped inside. She looked at him and shook her head. "What happened? You didn't get your face messed up doing what Dick wanted you to do."

"I had a fight with Buck Armand."

"I guess that was to be expected." She motioned to a chair at the table. "The water in the teakettle is hot. I'll clean your face up. I'll pour a cup of coffee for you, too. Have you had anything to eat?"

"Not for a long time." He tried to grin at her, but his lips wouldn't behave. "I feel like hell. Now that I stop to think about it, I'm hungry. I guess breakfast was the last time I et and that was before sunup. Maybe that's what's wrong with me."

"I wouldn't be surprised," she said.

She poured the coffee, then brought a bottle from the pantry and laced the coffee with whiskey. "Go ahead and drink," she said. "I'll see what I can do with your face and then I'll rustle something for you to eat." She stepped back and looked at him gravely. "You're a stubborn man, Morgan Dill. You're over your head when you start dealing with Dick Lamar. He can make a fox look like a fool."

Morgan sipped the coffee. As she brought a towel and a basin of hot water to the table, he said: "I ain't in any shape to argue with you."

She dropped one end of the towel into the basin of water, lifted it out, and squeezed it as dry as she could, then gently began to wipe the blood from his face. She examined each bruise and cut, then dabbed at them with the dry end of the towel, and finished by rubbing salve on them.

"Nothing very serious," she said. "Now I'll get you something to eat."

He drank the coffee and, closing his eyes, leaned back in his chair. His head still hurt and he had never felt so tired in his life. He was almost asleep when she said: "You'd better eat, Morgan. I'll talk while you're eating, then we'll decide what you're going to do."

"*We'll* decide?" He pulled his chair up to the table thinking that Jean was more like her sister than he had realized. Molly used to say things like

155

that. "I might as well make it plain. I'll decide."

Jean smiled. "All right, you decide. I'm going to lock the house. Somebody, either the sheriff or Armand, might think you'd come here and walk right in."

She was gone for two or three minutes, then she returned and locked the back door, and pulled the blinds in the kitchen. She sat down across the table from him and studied him for a moment before she spoke.

"I said I'd talk," she said. "I had no intention of deciding anything for you. I was going to tell you some things you probably don't know. After you hear them, you can decide all you want to." She hesitated, then added: "I know how Molly was and is, even now that she's married to Dick. I've always said I'd never try to boss a man, you in particular."

She had brought several slices of roast beef to the table along with bread, butter, and a quarter of a custard pie. She filled his coffee cup again and sat down. He watched her as he ate, thinking she wasn't much like Molly, after all. Jean didn't really look like her sister, not when he sat here and looked closely at her. Her hair was the same ebony black, so black that it held blue tints in the lamplight, her eyes were the same dark brown, and she was nearly the same size. The difference was in her expression. Molly had always been discontented and her face had showed it. Now that he thought about it, Morgan couldn't remember when she had been satisfied about anything. Jean was more straightforward, without any sign of being unhappy or expecting to be waited on and taken care of. Molly had always acted as if she were royalty, but Jean made no pretense of being anything more than she was. Then Morgan noticed something that he had not thought of before. Molly had always looked older than she was, perhaps because of the crow's feet around her eyes, but Jean looked young and fresh and very attractive.

Suddenly Jean laughed. "I guess we've both changed, haven't we, Morgan? While you're looking me over and wondering if I've really grown up, I've been looking you over and wondering if you've changed. You were a harum-scarum kind of fellow when you left here, you and Tully Bean and Johnny Bedlow. Sure, I was just a kid, but I knew a lot about you. It always seemed to me you had a lot of fun."

"I did," he said, "but I haven't had much fun since I left the basin."

He went on eating, realizing that he hadn't really thought much about it, but he had had a lot of fun when he'd lived here. Molly was always ready to go any time he could take her, and a man couldn't have had better partners than Tully Bean and Johnny Bedlow. They were all for it any time he suggested any hell-raising.

Morgan hadn't had a girl since he'd broken up with Molly and he hadn't formed any real friendships with other men since he'd left the basin. Now, thinking about Tully and Johnny, he told himself it would have been hell if he'd been forced into shooting them up there on the creek. Well, the night wasn't over. They might get on his tail again before morning.

For some reason Jean seemed reluctant to start talking, but she remained seated across the table from him, her hands folded in front of her. As Morgan reached for the pie, she said: "This is going to hurt you and I hate to do it, but you'd better know it just in case you're still in love with Molly. She never loved you. She's been a calculating, selfish bitch as long as I can remember. I ought to know. I used to get the short end of the stick time after time. That was when Ma was alive and the three of us lived here."

Morgan picked up the piece of pie from the dish and ate it with his fingers. He wasn't surprised by what Jean had said. He just hadn't ever admitted it to himself, but he'd known Molly pretty well, well enough to be sure that she was a person who made it a point to look out for herself first.

"She wanted to marry you as long as she thought you'd get at least half of the Rafter D," Jean went on. "At one time, before Celia married Buck Armand, I think Molly dreamed about you getting all of the ranch, but then it got to be common gossip in the basin that Celia would work it so you got nothing. Or at least you'd have nothing for three years and Molly was never one to wait. Dick began seeing her on the side and she encouraged him. You don't do much better than landing a banker for a husband, so she promised to marry Dick before she gave your ring back. Besides, she wouldn't have to work as hard if she married a banker."

Jean stopped as if wondering how he was taking it, then rose, and, going to the stove, picked up the coffee pot and brought it to the table and filled his cup. Morgan didn't say anything. He guessed that hearing this was the best medicine Jean could give him. He had never really got over being in love with Molly, although it had been a sort of festering sore in him because he had not understood why she had given the ring back. Now that he knew, the sore would heal. He didn't doubt what Jean told him. It was exactly the way Molly would operate.

Jean returned to her chair across the table from him. "One other thing you don't know is that Dick Lamar is broke and the bank is on the rocks. At least, there's a lot of talk along that line and Molly has hinted at it more than once. She feels sorry for herself, I guess, and wants sympathy. Anyhow, that was why I was so sure Dick was baiting a trap for you, though I didn't know what it was. The thing with Molly is that she's scared

159

she's going to lose her home and her position in the community as the banker's wife. Dick always has gambled a good deal. Lately he's been doing more of it. I think he's been stealing money from the bank and losing it at poker. It would account for his accusing you of robbing the bank. It's one way he can get into the clear."

Morgan picked up his cup and drank the rest of the coffee. He was still tired, so tired he couldn't think straight. His head didn't hurt as much as it had, but he felt as if he were glued to his chair and lacked the energy to free himself. He rolled and fired a cigarette, thinking he would ask Jean to let him sleep for an hour, then he'd look Lamar up and he'd get the truth out of him if he had to half kill him.

"I'm going to have to sleep a while, Jean," he said. "Wake me in an hour and I'll get up and do what I have to do. I've never killed a man, but I may kill Lamar."

"You can sleep here, of course." But she didn't get up. Her eyes remained pinned on his face, a questioning expression in them. "Morgan, I keep wondering if this was all Lamar's idea. Or did Molly think of having him rob the bank and sending for you and making you the scapegoat?"

"I don't know who thought of that," he said, "but I guess I asked for the whole business. You see, it wasn't just that Lamar read about me being in the ruckus in Steamboat Springs and knowing I

160

was there because of it. I was mighty damn' mad when I heard the will read, it giving the running of the Rafter D over to Celia until I was twenty-five. Armand always treated me like I was the worst cowhand he had. If there was a dirty job on the ranch, I got it, so I figured I might as well work for somebody else rather than to stay at home. That's why I lit out for Steamboat Springs."

"It also was the main reason Molly broke her engagement to you and encouraged Dick Lamar," Jean said. "It's like I told you a while ago. Molly didn't aim to live on a cowhand's wages for three years."

Morgan nodded, understanding that Molly would feel that way. He said: "A few weeks ago I got to thinking how the will read and that my birthday was coming up, so I wrote to Lamar. I didn't want any part of the spread, knowing I couldn't work with Armand, but I did want some money. With Lamar being the administrator of the estate, I figured he'd know what Celia would do, so I told him I'd sell my half of the Rafter D for a reasonable figure in cash. I said I was going out to Oregon and have my own spread. That was why he sent for me, saying Celia would buy me out and for me to ride into town quiet-like and stay off Main Street. He said Celia wanted to deal with me and not bring Armand into the dickering, and that, if Armand saw me in town, there would be a hell of a ruckus."

"There would be, too," Jean said. "He's the meanest man in the basin. He's worse than when you knew him."

"I didn't think that was possible," Morgan said. "Well, I didn't have any idea what Celia would offer me, but nobody could call one thousand dollars a reasonable figure. That was what Lamar said Celia would give me. He had the money all counted out and in a canvas bag. Celia was talking about me getting five thousand. I guess Lamar must have stolen four thousand dollars. I got sore and lost my head, or I wouldn't have left town the way I did. I should have gone to Ed Smith as soon as I figured out what Lamar was up to, but I didn't. Likewise, I made a mistake riding out to the Rafter D which was probably what Armand and Celia figured I'd do. I think Armand aimed to kill me."

"It would be like him," Jean said.

He rose and rubbed his face. "I'm still not thinking straight. I'll be all right as soon as I get a little sleep."

Jean rose. "Morgan, did you ever kill a woman?"

"No. I'm not going to kill Molly, if that's what you're thinking about."

She nodded. "It was exactly what I was thinking. You're got plenty of reason to break her neck. I'm ashamed of myself, but I hate her. I've hated her ever since I was a child. She'd always been a lying, bitchy girl. She didn't change any when she grew up. What I'm trying to say is that it would get you into trouble if you killed her. She isn't worth it."

Funny thing, he told himself. He felt that he could kill Dick Lamar and Buck Armand, but he guessed that he felt sorry for Molly. Jean was thinking how she felt toward her sister and transferring those feelings to him.

"I won't do anything to her," he said.

Jean nodded, frowning. Molly must have hurt her a great deal, Morgan told himself. When he thought about his sister Celia and the way she had treated him, he could understand how and why Jean felt about Molly the way she did. He had known families in which there had been love and respect and understanding, but it had not been either his or Jean's luck to be born into such a family.

Jean led the way to a bedroom door and opened it. "You can sleep here," she said. "I'll wake you in an hour."

He followed her and sprawled across the bed, the moon throwing a pool of light across its foot. He fell asleep at once. It seemed only a moment later when Jean shook him awake.

"Get up, Morgan," she said. "Somebody's outside. In the barn."

XI

Ed Smith strode to the back door of the Rafter D ranch house, Tully Bean and Johnny Bedlow following. He wondered what he could say to a man like Buck Armand. The trouble was it wasn't just Buck Armand. He would be talking to Celia Dill Armand, to the ghost of old Abe Dill, in the tradition of arrogant power that had been built up over the years.

They crossed the back porch to the door, their spurs jingling. Ed knocked. Celia opened the door and stood there, her body almost filling the opening as she stared at Ed. She made no effort to step aside or to hide her hostility.

"I want to talk to Buck," Ed said.

"He's busy," Celia said in the arrogant way Ed had come to expect of everyone connected with the Rafter D. "What do you want to talk to him about?"

Ed looked past her to Armand, who was seated at the table, his left hand in a basin of water. He looked at Ed coldly, his face a mask of cuts and bruises. Suddenly Ed didn't care whether Celia was a woman or not. She had always acted as if she wanted to be a man and thought of herself as a man, and now he decided to treat her like one.

Besides, he was filled up to overflowing with Rafter D's pride and arrogance.

He lowered a shoulder and plowed into her, spinning her out of the doorway and slamming her against the wall. He strode straight across the room to Armand, watching him closely to see if he intended to draw his gun. He didn't look back, sensing that Tully and Johnny Bedlow had moved into the room behind him and would stop Celia from attacking him.

"I see you got tangled with a buzz saw," Ed said.

Armand was naked to the waist. A bottle of liniment was on the table next to the basin of water. Ed wished he had seen the fight. Morgan must have been hurt, but he had done a job hurting Buck Armand.

"You can see anything you want to," Armand grunted through swollen lips. "Just say your spiel and git."

"What happened when Morgan came out here?" Ed asked.

"None of your business," Armand snapped. "Turn around and slope out of here. I ain't answering any questions."

"Then put on your shirt," Ed said. "You look pretty well banged up, so we'll saddle a horse for you and head back to town. After you cool your heels for a while in one of our private rooms, you'll be glad to answer any questions I can think of."

"You think you're big enough to take me to jail?" Armand demanded.

"It's not a matter of what I think," Ed said. "We were talking just before we came in, Tully and me, about whether you or my office runs the basin. If you've got some doubts, which in the past you and Celia seem to have had . . . and old Abe had 'em, too . . . then I aim to settle 'em. As far as the law is concerned, my office does all the running. If you try to make your brand of law stick, I'll lock you up in jail so fast it'll make your head swim."

"That's pretty strong liquor you've been drinking," Armand said.

Celia had been standing close to the wall near the door. Now she moved to where Ed stood in front of Armand. "I'll tell you some things you'd better remember," she said. "It ain't a matter of who runs the basin. There's some things we won't allow and you'd better understand that now. We both know there was something wrong with Pa's will that left half of the Rafter D to Morgan. I ain't sure what it was. Or let's say I can't prove what it was, but I've got a hunch Judge Alcorn could tell you. Anyhow, we ain't giving any part of the outfit to Morgan. I was the one who took care of Pa. Me 'n' Buck here kept the spread going while all Morgan done was to horse around and raise hell. He deserves nothing and that's what he's gonna get."

"I didn't ride out here to argue with you about the will and Morgan," Ed said. "The court will take care of that. I'm looking for Morgan and I want to know what happened when he showed up and where he went after he left."

"He had a fight with Buck," Celia said. "I fetched Buck into the house and wiped off some of the blood. He sprained his left hand on Morgan's head and he's soaking it in hot water. Morgan rode off. We don't know where he went."

"What did Morgan do that put you on his tail?" Armand asked. "Did he rob the bank or something like that?"

Ed wondered why he would ask that question. He studied Armand's battered face for a moment, then he said: "We want him for questioning. I talked to Slim Turner before he left. He said you were sending him to Indian Springs to get the crew. Why?"

"We're gonna hunt Morgan," Armand said. "When we find him, we'll hang him. If he's hiding out in some house in town, we'll burn the town if it takes that to run him out of his hole. He stole the buckskin gelding he's riding when he left the basin three years ago. It's a Rafter D horse. You always hang a man for horse stealing, don't you?"

The horse had belonged to Morgan from the time it had been a colt. The sheer effrontery of Armand's words shocked Ed, even though he

167

had been familiar with the Rafter D's attitude toward law enforcement for a long time. He said: "Buck, this is what I've been trying to tell you. You lay a hand on Morgan . . . I don't care what the charge is . . . and I'll put you in jail. Not one of your crew. You! If you do hang Morgan, you'll be tried for murder."

"That's big talk, Sheriff," Armand said easily. "You were singing pretty low for a long time. How come you're talking so big now?"

Ed wasn't sure. He had swallowed his pride just as Judge Alcorn had, but after about so long a man discovers he can't go on swallowing. He has to do something. He had reached that point.

"Let's just say it's taken me a long time to get around to talking big," Ed answered. "If you figure I can't do it, stand up and make your play. Your right hand's in good shape."

Armand shook his head. "And take on three men? I ain't that good. Or that stupid. No, I'll wait till my boys get here and we'll see who's talking big. If you're trying to scare us into giving Morgan half of the Rafter D, it won't work, Sheriff."

"One thing, and you'd better think about it," Ed said. "You couldn't handle Morgan by yourself. You fetch your whole crew in to take one man and you and the Rafter D will be the laughing-stock of the basin."

Ed wheeled and strode out of the house. He

didn't say a word as he mounted and rode away, but he was sour-tempered, knowing he hadn't really accomplished anything. As far as cutting the Rafter D down to size, he hadn't even started. It was a job that would take some powder burning.

In the past he had let the situation drift. It had gone too far because it had been the easy thing to do. Now he thought about his wife and children; he thought about Morgan Dill and the unfairness of this situation in which he had been forced to look for a desperate man who might be innocent. Well, if he was going to get killed, he'd rather do it making his stand for the principle of law enforcement against the Rafter D than trying to arrest Morgan Dill.

When he reached the road, he reined up. He said: "Tully, looks to me like we'll be swapping lead with the whole Rafter D pack of wolves before sunup. I wish we had Morgan's gun on our side."

"So do I," Tully said. "I sure do."

"Morgan's going to get his half of the outfit," Ed said. "He'll make that will stand up in court. Well, you figure Morgan's still down here in the willows?"

If he were, he would hear what they were saying. Somehow it seemed of utmost importance for Morgan to hear, for him to know that they were his allies against Buck Armand and the Rafter D crew. But Tully, who had been examining the road, turned and said: "He went back to town. Leastwise somebody did recent-like. It must have been Morgan."

Ed nodded wearily. He guessed he had expected it. Now they faced the task of hunting Morgan in town where there were a dozen places for him to hide. The chances were Armand and his men would be hunting him before sunup, too.

"We'll get along to town and start looking," Ed said, "but I don't know where to start."

"Maybe with Lamar," Tully said. "Morg will make him talk or kill him."

"And then he'll face a murder charge," Ed said. "We'd better find him first."

"It sure done me good to hear you talking back there," Tully said. "I never was able to figure out why you and Judge Alcorn and everybody else kept pussyfooting around with that Rafter D outfit."

Ed didn't answer. He really didn't have an answer. Maybe it had become a habit. Or maybe Ed and Alcorn and the rest wanted to live so much they had been afraid to face the situation. All Ed knew for sure was that he was off his knees at last and he felt like a man for the first time in years. It was a good feeling, a hell of a good feeling. He wondered if Judge Alcorn and Sam Colter and the rest of the Twin Rocks people would ever have that feeling.

XII

Ed rode back to town in silence, Tully and Johnny Bedlow trailing him. It was going to be a long night, he thought, if they didn't get lucky and find Morgan. He judged they had until about dawn before Buck Armand would lead his men into Twin Rocks. Suppose that he hadn't found Morgan by that time? What would Armand do?

He turned this over in his mind as he rode. He got sick after he had thought about it a while. Armand was crazy, crazy enough to be convinced that he was above the law and could do anything and not be held responsible for it. Knowing that, Ed came to the only conclusion he could. Armand would burn the town, just as he had threatened, if he couldn't find Morgan.

How did you stop a man like Armand? Even if Ed persuaded Morgan to throw in with them, there were only four men to do the fighting. He knew and Armand knew that the town fathers like Judge Alcorn and Sam Colter and Baldy Miles would run for cover. They'd be worth nothing when it came to the final showdown. Well, there was only one thing he could do. Find Morgan and jail him for his own safety, then put a gun in his hand when it was time for the shooting to start. That was the only way he might prevent disaster, and he wasn't sure that would do the job. The odds were just too long.

When they reached the edge of town, Ed said: "We'll start at Dick Lamar's house. I don't think we'll find Morgan there, but it's like you said, Tully. It's the logical place where he'd start. If we're too late and he's killed Lamar, then there'll be hell to pay all around."

Lamar's house was on a side street one block from the bank. It was the biggest and finest residence in Twin Rocks, which was fitting for the town banker and had been one of the reasons that Molly Runyan had married Lamar. She had given some great parties here, or so Ed had heard. He didn't know from personal experience because he and his wife didn't belong to the select social set that was invited to Molly's parties, and that suited him and his wife perfectly.

The three men tied up at the hitch pole in front, Ed's gaze on the house that in the moonlight was a sort of ghostly monument to Lamar's position in the town's pecking order. It was a two-story structure with a mansard roof, the only brick residence in town. An iron fence ran along the front of the lawn. Ed glanced up at the balcony with its white balustrade and shook his head, wondering if Molly ever regretted not marrying Morgan and if she was happy, now that she had gone as high as she could in Twin Rocks' society. She probably wasn't happy at all, Ed guessed, and more than

172

likely had nagged Lamar about moving to Denver where she would have a new world to conquer. She'd never get there, Ed thought, if the gossip about the condition of Lamar's bank was true.

They crossed the porch. Ed yanked the bell pull, and, when no one answered, he yanked three more times. The glass in the front door was frosted, so he didn't have a clear view into the back of the house, but there was a light back there some-where. Now it seemed to be moving forward along the hall. A moment later the door opened and Lamar stood there, a lamp in his hand, and peered at the men who stood in front of him as if uncertain about what he would say and do.

"We want to talk to you," Ed said.

"I sure as hell don't want to talk to you," Lamar snarled. "All I give a damn about as far as the sheriff's office is concerned is getting Morgan Dill locked up in a cell."

"That's why we're here," Ed said. "Can we come in?"

"No," Lamar snapped. "I'm getting ready for bed. Molly has a headache. So have I, after what happened today. I don't know what I'm going to do. I don't have enough money to even open the bank in the morning."

Lamar started to shut the door, but Ed shoved his foot against it. He said: "We're coming in, Lamar. You'll have a bigger headache if you don't talk to us."

"Have you got a warrant?" Lamar screeched. "A man's home is his castle. You've got no right to force your way in here if you . . ."

Ed's patience snapped. Lamar had always irritated him. Now the irritation turned into fury. He smashed a shoulder against the nearly closed door, slamming it open and sending Lamar reeling back so that he almost dropped the lamp.

"Come on," Ed said to Tully and Johnny Bedlow. "Lamar just invited us in."

He strode along the hall to the back of the house where an open door showed a light. He had never been inside the house before, but he guessed there was some sort of study or sitting room in the back. He was right. Molly was sitting on a rosewood sofa, some embroidery on her lap.

He judged that it was Molly's private sitting room with its rocking chairs, their seats covered by thick cushions, the wine-red carpet, and the sewing machine that, he guessed, she seldom used. The paintings on the wall were of brightly colored flowers, each surrounded by a heavy gilt frame. A melodeon was set against the far wall, and he remembered that Molly had always been fond of music.

"Good evening, Sheriff," Molly said. "I hear Morgan is back in town."

"That's right," Ed said. "How's your headache?"

She was surprised. "Why, I don't have a headache right now. Why did you ask?"

"Your husband said you did."

She laughed. "Well, Dick lies a lot."

Lamar came in just as she said that and set the lamp on a claw-footed walnut stand in the middle of the room. "Sure I lied," he said. "I didn't want you in here upsetting our evening. Smith, you've made yourself a hell of a lot of trouble. I'm going to take this up with Judge Alcorn in the morning. I'll have you thrown out of office for breaking into my house. I don't have to stand for this, and I won't."

Ed nodded at Tully who was standing in the doorway, Johnny a step behind him. He said: "Tully, you and Johnny take this lamp and search the house to make sure that Morgan isn't in it somewhere. Look in places where Lamar could hide a body."

"My God!" Molly screamed. "You think we'd kill Morgan? I haven't even seen him. Anyhow, he's the last man in the world I'd want killed."

"I doubt that your husband feels the same way," Ed said dryly.

Lamar was speechless for a moment, his eyes bugging from his head. Then he said in a choked voice: "This is the damnedest outrage I was ever subjected to. Just who do you think you are, Smith?"

"I guess I could ask you the same question," Ed said, "but right now all I want is to know where Morgan is."

"You're looking in a mighty funny place," Lamar snapped. "Why do you think you'd find him here?"

"Because he's going to come here sooner or later to make you clear him of the bank robbery charge," Ed answered. "If it got to the place where you had a fight, he'd kill you or you'd kill him. I can see you're alive, so I figure there's a chance you got him and you hid the body until you could decide what to do with it later on."

Lamar snorted a laugh. "I never heard such hogwash in my life. He robbed me and lit out with the money. One thing you can count on is that he's too smart to stay around here."

"Your story don't hold up, Lamar," Ed said. "It's like Molly said a while ago. You lie a lot."

The banker wheeled to face his wife. "Why in God's name did you say that?"

For a moment Molly didn't answer. She continued embroidering, her eyes on the circle of cloth tightened between the two hoops. She was a beautiful woman, Ed thought. She was wearing a belted blue wrapper; her hair hung down her back in a shining black mass; her features were perfect by Ed's standards. Yet for all of her beauty, he sensed that she was far from contented. He had heard stories of her verbal battles with her husband. The neighbors told of hearing them screaming at each other far into the night.

Finally she looked up at Lamar. "Because you

do lie a lot. I know that you've never told me the truth about what you do in Grand Junction when you go there. I know that you've gambled and lost more money than you've ever admitted to anyone, and I believe you've slept with whores every time you've been in Grand Junction and lied to me when you came home."

"It's not true!" Lamar shouted. "It's not true at all. I told the truth about Morgan Dill holding me up. Now I'm broke, I tell you! The bank won't be able to open in the morning."

Ed shook his head. "It won't work, Lamar. Morg would be a fool to stop and hold up a bank when he came back at the time he was to inherit half of the Rafter D. Being a fool is one thing Morg isn't."

Lamar snorted. "You know Celia. She made him a piddling offer for his half of the ranch. He could take it or leave it. If he didn't take it, he got nothing. You know damned well that Armand wouldn't let him on the place. Dill knew it, too. Well, he aimed to get more than the five thousand dollars Celia offered him, so he took it the only way he could, by poking a gun into my belly."

"And I know Morgan," Molly said. "I don't believe he's capable of robbing a bank, yours or anyone else's."

"Maybe you knew him once," Lamar said, "but you don't know him now. He's a bad one, I tell you. He'd have killed me this evening without batting an eye. I was never so scared in my life. Now he's ten miles from here, Smith, and you're not even trying to find him. In the morning I aim to let this town know how you enforce the law."

Tully and Johnny Bedlow came into the room, Tully setting the lamp down. He said: "We didn't find nothing, Ed. I don't think he's here."

For a moment Ed stood looking down at Molly, wondering what Lamar would do to her after he left. He said: "Will you be all right, Molly?"

She looked up at him, surprised, her full red lips slightly parted. "Of course."

"Then I guess we'll look somewhere else," Ed said.

He wheeled and left the room, Tully and Johnny Bedlow following.

XIII

For a time Ed stood beside his horse, one hand on the horn as he tried to bring back into his mind everything that he could remember about Morgan Dill. It would take all night to search the barns in Twin Rocks. Almost every house had one. He didn't have all night, so the problem was where to start.

At last Ed said: "I never knew Morg as well as you two did. I've been trying to think where he'd go after being gone so long. He never had many friends in town except you boys. Now he's in trouble. He's probably hurting in a dozen places after his fight with Armand. He needs help, maybe something to eat and a drink, maybe some liniment and bandages. Now where would he go to get help?"

"I've been asking myself the same thing," Tully said. "I don't know, Ed. I just don't know. He won't go to Doc Bridges. He hated the old buzzard. He might go to my place. Or Johnny's."

"Not to mine," Johnny said quickly. "I was an idiot tonight, not shaking hands with him, but it's too late now. He probably thinks I don't want nothing to do with him."

"Well, mine then," Tully said. "He may figure that, even if I am a deputy, I wouldn't turn him in."

"All right," Ed said. "You go have a look at your place, Tully. Johnny and me will try the stables. I don't think he'd leave his horse in one of the stables, but we've got to make sure."

"If he's hurting bad," Johnny said, "he might leave his horse in a stable and crawl up into the mow, or maybe take a hotel room."

"No, he wouldn't do that," Tully said sharply. "If I know Morg, he'd have to just about be dead to do anything of the kind."

"We'll find out," Ed said. "I'll have a look at the Red Front stable. Johnny, you try Barney's. We'll wait for each other in front of the courthouse."

A few minutes later Ed rode through the archway of the Red Front stable and dismounted. A lantern was hanging from the wall just inside the door. He took it down and walked slowly along the runway, examining each horse, but he recognized most of them. None of the ones he didn't know was a buckskin gelding.

He went on out through the back door and checked the corral, but he still failed to find a horse that could have been Morgan's. There were several bays, a couple of blacks, and one sorrel, but no buckskins. This was what he expected, but still he was disappointed.

As Ed strode back along the runway, Uncle Joe Miller, the owner of the stable, came out of the little room that served as an office and held a cot that he slept on when he stayed in the stable overnight. He rubbed his eyes and squinted at Ed.

"I heered somebody prowling around out here," Miller said in his squeaky voice. "Now just what the hell are you up to this time of night? I reckon you ain't here to trade horses, are you?"

"No, I sure ain't," Ed agreed. "I'm looking for Morgan Dill. I thought maybe he'd left his horse here and got a hotel room."

"Dill?" Miller said. "I didn't know that young hellion was back in town. If he is, he can leave his horse somewhere else. I remember the time he set a bucket of water over the door of my office and tied a string to the doorknob. I came in late one night to go to bed, so tired I could hardly move, and damned if I didn't get soaked to the skin. What he couldn't think of, that damned depity of your'n could. Or Johnny Bedlow. No, sir, I ain't seen young Dill, and I ain't hankerin' to."

"All right, Joe," Ed said. "Go back to bed."

He mounted and rode the half block to the hotel, dismounted, and went inside. No one was behind the desk, so he tapped the bell, then gave the register a turn and checked the names of everyone who had registered that day. Morgan Dill was not among them, but that, of course, proved nothing.

A big woman came out of a room back of the lobby, stretching and yawning and scratching herself, then she saw who was at the desk and stopped, her face flushed with anger. "Well, by God, if it ain't the law. Now don't tell me your pretty wife kicked you out of your bed because you've been horsing around and you're looking for one?"

"Amanda," Ed said, "you can take a good mood in a man and turn it into a sour one without even trying. What you need is competition."

She laughed. "Naw, competition wouldn't change me for the better. Might even make me worse. Besides, no sense in two of us starving to death when I can do it by myself. It's enough for me to wonder how I'm gonna keep Dick Lamar and his stinking bank from taking over the hotel."

"I'm looking for Morgan Dill," Ed said. "I thought he might have taken a room here."

"Morgan?" She shook her head. "I didn't know he was back in town. I sure ain't seen hide nor hair of him. Say, did he come back to settle with that son-of-a-bitch of a sister of his?"

"He's back," Ed said, "and Lamar claims he robbed the bank. I've got to find him and talk to him before Buck Armand does."

"Can't help you," the woman said. "I wish I could. Morgan used to make some of the old fuddy-duddies mad the way he tore around, but I always liked his style. On the other hand, I wouldn't believe anything Dick Lamar said if he was standing on a knee-high stack of Bibles."

"Sorry I had to wake you up," Ed said.

"You're a liar," she said amiably. "You enjoyed doing it."

Ed grinned. "All right. I enjoyed it."

He walked out of the lobby, stepped up, and rode to the courthouse. Tully and Johnny were waiting for him.

"Any luck?" Ed asked.

"Not any," Tully said.

Johnny nodded. "Same here."

"Well, I guess I didn't expect any," Ed said sourly. "I just hoped we'd have some. Nothing to do but look in every barn in town and we just don't have that much time. Morgan wouldn't leave his horse outside for one of us to find."

He paused and scratched the back of his neck thoughtfully. "Maybe we can figure out which barns he wouldn't use."

"He wouldn't use Judge Alcorn's," Tully said, "or Doc Bridges's. Outside of them two, I don't know which one he'd pick or wouldn't pick. He might take one at random."

"At first I didn't think he'd go to Lamar's place," Ed said, "but now I figure he will. He was always short on patience. I can't see him wasting the night."

"Wait a minute," Johnny said. "I've got an idea. You recollect who you talked to this evening? I mean . . . in front of the bank?"

Ed stared at him blankly for a moment, then he remembered Jean Runyan's stopping him as he'd left the bank. "Yeah, I saw Jean Runyan, but what's that got to do with Morgan?"

"She knew he was in town," Johnny said. "She was almighty worried about him, so she must have been friendly with him. Morg would know that, so he might go to her place."

"Hell, yes," Ed said. "I should have thought of that sooner. We'll try it."

They rode to the end of the block, then turned off Main Street and rode up an alley past the rear of dark houses until they reached the Runyan barn. A light was burning in the kitchen, so Jean was still up. Ed wondered about that as he swung down.

"Johnny, stay with the horses," Ed ordered. "Tully, me and you will ease around the corner into the barn. I don't want Jean to let go at us with a shotgun."

Ed slipped around the corner of the barn, pausing a moment as he studied the lighted kitchen window and the fifty feet or more of back yard that was brightly lighted by the moon. No one could reach the rear of the house without being seen. If Morgan was inside and he saw anyone approaching the house, he'd cut loose with his six-shooter. At this distance and with this light, he couldn't miss.

Very slowly and gently Ed gave the turn pin a twist and opened the door, hearing the squeal of rusty hinges that seemed inordinately loud to his ears. He slipped inside, waited for Tully to follow, then closed and hooked the door shut. He scratched a match to life, jacked up the chimney of a lantern that hung near the door, and lighted the wick. He eased the chimney down, then heard Tully swear softly.

"That's his horse, all right," Tully said. "I'd know that gelding anywhere. I've rode beside him too many times to be mistook."

"Then he's inside," Ed said. "I'd gamble on it. That was a good hunch Johnny had."

He moved along the wall to where Morgan had left his saddle. For a moment he stood staring at the saddlebags, afraid of what he'd find in them.

He took a long breath, opened them, and took out a canvas sack marked Twin Rocks Bank. He groaned, and said in a low tone: "Well, this is the last thing I wanted to find."

Tully whistled. "Well, now, you don't think Lamar told the truth for once in his life?"

"Looks like it," Ed said.

He opened the sack and drew out a handful of gold coins. "I dunno, Tully," he said heavily, "I sure don't. I'll want to talk to Morgan before I make up my mind about him, but this looks bad. It's the kind of evidence that would make a jury send him to the Canon City pen."

Tully shook his head. "I still don't believe it, Ed. I just don't think a man like Morgan can change that much."

Ed wondered how much money was in the sack, and decided it couldn't be more than $800 or $900, $1,000 at the most. He said, "If we take this sack to Lamar and tell him where we found it, he'd say it proved his story and proves that Morgan's guilty, so we won't do no such thing. It strikes me that Lamar must have had more than this in the bank, and, if Morgan had cleaned his safe out the way he said, Morgan would have more."

"That's right," Tully said. "Let's go talk to him."

"Not just yet," Ed said. "Not unless you want to be the first to go to the back door."

Tully grinned. "No, I can't say I do. Old Morg

might be in the kitchen, watching with his iron in hand."

"Then we'll wait a spell," Ed said, "till we figure out how to get there without getting plugged."

XIV

For a time Morgan could not comprehend what Jean was telling him. He felt as if he were fighting his way upward through a suffocating blanket of fog. Jean shook him again, and her words beat against his ears: "Morgan, you've got to wake up. Somebody's in the barn. I don't know who it is, but it might be Buck Armand and some of his crew."

He sat up, and shook his head. His body ached in a dozen places where Armand's big fists had slugged him. Jean had not brought a lamp with her, but light fell through the open door from the kitchen. The pool of moonlight, too, was still on the foot of the bed. Still, she was an indistinct shape to him. He rubbed his eyes and blinked, but he could not bring her into sharp focus.

"Wait a minute," he said. "My head's fogged up. I just now got to sleep."

"You've been asleep for more than an hour," she said sharply. "I was sitting on the back porch when I heard horses in the alley. The men

186

dismounted. They were talking, but they kept their voices so low I couldn't make out what they were saying. Two of them went into the barn and closed the door."

His head was gradually clearing and everything that had happened since his arrival in Twin Rocks came back to him. His buckskin gelding was in the barn. Buck Armand or the sheriff or almost anyone would recognize the horse and would guess that he was around here somewhere.

He stood up. "I don't want to go out there and start shooting unless I have to. You might get hurt. If it's Armand, I'll have to. If it's the sheriff or someone else, maybe I won't. You go to the back porch and ask who it is. Let them come into the house if they want to. I'll stay here and keep the door open a crack so I can see what's going on. If they come in and start roughing you up to make you tell them where I am, I'll take a hand in the game."

She hesitated, her worried gaze on him. Suddenly her hands went out to him and gripped his shoulders. She said: "Morgan, if it's the sheriff, I want you to talk to him. I know Ed Smith. So do you. He's an honest man. You can't go on running from him and Buck Armand."

"Sure, he's an honest man," Morgan said bitterly, "but men like Dick Lamar and Judge Alcorn and the rest of the big roosters in town call the turn, and Ed listens. No, the only chance I've got is to make Lamar clear me. Don't tell them I'm here under any circumstances. It will make me burn some powder if you do and I don't want that."

Still she hesitated as if she knew he was wrong, but she didn't press it. She shook her head, saying—"I don't know why the good Lord ever created stubborn men."—and left the bedroom.

He closed the door, then moved across the room to the back window that looked out upon the yard. He heard Jean call: "Who's out there?"

Silence for a good minute, then a man answered. "It's Ed Smith, Jean. Tully's with me. We want to talk to you."

"Come on in," she said. "You can talk to me any time, even at one o'clock in the morning."

Silence again for a moment. Morgan guessed that Smith and Tully were talking it over. They probably were convinced he was in the house and were afraid he would start shooting the moment he saw them. Finally Smith yelled: "Jean, is Morgan with you?"

"No, of course not," she answered. "What makes you think he's here?"

"His horse is in the barn."

"He is?" she said as if surprised. "Well, maybe he's asleep out there somewhere."

Both men stepped out of the barn and ran toward the back porch, more afraid than ever, Morgan thought, that he'd open up on them any minute. Still, they had taken the chance, so they were gambling on his not shooting them. He quickly moved back to the door and opened it a crack, then drew his gun.

Jean was in the kitchen, standing by the stove. She asked as Smith came in: "Will you have a cup of coffee, Sheriff?"

"Sure will," Smith said, his gaze whipping around the room, fixing on the bedroom door for a moment, then going back to Jean. "You're sure Morgan ain't here?"

"Sure I'm sure," she said testily. "I ought to know who's in my house. Besides, he left town."

Tully came in then and remained near the back door. Neither man had changed, Morgan thought. He had never been particularly fond of Smith, but he had been very close to Tully and he found it hard to believe that his old friend had actually taken the deputy's job.

He wondered where Johnny Bedlow was. Probably in the alley somewhere, he decided, or maybe he'd gone around to the front to cut him off if he made a run for it. He doubted that Smith believed Jean, but that wasn't important. What was important was whether the sheriff would insist on searching the house. It meant trouble if he did, and right now Morgan wanted to avoid trouble with everybody except Dick Lamar.

Jean poured two cups of coffee and handed them to Smith and Tully, then she asked: "Just what were you two pussy-footing around in my barn for? I don't think I like that. If you've got something on your mind, you could come to the door and ask like men."

"We were looking for Morgan's horse, figuring that he'd be where his horse was," Smith said. "We know he went to the Rafter D and we thought he came back to town. Now that we've found his horse, we know he did."

Jean shrugged. "Like I said, I thought he'd left town, but I guess he is around here somewhere if his horse is in my barn."

Smith walked to the table and sat down. He said: "We've got to find him, Jean. Armand has sent for his crew and he'll bring 'em into town and tear the place apart till he finds Morgan."

"What will he do then?" Jean demanded.

"He says he'll hang Morgan for horse stealing," Smith said. "He claims that Morgan stole the buckskin, that the animal belongs to the Rafter D."

"That's ridiculous!" Jean cried. "Why, Morgan's had that horse for a long time. I remember him riding the horse when he was shining up to Molly."

"I know, I know," Smith said impatiently. "The trouble is, Armand's gone loco. He's got his greedy hands on the Rafter D and he don't aim to let go. He's worse now that Morgan gave him a whipping."

"He's got to let go of half of it," Jean said. "That half belongs to Morgan."

"That's the point," Smith said. "He won't settle

for Celia's half. If Morgan stays alive, he can take his share, so Armand's bound to find an excuse to kill him. Horse stealing will do."

"You'd have to bring him in for murder," Jean said. "He ought to know he can't get away with anything as wild as that."

"Armand is going to be hard to bring in on any charge," Smith said. "I've got one deputy. I can call on Johnny Bedlow and that's about the size of it. Everybody is scared of Buck Armand and you know it as well as I do. The Rafter D bulldozed this county for years when old Abe was alive. Well, Armand's worse because he's crazy and Abe wasn't."

"Are you sitting there telling me that Armand can ride in here with his crew and hang Morgan on a trumped-up charge like that and get away scotfree?" Jean shook her head. "Ed, you wouldn't let him?"

"How can three men stop him?" Smith demanded sourly.

She stood there, shaking her head. Tully said: "Jean, Morg was my best friend. I don't aim for Armand to get his hands on him, but you've got to help. We can protect Morgan if we can find him. If Armand finds him first, we can't. We want Morgan to give himself up."

"And just what will you do with him if he does?" Jean demanded.

"We'll put him in jail for his own protection,"

Tully said. "If Armand tries to break him out, we'll give Morgan a gun because he'll need it."

"If Armand finds out we don't have Morgan in jail," Smith said, "he'll burn the town, figuring that will make him show himself. If Morgan is in jail, the four of us can hold Armand off. I think we can whip him."

Morgan saw Jean wipe her eyes and for a terrible moment he thought she was going to give him away. One thing was certain. He wasn't going to jail. They might be on the level. He had never known Tully to lie to him. Still, he wasn't sure that Ed Smith saw the situation the way Tully did.

Tully and Smith were watching Jean. She was silent, biting her lower lip and dabbing at her eyes. Then Tully said: "Jean, you're bound to see Morgan since his horse is here. You know, and Morgan would know if he was here to hear me say it, that there's nothing I wouldn't do for him. Right now he's got a chance to do something for himself and the town. We need him. Now you tell him that."

"He didn't rob the bank!" Jean cried. "I'll never believe that he did. He'll find some way to make Lamar clear him. It seems to me that you'd do a better job if you got the truth out of Dick Lamar."

"We will," Smith promised. "We don't think Morgan robbed the bank, either, but right now Buck Armand is the dangerous man, not Lamar."

Jean threw up her hands. "All right, do it your way. I'll tell Morgan if I see him. Now why don't you go on back to the courthouse or go home or wherever you want to. I'm ready for bed."

Smith rose. "We'll go back to the courthouse. Get word to Morgan that we're expecting him." He started toward the door, then stopped. "Seems funny that you're up so late."

"Nothing funny about it," she snapped. "I couldn't sleep for worrying about Morgan and I'm still worrying. What you've told me about Armand doesn't help. I still probably won't be able to sleep."

"Just get word to Morgan that we need him," Smith said. "With his help, we can clean Armand's plow for him." He left.

Tully followed, until he reached the door, then he turned. "I'm not sure you believe us, Jean, but you've got to. What's more, you've got to convince Morgan that we're still his friends."

He went out. Jean didn't move until they were out of the light, then she left the house and crossed the yard to the barn. She returned in a few minutes and shut the kitchen door. She said: "They're gone, Morgan. You can come out now."

193

XV

After Ed Smith and his men left the house, Lamar returned to Molly's sitting room and stood looking down at her. To him she was the most beautiful and desirable woman in the world. He still loved her; at least he loved her as much as he was capable of loving any woman. The first year of their marriage had been wonderful, the happiest year of his life, but then something happened.

He was not sure what had gone wrong. Molly had been a lusty wanton in bed, then for no reason that he could put his finger on she had turned cold. That was the reason, he had told himself, that he had started going to Grand Junction, the reason for his gambling, the reason for his bedding down with cheap whores. There were lines of discontent around her eyes that had not been there when they were married. Her mouth used to turn up at the corners in a ready smile when he came home from the bank. Now it curled down in derision. She had not given a party for three months, and, when he pressed her for the reason, she had said languidly that she was too tired.

Suddenly all the bitterness and frustration that had been piling up in him boiled over. He said: "Why in God's name did you tell Smith I lied a lot? Were you trying to make him think I was lying about Dill holding me up?"

She had been working steadily on her embroidery, ignoring him as completely as if he wasn't in the room. Now she glanced up. "Why, yes, darling. That's exactly what I wanted him to think. You were lying, weren't you? You framed Morgan, didn't you?"

"Sure I did, but they don't know it," he said. "I can make it stick, too. I can send Dill to the pen for twenty years, and I can get Alcorn and Colter and some of the others to back me in starting a new bank. Do you hear, Molly? We can start over."

"No." She went on with her embroidery. "We can't start over. We're finished. You're finished in this town, too, and I can't stand a failure. I can't stand living in this stinking, dirty, little town, either."

This, he knew, was part of the trouble, although he had never taken it seriously. Now, looking at her flushed face, he knew that it had been a mistake. Maybe that was what had turned their marriage sour. She had been contented and happy that first year, then she seemed to feel she had done all she could in Twin Rocks and began nagging him about selling the bank and moving to Denver. He had never seriously considered it and had told her to shut up about it. They were living in Twin Rocks and she'd better be happy to have the best house in town.

He clenched his fists and wheeled around and walked across the room and back. He knew she was right about being finished in Twin Rocks. There had been too much talk about his trips to Grand Junction, too many rumors about the bank being on thin ice. Some of it had come back to him; there must be a great deal of it going around the community.

He hunkered down in front of her and took her hands. He said: "Listen to me, Molly. I love you. I don't want to give you up. We'll leave here. You've been wanting to go away. Now we'll do it."

She left her hands in his, limp and without life. Her eyes were scornful as she said: "What will we use for money? You're broke, aren't you?"

"Not quite," he answered. "I've got a paper that Buck Armand and Celia want. Dill signed it when he was in the bank this evening. It says that he gives up his share to the Rafter D for the money I gave him. It's worth five thousand dollars to Armand. I know they've got that much cash out there. Five thousand will take us a long ways."

"And what will we do then?" she demanded.

"I'll make more," he promised. "I've got ways of making money. I guess I'm as tired of Twin Rocks as you are. If we go somewhere else, some place where I'm not known, I can do all right. You know that. I did all right until you drove me away."

"Me drive you away?" She jerked her hands away from his. "Why are you blaming me? I didn't drive you anywhere."

"The hell you didn't."

He rose and backed away from her, hating her and wanting to put his hands on her white throat and choke the life out of her. She must be lying. She was smart. She had to know what she had done to him.

"You know what you've been," he said. "When we were first married, I couldn't have asked for a better wife, then you turned into an iceberg. I might as well have been sleeping with a dead woman."

"That wasn't what drove you away," she said scornfully. "You got big ideas about what you could do playing poker and all you did was lose the bank and your self-respect. Why you'd think I'd even want you to sleep with me is more than I know when I knew what you were doing in Grand Junction."

"You didn't know," he flung at her. "I never told you."

"You didn't have to," she snapped. "I knew, all right. You're crazy if you think that going to some damned whorehouse in Grand Junction would make me welcome you back into my bed."

"It wasn't that in the beginning!" he shouted. "You damned broke me the first year we were married. You spent money like water every time

197

you were in Denver. You've got dresses in your closet you've never worn. Nothing satisfied you, by God, *nothing!*"

Her right hand moved away from her drawing the thread tight, then the needle pierced the cloth, and she drew the thread tight again. Slowly she raised her head and looked at him, smiling in her tantalizing way.

"A banker should be able to support his wife, shouldn't he, darling?" she said.

This was the way she often treated him when they were fighting and it always drove him into a fury. But now he didn't want their conversation to go this way. His fists closed and opened; he felt his heart pounding. He knew he had lost her; still, he could not give up.

"Listen, Molly," he said earnestly, "I'll admit I've done some bad things to you, but I'll change. I promise. I want you to go with me when I leave. I'm going to saddle up and ride out to the Rafter D. I'll get my money and I'll be back before sunup. Will you be ready to go?"

She had started working on her embroidery again. Now she glanced up and nodded. "I'll be ready. What have I got to stay here for?"

"Good. We can start over. You'll see."

He stooped and kissed her. She did not respond. His lips were eager, but she gave nothing back to him. He straightened and again felt the compelling impulse to choke her, or slap her face until her head wobbled. Not now, he told himself. Later, maybe, if she didn't keep her promise.

He left the room and went into his bedroom. He had put away his gun when he'd come home from the bank. Now he opened a bureau drawer and took out the gun and belt. He checked the revolver, saw that there were five loads in the cylinder, and slipped it back into the holster. He looked at it for a time, wondering if he should take it.

He seldom wore a gun, and he wasn't very good with it, but he didn't think Buck Armand was, either. He didn't trust Celia and he trusted Armand even less. He'd better take it, he decided. They might try to cheat him out of his $5,000 and he wasn't standing still for that. He'd earned his money. He would be keeping his part of the agreement by delivering the paper signed by Morgan Dill.

Lamar buckled the gun belt around his waist and left the house, not taking the time to look in on Molly. He strode across the moon-drenched back yard to the barn, lighted a lantern, and saddled his black gelding. He blew out the lantern, led the horse out of the barn, closed the door, and stepped into the saddle.

He did not have any faith in Molly's promise to leave with him, and for the first time he considered going without her. He might just as well keep on riding after he left the Rafter D. He had nothing left here except his personal possessions and the furniture, and he couldn't sell any of it for any worthwhile sum.

The furniture was expensive. He'd bought it new when they were married, but who would buy it for anything like what he had paid? The house was mortgaged for more than it was worth. He wanted to laugh when he thought about it. Molly didn't know about the mortgage. She probably figured she could go right on living there. Well, she was in for a surprise!

He could decide about going on without her after he left the Rafter D. He had to go back through town anyway. Suddenly he was in a hurry. He wanted to get this settled and be on his way. He could no longer face his failure here. It was hard to believe he had actually reached this point.

When they were married, he had the world by the tail and a downhill pull; he was the most powerful and respected man in town. Now he was nothing. Even the stupid sheriff didn't believe his story. No one loved him. By God, when he thought about it, no one even liked him. He didn't have a friend in town. He could lay it all on Molly. Why had he sucked around after her all that time, trying to outmaneuver Morgan Dill and break his engagement to Molly, was more than he could understand.

He put his horse to a gallop, feeling the cool night breeze on his hot face. Why he had even tried to talk Molly into going away with him was more than he knew. He was better off without her. Then, slowly, he began to think about Molly and the first months of their marriage. Her face haunted him. He would never be free of her as long as he lived. No, he had to take her with him. If at the last minute she refused to go, he'd put his hands on her beautiful throat and he'd squeeze until she couldn't breathe. If he couldn't have her, no one else would, either. How could a man both hate and love a woman the way he hated and loved Molly? He didn't know. It made no sense at all, but that was the way it was.

He reached the fork in the road and turned off toward the Rafter D. He had to get his business done and hurry back to Twin Rocks. He had to know what Molly would do.

XVI

Morgan left the bedroom as soon as Jean told him that the sheriff and Tully had gone. Jean asked: "You heard them, didn't you, Morgan?"

"Sure I heard them," he answered. "You didn't believe them, did you?"

"Yes, I did," she said sharply, "and you ought to believe them just as much as I do. I've known both men as long as I can remember, and I know that, if there are two decent men in this world you can believe, it's Ed Smith and Tully Bean."

"There was a time when I would have agreed," Morgan said, "but I figure things are different now. It would be quite a feather in Smith's cap if he could throw me into the jug, and I'd say Tully has sold out to him. Johnny Bedlow, too, I guess."

"No, Morgan." She walked to him and put her hands on his arms. "Now you listen. Ed doesn't need any feathers in his cap, and Tully was and is your best friend. You can't go fighting all of them. You heard what the sheriff said about Buck Armand bringing his men in and that they needed your gun. Help them, Morgan. You'll be helping yourself, too."

He shook his head. "Maybe you're right about Smith not needing any feathers in his cap, but he wants to stay alive, doesn't he? He knows that, if he tries to take me, some of them will be dead. I've got to play it my way, Jean, and stay out of jail. Lamar has framed me and he can make it stick if I don't make him clear me."

"Just how do you think you're going to do that?" she cried. "Morgan, I tried to tell you the kind of man Lamar is. He'd never admit he framed you."

"I'll kill him if he doesn't," Morgan said.

"Oh, that's crazy!" Jean stamped her foot. "Hang for murder? What good would that do you? You heard the sheriff say he didn't believe you robbed the bank. He doesn't like Lamar any better than you do. Nobody does any more. Lamar hasn't got a friend in this town. Even if you came to trial, no jury would convict you."

"Then they wouldn't convict me if I killed him," Morgan said. "They'd probably build me a statue in front of the courthouse."

He wheeled away from her, not as sure of himself as he wanted Jean to believe. He couldn't think past the fact that Lamar had framed him, and Lamar was the one man who could clear him. He wouldn't have to kill him. All he had to do was to make Lamar *think* he was going to kill him.

He paused at the back door and turned to look at Jean, who was watching him with troubled eyes. She said: "Come back when you get done with Lamar. I won't go to bed. I certainly couldn't sleep if I did."

Morgan nodded, and left the house. He crossed the back yard in long, quick strides and stopped in the shadow of the barn, wondering if Smith and the others had slipped back after leaving and were waiting for him. He didn't think so. He was reasonably sure that Smith knew he was in the bedroom and was listening to the conversation. He probably was counting on Morgan's believing what he and Tully said.

He had to play his hand out, he told himself. He had been telling himself that for quite a while, he thought sourly, but it seemed he had no choice. If Smith and the others were waiting for

203

him, he'd shoot his way past them. That wouldn't help the situation, but again he told himself he had no choice.

He ran down the alley, keeping in the shadows, stopping to listen and look, and then go on. When he reached the rear of the Lamar house, he stopped, seeing that there was a light in one of the back rooms. This surprised him. He had supposed Lamar would be asleep in bed. He could be sure of one thing, he told himself wryly. Lamar's conscience wouldn't be keeping him awake.

Morgan hesitated for a moment, the thought crossing his mind that Molly might be the one who was up and he didn't want to see her, but he wasn't going to worry about that. It was a chance he was willing to take. He ran to the back porch, crossed it to the door, and knocked. A moment later he heard footsteps, then the door opened, and Molly stood there peering at him.

The light in the hall that fell through the open door behind Molly was very thin and it took her a moment to recognize him. He couldn't see her clearly, standing as she was with her back to the light, but it couldn't be anyone else except Molly.

"I want to see . . . ," Morgan began.

"Morgan," she squealed. "Oh, Morgan, I'm so happy to see you. Come in."

She pushed the screen door back and he stepped in, then she threw herself at him, her arms coming around him. She lifted her mouth for his kiss. When he made no effort to kiss her, she reached up and pulled his head down. This was the last thing he had expected and wanted, then he was glad she did it because her lips that had been so warm and exciting did nothing to him now. He knew beyond doubt that the spell she had cast upon him was completely broken.

She gave no indication that she noticed his lack of response. She took his hand that was nearest to her and squeezed it, then said: "Come on back into my sitting room, Morgan. I want to look at you. It's been so long."

She led him along the hall and into her sitting room, then turned and gazed intently at his face. She said, smiling: "You look good to me. I can't tell you how good. I have never felt so deserted and alone as I do tonight. I needed to see you. Dick's gone to the Rafter D to see Armand and your sister, and he left me here by myself. He's leaving the country and expects me to go with him. I don't have the slightest intention of doing anything of the kind, but then, if you hadn't come, I might have done it." She motioned to a nearby chair, sat down, and picked up her embroidery. "Sit down, Morgan. We've got so much to talk about. First I want you to know that I was absolutely stupid to let you leave the country without me and to marry Dick. He's been a truly terrible husband. Compared to you, he just isn't much man."

He sat down and looked at her. Apparently she

expected him to pick up where he'd left off, to forgive her for what she had done to him, and to marry her as soon as she divorced Lamar, and that, he thought bitterly, was unrealistic and completely stupid. He sat on the front of the chair, his back stiff, and tried to decide what to say to her.

"Did your husband tell you about him claiming that I robbed his bank?" Morgan said after a moment's silence.

"Oh, yes." She glanced up, smiling. "But I know you didn't do it. He framed you and he told me he had. I'll tell the sheriff if you're worried about it. It was silly. No one would believe what Dick said. He's a chronic liar, you know. I guess that's no news to you."

He took a long breath of relief. "I'm glad to know that you'll clear me. I've been worried."

"You shouldn't be," she said reassuringly. "I don't think Dick believes he'll succeed in blaming you for the bank's money being gone. Anyhow, he knows he's finished in Twin Rocks, so he went out to get five thousand dollars from Armand, and then he's leaving."

"How can he get five thousand out of Buck Armand?" Morgan asked.

"He said he had a paper you had signed giving up your claim to the Rafter D," she said. "I guess he must have been telling the truth or he wouldn't have ridden out to the ranch. I mean, he just

206

doesn't like to ride that well, but I didn't believe you'd sign any paper like that and throw away your share of the property that's rightfully yours."

"Let's say he tricked me," Morgan said.

He had been staring at her, thinking she had changed a great deal in the time he had been gone. He had trouble deciding what the change was. She was not as pretty as he remembered her. She looked much older, with lines of discontent around her eyes. He guessed that was the biggest change. Some people seem not to be changed by time, but Molly Lamar was not one of them.

"Well, I know one thing," she said. "Dick will go to prison if he doesn't get away, or if he can't prove to Smith that you're the one who robbed the bank. If I tell the sheriff what I know, then I guess he will go to prison, won't he?"

She was making herself plain enough, he thought. She was really saying that, if he wanted her, she could clear him. He rose, telling himself that if it came to bargaining like that, he'd take his chances surrendering to Ed Smith.

She threw the embroidery down and jumped up as Morgan said: "I'll stop by later and see Lamar."

"No!" she cried. "He won't be here more than a minute when he stops to get me. You'll miss him. He'll want me to go with him and I'll tell him I'm not going, and then he'll leave. He'll have to. Don't you see, Morgan? I'll tell him plain out that I'll testify for you. I'll tell the sheriff what he old me. That's all it'll take to clear you, isn't it?"

He shook his head. "He'd swear you were lying. It would be better if I got a confession out of him."

He backed toward the door. She said in a frantic tone: "Morgan, please stay here till he comes. I'm afraid of what he'll do to me if I don't go with him. After he leaves, I'll go with you to the sheriff's house and we'll get him out of bed and I'll tell him."

He found it hard to believe that Molly thought she could roll back the years this way and go right on as they had when he was so much in love with her that he didn't have a thought for anything or anyone else. Yet that certainly was what she was thinking, but, then, she never had been realistic. To her the world had always been what she wanted it to be.

"It won't work, Molly," he said brusquely. "We can't pick up where we left off."

He wheeled toward the door, hearing her cry out: "Yes, we can, Morgan! Let me show you that we can!"

He was in the hall by then. He kept going, across the porch and the back yard. Without thought he turned toward Jean's house, feeling empty and frustrated. Molly wouldn't testify for him unless he bowed to her every whim.

He still had to see Lamar. It was his only chance, but if Molly was telling the truth about the banker's leaving town, there was small chance he would find the man. On the other hand, he wasn't staying here until Lamar showed up. Right now all he wanted to do was to put some distance between himself and Molly.

XVII

Lamar tied his horse in front of the Rafter D ranch house, noting that there was a light in the front room, so some of them were up. He was glad. He didn't want to waste time pounding on the door and waiting for Armand to get dressed. The sooner he got this over with and started back to town the better.

He walked up the path to the front door, uneasiness beginning to work through him. He hadn't felt it before because his mind had been on Molly and his slide from the pinnacle of respectability into poverty and oblivion. A few months after he had left Twin Rocks no one would remember him unless they blamed him for the bank's going under. He would just as soon that they forgot him as to remember him that way.

He crossed the porch and knocked, not sure why this sudden fit of uneasiness had struck him unless it was the simple truth that Buck Armand was a hard and unpredictable man to deal with. He was given to terrible fits of temper, and, if he thought of something to blame Lamar for, the next few minutes were going to be hell.

Celia opened the door, saw who it was, and said with cold contempt: "Oh, it's you, Lamar. Come in."

No respect for him, Lamar thought bitterly as he stepped into the living room. There had been a time not so long ago when no one, not even Celia Armand, would have thought of addressing him as anything but Mr. Lamar. Slowly and insidiously this respect that a community naturally holds for its banker had eroded until it no longer existed. To hell with it, he thought sourly as he nodded at Armand who was sitting on a battered leather couch. He wouldn't be around very much longer to think about minor things such as his fading dignity and respect.

"Howdy, Buck," he said.

Armand gave him a bare half-inch nod, not taking the trouble to speak. Uneasiness grew in Lamar and spread down into his belly like a paralyzing liquid that froze his insides. Armand was in an evil mood. His battered face looked as if he had tangled with a grizzly, but Lamar decided it would be a mistake to ask what had happened.

"Morgan Dill's back," Lamar said.

"We know it," Armand grunted. "Did you get the paper?"

Lamar nodded. "It worked just as we planned.

He didn't like the notion of signing the paper, but my gun was a powerful persuader."

"All right, all right," Armand said impatiently. "Let's have the paper."

"It's right here." Lamar patted his coat pocket. "Let's see the money."

"You think you're going to get the money before I see the paper?" Armand demanded. "You're crazy. For all I know you may have forged his signature."

"I'll know it," Celia said. "I've seen Morgan's handwriting often enough."

Lamar looked from Armand's bruised face to Celia's fat one with the drooping jowl. In all of his life, he told himself, he had never seen two more disagreeable people. The uneasiness had turned to fear as he decided he'd give them the paper and take his money and get out. He reached into his coat and drew out the folded sheet of paper. He handed it to Celia.

"Look at the signature all you want to," he said. "It's his, all right. Maybe a little shaky, him sitting there under my gun when he signed, but it's his."

Celia held the paper close to the lamp and studied it a moment. She nodded as she handed it to her husband. "It's Morgan's, all right."

Armand gave a quick glance. He said: "I'm satisfied if Celia is."

Armand sat motionlessly. Celia moved away from him toward the stand in the middle of the room and stood staring at Lamar. The banker looked from one to the other and back. Neither showed any intention of going after the money. The horrible fear raced through his mind that they weren't going to give it to him.

"Where's my five thousand?" Lamar demanded.

"What five thousand?" Armand asked with bland innocence.

"By God, you're not weaseling out of it. I made an agreement with both of you and I kept my part. I expect you to keep yours."

Armand shrugged his thick shoulders. "You can expect what you damn please."

"If you don't give it to me," Lamar threatened, "I'll tell the whole plan to Smith."

"Go ahead," Armand said. "You'll be in the jug with us."

Sweat began pouring down Lamar's face. He took a handkerchief from his pocket and wiped his face. He asked hoarsely: "You're refusing to give me the money?"

"I've got a convenient memory," Armand said. "Right now I can't remember making any agreement with you that's concerned with five thousand dollars. You wanted an arrangement that covered your own thievery, and this deal with Morgan was just what you needed. That's profit enough for you. Now you can walk out of here and look Ed Smith in the face and you'll know he can't touch you. Otherwise, you'd be headed for Canon City.

I guess the pen down there ain't so bad, but I don't think you'd like it, being used to all the comforts you are."

The bald-faced effrontery turned Lamar's fear into anger. He found it hard to believe that Armand was serious, but there was no trace of humor in the broad, bruised face. Only cold contempt. The anger grew until it turned into rage. He began to tremble.

"I've got to have the money," Lamar said in a tight voice. "I'm leaving town and there's nothing left in the bank. I gave all the cash that was in the safe to Dill. I counted on your keeping your word. I've got to have a stake when I leave here. I won't walk out of this house until I get it."

"Oh, you'll be walking out pretty soon," Armand said, "if you're able to walk. I'm riding out and I sure ain't leaving you here with my pretty wife. So why don't you just get on your horse and ride back to town?"

Lamar thought about Molly and how he had promised her he'd have $5,000. She would never leave with him unless he had it. She had no respect for a man who was broke. He had a chance to regain her respect if he had money; he had no chance whatever if he didn't have any.

He didn't move. All the fear and uneasiness was gone from him now. In its place was a cold fury such as he had never known before in his life. He rubbed his hands up and down against his pants legs; he felt the weight of the gun and a compelling urge to reach for it swelled up in him. Armand's hands were palms down on his thighs. They looked swollen. If they were, Armand would have trouble handling his gun.

"Armand," Lamar said slowly, "you'd better know something before you make up your mind to cheat me. I've gone downhill until I've reached the bottom. The money you owe me is all I've got coming from anyone. I know you've got it. You withdrew more than that a few days ago. I tell you I'm going to have it if I have to kill you."

"Give it to him," Celia said wearily. "He's right. We made an agreement."

Armand was on his feet, a malicious grin tugging at the corners of his swollen mouth. He said: "You couldn't kill me if I gave you the first five shots. You just don't have the guts, banker man. If you had, you wouldn't be where you are, yelling about being broke and begging me for money. No, Celia, I won't give it to him. Look at him, shaky and scared so he's turned white. Or maybe it's green. I guess a man turns green when he's scared, don't he?"

"Give it to him and get him out of here," Celia said. "He makes me sick just looking at him."

"Yeah, he makes me sick, too," Armand said. "Mosey on out of here before I throw up."

It was bad enough to have a promise broken and not get the money that was due him; it was worse to be insulted after he had done exactly what he had bargained to do. It was unfair and wrong, but there was no use to go on begging. He knew Armand well enough to be sure that he would not change his mind. Still, knowing that, he continued to beg.

"You don't understand," he said, so tired he found it hard to make the words come. "You see, I've got to have that money. Molly won't go with me unless I do and she's got to go. That means you've got to give it to me. I'll say please and get down on my knees and do any damned thing you want me to do. Just keep your promise."

Armand looked at him, his lips curled in disgust. "Get out, banker. Go back to town and look in your safe. Maybe a few nickels are left for a man who will say please and get down on his knees."

Lamar took a long breath as all self-control left him. What he did was not the result of a cool, rational decision. It was simply the reflex action of a man who knew there was nothing left for him if he walked out of this house empty-handed. The thumb of his right hand was hooked under his waistband. Now he jerked it out and wrapped his hand around the butt of the gun and lifted it from leather.

Armand's first bullet struck him in the chest and knocked him down. It was like the blow of a sledge-hammer. He couldn't breathe; he knew he had dropped his gun and his hand began searching for it. He had heard the roar of the shot; he had heard Celia's scream, and now Armand's brutal face seemed to be detached from his beefy shoulders and was floating in space in front of him, then the Colt roared again and Dick Lamar saw and heard nothing more.

"You idiot!" Celia screamed. "You didn't have to kill the little weasel. All you had to do was to take his gun away from him. I never saw a man make a slower draw in my life. You could have walked over to him and taken the gun away from him before he pulled the trigger."

Armand shoved his gun back into the holster. "Maybe I could have," he said. "Maybe not. I reckon it don't make any difference, but I liked the notion of fixing it so his mouth was shut for good. Now he won't be making no deal with Smith and telling him how he got the idea of framing Morgan." For just a moment Armand stared at the motionless body. He said—"No guts."—and started toward the front door.

XVIII

Celia stood motionlessly, her gaze on Lamar's body. At first she had been stunned, then angry, and now she was furious. She was used to violence, she had seen men killed, but this had been so unnecessary. She'd had no use for the banker, for he had been a willing tool from the beginning. Still, he was in no way a threat to Buck or her. He had been too deeply involved in hers and Buck's plotting to talk. There had simply been no good reason for killing him.

Armand had almost reached the front door when she said: "Buck."

He stopped, then turned slowly. "What the hell do you want?"

"I said you were an idiot," she said. "Well, you're worse. You're a god-damned fool. You didn't accomplish anything by killing Lamar. All you did was to complicate our situation. What are you going to do with the body? How are you going to explain his killing to the sheriff?"

"Do whatever you want to with the body," he said. "It's your problem. I'll leave him here with you."

"No you don't!" she shouted. "I didn't kill him. You did. Now get rid of him."

He shrugged, started to say something, then decided against it, and shut his mouth. Once more he turned toward the door. Celia screamed: "I asked you what you're going to say to the sheriff! Now you'd better tell me because he may ride out here again."

Once more he turned to face her. "We don't need to explain nothing to the star toter."

"If he shows up here again and finds the body, we can't just . . ."

"Say it was an accident."

"He wouldn't believe that," she said scornfully. "And another thing. You're a damned crook as well as an idiot. We did make a bargain with Lamar. It was easier and smarter to keep it than to kill him. What the hell is the matter with you?"

"You're a bigger idiot than I am," he said harshly. "Anybody would be an idiot to give that tinhorn five thousand dollars. You're a good one to call me a crook. I guess a woman who would do all you've done to cheat your brother out of his share of the spread is as big a crook as anyone could be."

"You were in it from the beginning!" she cried. "It was your idea. You were the one who went to Lamar. . . ."

"Oh, shut up." He walked slowly toward her, his fists clenched. "I've had all of your caterwauling I can stomach. You're nothing but a fat old sow who married me because you wanted a man. You'd have done anything to get a husband, only nobody but me was fool enough to take the bait."

"Don't call me a fat old sow!" she shrieked, her face red. "I'm not a nothing as long as the Rafter D is mine. I've always kept my word and my father always kept his. You're the one who's a nothing. A chiseler and a murderer. That's what you are. Now get off my ranch."

He stood very close to her. Suddenly he laughed. "You think you can order me off this spread?

You think for a minute the crew would take orders from you? Well, now, that makes you the real idiot. No, you can't get rid of me by ordering me off the ranch." He scratched his chin, his eyes narrowing thoughtfully. "But maybe I'd better get rid of you."

She stared at him, the fury in her giving way to terror. She read murder in his face, cold, premeditated murder, the fulfilling of a plan that had long been in his mind. Then she lost all control and struck him on the side of the face, a hard blow that rocked his head. She had lost her ability to reason, but the instant she hit him, instinct told her she had done the wrong thing, that she was likely to trigger the killing hunger that was in him. She whirled away and tried to run, but he caught her before she reached the kitchen door. He yanked her around and hit her in the belly as he would have hit a man.

Breath was knocked out of her, making a strange wheezing sound. She was on the floor, although she had no memory of falling. She had a crazy feeling that time was suspended, that she was floating and turning in the air. She could not breathe; she had a terrible feeling that she was paralyzed.

Armand stood rubbing his knuckles as he looked down at her. He said: "Later, my good wife. Later."

This time, when he turned to the front door,

he kept going. Celia still could not move, but breath was beginning to come back into her lungs now, very slowly and very painfully. She was conscious, yet she couldn't move.

She heard Armand ride away. With a clarity of vision that shocked her, she realized she had been very close to death, that she had been spared only because killing her had not fitted Armand's timing. She had long suspected that he had murdered her father. Now, after seeing Armand gun down Lamar and then stare at her with the naked lust to kill so plainly written on his face, she knew beyond any doubt that he had murdered Abe Dill, that he was moving along a carefully schemed line, and he was intent on keeping everything in perfect order. Her murder would come later after Morgan had been disposed of. She had to leave before he returned or he would kill her even if it wasn't the proper moment.

She discovered she was able to move. Slowly she got to her feet, breath coming easier now. She sat down on the couch and wiped sweat from her face. Her belly hurt, not only from the blow Armand had given her, but from the fear that was like a cold stone in her abdomen. She had been afraid of Armand before, but not like this. His mask was off at last; for the first time she had seen the real Buck Armand, a man her father had trusted but had never really known.

For a moment she thought about Abe Dill, the

man his neighbors had called Lucifer Dill. She understood why. He had always been a brutal and grasping man, one who had simply bulldozed others out of his way until he had gained his objective, but she had never known him to break his word, to fail to keep a promise. Now, staring at Lamar's stiffening body, she was ashamed. She told herself that Buck Armand had brought himself to the lowest possible point that a human being could and in spite of herself she was a part of it.

She knew, then, what she would do. A shiver slid along her spine. For some illogical reason she had a feeling she would not live until morning, an insight that brought cold sweat breaking through her skin. She didn't know how she would die, or at whose hands, but one thing must be done first. Buck Armand had to hang for killing Dick Lamar. She would see that he did. Somewhere along the line she had to clear Morgan. Not that she had suddenly discovered any real love for her brother. It was simply a matter of getting at her husband. If by any chance she lived through the night, she would need Morgan's help.

She rose and left the house, walking slowly and bent forward at the hips. One hand was held against her belly. When she reached the barn, she lighted a lantern and harnessed a team. Leading the horses out of the runway, she hooked them to the buckboard, and drove to the front of the house.

Celia wasn't sure that she could do what she had to do. Her belly had never hurt like this in her entire life and she began to wonder if Armand's blow had damaged her insides. Maybe that was why she had this crazy premonition of death. It was a new sensation to her. She had never really thought much about dying. She had always been a strong, dominating woman who had been able to shape life the way she wanted it, but now her world had slid out from under her.

All the time she had thought she was using Armand, he had actually been using her, working steadily and patiently toward his goal. To him she had been nothing more than the fat old sow he had called her. He must have hated her all this time with a passion, she thought bitterly. He probably had been filled with disgust every time he had touched her.

Slowly she got out of the buckboard and walked into the house, still moving in that painful, bent-over position. Normally she could have picked Lamar up and carried him to the rig, but she knew she couldn't do that now. She blew out the lamp, then took hold of the banker's feet and pulled him through the front door to the porch. She stopped to rest, panting and holding her belly, then went on to the buckboard, the head of the corpse hitting each step with a dull *thwacking* sound as she pulled the body off the porch.

When she reached the buckboard, she had to

stop again to rest. The pain was worse now, a deep, stabbing pain that was like a knife thrust deeply into her abdomen. Somehow she had to get the corpse into the buckboard, but that required a straight lift and she couldn't do it.

She wiped her face with a sleeve. When she thought about Armand coming back with his crew and finding her here, she knew she could lift the body regardless of the pain. She stooped, slipped her hands under his shoulders and legs, and lifted him into the buckboard, and then nearly fainted from the pain. For a time she clung to a wheel, tears running down her cheeks. Each breath sent a deeper thrust of pain into her belly than she had felt. She knew with a greater certainty than before that she would die tonight and death was better than living if she had to suffer like this.

She did not know how long she remained that way, her hands clutching the wheel, her eyes closed, the tears running down her face and leaving their salty taste in her mouth. Time was not normal seconds and minutes to her, but seemed to run on and on like an endless river. She remembered when she had been very sick one time with scarlet fever and had almost died, and it had seemed to her that each feverish minute had been an hour. It was that way now.

She couldn't stay here no matter how much she hurt. Help was in town, not on the Rafter D.

Slowly she eased into the seat. Taking the lines, she drove across the moon-lighted yard and started down the road toward Twin Rocks.

Yes, she would see to it that Buck Armand died with a rope on his neck for the murder of Dick Lamar. She must survive the night, she told herself, and then she would live a long time, for Buck would not be around to murder her.

XIX

Ed Smith tied his horse in front of the court-house, stepped up on the boardwalk, and waited for Tully and Johnny Bedlow to dismount and tie. The courthouse was an ugly frame building that needed paint. Now it loomed ahead of him, a gaunt ungainly shape in the moonlight. The yard showed no pretense of a lawn, but held a splendid growth of dog fennel and various other weeds.

Whenever Ed stopped to think about it, the neglect that the county showed the courthouse seemed to him to be indicative of the feeling that the local people had for the law. The courthouse was a symbol of the law. The influence the Rafter D exerted on the law was one reason for that feeling, and it would exist as long as the Rafter D ran the county. Tonight, Ed told himself grimly, that influence would end.

No one had said a word on the way back from Jean Runyan's house. Now Tully stepped up on the boardwalk to stand beside Ed. He asked: "Think he'll come in?"

"Damned if I know," Ed answered. "You can come nearer telling me than I can tell you."

"He was in that bedroom," Tully said thoughtfully. "I'd bet on it, so he heard all we said. I think he'll come in after he's thought about it a while. Trouble is he may be too late."

Johnny joined them, and they walked around the corner of the courthouse to the jail, a small, stone building on the west side of the courthouse. Ed went in first, lighted a lamp, and sat down in his swivel chair at his spur-scarred desk. It was an ancient piece of furniture that went back to the day the courthouse and jail were built and that was a long time ago. Ed had often thought about asking for a new desk and chair, but he hadn't because he knew it would be a waste of time. Asking for anything that required tax money was a waste of time.

"It's gonna be a long wait," Tully grumbled. "I wish to hell Morg would come in. At least, we'd have him to talk to."

"Won't be long," Johnny Bedlow said. "Ain't more'n two, three hours till daylight, then we'll have plenty of excitement."

"We will for a fact," Tully agreed somberly.

Ed glanced at the metal door that opened into the corridor that divided one big cell from two small ones. The jail was empty as it usually was except on Saturday nights when Ed normally picked up a few drunks and held them here until they sobered up.

Ed's duties were seldom demanding. He guessed that more had happened tonight of a lawless nature than in all the previous time he had carried the star. It was a wonder he had been allowed enough money to pay one deputy. He thought moodily that he'd have a job getting Johnny's wages for the time he had put in tonight.

His gaze went on around the office to the gun rack near the door, to the calendar on the wall that pictured a girl in a very short dress. It was a disgrace to the county, Judge Alcorn grumbled, and Ed remembered replying sourly that, if the judge didn't like the scenery here, he could go back to his own office. Several Reward dodgers yellowed by age were tacked to the wall beside the calendar, all showing outlaws' fierce, mustached faces. Chances were every one of them was dead or in jail somewhere.

He rose and paced the length of his office and back. He couldn't stand it here another minute. He said: "I'm going home for a little while. Mary's probably sitting up, worrying about me."

"Go ahead," Tully said, still grumpy. "I wish I had a wife who was sitting up, worrying about me."

"Especially a pretty one like Mary," Johnny said, grinning. "You're a lucky man, Ed."

"I figure I am," Ed agreed.

He looked at Tully, who didn't meet his gaze. He had seldom seen his deputy in a mood as low as this. He understood how Tully felt about Morgan Dill, how much pressure Tully had been under all evening. He said: "I think he'll come in, Tully. You might as well quit worrying."

"Hell, I ain't worryin'," Tully snapped. "I'm as happy as the first robin in spring. I just wish it was sunup and I had my sights on that goddamned Buck Armand."

"He'll be here soon enough," Ed said, and left the jail.

He mounted and rode to his house, thinking how uneventful the months had been since he had taken the star. He had never been forced to face a tough situation before, at least against odds like this. Oh, he'd gone after wanted men and brought them in, but that wasn't facing the Rafter D crew.

The fact was he had never really been tested. Well, he'd be tested before this was over, he told himself sourly, and admitted that he would feel better if Morgan was in the jail with them. Funny thing, he thought, as he strode up the path to the front door. He was supposed to arrest Morgan Dill, and yet he was thinking that he needed Morgan because he was a fighting man, and Ed had mentally leaned on him ever since he'd heard what Buck Armand planned to do.

He opened the front door and stepped into the living room. A lamp was burning on the oak stand in the middle of the room. He saw that Mary was curled up on the couch, an afghan pulled over her. She stirred as he crossed the room to her and sat up and yawned.

"Must be two o'clock," she said.

He nodded. "About."

"Ed, did you find the Dill boy?"

He shook his head as he drew up a chair and sat down beside her. "We know where he is, or think we do. We hope he'll turn himself in. We could have gone after him, but some of us would have been dead, if we had."

"You're learning." She reached out and took his hand. "I'm glad."

He knew what was in her mind. She had often accused him of rushing into a situation before he looked. He winked at her as he said: "Give me credit."

"Oh, I do. I do."

"I don't suppose you've slept any tonight."

"Not much," she admitted. "Tell me what's happened."

He told her, adding: "Armand might be bluffing, but I've played poker with him and I found out he ain't a bluffer. He waits until he's got the power, then he tears you apart. I think he'll play this hand the same way."

"How many men will he bring?"

"I don't know. Maybe ten. Maybe twelve."

"And there's three of you?"

"Four, if Morgan Dill turns himself in. He'll fight with us. The thing is he may not make up his mind in time to be of any help."

They sat in silence for a time, holding hands and being very much aware that these minutes might be the last they would spend together. Presently Mary said: "Remember the time we rode up to Coogan's Falls and the storm caught us and we had to stay there all night?"

He laughed. "How could I forget it? Your dad dusted off his shotgun when we got back. If it hadn't been for that, I don't think we'd ever have had the courage to tell him we were getting married."

She nodded, smiling as old memories came back to her. She said: "We've had a good life, Ed, and I've been a very happy woman. I don't envy anyone in this whole, wide world."

"Not even Molly Lamar in her fine big house?"

"Molly least of all."

"I ain't looking forward to getting killed," Ed said somberly, "but it ain't so much that I'm afraid to die that bothers me. I'd never have run for sheriff if I felt that way. What worries me the most is that I've helped bring some children into the world and I want to help raise them. I won't leave you very well fixed, either."

She squeezed his hand. "Don't worry. Not for a

minute. Sure, it'll be hard, but I'm young and strong and I'll make out." Then in spite of herself she began to cry. "I'm sorry." She wiped her eyes and shook her head. "I didn't aim to do that. It's just that I love you so much that I can't even bring myself to think how it would be if you weren't here."

He rose. "We're borrowing trouble and there's no sense in that. Maybe I'll make out all right."

She stood up, her head tipped back, worried eyes on him. She asked: "You think Armand actually will burn the town if he doesn't find Morgan Dill?"

"I think Buck Armand is crazy enough to do anything," Ed said. "He stood in old Abe's shadow for a long time and now he figures on making his own shadow. He's going to be damned sure that he throws a longer one than Abe ever did. If it comes to that, get the kids out of the house. You'd better get them clear out of town."

"I'll take care of them," she said. "Don't worry about us."

She put her arms around him and hugged him hard, then tipped her head back for his kiss. "I'm proud of you, Ed. I never knew how proud until tonight. Some men would have had business elsewhere."

He nodded, remembering how Caleb Mason, who had carried the star for years, always said that time would solve anything and he made it a habit to go fishing when anything that threatened danger loomed ahead.

He kissed her, her lips sweet and warm. He ran a hand down her back and patted her behind. "Go to bed, honey. No use wasting the whole night."

She shook her head. "I'll keep my clothes on and stay here on the couch. Send for me if you need me."

He nodded and turned away quickly, not wanting her to see his expression. When he was outside, he blew his nose and swallowed, wondering if anyone ever found security in this life. He guessed not. Security wasn't a part of man's heritage on earth.

Mounting, he rode back to the courthouse. He dismounted and for a while stood on the board-walk, his head cocked, listening, but he heard nothing. It wasn't time yet and he wondered why he had stopped to listen for Rafter D's approach. Maybe his nerves were beginning to crack. If he could meet a danger head-on, he could handle it, but waiting had always been hell for him.

When he went into the jail, Tully and Johnny Bedlow were playing cards. He asked: "Anything happen?"

"Not a thing," Tully answered.

"Quiet as a tomb," Johnny added.

Tully scowled at him. "Now that's a hell of a thing to say."

"Ain't it now?" Johnny agreed. "I'll change it. This is a good night for murder."

"Oh, for God's sake," Tully growled.

Ed sat down at his desk, thinking that Johnny's attempt at humor had failed. There was nothing to do now but wait.

XX

Morgan returned to Jean Runyan's house after he left Molly Lamar because he didn't know where else to go or what to do. He felt trapped. He wanted nothing from Molly. He never wanted to see her again, but he'd have to if he went back to force a confession out of Dick Lamar.

As he crossed the yard to Jean's back door, he asked himself again if Molly had been lying about her husband's leaving town. If she was telling the truth, just how bad did he want to get that admission of guilt out of Lamar? He honestly didn't know. Maybe Lamar wouldn't admit anything regardless of what Morgan did to him. Maybe he'd been foolish to come back to town. He was tempted to saddle up and ride away and say to hell with all of it. He knew at once he could not. He had never ridden away from anything and he wasn't starting now.

Well, he'd talk to Jean, if she was still awake, drink another cup of coffee, and wind up going back to the Lamar house. Perhaps he could catch the banker outside. Anyhow, he shouldn't let Molly get to him the way he had. He didn't know why it had happened. He was certain he no longer loved her; he knew he was far better off the way it had turned out. It was just that seeing her and having her throw herself at him brought back all the old dreams that were broken, dreams that had been good at the time, but now seemed childish. More than that, it had hurt him to see Molly trample on her pride and beg him to take her back. She had been a proud woman. Now all she could think of was to jump from one man who could no longer take care of her to a man who could.

He stepped into the kitchen and stopped, his hand dropping to his gun. Someone was with Jean in the front room. For a moment he stood motionlessly, trying to place the man's voice and failing, then Jean called: "That you, Morgan?"

He didn't answer. He eased across the kitchen, staying close to the wall so he could not be seen by anyone who was in the other room. He heard Jean say: "I was sure someone came in. I'll go see."

He stepped through the doorway, his gun in his hand. He said: "It's me, all right." Then he stopped, breathing hard, his gun lined on the man. It was Judge Alcorn.

"Well, by God, Jean," he said in a low tone as if he could not believe what he saw. "You sold me out. You set a trap for me."

"I did no such thing," she said angrily.

"Don't tell me the judge just wandered over here at this time of night because he couldn't sleep. You knew I'd be back, so you went after him, didn't you?"

"Yes, I did," she said resentfully. "Sometimes you act as if you don't know who your friends are, Morgan Dill. You're so stubborn you don't even think straight. All I wanted was to get you to talk to the judge. Now sit down and talk while I get the coffee."

"It really isn't much of a trap, is it, Morgan?" the judge said. "You've got the gun on me. I sure don't have one on you."

Morgan looked down at the gun in his hand, then raised his gaze to Alcorn's face. He had forgotten how old and frail the judge was. Or perhaps Alcorn had aged more in the three years Morgan had been gone than he normally would have. In any case he had nothing to fear from Judge Alcorn. Liver spots covered the backs of his claw-like hands. His thin face was as deeply lined as the last apple in the barrel late in spring. Suddenly Morgan was ashamed. He had been going on the basis that he could not trust anybody. Maybe Jean was right. He guessed he didn't know who his friends were.

He holstered his gun and held his hand out to Alcorn. "Seems like I was out of line, Judge. Will you shake hands?"

"Of course, I'll shake hands." Alcorn rose and gripped Morgan's hand, his gaze boring into the younger man's face. "You went away a boy, Morgan, and now I've got to quit thinking of you as a boy. You came back a man. I'm glad to see you. I'm hoping you'll be our ally. We need one."

Morgan remembered what Tully and Ed Smith had said about needing him and his gun, and now Judge Alcorn was saying the same thing.

"I don't savvy this, Judge," Morgan said. "Tully and the sheriff were here a while ago trying to soft-soap Jean into talking me into giving myself up. They claimed they'd be needing me, that Buck Armand was bringing the Rafter D to town to find me and hang me for horse stealing, and they'd burn the town if they didn't find me. It sounded like hogwash to me."

"It's no hogwash. I would put nothing past Buck Armand." Alcorn motioned toward a chair. "Sit down, Morgan. I've got some things to say to you and I want you to listen. That's why I got out of bed to talk to you."

Jean came in with the coffee. Morgan took a cup and sat down. "I guess I jumped the gun, Jean," he said. "I'm sorry."

"You ought to be," she snapped. "I'm getting tired of trying to help a man who won't be helped. If you're not going to listen to the judge, then I'll quit trying to help you."

He sipped his coffee, quick rebellion boiling up

in him. They didn't know, he told himself. He was the one who had been framed. He was the one who had looked into the muzzle of Lamar's gun. He was the one who had fought for his life with Buck Armand. He was the one whose sister had hit him over the head and knocked him cold. He was the one Ed Smith wanted to lock up in his stinking jail. Well, he'd listen, and then he'd get up and walk out. To hell with Jean. If she didn't want to help him, then he sure didn't want her help.

"I had called a meeting in my office before we knew you were back in town," Alcorn said. "Sam Colter and Baldy Miles were there along with Ed Smith. I guess folks think that Colter and Miles and me kind of run things in Twin Rocks. We did, I suppose, years ago, but we don't any more. I hate like hell to admit this, but we're all scared. Well, we were talking about your coming back, seeing as your birthday is coming up now, and we agreed that you and Johnny Bedlow and Tully Bean had been pretty harum-scarum when you were boys, but we've seen Johnny and Tully settle down. Tully's a deputy and a good one. Johnny's got his barbershop and he's doing fine. We figured you'd settle down, too, when you got back."

Rebellion was still high in Morgan. He said angrily: "I came back with the idea of getting a decent deal out of Celia. As far as settling down is concerned, I'd like to, but all I got was a frame-up from your honest banker."

"I know," Alcorn said quickly. "Jean has been telling me what happened tonight. I don't believe for a minute that you held up the bank."

"Ed Smith does," Morgan snapped, "and he's the one who's looking for me."

Alcorn shook his head. "Ed doesn't believe it, either. It's just that he's got to hold you till this is cleared up. You see, none of us trusts Lamar. We've been worried about him for quite a while, but we didn't know what to do. Of course, we never dreamed he'd work a deal with Celia and Armand, and that's exactly what he'd done. I'm sure of it."

"What happened at Lamar's house when you went over?" Jean asked.

Morgan told her, adding: "Maybe I never really knew Molly. Not the way you did, living with her and growing up with her and all, but I still can't believe she used to be like she is now. I couldn't have been that blind."

"She's worse," Jean admitted. "Once she got a taste of Twin Rocks' social life, she wasn't satisfied with anything Lamar did for her. She used to envy the women who were the high mucky-mucks of town, but it wasn't enough when she got to be one."

Morgan shook his head, still not believing that the Molly he had been in love with could have been that foolish, but the Molly he had seen tonight could. They were two different women, and this was the part he could not understand, that the Molly he had loved simply did not exist.

"The part I want you to know," Alcorn said, "is that Lamar's not the problem. Maybe he is the way you see it, but he's not. I think Molly will clear you, if I talk to her, so you don't need to get a confession out of Lamar. I suggest you don't go back there. You might end up killing him, and then you'd have more trouble than we can handle."

"I feel like killing him," Morgan admitted, "but I'm in more trouble now than I can handle if Lamar doesn't clear me. If I don't stick around after Molly, she won't tell the truth."

"I'll get it out of her," Alcorn said. "I'm slow making my point, but what I've been trying to say is that Buck Armand is the dangerous one. You'll remember that your pa was high-handed and hard to get along with. He got what he wanted from the town and we swallowed our pride to give it to him." The judge jabbed a finger at Morgan. "The difference is that Abe Dill was sane and knew where to stop. Armand is crazy and he won't stop at anything once he decides to do it. He wants it all, and I've got a hunch that getting all of it means killing you and Celia. He looks down on any of us who represent the law, and that means he thinks we can't stop him."

"Even if I'm cleared of robbing the bank,"

Morgan said, "I won't get my share of the Rafter D. I signed a paper. . . ."

"Jean told me," Alcorn interrupted, "but I can assure you that the agreement you signed will not hold up in my court. You signed under duress and that robs it of any legality."

"Well, it still goes back to proving that I'm telling the truth," Morgan said, "so we're right where we started. Judge, I tell you I will not rot in Ed Smith's jail."

"Nobody expects you to," Alcorn said sharply. "Armand's riding high right now. I'm sure he thinks he's got everything in the palm of his hand. One thing he's been up to is to force the small outfits to throw in with him when he makes his drive to the railroad. I'm not sure just what his angle is, but you can be sure he's got one. Another thing is he owes money to both Colter and Miles, but it's plain enough that he doesn't aim to pay either of them. He's making his own law, Morgan. That's why he believes he can come to town and hang you, or burn the town to force you into the open, and nobody will touch him."

"The crew won't stick with him when it comes to something like burning the town," Morgan said.

"You don't know the Rafter D men," Alcorn said. "Not many of them anyhow. He fired most of the hands you knew and hired toughs who will take his orders. Just two or three like Slim Turner are left. He pays better than average wages, so they've got a good deal and they know it." He shook his head. "No, they'll do what he tells them no matter how unreasonable or criminal it is. Maybe Turner and the other old hands won't, but there's not enough of them to change anything."

"I don't savvy this," Morgan said. "You don't have any fighting men in town, but you could recruit some of the small ranchers you were mentioning. As I remember it, there's fifteen or twenty little spreads in the county."

"There's not that many now," Alcorn said. "The Rafter D has swallowed some of them and the rest are too scared of Armand to buck him. Anyhow, there isn't time. Armand will be here in another hour or so. You don't seem to savvy that. Your gun could make the difference."

They were watching him, waiting for him to say he would give himself up, that he would fight alongside Ed Smith and his deputies, that he would help save a town that wanted to jail him for a crime he had not committed. That wasn't exactly true about the town wanting to jail him, he admitted to himself. Most of the old and retired people who lived in Twin Rocks did not even know what had happened, but Ed Smith represented the law and he wanted to jail Morgan.

He shook his head. "I'm sorry, Judge. Ed Smith can maybe kill me, but he's not going to lock me up in his lousy jail as long as I'm alive."

240

XXI

The ride into town was the most agonizing experience in Celia's life. The wheels seemed to find all the bumps and holes in the road and each bounce drove a knife thrust of pain through her abdomen every time she hit bottom. On more than one occasion she thought she would faint. She rode bent forward, one hand holding the lines, the other pressed against her belly.

She reached Twin Rocks before sunup, the first color of dawn showing in the eastern sky. She pulled to a stop in front of the courthouse and for a time sat motionlessly in the seat, her eyes closed, and waiting for the pain to ease off.

In spite of the pain, there seemed to be a startling clarity to her thinking. She had no regrets for what she had done in her life except for one thing. Her mistake had been to marry Buck Armand. She had thought more than once about killing him and now she wished she had. She'd had both means and opportunity. By waiting, she had given him a chance to kill her. She didn't know what the blow he had given her had done to her, but she thought she was dying. It was too bad, she told herself bitterly, to die and leave Buck Armand alive.

Now Morgan would have all of the Rafter D if

he lived. If, by some miracle, she did not die, she would own half the ranch and she would need Morgan to run the outfit. She could get along with him if she had to. He was honest. He knew the cattle business. He was a good worker. The truth, then, was plain. Instead of fighting Morgan and trying to cheat him out of his share of the Rafter D and marrying Armand to help achieve her goal, she should have accepted Morgan as a partner and worked with him. It was too late now to live those years over, but, if she didn't die, the future was going to be different.

She eased out of the seat, and then, with her feet on the ground, she had to hold to the side of the buckboard to keep from falling. Maybe she would live, she told herself, live long enough to get rid of Armand, and, if she lived that long, she might keep right on living. Her thoughts focused on her husband. God, how she hated him. She had hated many people in her life, but none the way she hated Buck Armand. Slowly her thoughts turned to Morgan. She would have to convince him that he could get along with her. He must be around here somewhere. She wanted to talk to him. That was strange, too, something she had never dreamed she would want to do.

She gritted her teeth against the spasm of pain. Her head was swimming and the street was turning around like a giant top. She realized then she was not thinking as clearly as she thought she was. Now the only thing she wanted to do was to lie down and not think at all.

She was aware that there were men around her and one was asking: "What's wrong, Missus Armand?"

She recognized Ed Smith in the thin light. Two other men were standing beside him. They'd be Tully Bean and Johnny Bedlow. She said: "Buck hit me in the belly before he left the ranch. I guess he did something bad to my insides. I hurt like hell."

"We'll get you into the jail where you can lie down," Smith said. "Tully, give me a hand."

"Bean, put my rig away," Celia ordered. "The carcass is Dick Lamar. Buck shot and killed him tonight. Get him over to the undertaker."

Tully hesitated, glancing at Smith. The sheriff said: "All right, Tully. Do what she said. Johnny, you can help me."

She was a heavy woman, but somehow they got her into the jail, dragging her more than carrying her. She lay down on one of the bunks in the big cell and closed her eyes. She groaned, gritting her teeth as another spasm of pain struck her.

A moment later, when the worst of the pain had passed, she asked: "Get the doc, Smith. Maybe he can help."

"Doc Bridges is out of town, Missus Armand," Johnny said. "Missus Downey's having her baby."

"Oh, hell, then I've got to lie here and grunt," she muttered. "I guess you know Buck's bringing the crew to town. They'll be along pretty soon. He's bound to get Morgan."

"We're expecting 'em," Smith said.

"He murdered Lamar," Celia said. "Shot him down like a skunk. It was murder, I tell you. You've got to arrest him and hold him for murder."

Smith was silent for a moment, then he said: "All right, Missus Armand, we'll take care of it."

"You'll have a hell of a job doing it," she said. "He'll try to tell you that Lamar had a gun, that it wasn't murder. Well, Lamar had a gun, all right, but he shouldn't have tried to draw. Anybody could have done better. It was murder, all right, same as shooting a baby. Just 'cause he had a gun didn't stop it from being murder."

"Why did he kill Lamar?" Smith asked.

"Lamar wanted money. We'd made a deal. . . ." She stopped, realizing that she had started to incriminate herself. "They had a row. That was all. Lamar lost his head. He tried for his gun, but he never had no chance at all."

She was silent, one hand over her abdomen, her eyes still closed. She groaned in spite of herself and gritted her teeth to keep from groaning again. "My God, it hurts. I'll bet he busted my liver."

"Why did he hit you?" Smith asked.

"We had a row, too," she said. "Over him killing Lamar. We called each other some names, and finally I lost my temper and hit him. It was a mistake. He can hit harder than I can." She didn't bother to say anything for a time, then she asked: "You don't think Doc will get back pretty soon?"

"I doubt it," Smith said. "The Downeys live 'way up Rock Creek."

"What are we going to do when Buck gets to town?" she asked. "He won't let nothing stop him till he finds and hangs Morgan. You know as well as I do that Morgan can't fight the whole crew."

"We're hoping that Morgan will come in," Smith said. "If he does, the four of us can hold Buck and the boys off. This jail is solid."

"You don't know Buck," she said. "I've lived with him and quarreled with him and slept with him, and, by God, I know him. Morgan's in town, ain't he?"

"Yeah, he's here."

"You know where?"

"We think he's in Jean Runyan's house."

"You think?" She opened her eyes. "Don't you know?"

"Not exactly. We ain't seen him, but we found his horse in Jean's barn, so we figure he's in her house."

"You told him about Buck coming after him?"

"We told Jean. She kept saying he wasn't there, but I'm sure she was lying."

"Morgan's stubborner'n a mule," she said. "Why didn't you bring him in for his own protection?"

245

"He wouldn't have come," Smith answered. "We figured we'd wind up killing each other if we forced him. What about the bank robbery that Lamar accused Morgan of? You know anything about it?"

"Sure I know about it," she said. "You don't think a Dill would rob a bank, do you?"

"No, but we want to know what did happen?"

"Lamar robbed it hisself," she said, "which same you could have guessed. He's been losing money gambling and the bank was broke, so he comes to Buck with the notion of framing Morgan, figuring that Morgan would come back to Twin Rocks if he had a little push, this being close to his birthday. Buck was to give Lamar five thousand dollars for framing Morgan, but Buck didn't keep his word. That was what made Lamar so mad he pulled his gun."

"So Morgan had nothing to do with it?"

"Hell, no!"

"Will you swear to that in court?"

"If I live that long," she said.

She had finally got around to telling Smith without leaving herself wide open. She'd never tell anyone that she was into the scheme as deeply as Buck was. If the damned fool had only paid Lamar as he had agreed, they wouldn't be in the fix they were now and she could have said to hell with Morgan. Now Buck was coming with his men and they were past the point of working anything out. Morgan had to be kept alive. The only chance of doing that was getting him to come here.

"I want to see Morgan," she said. "Go get him. Tell him I can clear him and he won't be in no more trouble."

"I dunno if he'll come," Smith said.

"Try," she urged. "If you tell him I want to see him to make a reasonable deal for his share of the Rafter D, he'll come."

"All right, Johnny," Smith said. "Go tell him."

Johnny Bedlow left the jail. Smith remained beside the bunk. For a long time Celia lay there, groaning, sweat running down her face. Then she said: "Smith, I aim to kill Buck. Don't arrest me for murder. It'll be an execution. His men won't stand with him. I'm the one who owns the Rafter D and I pay 'em. I'll remind 'em of that, and then I'm going to kill him."

Smith, still looking down at her, wished it was that simple.

XXII

Morgan sat in Jean Runyan's living room, feeling Jean's and Alcorn's eyes on him. He was uncomfortable, and, in spite of himself, he felt a little guilty. Suppose Buck Armand did come to town with the Rafter D crew and burn every building trying to root him out of his hiding place? It wouldn't happen. He was sure of it, but, if it did, he would feel guiltier than ever. He shifted in his chair, feeling his face get red.

He started to tell them to quit staring at him, that he had a right to make his own decisions whether they were wrong or not, and that he was the one who would rot in the county jail if Ed Smith arrested him. He didn't say any of those things because he heard steps on the porch, and then a man's heavy knock.

Morgan jumped up and drew his gun. He motioned for Jean to answer the knock as he backed into the kitchen. Jean opened the door and said something, then he heard her say: "Come in. Morgan's here."

He swore softly, thinking that it might be Ed Smith and Jean was not going to play the game his way any longer. There was no sense in pretending he wasn't here, so he stepped through the door, his gun still in his hand. Johnny Bedlow stood there, his Colt still in his holster.

"Damn it, Morg," Johnny said testily, "put up that gun. You've set everybody on their ear tonight. It's time you came back down to earth and listened to reason."

Morgan didn't say anything for a moment, the sharp memory of Johnny's refusing to shake hands with him crowding into his mind. Tully was the more opinionated of his two friends, the one who used to give him an argument when they disagreed on anything, but Johnny had always been the easy-going one, so Morgan still could not understand why Johnny had acted the way he had.

Because he hesitated, not speaking and not holstering his gun, Johnny said angrily: "I said put it up. I'm not here to make any trouble for you. My gun's not in my hand, either, but it would have been if I'd intended to take you in. Now, what the hell are you worried about?"

Morgan knew he could outdraw Johnny if it came to that. Johnny had never been one to lie or deceive him, and he didn't think he was now. Slowly he lowered the gun and dropped it into leather. He said: "I was glad to see you when I first got to town, but you weren't glad to see me. Why?"

"You mean why didn't I shake hands with you?" Johnny asked. "Well, I'm sorry I didn't, but the reason wasn't because I wasn't glad to see you. I was scared. I'd heard Buck Armand talk in the barbershop about what he would do to you if you ever came back to Twin Rocks. I didn't expect to see you, and, when I did, all I could think of was to tell Ed Smith. I thought he could protect you."

"I never saw the day I needed to have Ed Smith's protection," Morgan said hotly.

"I know that," Johnny admitted. "I acted on

the spur of the moment and I'm sorry I didn't shake hands with you, but I didn't come here to apologize. I came to tell you that your sister is in Ed's office and she wants to see you."

"To hell with her," Morgan said harshly. "She saw me once tonight. She sure didn't act like she wanted to see me then."

"Things have changed," Johnny said. "You'd be a fool if you didn't go, though I reckon you are pretty much of a fool, playing hard to find all night the way you've been doing."

Morgan was tempted to tell him to get out and let him alone, but he hesitated, wondering what had changed. Before he could ask, Jean said: "He had reason to play hard to find, with Ed acting like he believed Lamar's story, but maybe it's time to stop playing that game. What's changed?"

"For one thing, Armand shot and killed Lamar tonight," Johnny said. "Seems that they had a deal to frame Morgan on this bank-robbing business and Lamar was to get five thousand dollars, but Armand wouldn't keep his word. Lamar got mad and tried for his gun, and Armand killed him. Celia says it was murder."

"It would be," Morgan said bitterly. "Armand's fast with a gun and Lamar wasn't. He had to have you looking down the barrel." He sucked in a long breath and shook his head. "Now who's going to clear me?"

"Celia," Johnny answered. "That's one thing she

wants to see you about. She said to tell you she would. She didn't say how much she was in the deal with Lamar, but she's pretending it was all Armand."

"She was in it up to her neck," Morgan said. "If she was lying about that, maybe she's lying about clearing me."

"I don't think so," Johnny said. "You see, she and Armand got into a big row. She hit him, and then he really gave her one in the gut. She's hurt. I don't think she's putting on. She thinks he boogered up her insides. Doc Bridges is out of town, so she's having to grit her teeth and stand it. She says that she's going to fire Armand, so I suppose she figures she needs you to run the place. I'm guessing about that, but it seems logical. Anyhow, she said to tell you that she'll make you a reasonable deal for your part of the spread, so maybe she just wants to buy you out."

Morgan stared at Johnny as he thought about it. Lamar couldn't clear him and he still had no faith that Molly would when the time came. Maybe Celia was his only chance. Sure, Ed Smith could say he didn't believe Morgan robbed the bank, but the shadow would still be on him until he was finally and completely cleared.

"Well?" Jean said tartly. "This is what you've been looking for. You still going to be stubborn about turning yourself in?"

"No," Morgan said. "I guess it's time to see

what Smith will do, but you'd better savvy one thing, Johnny. He ain't putting me in jail."

"He don't want to," Johnny said, "but we'll sure need your gun when Armand comes to town."

"You'll have it," Morgan said, "if this turns out the way you've been saying."

"I'll come down to the jail," Alcorn said. "I'm old, but I can still pull a trigger."

Johnny shook his head. "No. I don't believe you could shoot straight if you did pull a trigger. I reckon Ed would tell you that you're more important sitting in the courtroom than you are trying to play deputy."

Alcorn sat back, plainly relieved. "I guess I am at that," he said.

Morgan strode to the door. He paused to look back at Jean. "If I don't see you again . . ."

"Don't say that!" she cried. "Don't even think it. You've got to see me again and don't you ride out of town without coming back here."

"I'll be back if Celia's telling the truth," he said. "I mean, if she does what she says she will."

"I think she will," Johnny said. "She's hurting too much to lie to you or us, or make a promise she didn't aim to keep. She thinks Armand busted up her liver when he hit her. I've got a hunch she thinks she's dying."

"She's too tough to die from getting hit in the belly," Morgan said.

He left the house and turned toward the

courthouse, Johnny keeping step with him. They were silent, Morgan thinking that the old spirit of partnership with Johnny Bedlow was gone. It would be the same with Tully Bean. Too much had happened, he thought sadly, to pick up his life the way it had been when he'd left. Even if Celia meant what she had told Johnny, he could not work with her or for her.

When they reached the courthouse, Johnny said: "She's in the jail. She had to lie down and that was the only place we could put her right then."

Johnny led the way into the sheriff's office. Ed Smith stood beside his desk, anxious eyes on Morgan. He said: "I'm glad to see you, Morg. I've been hoping you'd come in."

"I'm here to see Celia," Morgan said. "If you've got a notion about jailing me . . ."

"I don't," Ed said. "Celia's cleared you. I guess Johnny must have told you."

"He told me," Morgan said, "but I figured it might be a trap."

Ed sighed. "I'm sorry you even thought that. I'll say it again. Celia has cleared you. The law doesn't want you, but we need you as a deputy. I'll remind you that you're the reason Armand is bringing his crew into town. I figure the four of us can give him a pretty warm reception."

"That you, Morgan?" Celia called from a cell.

Ed tipped his head toward the door that opened

into the cells. "Go ahead. She's been fretting about you not getting here in time."

Morgan crossed the room to the door that led into the cells. Celia lay on her back, her face contorted with pain. When she saw Morgan, she grumbled: "Took you long enough."

"I see your disposition hasn't improved much," Morgan said.

"I've got reason to have a bad disposition," she snapped. "That god-damned Buck hit me. . . ."

"Johnny told me," Morgan said. "Smith also says you've cleared me of the bank robbing frame-up."

She nodded. "But that's not the reason I sent for you. I'm getting rid of Buck. I'll divorce him as soon as I can, and I'm firing him the next time I see him. If I live and if it ever comes to court, I'll swear you had nothing to do with any bank robbery. What I wanted to see you about was the Rafter D. We've got to make a deal. . . ."

A spasm of pain knifed through her and she stopped, her face turning pale. She groaned, her lips twitching until the worst of the pain had passed. Morgan, watching her, could not doubt her agony. She had never been one to play-act about anything.

"You'll live," he said. "Just hang on till the doc gets here."

"Oh, I'll hang on," she said, "but I dunno how bad off I am." She chewed on her lower lip a moment, then she added: "You know how much I think of the spread. Nothing else means anything to me. It was the same with Pa. That's why I married Buck, and it's why I've tried to hornswoggle you out of your share. I'd still do it if I could, but I've learned one thing since Buck hit me. I can't go it alone. I've got to have a man I can trust. That's you. I'll buy you out, if you want to sell, but I want you to ramrod the outfit. Or if you want to run the ranch as partners, we'll do that."

She had been brought down a long way, he thought, to talk like this. He didn't think he'd ever hear her say she couldn't go it alone. Maybe she'd been brought to the place where she did mean it.

"All right," Morgan said. "When this is over, we'll get hold of Judge Alcorn and draw up whatever papers we need. I'm not sure it'll work, but we'll try."

"That's all I ask," she said, closing her eyes. "Just try."

XXIII

Ed Smith heard most of what was said between Morgan and his sister. Celia Armand had always been an obstinate, proud woman who had never asked anything from anybody with the exception of her father. Now she was broken. Ed wasn't sure what had broken her. It might have been the physical suffering that came from receiving Armand's blow, or it might have been the fact that her husband had struck her and walked out, forcing her to face the biggest mistake she had ever made in her life. She had never been one to admit making a mistake, but now she could not avoid it.

Morgan joined Ed, glancing at him questioningly as if asking whether Celia had meant what she'd said. Ed jerked his head toward the door. They stepped outside into the pale morning light. For a time there was only silence, the world not yet awake, then a rooster crowed and from somewhere at the other end of Main Street a dog barked.

"It ain't like Celia," Ed said. "I guess that's what you were thinking."

Morgan nodded, his expression grim. "I was saying to myself when I was coming here with Johnny that I couldn't work with Celia or for her. Now I'm not so sure. Maybe she's really changed. But then maybe, when she quits hurting, she'll be just as ornery as ever."

"Maybe," Ed said, "but I've known people who were changed because of what happened to 'em. It sure did something to Celia when Armand hit her the way he did. Not physically so much. It destroyed something in her. Pride, maybe."

"I guess you didn't hear what she said right there at the last," Morgan said. "She lowered her voice so nobody else would hear. She claims that Armand murdered Pa. You ever think of that?"

"No," Ed said, "but it's possible. He'd do anything that would get him what he wanted, and he's wanted the Rafter D as long as he's been in the country."

"She also says he'll kill her after he finishes me," Morgan went on. "He's a mad dog, Ed."

"He's that, all right," Ed agreed, "though I'm not sure all of his men are. Most of 'em are new, cowboys he's hired after your pa died. There's just two or three old hands who ain't saints, but they ain't cold-blooded killers, neither."

"Slim Turner, for instance," Morgan said.

Ed nodded. "I can think of a couple more, but three ain't enough to stop 'em, and some of the others, like the Idaho Kid, are plain poison. I figured Armand would wind up firing all the old hands, but he never got around to cleaning house. Maybe Celia wouldn't stand for it."

"He'd have to have a reason for firing them or Celia would have raised hell," Morgan agreed. "Chances are he wasn't quite ready for a showdown."

There was a moment of silence, both men thinking about what had been said, then Ed muttered: "This waiting is making my insides crawl. It's been that way most of the night. I guess

I've got time to go tell Missus Lamar about Dick being killed. I should have done it sooner, but I wanted you to get here first. Tully ought to be back any minute."

"Go ahead," Morgan said. "I'll stay here."

Ed crossed the weed-covered yard to his horse, glad to be on the move even for a few minutes. The waiting was worse as the showdown came closer. He had plenty of water in the jail, and he could lock the door and put shutters on the windows and hold out all day if Armand decided to lay siege to the jail.

The prospect of defending the jail didn't worry Ed, but if Armand chose to burn the town to force Morgan into the open, the whole game was changed. He thought of his wife and children, of the other women and children in town, and he knew he could not stay inside the jail if that happened.

A prickle of fear ran down his spine. Once he and his deputies left the safety of the jail, the odds being what they were, they'd all be killed. The other alternative was to give up Morgan and that was even more unthinkable. If Buck Armand got his way now, there would be no living with him, and Ed would be killed sooner or later. Celia could very well be right in saying that Armand had killed her father and would find a way to kill her.

He mounted and rode to the Lamar house. No

light showed at any of the windows. He dismounted, tied, and walked to the front door, thinking that Molly Lamar would have stayed up all night waiting for her husband's return, if she were any other woman, but Molly was in a class by herself.

He jerked the bell pull three times, but no one answered. He pounded on the door with his fist, making enough noise, he thought, to wake the neighbors. Presently he heard someone coming. The door opened and Molly stood there, a lamp in her hand. She was, he thought, a very sleepy-looking woman, and it took her a moment to recognize him.

"Oh, it's you, Sheriff," she said in a listless voice. "Come in. I guess I don't need the lamp, do I. I didn't know it was daylight. I've been asleep."

She led the way back along the hall to her sitting room and set the lamp down. Then she turned and faced him. "Why are you here, Sheriff? If it's about that hold-up, I can tell you right now that Morgan Dill had nothing to do with it. Dick's been dipping into his safe for months to get money to gamble with, and he framed Morgan to hide the shortage of funds and make folks think Morgan took the money. He had a deal with Buck Armand so Morgan would have to leave the county."

Ed hesitated, surprised that she volunteered the information this way, information that would have ruined her husband if he were still alive. He said: "Thanks for telling me. I figured it was that way."

She sat down in a rocker, her hands fluttering uncertainly in front of her before she folded them and let them drop to her lap. "I should have told you before," she said, "but I just didn't know what to do. You see, nobody loves me any more. Dick went out to the Rafter D to get some money that Armand owed him over this deal they'd made, then he was leaving town and taking me with him." She paused and dabbed at her eyes, before she went on: "He didn't come. Morgan was here for a while. He left and didn't come back. I told him I'd clear him of the bank robbery if he . . . well, you know. . . ." Her voice trailed off.

"I understand," Ed said, knowing exactly what she meant. "Missus Lamar, I've come to give you some sad news. Your husband was shot and killed tonight by Buck Armand. It seemed that they quarreled about that money you mentioned."

"Dick's . . . dead?" She looked at him blankly, as if not believing it, then she shook her head. "That's funny, Sheriff. You know, Dick was a terrible coward. I can't imagine him having enough trouble with a man like Buck Armand to get himself killed."

"Missus Armand says it was murder," Ed said. "The body is at the undertaker's if you want to see it."

Her hands unfolded and fluttered in front of her again, and dropped back to her lap. "No, I don't want to see the body. I don't want to have anything to do with him again. Never! Somebody else will have to arrange for the funeral. I don't know what to do."

"It will be taken care of," Ed said.

As he turned to leave the room, she said: "If you see Morgan, tell him to come and see me. He's all I've got left."

He walked out of the room. She was a strange one, he thought. She certainly wasn't grieving over Lamar's death; she didn't even act as if she were shocked by the news. Ed had a feeling she cared more about Morgan than her husband, that she had been deeply hurt by his not coming back to her, but that made very little sense, considering the way she had thrown him overboard to marry Dick Lamar. Well, there had never been very much about Molly that did make sense.

He rode back to the courthouse, the sun showing a full red circle above the eastern hills. He dismounted and tied, again pausing to listen, but he heard nothing. It was time, he thought. He walked slowly to the jail, noting that Tully stood in the doorway.

"You get everything taken care of?" Ed asked.

Tully nodded. "Funny thing, though. I didn't think the business about Lamar's bank was generally known in town, but that damned undertaker wanted to know who was going to pay him. Maybe he'd heard that the bank was robbed last night and he figured there wasn't any money left. . . ."

Ed held up a hand. He said: "Listen." The steady drumbeat of hoofs came to him. The moment was now. He said: "They're coming."

XXIV

When Morgan heard Ed Smith say they were coming, he pushed past Tully and stepped outside asking: "How do we play this, Sheriff?"

For a moment Ed didn't answer. Morgan, looking at him, saw the corners of his mouth twitch. He sensed the fear that was in the man and for an instant he thought the lawman was going to cave, but he regained control of himself.

"We play it tough," Ed said. "I'm glad the waiting's over. I thought the damned night would never end." He motioned for Morgan and Tully to go back inside. "If Armand wants to root us out of here, he's got a job to do."

He followed Morgan and Tully inside and, going to the gun rack, passed out three rifles, then kept the last one. He went to his desk, opened a drawer, took out several boxes of shells, and laid them on top of the desk. "Check your Winchesters," he said. "I think they're all loaded, but be sure. Better load your pockets with shells."

He saw that the magazine of his rifle was full, then moved to the door. He paused, glancing along the wall. He said: "Stand by the windows and let 'em have it the first shot they fire. We can put the shutters up, but we'll wait and see what they do. I just don't believe Armand's got the patience to sit it out all day with us in here."

The threat to burn the town was in all of their minds, Morgan knew. He would have considered it a bluff with any man but Buck Armand. The only way to stop him was to give himself up. If it came to that, he'd walk out with his gun blazing and end up getting killed by the Rafter D men who worked for a ranch that partly belonged to him. It couldn't end that way, he thought. It just couldn't, but if it did, he'd take Buck Armand with him.

"Give me a rifle!" Celia called. "I can shoot as good as any of you, though I don't figure it's gonna come to that. I aim to put a stop to this business when they get here."

"Stay where you are," Ed said. "It's got past the place where you can stop it."

He stepped back through the doorway and stood in front of the jail, his Winchester held at the ready. Morgan could see the riders now at the edge of town, a dust cloud rising behind them. Ed said: "If they charge us, I'm coming back in *pronto*. Tully, you slam and bar the door. I don't think they'll do that, though. Armand knows we'd cut 'em to ribbons."

The Rafter D men reached the corner of the block and stopped, Armand holding up a hand. Dust swept by them and was gone. Morgan, making a quick count, saw an even dozen. Slim Turner was in the rear of the pack. He recognized Quince Curry, but he didn't know any of the others.

"All right, Smith!" Armand yelled. "You know why we're here!"

Smith stood motionlessly, a lean, straight-backed man, the early morning sun casting his long shadow across the weed-covered yard. "Looks like you're taking an early morning ride!" he yelled back.

"Don't get smart, you jackass!" Armand shouted. "I want Morgan Dill! We're hanging him for stealing a horse from the Rafter D when he left the country in a hurry! Have you got him?"

"He's here!" Ed answered.

"Well, then, by God, send him out!" Armand bellowed. "We've been riding all night and we're tired, so let's get it over with!"

"Come and get him!" Ed said.

That jolted Armand. He snarled: "You think we can't do it?"

"It'll cost you!" Ed said. "There's four of us and we shoot damned straight, so let's see you try it!"

"We ain't gonna bust your door down," Armand

264

said, "if that's what you're figuring on us doing! We'll give you just ten seconds to send him out! If he don't come, we're starting at the west edge of town and we'll burn one house at a time till you see the light! We don't aim to hurt nobody else, so we'll get the people out of the houses, but you'll have no town left! Now start counting or push him through the door!"

Before Ed could say a word, Celia shoved past him and walked out of the jail. She still bent forward at her waist; she still had one hand against her belly. She called: "Don't start no counting! I've got something to say to all of you!"

"Get back inside!" Armand bawled. "My God, Celia, have you lost the few brains you used to have?"

She kept walking, moving slowly as if each step hurt her. When she was halfway across the yard, she stopped. "I guess this is close enough for all of you to hear me," she said. "You boys turn around and ride back to the Rafter D. I've let this son-of-a-bitch I married run my spread too long, so I'm firing him now, and I'll divorce him as soon as I can. From now on my brother Morgan is running the outfit. Now head back. There'll be no shooting and no town burning. I'm the one who pays you and don't you forget it."

For a moment there was only a stunned silence, the men frozen in their saddles as they stared at her. Morgan, watching, admired Celia more than he ever had in his life. It took guts to walk out there as she had.

"Go on!" Celia cried impatiently. "Git!"

From somewhere in the rear of the cluster of riders a six-gun roared. Celia went back and down into the weeds of the yard. An instant later a second gun was fired and one of the riders spilled out of his saddle.

"It was the Idaho Kid!" Slim Turner yelled. "He won't shoot no more women! We didn't come here to kill our boss! I've had enough! Let's ride!"

"Me, too!" Quince Curry said.

"No, you don't!" Armand bawled. "You'll stay right here till I tell you to ride!"

It was time to sit in on the game, Morgan knew. He put his rifle down and stepped through the door, calling: "Buck, I hold you personally responsible for the murder of my sister! This is between you and me. There's no sense of anybody else getting hurt. Now, if you ain't yellow all the way through, you'll get off that horse and we'll settle this right now, just the two of us."

Armand sat hunched over the saddle horn like a great toad. This was not to his liking, Morgan sensed, not the way he had pictured it to himself, but he was cornered. If he refused, he lost status in front of his men and he would never command again.

Morgan paced toward Armand, his right hand brushing the butt of his gun, his giant shadow moving across the yard. Armand stepped down slowly, grudgingly, and started toward Morgan, his round face hard set and ugly with fury. Suddenly, as if he had lost all self-control, he began to run toward Morgan, his right hand sweeping his gun from leather.

Armand fired first, the slug kicking up dust at Morgan's feet. Morgan drew, felt the hard butt of the gun against his palm, then the kick of that gun as he pulled the trigger. Powder flame was a brilliant burst of fire in the pale morning light. The thunder of the two shots rolled through the sleeping town. Morgan stood motionlessly, waiting. He did not fire again.

Armand stopped his headlong rush as suddenly as if he had run straight into an invisible wall. His head tipped forward and he broke at knee and hip and collapsed, his gun falling from his hand. Face down in the weeds, he made one final effort to reach his gun, impelled by the driving hate he had for Morgan, but the strength was not in him. His hand fell back to the ground, his fingertips a good six inches from the handle of the gun.

Holstering his Colt, Morgan looked at the men in the street. He said: "If you boys want to go on working for Rafter D, you'd better head back to it. I'll be out later today."

For a moment they sat motionlessly as if still frozen by what had happened, then Slim Turner said: "I guess we'd better ride if we want to keep our jobs." He turned his horse and rode away. Quince Curry followed, the others slowly falling in behind them.

Ed Smith and Tully had run from the jail and were picking Celia up as Morgan turned. They carried her inside, Morgan a step behind them. They put her down on the bunk she had occupied before she ran out of the jail. If she had stayed inside, Morgan thought, she would have lived, but now she was dying and the knowledge was in her eyes as she turned them to Morgan's face. She held up a hand and he took it.

Strange, he thought, that she had hated him and fought him most of his life, yet now, with death only seconds away, she reached for his hand. He should say something, but he didn't know what to say that would make any sense at a time like this. He could not bring himself to lie and tell her she was going to be all right.

"Is that bastard of a husband of mine dead?" she asked.

"He's dead," Morgan answered.

"Good," she said, her voice so low Morgan could barely hear what she said. "I'll soon be seeing him in hell." Blood bubbled at the corners of her mouth in a crimson froth. "It's yours without no more trouble, Morgan, the whole damned layout. Make it a good spread like Pa did." She stopped and Morgan thought she was gone, but a moment later she added: "Funny how it started out, ain't it? All of my scheming didn't get me nowhere."

A moment later she was dead. He turned and walked out into the morning sunlight. It was indeed funny, he thought. He wasn't sure what had prompted Celia to run out of the jail unless she had been determined to show the crew that she was the boss, to get the best of Buck Armand in front of the men who were important to both of them. One thing was plain. It was her death that had made possible the duel between him and Armand, shocking the men into immobility. If Morgan had walked out of the jail before Celia made her appearance, he would have been cut down by a dozen slugs, and so, regardless of her intentions, his sister had saved his life.

He moved slowly along deserted Main Street, knowing that he had much to do. One thing was essential, to give everyone in the county a different image of the Rafter D than they'd had through the past years. It would still be the biggest and most powerful ranch in the county, but the power would be used in a different way than it had been in the past.

He did not see Jean Runyan come around the corner until she was within a few feet of him. Then he heard her cry out in a nearly hysterical voice: "Are you all right, Morgan? I heard the shooting. The judge didn't want me to come, but I had to. Are you all right?"

"Of course, I'm all right," he said as he took her into his arms. "The judge was right. If there had been a big fight, it wouldn't have been safe for you to be on the street."

She buried her face against his shirt and began to cry.

He asked: "What are you crying about? I just told you I was all right."

She said, her voice muffled: "I'm crying because I'm so happy that you're still alive."

"Now that's a good reason to cry, ain't it?" he asked. "I'd better warn you about something now that the trouble is over. I'm aiming to court you, and then I'm going to marry you."

She tipped her head back and smiled up at him. "Can't we just skip the courting and get married? I loved you when I was a little girl, but you didn't have eyes for anyone but Molly. I don't want to wait. I don't want to wait at all."

He laughed softly and kissed her. "Why, when you get right down to it, I don't want to wait, either."

Duke of Wellington of George IV in July 1821.[1] And in March 1827 Stephen Lushington, M.P., Secretary of the Treasury, still attributed to the king the absolute and unqualified choice of his ministers;[2] while Canning, in language curiously reminiscent of that held by Bute sixty-five years earlier, inveighed against aristocratic 'confederacies', and discoursed on 'the real vigour of the Crown when it chooses to put forth its own strength'.[3]

When in 1834 William IV had dismissed the Melbourne Government, Peel claimed a 'fair trial' for the ministers of the king's choice; and its semblance was conceded by the Whigs who, having won the ensuing general election, refrained from a direct vote of censure on the Address.[4] As late as 1846, Wellington and Peel, at variance with a majority of their party, harped on their position and duties as Ministers of the Crown and declared that, were they to stand alone, they would still have 'to enable Her Majesty to meet her Parliament and to carry on the business of the country'.

> I was of the opinion [declared Wellington] that the formation of a Government in which Her Majesty would have confidence, was of much greater importance than the opinions of any individual on the Corn Laws, or any other law. . . .

And Peel, whose ideas of an independent executive similarly seemed to hark back to the earlier period, thus attempted to define his position:

> I see it over and over again repeated, that I am under a personal obligation for holding the great office which I have the honour to occupy . . . that I was placed in that position by a

[1] *The Diary of Henry Hobhouse (1820–7)* ed. A. Aspinall, p. 67; see also *The Journal of Mrs. Arbuthnot*, 27 June 1821, ed. F. Bamford and the Duke of Wellington, vol. i, p. 103.

[2] S. R. Lushington to Sir Wm. Knighton, 26 March 1827: *Letters of King George IV*, ed. A. Aspinall, vol. iii, pp. 207–10.

[3] G. Canning to J. W. Croker, 3 April 1827: *The Croker Papers*, ed. L. J. Jennings, vol. i, p. 368.

[4] See G. Kitson Clark, *Peel and the Conservative Party. A Study in Politics, 1832–41*, pp. 211–12, and 237–8.

C

party.... I am not under an obligation to any man, or to any body of men, for being compelled ... to undergo the official duties and labour which I have undertaken....

And next:

> I have served four Sovereigns.... I served each of those Sovereigns at critical times and in critical circumstances ... and ... there was but ... one reward which I desired ... namely, the simple acknowledgment, on their part, that I had been to them a loyal and faithful Minister....

To this Disraeli retorted that the queen would never have called on Peel in 1841 had he not 'placed himself, as he said, at the head of the Gentlemen of England'.

> I say [continued Disraeli] it is utterly impossible to carry on your Parliamentary Constitution except by political parties. I say there must be distinct principles as lines of conduct adopted by public men....
> Above all, maintain the line of demarcation between parties; for it is only by maintaining the independence of party that you can maintain the integrity of public men, and the power and influence of Parliament itself.[1]

Here then were two conceptions of the ministers' relations to Crown and Party: one reflecting the past but still adducible without patent absurdity; the other, much more in harmony with the realities which then were shaping, and which, once shaped, were soon to be mistaken for primordial elements of the British Constitution. The past and the future, capable of neat definition, impinged on a period of mixed character, first, by a theoretical carry over, and next, by historical antedating. As a result, 'by a double distortion', to quote Mr. Sedgwick's summing up, George III 'has been represented as having endeavoured to imitate the Stuarts when he ought to have anticipated Queen Victoria'.[2]

---

[1] Hansard, vol. lxxxiii, 3rd series, 22 January 1846, cols. 92–3, 120, and 123.

[2] *Letters from George III to Lord Bute, 1756–1766*, ed. Romney Sedgwick, Introduction, p. viii.

3

According to contemporaries the complex system of the 'mixed form of government' combined 'by skilful division of power' the best of the monarchy, aristocracy, and democracy; and it was viewed by them with pride and satisfaction. Mechanically minded and with a bent towards the ingenious, they relished its 'checks and controls', and the 'mutual watchfulness and jealousy' which its delicate balance demanded from all concerned; and they cherished a constitution which safeguarded their rights and freedoms when 'in almost every other nation of Europe' public liberty was 'extremely upon the decline'.[1] George III, that much maligned monarch, was truly representative when, abhorring both 'despotism' and 'anarchy', he extolled 'the beauty, excellence, and perfection of the British constitution as by law established'.[2] What was bound to escape contemporaries was the insoluble contradictions of a political system which, incongruously, associated a royal executive with parliamentary struggles for office. Yet the two had to coexist in an organic transition from royal to parliamentary government.

A parliamentary régime is based on the unhindered alternating of party-governments. But while contending party leaders can in turn fill the office of prime minister, how could the king freely pass from the one side to the other, and in turn captain opposite teams? It was far more consonant with his position to try to heal 'the unhappy divisions that subsist between men' and form an administration from 'the best of all parties' than to quit 'one set of men for another'. Could he give up with unconcern the ministers whom he had chosen and upheld, and in whose actions and policy he had participated? In 1779 it was but natural for him to stipulate that on a change of government past measures should 'be treated with proper respect' and that 'no blame be laid' on them. And here is a naive but sincere statement of his position: 'I have no wish but for the prosperity

[1] David Hume, *Essays Moral, Political, and Literary* (1742).
[2] *Correspondence of King George III*, vol. iv, pp. 220–1, no. 2451; the King to Lord North, 14 November 1778.

of my Dominions therefore must look on all who will not heartily assist me as bad men as well as ungrateful subjects.' And on another occasion: '... whilst I have no wish but for the good and prosperity of my country, it is impossible that the nation shall not stand by me; if they will not, they shall have another King.'[1] He did not think in terms of parties; but their existence prevented the king, while he remained the actual head of the executive, from leading an undivided nation.

Yet it was impossible to eliminate party from parliament: an assembly whose leaders contend for office and power was bound to split into factions divided by personal animosities and trying to preserve their identity and coherence in and out of office. Consequently when in office they laid themselves open to the accusation of monopolizing power and of 'keeping the King in fetters'; in opposition, of distressing the government with intention to 'storm the Closet' and force themselves, unconstitutionally, on the king. No consistent defence of parties was possible under the 'mixed form of government', and this undoubtedly retarded their development and consolidation. To Bolingbroke parties when based on a 'difference of principles and designs' were 'misfortune enough', but if continued without it an even greater misfortune, for then they were mere 'instruments of private ambition'.[2] David Hume denounced them as subversive of government and begetting 'the fiercest animosities' among fellow citizens; but he next conceded that to 'abolish all distinctions of party may not be practicable, perhaps not desirable, in a free government'.[3] Burke squarely contended that party-divisions were, for good or evil, 'things inseparable from free government'; and in his well-known eulogy of party as a union of men endeavouring to promote the

---

[1] *Correspondence of King George III*, ed. Sir John Fortescue, vol. i, p. 375, no. 353, the King to Pitt, 15 July 1766; vol. iv, p. 517, no. 3875, the King to the Lord Chancellor, 11 December 1779; vol. iv, p. 507, no. 2865, same to same, 3 December 1779; vol. vi, p. 151, no. 3973, the King to Lord North, 4 November 1782; vol. iv, p. 65, no. 2230, same to same, 17 March 1778.

[2] *A Dissertation upon Parties* (1734).

[3] op. cit., part I, essay VII, 'Of Parties in General', and part II, essay XIV, 'Of the Coalition of Parties'.

national interest on a common principle, gave a forecast of parliamentary government. Men so connected, he wrote, must strive 'to carry their common plan into execution with all the power and authority of the State'; in forming an administration give 'their party preference in all things'; and not 'accept any offers of power in which the whole body is not included'.[1] While professing adherence to the Revolution Settlement, by implication he eliminated the rights of the Crown, and obliquely argued that in fact the royal executive had ceased to exist, replaced by the monstrous contraption of a cabal set on separating 'the Court from Administration'. The 'double Cabinet', a product of Burke's fertile, disordered, and malignant imagination, long bedevilled his own party and their spiritual descendants.

That the House of Commons might ultimately 'engross the whole power of the constitution', wresting the executive from the Crown, was apprehended by Hume. How then could they be 'confined within the proper limits'?

> I answer [wrote Hume] that the interest of the body is here restrained by that of the individuals. . . . The Crown has so many offices at its disposal, that, when assisted by the honest and disinterested part of the House, it will always command the resolutions of the whole so far, at least, as to preserve the antient constitution from danger.

He thus discerned within the House itself the main obstacle to parliamentary government: a majority of its members were as yet by their ideas, interests, and pursuits, unfitted for a system of party politics.

4

Parliamentary struggles for office necessarily produce a dichotomy of 'ins' and 'outs'; and two party-names were current since the last quarter of the seventeenth century: hence in retrospect the appearances of a two-party system. In reality three broad divisions, based on type and not on party, can be distinguished in the eighteenth-century House of Commons:

[1] *Observations on a late State of the Nation* (1769); and *Thoughts on the Cause of the Present Discontents* (1770).

on the one side were the followers of Court and Administration, the 'placemen', *par excellence* a group of permanent 'ins'; on the opposite side, the independent country gentlemen, of their own choice permanent 'outs'; and in between, occupying as it were the centre of the arena, and focusing upon themselves the attention of the public and of history, stood the political factions contending for power, the forerunners of parliamentary government based on a party-system. Though distinct, these groups were not sharply separated: wide borderlands intervened between them, in which heterogeneous types moved to and fro.

The Court and Administration party was a composite, differentiated body; but common to them all was a basic readiness to support any minister of the king's choice: even in their parliamentary capacity they professed direct political allegiance to the Crown, either on a traditional semi-feudal, or on a timeless civil-service basis, or merely as recipients, in one form or another, of the king's bounty; and adherence to the king's government, so long as compatible with conscience, was far more consonant with the avowed decencies of eighteenth-century politics than 'formed opposition'. A second, concomitant, characteristic of the group was that whether they were great noblemen, or minor ministers of an administrative type, or hard-working officials, or political parasites, they tried through a direct nexus with the Crown to secure permanency of employment: wherein they were, by and large, successful. A third common feature, induced by natural selection and inherent in the character of the group, was that its members did not play for the highest political prizes: peers of the first rank and great wealth and desirous of making a figure in the country, or great orators or statesmen in either House, would well-nigh automatically move into the centre of the arena and take their place among the leaders of political factions.

Here are examples of non-political groups in Court and Administration. The Brudenells were in the second half of the eighteenth century prominent at Court, and although they invariably had two, and mostly three, peerages, and at least four seats in the Commons—'I do not think', says their historian, Miss Joan Wake, 'that they were ever much interested in politics.'[1] The Secretaries of the Admiralty were civil servants with expert technical knowledge, and though from Pepys to Croker they sat in parliament, in the eighteenth century not one went out on a change of government. Croker resigned with Wellington in 1830; 'till our own day', he wrote in 1857, 'the Secretary was not looked upon as a political officer, did not change with ministries, and took no part in political debate'.[2] The Secretaries of the Treasury, forerunners *inter alia* of the modern Parliamentary Whips, were civil servants concerned in the management of the House of Commons. In 1742, the Duke of Bedford took it for granted that Walpole's Secretary of the Treasury, John Scrope, would be dismissed, 'through whose hands such sums of money have passed, and who refused to give any answer to the Secret Committee about those dark transactions. . . .'

> . . . what your Grace mentions is absolutely impracticable [replied Pulteney]. Mr Scrope is the only man I know, that thoroughly understands the business of the Treasury, and is versed in drawing money bills. On this foundation he stands secure, and is as immovable as a rock. . . .[3]

When in May 1765 the king was obliged to take back the Grenvilles, they meant to exact explanations from some Members of Parliament who held quasi-civil service posts and of whose attachment they felt uncertain; but they dropped this design when told by one of them that

> he would faithfully support the administration of which he was a part but that he would on no consideration combine with any body of subjects against the undoubted right of the Crown to name its own officers. . . .[4]

[1] Miss Wake, when sending me the eighteenth-century chapters of her forthcoming book, used the sentence quoted above in a covering letter.

[2] *The Croker Papers*, ed. J. L. Jennings, vol. i, p. 81.

[3] The letters are printed in the *Bedford Correspondence*, ed. Lord John Russell, vol. i, pp. 4–8. Their text reproduced above is corrected from the originals at Woburn Abbey. In the letter from Bedford to Pulteney the editor through a slip omitted 'about those dark transactions' followed by fifteen more words.

[4] From Gilbert Elliot's 'Account of the crisis of May–June 1765', Elliot MSS. at Minto House, vol. vii, no. 3; reproduced from a copy in the Liverpool Papers, Add. MS. 38335, ff. 120–33, in N. S. Jucker, *The Jenkinson Papers*, p. 367.

And in 1827 J. C. Herries, M.P., Secretary of the Treasury, thus defined his position:[1]

> I am pursuing my own laborious vocation. . . . I am not in the following of any party. My business is with the public interests and my duty to promote the King's service wherever I am employed.

Horace Walpole admitted that among the 'Treasury Jesuits', as he called them, were 'some of the ablest men in the House of Commons, as Elliot, Dyson, Martin, and Jenkinson'; yet he ascribed to 'secret influence' their continuance in office 'through every Administration', and echoed Burke in calling them 'the Cabinet that governed the Cabinet'.[2]

Whether a post was held by quasi-civil service tenure often depended on its holder. Lord Barrington, M.P., never out of employment between 1746 and 1778, was nineteen years at the War Office under Newcastle, Devonshire, Rockingham, Chatham, Grafton, and North; but Henry Fox as Secretary at War was a front-rank politician. Soame Jenyns, a littérateur of distinction and with good connexions, held the post of a Lord of Trade from 1755 till he left parliament in 1780; for Charles Townshend it was the first step in his political career. The character of Court offices was even more uncertain: Lord Hertford, the head of an eminently political family, who between 1751 and 1766 had been Lord of the Bedchamber, Ambassador to Paris, Lord Lieutenant of Ireland, Lord Steward, and then from 1766 onwards, Lord Chamberlain, wrote to the king on the fall of the North Administration: 'Let me . . . as a personal servant to your Majesty, not be involved with Ministers to whom I have never belonged. . . .'

Not 'to belong to Ministers' was sometimes raised to the level of a principle. Harry, sixth Duke of Bolton, early in the reign of George III sided with the Opposition and rejoined them in 1770; but on succeeding to the dukedom in July 1765, declared that in future

---

[1] J. C. Herries to Sir Wm. Knighton, 27 February 1827, *Letters of King George IV*, ed. A. Aspinall, vol. iii, p. 200.

[2] Horace Walpole, *Memoirs of the Reign of King George III*, vol. ii, p. 221; vol. iv, pp. 75–76.

his attachment shall be to the Crown only—that he sees how contemptible, and weak it is for a peer of England independent as he is, and with a great estate, to be dragged along in the suite of any private man or set of men whatever; and to become the mean instrument of their views, their faction, or ambition.

And Lord Egmont declared in the Cabinet on 1 May 1766: '. . . that I had no predilection for this or that set of men—that my first duty was to Your Majesty.' Or again, in January 1783, Lord Hood, when put up in his absence as candidate for Westminster, wrote that though he had no ambition for a seat in the House of Commons, he would accept, but would then 'studiously steer clear . . . of all suspicion of being a *party man* . . . for or against the Minister', as he thought this 'unbecoming a military servant of the King'.[1]

To sum up: so long as government was truly the king's own business, and the king's permanent servants could sit in parliament, there was nothing reprehensible or illogical in members refusing, from legitimate interest or on grounds of conscience, to commit themselves to parties and leaders.

5

The country gentlemen (and certain urban counterparts of theirs)[2] were the very antithesis of the Court party. Their watchword was independence: attachment to the Crown but no obligations to ministers. They entered the House with a sense of duty to the public; their ambition was primacy in their own 'country' attested by being chosen parliamentary representatives for their county or some respectable boroughs (or else they sat for complete pocket boroughs of their own, preferably without voters for whom favours might have to be obtained from

---

[1] *Correspondence of King George III*, ed. Sir John Fortescue, vol. i, p. 27, no. 21, Lord Hertford to the King, 3 April 1782 (misdated by the editor as 1762); vol. i, p. 158, no. 134, Egmont to the King, 12 July 1765; vol. i, p. 300, no. 304, same to same, 2 May 1766; vol. vi, p. 209, no. 4062, Lord Hood, 16 January 1783.

[2] Men like John Barnard or William Beckford—rich business men not seeking government contracts but representative of the independent business community.

Administration). Office, honours, or profits might have impaired rather than raised their standing;[1] the sovereign had therefore little occasion to disappoint them, or the minister to reward them; and they were treated with the respect due to the independent part they played. They were critical of financial extravagance on Court, sinecures, or on costly (and unnecessary) wars; and they were suspicious, or even contemptuous, of the ways of courtiers and politicians; they loathed government contractors and pensioners in the House—the locusts that devoured the land-tax—and were easily roused against them. But not playing for office, they were not bound to factions: when on 12 February 1741, the Opposition Whigs moved for Walpole's dismissal, 25 country gentlemen normally in opposition to him voted against the motion, while 44 left the House.[2]

Governor Pitt wrote to his son on 16 January 1705:[3]

> If you are in Parliament, show yourself on all occasions a good Englishman, and a faithful servant to your country ... Avoid faction, and never enter the House pre-possessed; but attend diligently to the debate, and vote according to your conscience and not for any sinister end whatever. I had rather see any child of mine want than have him get his bread by voting in the House of Commons.

About 1745 the story was told[4] that a peerage had been offered

[1] With regard to honours the position had changed by the beginning of the 19th century: numerous peerages had been conferred by Pitt on leading county families, and seem to have stimulated further applications. On 5 November 1814, Lord Liverpool, having repeatedly discussed the creation of peerages with the Prince Regent, wrote to E. Wilbraham Bootle, M.P., that in order to keep the number within reasonable bounds, it was found necessary 'explicitly to refuse the application of every country gentleman, whatever his fortune or pretensions', and confine new peerages 'either to persons who had claims on the ground of some public service, official or in the field', or 'who were already Scotch or Irish peers'. (Add. MS. 38260, f. 96.)

[2] Rev. H. Etough to Rev. Dr. Burch, n.d., Coxe, *Memoirs of Sir Robert Walpole*, vol. iii, pp. 562–3.

[3] H.M.C. *Fortescue MMS.*, vol. i, p. 18.

[4] H.M.C. *Hastings MSS.*, vol. iii, p. 49; Lord Hastings to his father, Lord Huntingdon, n.d.: 'This I had from Sir Walter Bagott's son, who had it from his father.'

to Sir Watkin Williams Wynn (M.P. for County Denbigh from 1722 till his death in 1749):

> ... his answer was that as long as His Majesty's Ministers acted for the good of their country, he was willing to consent to anything; he thanked His Majesty for the Earldom he had sent him, but that he was very well content with the honours he had and was resolved to live and die Sir Watkin.

And the boast of the typical country gentleman was that he was neither the minion of Administration nor the tool of faction.

Originally the country gentlemen tried to exclude all office-holders from the House; their failure left the door open for parliamentary government. But as a rule they practised what they had preached—it would have been a handicap for a knight of the shire, relying on the support of the country gentlemen, to hold office or to have received personal favours from government: in 1830 Sir Thomas Gooch, M.P. for Suffolk 1806–30, had to make excuses on the hustings for having solicited a Crown living for his son.[1] Before about 1830 even 'too marked a party line' was apt to be considered incompatible with true independence: in 1806, W. R. Cartwright (M.P. for Northamptonshire 1797–1830) was criticized for having consistently supported Pitt when 'a Knight of the Shire should vote as an individual and not as a party man'.[2] In a speech in parliament, on 21 January 1819, Sir George Sinclair, M.P. for Caithness, thus defined the attitude of the country gentlemen:[3]

> ... neither to withhold entirely their confidence from Government, nor implicitly to sanction their proceedings; sometimes to oppose their measures, but never to impeach their motives—to combine political candour with constitutional vigilance—rather predisposed to approve than predetermined to condemn; resolved to favour but not to flatter; to controul, but not to embarrass.

And he rightly added:

---

[1] *Suffolk Chronicle*, 14 August 1830.
[2] See E. G. Forrester, *Northamptonshire County Elections and Electioneering, 1695–1832*, p. 92.
[3] *Parliamentary Debates*, vol. xxxix, cols. 55–59.

I am well aware that no individual is more obnoxious to both parties than one who will not absolutely bind himself to either.

Thus the country gentlemen had this in common with the Court group that they too, though for widely different reasons, refused to be tied to parliamentary parties and leaders; further, that they also were neither orators nor leaders: for again, any one of them who rose to such pre-eminence, automatically joined the politicians in the central arena.

6

Little needs to be said about the outstanding, historical figures among the politicians: these were the men who played for the highest prizes, for Cabinet posts and the conduct of the king's business in administration and parliament. It was in their power to procure ease to the king's affairs in parliament, or to obstruct them; they could therefore claim the king's favour, and in a crisis compel it. But who were the rank and file of the political factions? In the first place the relatives, friends, and dependants of great peers usually returned for seats at their disposal; and next, the political following of Commoners who could aspire to the highest offices and hunt as equals with the oligarchical groups. But these followers, in search of places or profits, did not differ essentially from the minor ministers or political parasites of the Court party. In fact, the same men are found at various times on either side of the fence, and happiest when there was no fence: when their group was so firmly established in office that it could hardly be distinguished from the Court party.

Though there were three main groups in the eighteenth-century House of Commons, in action there could be but two: the ayes and the noes, the Government party and the Opposition—which fact has reinforced the delusion of a two-party system. The Government side was invariably a junction of the Court party with a group of politicians; to the attractive force of Crown patronage was added the political ability of parliamentary leaders. When the dissolution of the first Rockingham Administration seemed imminent in January 1766, members forming the core of the official group, in a survey of the political scene, thus described their own position:[1]

> Those who have always hitherto acted upon the sole principle of attachment to the Crown. This is probably the most numerous body and would on trial be found sufficient to carry on the publick business themselves if there was any person to accept of a Ministerial office at the head of them, and this is all they want.

In other words, the Court could supply numbers and workers but not political leaders and a parliamentary façade—for this in 1766 it had to turn to the Rockinghams, or the Grenvilles and Bedfords, or to Chatham. Even when the leading minister was the king's choice—Bute in 1762, Chatham in 1766, North in 1770, or Pitt in December 1783—the king had often to accept some ministers displeasing to himself. But when his relations with the dominant political group were distant or uncertain, he would try to introduce into the Cabinet some ministers of his own: thus Northington and Egmont entered the Grenville and the first Rockingham Administration, and Thurlow those of Rockingham and Shelburne in 1782–3; and it gave rise to comment in March 1783 when the king was not allowed a single member of his own choice in the Coalition Government.[2] The theory of the Cabinet as a joint board of king's men and politicians was, unconsciously, formulated by Horace Walpole when the Duke of Richmond, in discussing Cabinet reconstruction in 1767, objected to Camden because he 'would be the King's'—'I asked', writes Walpole, 'if they expected that every man should depend on King Rockingham, and nobody on King George.'[3]

When a First Minister was known to enjoy the favour of the king, the Court party would naturally adhere to him; and every group of politicians in power tried to fill places at Court, administrative posts, and seats in government boroughs with their own men; these, if their group long continued in office, would

[1] N. S. Jucker, *The Jenkinson Papers*, pp. 405–6.

[2] Horace Walpole, *Last Journals*, vol. ii, p. 500.

[3] Horace Walpole, *Memoirs of the Reign of King George III*, vol. iii, p. 47.

permeate the Court party and coalesce with it. But if then a separation supervened, it remained to be seen how much government property the politicians would get away with—places for life, reversions, parliamentary seats, etc.—and how many friends, glued to the flesh pots, they would have to part with. Moreover, men who had long 'upheld the rights of the Crown', condemning 'formed opposition' as factious and disrespectful to the king, found it difficult to enter it themselves: as was seen in the case of Newcastle in 1762, and of Wellington in 1830.[1]

In normal circumstances the king's authority and support were sufficient to keep the average group of politicians in office, but no government could survive for long if either the king or public opinion turned definitely against them. Between 1742 and 1832 the country gentlemen and their city counterparts increasingly became the spokesmen and indicator of public opinion; and that group, about a hundred strong, when solid would carry with it a good many men of its own type and class but of less pronounced independence and normally voting with the Court or with political groups. When in 1764, over General Warrants, a great many of the country gentlemen voted with the Opposition, the Government was in serious danger.[2] When in February 1781, 59 out of 80 English knights of the shire, were listed by John Robinson, Secretary of the Treasury, as opposition,[3] the end was near; and when on 18 March 1782, Thomas Grosvenor informed North 'in his own name, and in those of some other country gentlemen' that they would withdraw their support from his Government, its fate was sealed. Even members of the Court party were now breaking away, or at least absenting themselves from the House: some from conviction, others from caution. When Wellington was defeated on 15 November 1830, only 15 out of 82 English county members voted for him and 49 against; and in 1831 'only six . . .

[1] See *Three Early Nineteenth Century Diaries*, ed. by A. Aspinall, Introduction p. xxxv: 'Wellington said that he could not bear the idea of being in opposition: he did not know how to set about it.'
[2] See my book, *England in the Age of the American Revolution*, p. 232.
[3] Abergavenny Papers.

English county-members in the new House were anti-Reformers'.[1]

Unengaged in struggles for office, the independent country gentlemen were a retarding element in the growth of parliamentary government, but the charge of favouring 'prerogative', sometimes levelled against them, was as uncorrelated to political realities as were their own attempts at constructive action—for instance in the confusion after the fall of North, when the weight of the independent members was felt more than under stable conditions. Thus early in 1784, 78 members—the St. Albans Tavern group—endeavoured to contrive a reconciliation between Pitt and Fox and a coalition which was probably desired by neither, and least of all by the king: for these country gentlemen party wrangles were meaningless, and a nuisance if likely to bring on the dissolution of a parliament which had run only half its course. Another, even more naive, move in 1788 is set forth in a circular[2] endorsed by 30 Lords and Commoners. In this 'such Members of the two Houses as hold themselves independent of, and unconnected with, the parties that now exist, and are desirous of contributing their best endeavours to promote the general interests of the Country', were invited, while not considering themselves 'under any restraint, or tied down to follow the sentiments of the majority', to 'act in unison with each other. And here is the 'Analysis of the House of Commons' given in the circular:

1. Party of the Crown   185
   This party includes all those who would probably support his Majesty's Government under any Minister, not peculiarly unpopular.
2. The Party attached to Mr. Pitt   .   .   .   52
   Of this party were there a new Parliament, and Mr. P. no longer Minster, not above twenty would be returned.

[1] See *Three Early Nineteenth Century Diaries*, Introduction, pp. xxii–xxiii and xxxvi.

[2] The circular headed 'Proposals' is in the Braybrooke Papers, in the Essex Record Office, Chelmsford (D/DBy C9/44).

3. Detached Parties supporting the present Administration viz:
   1. Mr. Dundas 10
   2. Marquis of Lansdowne . . . 9
   3. Earl of Lonsdale 9
   4. East Indians 15
4. The independent or unconnected Members of the
   House . . . . . . [108][1]
   Of this body of men about forty have united together, in conjunction with some members of the
   House of Peers in order to form a third party
   for the purpose of preventing the Crown from
   being too much in the power of either of the two
   other parties who are contending for the government of the country, and who (were it really
   necessary) might with the assistance of the
   Crown, undertake to make up an administration
   to the exclusion both of Mr. Pitt and Mr. Fox,
   and of their adherents.
5. The Opposition to the present Administration
   1. The Party attached to Mr. Fox . . 138
   2. Remnants of Lord North's Party . . 17
6. Absentees and Neutrals 14

The names of Whig and Tory do not appear in this list, nor in
any other compiled in those years; nor have I used them so far
in this lecture, for they explain little, but require a good deal
of explaining.

7

Whig and Tory were 'denominations'—names and creeds—
which covered enduring types moulded by deeply ingrained
differences in temperament and outlook. But when was a clear
party division covered by them? Even before 1714 some scholars
now discern merely a number of groups and connexions of a
Tory or a Whig hue, or of uncertain colouring; for hardly ever
was there anything like straight party voting. About the middle
of the century the names were deprecated, described as out-

---

[1] The number is not given here, but lower down in a summary list of
the parties.

worn and meaningless, and yet they were used; for names there must be in a political dichotomy, even if their meaning is uncertain and their use misleading. In parliament even under the first two Georges disaffected Whigs supplied the most inveterate leaders of the Opposition and most of its voting strength. But in a good many constituencies the names of Whig and Tory still corresponded to real divisions: partly perhaps because local factions could hardly have been denoted as 'Government' and 'Opposition', and partly because the most enduring distinction between Tory and Whig—High Church *versus* Low Church and Dissent—retained more vitality and significance in local struggles than at Westminster.

A ruling group will always try to place its opponents under a ban, and the natural consequence of the practice of Walpole and the Pelhams was that anyone who wished to play at politics and for office, adopted the name of Whig: the Finches, Seymours, Legges, Leveson-Gowers, Wyndhams, Foxes, etc. In fact by 1750 everyone at Court, in office, and in the centre arena was a Whig, while the name of Tories, by a process of natural selection, was left to the residuum who did not enter politics in pursuit of office, honours, or profits, that is, to the country gentlemen and to the forerunners of urban radicals.

The nomenclature, as further developed in the first decade of George III's reign, is correctly stated by Horace Walpole in a passage of his *Memoirs*, penned late in 1768, or more probably in 1769:[1] 'The body of the Opposition', he says, 'still called itself Whig, an appellation rather dropped than disclaimed by the Court'; 'the real Tories still adhered to their old distinctions ... and fluctuated according as they esteemed particular chiefs not of their connexion ...'; but 'their whole conduct was comprised in silent votes...'. Thus Walpole knew the difference between 'real Tories' and the Court Whigs who had become the 'Tories' of Opposition Whig pamphleteers; but as he habitually flavours accurate perceptions with current cant, a footnote, added in the 1780's, emphatically asserts that Lord North 'was a Tory'. About the same time Burke, in a letter of 24

[1] Horace Walpole, *Memoirs of the Reign of King George III*, vol. ii, p. 67.

D

December 1782, describes the phalanx of 130–50 placemen and place-hunters ranged behind North to secure the survival of places, refers to them as 'the body, which for want of another name, I call Lord North's'; and then adds: 'I ought to have excepted out of the profligates of Lord North's corps five or six Tories who act on principle, such as it is.'[1] Less than two months later, the Rockinghams formed a coalition with the 'profligates' by conceding to them that nothing more should be done 'about the reduction of the influence of the Crown' by economical reform.

Who were now the 'Tories'? The younger Pitt never used the name and after his death his successors went merely by that of 'Mr. Pitt's friends' (apparently George Canning was the only one who occasionally called himself a 'Tory'). On 5 October 1809, Perceval wrote to Lord Melville:[2]

> Our Party's strength, dismembered as we are by Canning's and Castlereagh's separation from us . . . has lost its principle of cohesion. We are no longer the sole representatives of Mr. Pitt. The magic of that name is in a great degree dissolved, and the principle on which we must most rely to keep us together, and give us the assistance of floating strength, is the public sentiment of loyalty and attachment to the King. Among the independent part of the House, the country gentlemen, the representatives of popular boroughs, we shall find our saving strength or our destruction.

In short: here is once more the basic structure of eighteenth-century parliamentary politics, with increased regard for the country gentlemen but no trace of a two-party system, or at all of party in the modern sense; and the group which in 1760 went by the name of Tories, a generation later is referred to simply as 'independent country gentlemen', the name of Tory being practically in abeyance. It is the history of those party-names, and how they were applied, which calls for careful study free of confusion between names and realities, or rather between the differing realities which the same names were

---

[1] See E. B. de Fonblanque, *Political and Military Episodes . . . from the life and correspondence of . . . John Burgoyne* (1876), pp. 418–21.
[2] Perceval MSS.

made to cover; and next the history must be traced of party realities as shaped by interaction between the constituencies and the House of Commons. Nineteenth-century parliamentary historians now seem agreed in deferring the full emergence of the modern party till after the Second Reform Bill: what preceded it were intermediary forms which should not be treated anachronistically in terms of a later age.

With regard to the second half of the eighteenth century, the idea of party conducive to parliamentary government is usually linked up with the Whigs; which, for what it is worth, is a matter of nomenclature rather than of ideology: the politicians, and not the Court group or the independent country gentlemen, were the party-forming element, and the politicians called themselves Whigs. But among the politicians the attitude to sovereign and party did not depend on the degree of their Whiggery: those who enjoyed the favour of the Crown, and coalesced with the Court party, were naturally less of a party-forming element that those in disfavour, or uncertain of royal support, who had therefore to rely primarily on parliament and seek to form their following into a coherent party. This was specially true of political groups which had forced themselves on the king: the Grenvilles after September 1763, the Rockinghams in 1782, and the Coalition in 1783.

The fourth Duke of Devonshire, the 'prince of the Whigs', was in every way an outstanding personality among them: disinterested and generous, he acted from a sense of duty but according to the canons of the time. As Lord Chamberlain he had to deal in August 1761 with a crisis in the King's Bedchamber.

> Lord Huntingdon Groom of the Stole [he writes] came to Lord Ashburnham who was in waiting and told him that he would put on the King's shirt. His Lordship reply'd to be sure if he pleased but then he must take the whole waiting. The other said no, I will only put on the shirt, Lord Ash[burnham] said I give you notice if you do it I shall quit the room. . . .

And so he did. Lord Rockingham and other Lords of the Bedchamber agreed with Ashburnham, 'were much dissatisfy'd, thought it lowering their employments, and that they could not stay'; but when Bute became 'very warm' over the matter Devonshire warned him that if five or six of the most considerable lords threw up their employment as beneath them, others too would quit, and Bute 'would get nobody to take it that was worth having it'. The late king, said Devonshire,

> had piqued himself on raising the Bedchamber by getting men of the first rank for them to take it, and that [if] it was lower'd they certainly would not remain in, that it was a very cheap way of keeping them steady to support Government.[1]

Indeed, in 1761 the Lords of the Bedchamber included seventeen peers controlling at least double the number of seats in the House of Commons, and three courtesy lords, all in the House; and Devonshire was giving the right advice on how to put Court offices to the best use in managing parliament. But in that advice, given by a leading Whig at the end of the so-called Whig era, there is nothing which would even distantly foreshadow parliamentary government based on party.

For that, owing to circumstances, we have to turn much rather to the Grenvilles. Two months after the king had, in August 1763, unsuccessfully tried to get rid of them, a by-election occurred in Essex, and on 28 October, John Luther, one of the candidates called on Lord Sandwich, and expressed his concern at hearing that Sandwich was taking a part against him.

> I told him[wrote Sandwich to Rigby] that I considered myself meerly with regard to Essex as a party man, that my interest and that of my best friends was at stake, as far as related to the support or downfall of the present Administration . . . that I had seen Mr. Conyers, who had told me that he embarked himself in my system, and that he meant if he succeeded, to be a true and steady friend to *this* Administration. Mr. Luther answered me that he had given the same assurances to Mr. Grenville . . . that he was a friend to *Government*, . . . I said that *Government* was a loose word . . . was he a friend to *this* Administration, and more so to *this* than he should be to any Administration of which Mr. Pitt was a member, at that he smiled and hesitated a little, but

---

[1] Devonshire MSS. 260. 339.

soon answered that he was a friend to this Administration and
would shew himself as such while they acted *consistently*.... I
answered ... that his own words obliged me situated as I am to
act against him; that this country must be governed by combinations of people, and that those who would act in the combination
that I belonged to would have a right to my support. ...

But Luther, according to Sandwich, kept a back door open by
constituting himself 'the judge of what was *consistency* in the
Administration'.[1]

Or again, in 1764 the Grenvilles intervened in East India
Company elections (the first government to do so), with the
purpose of helping Clive to get back his *jagir*, he having
pledged himself to support them in or out of office—to which
promise he adhered. And when they and the Bedfords were
turned out by the king, they withdrew their men from Administration and the Court; whereas a year later, the Rockinghams showed so little understanding of party management that
they left Chatham whomever he chose to retain. Ideas and a
political practice are things of slow growth; parliamentary
government, wise as it is as a system, was not born like Pallas
Athene.

To sum up: Parliamentary government based on the party-
system, is not an ingenious device, the product of creative
thought, for which credit is due to one set of men, while another is to be blamed for lack of foresight or virtue in not
anticipating it. Its bases are deep down in the political structure
of the nation, which was being gradually transformed during
the period of so-called mixed government. An electorate thinking in terms of nation-wide parties is its indispensable basis;
and it is therefore at least as much in the constituencies as in
parliament that the growth of these parties will have to be
traced. In the eighteenth century parliament was without that
background of enfrancmised masses thinking in terms of party;
it was to a high degree a closed arena, with its own life and
divisions, still dominated by Court and Country on the peri-

[1] Sandwich MSS.

phery, but containing the forerunners of political parties in the centre. To clear up these antecedents must be the contribution of us, eighteenth-century historians, to the essential work on the least explored period of British constitutional history, the nineteenth century, now started by a group of keen, able, and what is important, mostly young, historians.

4

KING GEORGE III:
A STUDY OF PERSONALITY

(Academy of Arts Lecture, 1953)

THERE WERE three large pictures of George III at the exhibition of Royal Portraits arranged by the Academy of Arts in the Spring of 1953. Looking at the first, by Reynolds, painted when the King was 41, I was struck by the immaturity of expression. The second, by Lawrence, painted in 1792 at the age of 54, depicts him in Garter robes; face and posture seem to attempt in a naive, ineffective, and almost engaging manner to live up to a grandeur which the sitter feels incumbent on him. The third, by Stroehling, painted in November 1807, at the age of nearly 70, shows a sad old man, looking dimly at a world in which he has no pleasure, and which he soon will not be able to see or comprehend.

A picture in a different medium of the King and his story presents itself to the student when in the Royal Archives at Windsor he surveys the papers of George III. They stand on the shelves in boxes, each marked on a white label with the year or years which it covers. The eye runs over that array, and crucial dates recall events: 1760, '65 and '67, '74 and '75, '82 and '83, 1789, '93, '96, 1802, 1805—the series breaks off in 1810; and brown-backed volumes follow, unlabelled: they contain the medical reports on a man shut off from time, which means the world and its life.

Fate had made George III ruler when kings were still expected to govern; and his active reign covered half a century

39

during which the American conflict posed the problem of Imperial relations, while at home political practice constantly ran up against the contradiction inherent in the then much belauded 'mixed form of government': personal monarchy served by Ministers whose tenure of office was contested in Parliament. Neither the Imperial nor the constitutional problem could have been solved in the terms in which the overwhelming majority of the politically minded public in this country considered them at the time; but George III has been blamed ever since for not having thought of Dominion status and parliamentary government when constitutional theory and the facts of the situation as yet admitted of neither.

In the catalogue, *Kings and Queens*, on sale at the exhibition, the introduction dealing with the reign of George III gave the traditional view of his reign:

> Conscientious and ambitious, he tried to restore the political influence of the Crown, but his intervention ended with the humiliating American War of Independence.

Conscientious he certainly was, painstakingly, almost painfully, conscientious. But was he ambitious? Did he try to exercise powers which his predecessors had relinquished, or claim an influence which was not universally conceded to him? And was it the assertion of Royal, and not of Parliamentary, authority over America which brought on the conflict and disrupted the First British Empire?

Let us place ourselves in March 1782. Dismal, humiliating failure has turned public opinion, and the House of Commons is resolved to cut losses and abandon the struggle; it is all over; Lord North's government has fallen; and the King is contemplating abdication. He has drafted a message to Parliament (which was never sent); here are its first two paragraphs:

> His Majesty during the twenty-one years he has sate on the throne of Great Britain, has had no object so much at heart as the maintainance of the British Constitution, of which the difficulties he has at times met with from his scrupulous attachment to the rights of Parliament are sufficient proofs.

His Majesty is convinced that the sudden change of sentiments of one branch of the legislature has totally incapacitated him from either conducting the war with effect, or from obtaining any peace but on conditions which would prove destructive to the commerce as well as essential rights of the British nation.[1]

In the first paragraph the King declares his unswerving devotion to the British Constitution, and shows himself conscious of his difficulties in America having arisen through 'his scrupulous attachment to the rights of Parliament'; the second paragraph pointedly refers to the Commons as 'one branch of the legislature', and gives the King's view of the American war: he is defending there the vital interests and essential rights of the British nation.

A year later, in March 1783, when faced by the necessity of accepting a Government formed by the Fox-North coalition, George III once more contemplated abdication; and in a letter (which again was never sent) he wrote to the Prince of Wales:

The situation of the times are such that I must, if I attempt to carry on the business of the nation, give up every political principle on which I have acted, which I should think very unjustifiable, as I have always attempted to act agreable to my duty; and must form a Ministry from among men who know I cannot trust them and therefore who will not accept office without making me a kind of slave; this undoubtedly is a cruel dilemma, and leaves me but one step to take without the destruction of my principles and honour; the resigning my Crown, my dear Son to you, quitting this my native country for ever and returning to the dominions of my forefathers.

Your difficulties will not be the same. You have never been in a situation to form any political system, therefore, are open to addopt what the times may make necessary; and no set of men can ever have offended you or made it impossible for you to employ them.[2]

Alongside this consider the following passage from a letter which George III wrote on 26 December 1783, after having

[1] Fortescue, *Correspondence of King George III*, vol. v, no. 3061.
[2] Windsor MSS.

dismissed the Coalition and while he was trying to rally support for the newly formed Administration of the younger Pitt:

> The times are of the most serious nature, the political struggle is not as formerly between two factions for power; but it is no less than whether a desperate faction shall not reduce the Sovereign to a mere tool in its hands: though I have too much principle ever to infringe the rights of others, yet that must ever equaly prevent my submitting to the Executive power being in any other hands, than where the Constitution has placed it. I therefore must call on the assistance of every honest man ... to support Government on the present most critical occasion.[1]

Note in these two passages the King's honest conviction that he has always attempted to do his duty; that he has been mindful not to infringe the rights of others; but that it would be equally wrong in him to submit 'to the Executive power being in any other hands, than where the Constitution has placed it.' And while I do not for a moment suggest that these things could not have been done in a happier manner, I contend that the King's statements quoted above are substantially correct.

In the eighteenth century, a proper balance between King, Lords, and Commons, that is, the monarchical, aristocratic, and representative elements of the Constitution acting as checks on each other, was supposed to safeguard the property and privileges, the lives and liberty of the subjects. Single-Chamber government would have been no less abhorrent to the century than Royal autocracy. The Executive was the King's as truly as it is now of the President in the United States; he, too, had to choose his Ministers: but from among Parliamentary leaders. And while aspirants to office swore by the 'independency' of the Crown and disclaimed all wish to force themselves on the King, if left out they did their level best to embarrass and upset their successful rivals. The technique of Parliamentary opposition was fully established long before its most essential aim, which is to force a change of government, was recognized as legitimate; and because that aim could not be avowed in its innocent purity, deadly dangers threatening the Constitution, nay the life of the country, had to be alleged for justification.

[1] Windsor MS. 5709.

Robert Walpole as 'sole Minister' was accused of arrogating to himself the powers of both King and Parliament; the very tame Pelhams, of keeping George II 'in fetters'; Bute, who bore the name of Stuart, of 'raising the standard of Royal prerogative'; and George III of ruling not through the Ministers of his own choice whom he avowed in public, but through a hidden gang of obscure and sinister 'King's friends'. It is obviously impossible here to trace the origin and growth of that story, or to disprove it by establishing the true facts of the transactions to which it has become attached—it was a figment so beautifully elaborated by Burke's fertile imagination that the Rockinghams themselves finished by believing it, and it grew into an obsession with them. In reality the constitutional practice of George III differed little from that of George I and George II. William Wyndham was proscribed by the first two Georges as a dangerous Jacobite, and C. J. Fox by the third as a dangerous Jacobin; while the elder Pitt was long kept out by both George II and George III on personal grounds. But for some the Royal veto and Royal influence in politics lose their sting if exercised in favour of successful monopolists in Whiggery.

I go one step further: in the eighteenth century the King had to intervene in politics and was bound to exercise his political influence, for the party system, which is the basis of Parliamentary government, did not exist.[1] Of the House of Commons itself probably less than half thought and acted in party terms. About one-third of the House consisted of Members who looked to the King for guidance and for permanency of employment: epigoni of earlier Courts or forerunners of the modern Civil Service; and if they thus pursued their own interest, there is no reason to treat them as more corrupt than if they had done so by attaching themselves to a group of politicians. Another one-fifth of the House consisted of independent country gentlemen, ready to support the King's Government so long as this was compatible with their conscience, but averse to tying themselves up with political groups: they did not desire office, honours, or profits, but prided themselves on the disinterested and independent line they were pursuing; and they rightly

[1] For a fuller discussion of this point see above, pp. 21–32.

claimed to be the authentic voice of the nation. In the centre of the arena stood the politicians, their orators and leaders fighting for the highest prizes of Parliamentary life. They alone could supply the façade of governments: the front benches in Parliament. But to achieve stability a Government required the active support of the Crown and the good opinion of the country. On matters about which public opinion felt strongly, its will would prevail; but with the House constituted as it was, with the electoral structure of the unreformed Parliament, and an electorate which neither thought nor voted on party lines, it is idle to assume that modern Parliamentary government was possible.

I pass to the next point: was George III correct in saying that it was 'his scrupulous attachment to the rights of Parliament' which caused him the difficulties in America? Undoubtedly yes. It was not Royal claims that the Americans objected to, but the claims of 'subjects in one part of the King's dominions to be sovereigns over their fellow-subjects in another part of his dominions.'[1] 'The sovereignty of the Crown I understand,' wrote Benjamin Franklin; 'the sovereignty of Britain I do not understand. . . . We have the same King, but not the same legislature.' Had George III aspired to independent Royal Power nothing could have suited him better than to be Sovereign in America, the West Indies, and possibly in Ireland, independent of the British Parliament; and the foremost champions of the rights of Parliament, recalling the way in which the Stuarts had played off Ireland and Scotland against England, would have been the first to protest. But in fact it would be difficult to imagine a King simultaneously exercising in several independent countries executive powers in conjunction with Parliamentary leaders. It will suffice to remember the difficulties and jealousies which Hanover caused although itself politically inert. The two problems which George III is unjustly accused of having mismanaged, those of Imperial and constitutional relations, were interconnected: only after responsible government had arisen did Dominion status within the Commonwealth become possible.

[1] Benjamin Franklin to the Rev. Samuel Cooper of Boston, 8 June 1770.

Lastly, of the measures which brought on the American conflict none was of the King's making: neither George Grenville's Stamp Act, nor the Declaratory Act of the Rockinghams, nor the Townshend Duties. All that can be said against him is that once the struggle had started, he, completely identifying himself with this country, obstinately persevered in it. He wrote on 14 November 1778:

> If Lord North can see with the same degree of enthusiasm I do, the beauty, excellence, and perfection of the British Constitution as by law established, and consider that if any one branch of the Empire is alowed to cast off its dependency, that the others will infalably follow the example...he...will resolve with vigour to meet every obstacle...or the State will be ruined.[1]

And again on 11 June 1779, expecting that the West Indies and Ireland would follow:

> Then this island would be reduced to itself, and soon would be a poor island indeed.[2]

On 7 March 1780:

> I can never suppose this country so far lost to all ideas of self importance as to be willing to grant America independence, if that could ever be universally adopted, I shall despair of this country being ever preserved from a state of inferiority and consequently falling into a very low class among the European States...[3]

And on 26 September 1780:

> ...giving up the game would be total ruin, a small State may certainly subsist, but a great one mouldering cannot get into an inferior situation but must be annihilated.[4]

When all was over, Lord North wrote to the King on 18 March 1782:

> Your Majesty is well apprized that, in this country, the Prince on the Throne, cannot, with prudence, oppose the deliberate resolution of the House of Commons... Your Majesty has graciously

---

[1] Fortescue IV, no. 2451.   [2] *Ibid.*, no. 2649.   [3] Fortescue V, no. 2963.
[4] *Ibid.*, no. 3155.

and steadily supported the servants you approve, as long as they could be supported: Your Majesty has firmly and resolutely maintained what appeared to you essential to the welfare and dignity of this country, as long as this country itself thought proper to maintain it. The Parliament have altered their sentiments, and as their sentiments whether just or erroneous, must ultimately prevail, Your Majesty ... can lose no honour if you yield at length ...

Your Majesty's goodness encourages me ... to submit whether it will not be for Your Majesty's welfare, and even glory, to sacrifice, at this moment, former opinions, displeasures and apprehensions (though never so well-founded) to ... the public safety.[1]

The King replied:

I could not but be hurt at your letter of last night. Every man must be the sole judge of his feelings, therefore whatever you or any man can say on that subject has no avail with me.[2]

What George III had never learnt was to give in with grace: but this was at the most a defect of character.

2

Lord Waldegrave, who had been Governor to the Prince of Wales 1752–6, wrote in 1758 a character sketch of him so penetrating and just that it deserves quoting almost in full.[3]

The Prince of Wales is entering into his 21st year, and it would be unfair to decide upon his character in the early stages of life, when there is so much time for improvement.

A wise preamble: yet a long and eventful life was to change him very little. Every feature singled out by Waldegrave finds copious illustration in the fifty years that followed (in one case in a superficially inverted form).

His parts, though not excellent, will be found very tolerable, if ever they are properly exercised.

He is strictly honest, but wants that frank and open behaviour which makes honesty appear amiable. ...

[1] Fortescue V, no. 3566.   [2] *Ibid.*, no. 3567.
[3] James, 2nd Earl Waldegrave, *Memoirs* (1821), pp. 8–10.

His religion is free from all hypocrisy, but is not of the most charitable sort; he has rather too much attention to the sins of his neighbour.

He has spirit, but not of the active kind; and does not want resolution, but it is mixed with too much obstinacy.

He has great command of his passions, and will seldom do wrong, except when he mistakes wrong for right; but as often as this shall happen, it will be difficult to undeceive him, because he is uncommonly indolent, and has strong prejudices.

His want of application and aversion to business would be far less dangerous, was he eager in the pursuit of pleasure; for the transition from pleasure to business is both shorter and easier than from a state of total inaction.

He has a kind of unhappiness in his temper, which, if it be not conquered before it has taken too deep a root, will be a source of frequent anxiety. Whenever he is displeased, his anger does not break out with heat and violence; but he becomes sullen and silent, and retires to his closet; not to compose his mind by study or contemplation, but merely to indulge the melancholy enjoyment of his own ill humour. Even when the fit is ended, unfavourable symptoms very frequently return, which indicate that on certain occasions his Royal Highness has too correct a memory.

Waldegrave's own endeavour was to give the Prince 'true notions of common things.'[1] But these he never acquired: which is perhaps the deepest cause of his tragedy.

The defect Waldegrave dwells upon most is the Prince's 'uncommon indolence', his 'want of application and aversion to business'. This is borne out by other evidence, best of all by the Prince's own letters to Bute:[2]

July 1st, 1756: I will throw off that indolence which if I don't soon get the better of will be my ruin.

March 25th, 1757: I am conscious of my own indolence . . . I do here in the most solemn manner declare, that I will throw aside this my greatest enemy . . .

[1] *Ibid.*, p. 64.
[2] See *Letters from George III to Lord Bute* (1939), edited by Romney Sedgwick, from which all such letters are quoted. Mr Sedgwick's edition is a masterpiece of scholarship. To mention but one aspect: from internal evidence he has succeeded in dating some 330 undated letters.

September 25th, 1758: .... that incomprehensible indolence, in-
attention and heedlessness that reigns within me ...

And he says of his good resolutions: 'as many as I have made
I have regularly broke'; but adds a new one: 'I mean to
attempt to regain the many years I have fruitlessly spent.'

December 19th, 1758: ... through the negligence, if not the
wickedness of those around me in my earlier days, and since
perhaps through my own indolence of temper, I have not that
degree of knowledge and experience in business, one of my age
might reasonably have acquir'd ...
March 1760: ... my natural indolence ... has been encreas'd by
a kind of indifference to the world, owing to the number of bad
characters I daily see ...

By shifting the blame on to others, he tries to relieve the bitter
consciousness of failure: which is one source of that excessive
'attention to the sins of his neighbour' mentioned by Waldegrave. Indeed, George III's letters, both before and after his
accession are full of it: 'the great depravity of the age', 'the
wickedest age that ever was seen', 'a degenerate age', 'probity
and every other virtue absorb'd into vice, and dissipation'; etc.
'An ungrateful, wicked people' and individual statesmen alike
receive castigation (*in absentia*) from this very young Old Testa-
ment prophet. Pitt 'is the blackest of hearts', 'the most dis-
honourable of men', and plays 'an infamous and ungrateful
part'; Lord Temple, an 'ungrateful arrogant and self-sufficient
man'; Charles Townshend is 'a man void of every quality',
'the worst man that lives', 'vermin'; Henry Fox, a man of
'bad character', 'void of principles'; Lord Mansfield is 'but
half a man'; the Duke of Bedford's character 'contains nothing
but passion and absurdity'; etc. As for George II, the Prince felt
ashamed of being his grandson. And on 23 April 1760, half a
year before his accession, aged twenty-two he wrote to Bute:
'... as to honesty, I have already lived long enough to know
you are the only man who possesses that quality...'

In Bute he thought he had found the tutelary spirit who
would enable him to live up to his future high vocation. Here
are further excerpts from the Prince's letters to him:

July 1st, 1756: My friend is ... attack'd in the most cruel and horrid manner ... because he is my friend ... and because he is a friend to the bless'd liberties of his country and not to arbitary notions ...

By ... your friendship ... I have reap'd great advantage, but not the improvement I should if I had follow'd your advice ... I will exactly follow your advice, without which I shall inevitably sink.

March 25th, 1757: I am resolved ... to act the man in everything, to repeat whatever I am to say with spirit and not blushing and afraid as I have hitherto ... my conduct shall convince you that I am mortified at what I have done and that I despise myself ... I hope this will persuade you not to leave me when all is at stake, when nobody but you can stear me through this difficult, though glorious path.

In June 1757 Leicester House were alarmed by rumours of an alliance between the Duke of Newcastle and Henry Fox, and were ascribing fantastic schemes to the Duke of Cumberland. The Prince already saw himself compelled to meet force by force or to 'yield up the Crown',

for I would only accept it with the hopes of restoring my much beloved country to her antient state of liberty; of seeing her ... again famous for being the residence of true piety and virtue, I say if these hopes were lost, I should with an eye of pleasure look on retiring to some uninhabited cavern as this would prevent me from seeing the sufferings of my countrymen, and the total destruction of this Monarchy ...

August 20th, 1758: ... by ... attempting with vigour to restore religion and virtue when I mount the throne this great country will probably regain her antient state of lustre.

Was this a Prince nurtured in 'arbitrary notions', ambitious to make his own will prevail? or a man with a 'mission', striving after naively visionary aims? No doubt, since early childhood it must have been rammed into him, especially when he was being reproved, to what high station he was born; and disparaging comparisons are said to have been drawn between him and his younger brother. He grew up with a painful consciousness of his inadequacy: 'though I act wrong perhaps in

E

most things', he wrote on one occasion. Excessive demands on a child, complete with wholesome exhortations, are fit to reduce it to a state of hebetude from which it is not easy to recover. A great deal of the pattern of George III's behaviour throughout life can be traced back to his up-bringing.

He spent his young years cut off from intercourse with boys of his own age, till he himself ceased to desire it. Bubb Dodington notes in his *Diary* on 15 October 1752, that the Princess Dowager of Wales

> did not observe the Prince to take very particularly to anybody about him, but to his brother Edward, and she was glad of it, for the young people of quality were so ill-educated and so vicious, that they frightened her.

And so they did him for the rest of his life. Isolation by itself would be apt to suggest to a child that there was something wrong with those he had to shun; but this he was probably told in so many words. On 18 December 1753, Dodington records another talk with the Princess:

> I said, it was to be wished he could have more company. She seemed averse to the young people, from the excessive bad education they had, and from the bad examples they gave.

So the boy spent joyless years in a well-regulated nursery, the nearest approach to a concentration camp: lonely but never alone, constantly watched and discussed, never safe from the wisdom and goodness of the grown-ups; never with anyone on terms of equality, exalted yet oppressed by deferential adults. The silent, sullen anger noted by Waldegrave, was natural to one who could not hit back or speak freely his mind, as a child would among children: he could merely retire, and nurture his griefs and grievances—and this again he continued through life. On 3 May 1766, during a political crisis, he wrote to Bute: 'I can neither eat nor sleep, nothing pleases me but musing on my cruel situation.' Nor could he, always with adults, develop self-reliance: at nineteen he dreamt of reforming the nation, but his idea of acting the man was to repeat without blushing or fear what he had to say.

For the pious works which were 'to make this great nation happy' Bute's 'sagacious councils' were therefore indispensable. When in December 1758 Bute expressed doubts whether he should take office in the future reign, the Prince in a panic searched his own conscience:

> Perhaps it is the fear you have I shall not speak firmly enough to my Ministers, or that I shall be stagger'd if they say anything unexpected; as to the former I can with great certainty assure that they, nor no one else shall see a want of steadiness either in my manner of acting or speaking, and as to the latter, I may give fifty sort of puts off, till I have with you thoroughly consider'd what part will be proper to be taken . . .

George III adhered to this programme. On his grandfather's death he waited to hear from Bute what 'must be done'. When expecting Pitt at a critical juncture: 'I would wish to know what I had best say. . . .' With regard to measures or appointments: 'I have put that off till I hear my Dear Friend's opinion'; 'If this [is] agreeable to my D. Friend I will order it to day . . .'; 'I desire my D. Friend to consider what I have here wrote, if he is of a contrary opinion, I will with pleasure embrace it'. And when in November 1762 Bute declared he would retire on conclusion of peace:

> I had flattered myself [wrote the King] when peace was once established that my D. Friend would have assisted me in purging out corruption . . . ; . . . now . . . the Ministry remains compos'd of the most abandon'd men that ever had those offices; thus instead of reformation the Ministers being vicious this country will grow if possible worse; let me attack the irreligious, the covetous &c. as much as I please, that will be of no effect . . . Ministers being of that stamp . . .

Two years on the throne had worked little if any change in his ideas and language; nor did the next twenty. The same high claims on himself, and the same incapacity to meet real situations he was faced with: hence his continued dependence on others. By 1765 he saw that Bute could not help him, by the summer of 1766 he had written off Bute altogether. In the spring of 1765 he turned to the Duke of Cumberland, the bugbear of his young years: 'Dear Uncle, the very friendly and warm part you have taken has given me real satisfaction....'[1] And to Pitt, 'the blackest of hearts': 'My friend for so the part you have acted deserves of me....'[2] In July 1765 Cumberland formed for him the Rockingham Administration and presided over it a quasi-Viceroy; but a few months later Cumberland was dead. In July 1766 Chatham formed his Administration; but a few months later his health broke down completely. Still George III clung to him like a molusc (a molusc who never found his rock). 'Under a health so broken,' wrote Chatham, 'as renders at present application of mind totally impossible....'[3] After nearly two years of waiting for his recovery, the King still wrote: 'I think I have a right to insist on your remaining in my service.'[4] Next he clung to the ineffective Grafton who longed to be relieved of office; and when Grafton resigned, the King wrote to him on 27 January 1770:

> My heart is so full at the thought of your retiring from your situation that I think it best not to say more as I know the expressing it would give you pain.[5]

Then came North. Totally unequal to the difficulties of the American crisis, in letter after letter he begged the King to let him resign. Thus in March 1778:

> Lord North cannot conceive what can induce His Majesty, after so many proofs of Lord North's unfitness for his situation to determine at all events to keep him at the head of the Administration, though the almost certain consequences of His Majesty's resolution will be the ruin of his affairs, and though it can not ward off for a month that arrangement which His Majesty seems to apprehend.[6]

But the King would not hear of it. July 2nd, 1779: 'no man has a right to talk of leaving me at this hour....'[7] October 25th, 1780: he expects North 'will show that zeal for which he has been conspicuous from the hour of the Duke of Grafton's desertion.[8]

[1] Fortescue I, no. 74.   [2] *Ibid.*, no. 94.
[3] *Ibid.*, no. 538.   [4] Fortescue II, no. 669.   [5] Grafton MSS.
[6] Fortescue IV, no. 2241.   [7] *Ibid.*, no. 2696.   [8] Fortescue V, no. 3165.

George III's attitude to North conformed to the regular pattern of his behaviour. So did also the way in which after a while he turned against North in bitter disappointment. By the '70s the King spoke disparagingly of Bute and Chatham; and in time his imagination enabled him to remember how on the day of his accession he had given the slip to them both. A month after Grafton had resigned, George III wrote to him: 'I . . . see anew that the sincere regard and friendship I have for you is properly placed. . . .'[1] Somewhat later his resignation changed into 'desertion'. When North resigned: 'I ever did and ever shall look on you as a friend as well as a faithful servant. . . .'[2] But incensed at the new situation he soon started attacking North, and treated him niggardly and unfairly over his secret service accounts. George III's attachment was never deep: it was that of a drunken man to railings—mechanical rather than emotional. Egocentric and rigid, stunted in feelings, unable to adjust himself to events, flustered by sudden change, he could meet situations only in a negative manner, clinging to men and measures with disastrous obstinacy. But he himself mistook that defensive apparatus for courage, drive, and vigour, from which it was as far removed as anything could be. Of his own mental processes he sometimes gave discerning though embellished accounts. Thus to Bute in 1762: 'I . . . am apt to despise what I am not accustom'd to . . .' And on 2 March 1797, to the younger Pitt when criticizing the way measures were weakened in passing through Parliament:

My nature is quite different I never assent till I am convinced what is proposed is right, and then . . . I never allow that to be destroyed by after-thoughts which on all subjects tend to weaken never to strengthen the original proposal.[3]

In short: no after-thoughts, no reconsideration—only desperate, clinging perseverance.

Still it might be said: at least he broke through his indolence. Yes, indeed: from pathologically indolent he turned pathologically industrious—and never again could let off working;

---

[1] March 2nd, 1770, Grafton MSS.   [2] Fortescue V, no. 3593.
[3] Windsor MSS.

but there was little sense of values, no perspective, no detachment. There is a legend about a homunculus whose maker not knowing what to do with him, bid him count poppy-seed in a bag. That George III was doing with his own busy self. His innumerable letters which he copied in his own hand, or the long documents transcribed by him (he never employed an amanuensis till his eye-sight began to fail) contain some shrewd perceptions or remarks, evidence of 'very tolerable parts if . . . properly exercised'. But most of his letters merely repeat approvingly what some Minister, big or small, has suggested. 'Lord A. is very right. . .'; 'General B. has acted very properly . . .'; 'the minute of Cabinet meets with my fullest concurrence . . .'; 'Nothing can more deserve my approbation than'—whatever it was. But if a basic change is suggested, his obstinacy and prejudices appear. On 15 March 1778, in a letter to Lord North, he makes an unusual and startling admission:

> I will only add to put before your eyes my most inmost thoughts, that no advantage to this country nor personal danger can ever make me address myself for assistance either to Lord Chatham or any other branch of the Opposition. . . .[1]

As a rule he would sincerely assert, perhaps with somewhat excessive ostentation, that first and foremost he considered the good of the country. When told by Bute that it would be improper for him to marry Lady Sarah Lennox, he replied: 'the interest of my country ever shall be my first care, my own inclinations shall ever submit to it' (and he added: 'I should wish we could next summer . . . get some account of the various Princesses in Germany'—and he settled down to 'looking in the New Berlin Almanack for Princesses'). When considering withdrawal from the German War, he wrote (with a sidelong glance at the late King) about the superiority of his love 'to this my native country over any private interest of my own. . . .' He was 'a King of a free people'; 'I rely on the hearts of my subjects, the only true support of the Crown,' he wrote in November 1760. They will not desert him—

[1] Fortescue IV, no. 2221.

if they could be so ungrateful to me who love them beyond anything else in life, I should then I realy believe fall into the deepest
melancholy which would soon deprive me of the vexations of this
life.

The same note, of love for this country and trust that his
subjects would therefore stand by him, continues for almost
twenty years. But gradually other overtones begin to mix with
it. He had become the target of virulent attacks and unjust
suspicions which he deeply resented. Thus to Lord North on
7 March 1780: '...however I am treated I must love this
country.'[1] And to the Prince of Wales on 14 August 1780:

> The numberless trials and constant torments I meet with in
> public life, must certainly affect any man, and more poignantly
> me, as I have no other wish but to fulfill my various duties; the
> experience of now twenty years has convinced me that however
> long it may please the Almighty to extend my days, yet I have
> no reason to expect any diminution of my public anxiety; where
> am I therefore to turn for comfort, but into the bosom of my own
> family?[2]

And he appealed to his son, the future George IV, to connect
himself only with young men of respectable character, and by
his example help 'to restore this country to its former lustre'
—the old tune once more. And, in another letter:

> From your childhood I have ever said that I can only try to save
> my country, but it must be by the co-operation of my children
> only that I can effect it.[3]

In the 1780s there is a more than usually heavy crop of bitter
complaints about the age by one 'righteous overmuch': 'it has
been my lot to reign in the most profligate age', 'depravity of
such times as we live in', 'knavery and indolence perhaps I
might add the timidity of the times....' And then:

> I thank Heaven my morals and course of life have but little
> resembled those too prevalent in the present age, and certainly of
> all objects in this life the one I have most at heart, is to form my
> children that they may be useful examples and worthy of imita-
> tion...[4]

[1] Fortescue V, no. 2963.   [2] Windsor MSS.
[3] *Ibid.*   [4] Windsor MSS.

With the King's disappointments in country and son another note enters his letters. He warns the Prince—

> in other countries national pride makes the inhabitants wish to paint their Princes in the most favourable light, and consequently be silent on any indiscretion; but here most persons if not concerned in laying ungrounded blame, are ready to trumpet any speck they can find out.[1]

And he writes of the 'unalterable attachment' which his Electoral subjects have shown to their Princes. When George III went mad in 1788, he wanted to go back to Hanover. Deep down there was a good deal of the Hanoverian in him.

His insanity was a form of manic-depression. The first recorded fit in March 1765 was of short duration, though there may have been a slight relapse in May; and a year later he wrote to Bute—

> if I am to continue the life of agitation I have these three years, the next year there will be a Council [of] Regency to assist in that undertaking.

During the next twenty-three years he preserved his normal personality. The attack in 1788 lasted about half a year: the King was over fifty, and age rendered complete recovery more difficult. His self-control weakened and his irritability increased. He was conscious of a growing weakness. Yet there was something about him which more and more endeared him to the people. He was never popular with London society or the London mob; he was much beloved in the provinces—perhaps it was his deeper kindness, his real piety, and sincere wish to do good which evoked those feelings. These appear strikingly, for instance, in his own account of his journey to Portsmouth in 1788,[2] and in Fanny Burney's account of his progress through Wiltshire in 1789.[3] He was not a politician, and certainly not a statesman. But in things which he could judge without passion or preconceived ideas, there appears basic honesty and the will to do the right thing. I shall limit myself to two examples.

---

[1] *Ibid*.   [2] Windsor MSS.
[3] Fanny Burney, *Diary* (1905), vol. iv, pp. 310–11.

When in 1781 a new Provost was to be appointed at Eton, George III insisted on choosing a man 'whose literary tallents might make the appointment respectable ... for Eton should not be bestowed by favour, but merit'.[1] And when in 1787 a new Lord Lieutenant had to be chosen for Ireland, the King wrote to the younger Pitt about the necessity

> of looking out for the person most likely to conduct himself with temper, judgement, and an avowed resolution to avoid partiality and employ the favours he has to recommend to with the justice due to my service and to the public. ... When I have stated this Mr. Pitt must understand that I do not lean to any particular person ... when I state that a Lord Lieutenant should have no predelection but to advance the public good I should be ashamed to act in a contrary manner.[2]

I have given here a picture of George III as seen in his letters, 'warts and all'. What I have never been able to find is the man arrogating power to himself, the ambitious schemer out to dominate, the intriguer dealing in an underhand fashion with his Ministers; in short, any evidence for the stories circulated about him by very clever and eloquent contemporaries. He had a high, indeed an exaggerated, notion of royalty but in terms of mission and duties rather than of power; and trying to live up to this idealized concept, he made unreasonable demands on himself. Setting himself unattainable standards, he could never truly come to grips with reality: which condemned him to remain immature, permanency of inner conflict precluding growth. Aware of his inadequacy, he turned to others and expected them to enable him to realize his visionary program (this appears clearest in his relations with Bute); and he bitterly reproached them in his own mind, and blamed the age in which he lived, for his own inevitable failure. The tension between his notions and reality, and the resulting frustration, account to a high degree for his irritability, his deep-seated resentments, and his suppressed anger—for situations intolerable and disastrous for himself and others; and it may have been a contributory factor in his mental breakdowns. The desire to escape from

---

[1] Fortescue V, no. 3455.   [2] Windsor MSS.

that unbearable conflict repeatedly shows itself in thoughts of abdication which must not be deemed insincere because never acted upon (men of his type cannot renounce their treadmill). He himself did not understand the nature and depth of his tragedy; still less could others. There was therefore room for the growth of an injurious legend which made that heavy-burdened man a much maligned ruler; and which has long been accepted as history.

COUNTRY GENTLEMEN IN PARLIAMENT
1750—84
(Enid Muir Lecture, 1954)

IN COMMON parlance 'country gentlemen' can be equated with commoners possessed of armorial bearings and landed estates. but the term denotes also a way of life: Colonel John Selwyn was a country gentleman, but no one would describe his son George Augustus Selwyn, the wit, as such—a rustic touch is implied in the term. And there are outer rings to the indisputable core of any social group. At what point do men in the line of succession to a peerage merge back into the country gentry? And what about Irish peers, especially those with nothing Irish to them except their titles? In the mid-eighteenth-century House of Commons, excluding sons of British and Scottish peers on the one flank (an average of about 80) and those with 'no claim to arms' on the other (less than 30) we are left with about 80 per cent of the total. Yet in Parliament the term 'country gentleman' is never made to cover anything like four-fifths of the House; its character is residual: certain categories are subtracted, and not the same by everybody, and what is left is called country gentlemen.

There are elaborate lists in the Newcastle Papers[1] analysing the House of Commons as it emerged from the general election of 1754; and the results appeared of sufficient importance to Lord Hardwicke to copy them out for his own use.[2] A peculiar feature of these lists is that, having abstracted several professional groups—officers in the Army or Navy, placemen, mer-

---

[1] Add. MS. 33034, ff. 169–181. [2] Add. MS. 35876, f. 1.

chants and planters, and practising lawyers—they describe the rest as 'country gentlemen', including among them even courtesy lords. Roughly the category is meant to denote men without professional interests and in less obvious dependence on Administration. And in fact while in the professional groups only 25 are classed as against the Administration, 6 as 'doubtful', and 170 as 'for' (yielding an over-all majority of 139) among the country gentlemen the corresponding figures are 124, 28, and 162, leaving a narrow margin of 10.

Still, these 'country gentlemen' on both sides formed groups of a mixed character. Among the 162 friends of the Administration a great many, while they held no places or pensions, depended on Government support for their seats, and drew heavily on official patronage for their relatives, friends, and most of all their constituents; others were connected with peers or leading politicians in office; and it was a small and shrinking group of truly independent Whigs of the country gentleman type which differed basically from holders of places, commissions, or contracts. Similarly on the Opposition side a distinction should be drawn between mere 'outs' panting to get in, and the real independents; but of the 152 country gentlemen classed in 1754 as 'against' or 'doubtful', at least two-thirds were such independents.

The distinguishing mark of the country gentleman was disinterested independence: he should not be bound either to Administration or to any faction in the House, nor to a magnate in his constituency; if a knight of the shire, he should owe his election to the free choice of the gentlemen of the county, and if a borough Member, he should sit on his own interest: so as to be free to follow in the House the dictates of his own judgement and conscience. The monumental inscription in the church of St. Mary, Astbury, for Richard Wilbraham Bootle, M.P. for Chester 1761–90, reads: 'in Parliament his conduct was uniform in the support of his King and his country, in the respectable character of an independent country gentleman.' And a newspaper about 1780[1] described him as

---

[1] Some 25 years ago I picked up, I do not remember where, a book of newspaper cuttings headed 'Parliamentary Characters. From the *Public*

one of the most independent Members in the House. He attaches himself to no party, but is governed in the vote he gives, by the unbiased suggestions of his judgment, and the fair operation of that influence only which originates in the several arguments he hears. . . .

A similar attitude was taken by Lord Belasyse, son of the Earl Fauconberg, but in character and outlook a Yorkshire country gentleman, when he wrote to his father on 20 April 1769:[1]

> Last Saturday I sat twelve hours in the House of Commons without moving, with which I was well satisfied, as it gave me the power from the various arguments on both sides of determining clearly by my vote my opinion. . . .

And about William Drake, Member for his own pocket borough of Agmondesham during half a century, 1746–96, a newspaper wrote in the early 1780s:[2]

> . . . the late Earl Temple took great pains to enlist this gentleman under the banners of the Chatham party; but tho' Mr. Drake uniformly supported the measures of that great statesman, he could never be prevailed upon to form a partial connection which might deprive him of the constitutional freedom of sentiment which *ought* to be the characteristic of a British senator. . . .

Here was a conception of Parliamentary duties radically different from our own: such Members did not deem it a function of Parliament to provide a Government—the Government to them was the King's. Their duty was to support it as long as they honestly could, while judging of questions which came before them with the impartiality and disinterestedness of a jury.

Ledger, 1779; and *The English Chronicle*, 1780 and 1781.' The cuttings are not dated nor marked with the name of the newspaper. At the end there are some cuttings and papers referring to William Strahan, M.P., the printer, and his wife, which suggests that the book may have been started by him, and completed by someone connected with him.

[1] Fauconberg MSS. in the possession of Captain Malcom Wombwell, at Newburgh Priory, Yorks.

[2] G. Eland on 'The Shardeloes Muniments' in *Records of Buckinghamshire*, p. 294. The cutting can be dated approximately from internal evidence.

As late as 1793, R. B. Jenkinson (subsequently second Earl of Liverpool and Prime Minister) in a debate on Parliamentary Reform,[1] described 'the landed interest, or country gentlemen', as seldom ambitious of exercising Government functions.

> Indeed, it may, perhaps, be more proper that such persons should be employed in watching over the conduct of those who exercise the functions of executive Government, than that they should be employed in exercising those functions themselves.

In short, not partisans but judges; and therefore without party label.

Things were as yet somewhat different about 1750 when 'independent country gentlemen' was well-nigh a synonym for Tory. Between 1688 and 1714, Whigs and Tories alike had a Court and a country wing, and neither side being permanently in office, the balance of that double division was maintained. But during the Walpole-Pelham era, the Tories' forty years in the desert, the Court-minded among them, that is most of the nobility and the 'flesh-potters', drifted over to the 'Whigs', while among these the country gentlemen were being gradually absorbed by the Administration group. Thus the Tories were losing their Court, and the Whigs their country wing.

It would indeed have been wholly unnatural, and even priggish, for a supporter of Administration, by a self-denying ordinance to preclude himself from ever asking a service or favour of his friends in office. It was merely a question of how frequent and urgent such requests were, whether the favours were for the Member himself or for others, and what conclusions were drawn from their being granted or refused; most of all, how far the Member would go against his own convictions in his support of Administration. There were country Whigs of an older stamp: such as John Garth (born in 1701), M.P. for Devizes 1740–64, who in 1755 could speak of 'fifteen years' of 'constant and steady concurrence in support of the measures of Government in Parliament without any assistance or return';[2] Robert More (born in 1703). M.P. for Shrewsbury,

---

[1] *Parliament Register* (1793). vol. xxxv, p. 389.
[2] See 'Charles Garth and his Connexions', by L. B. Namier, in *The English Historical Review*, 1939.

who claimed to have been chosen 'without solicitation, without influence of Minister of State or Lord', in 'contempt for the influence of the greatest';[1] John White (born 1699), M.P. for East Retford, and John Page (born 1697), M.P. for Chichester, two strong independent characters. There were also some younger men, such as Brooke Forester (born 1717), M.P. for Much Wenlock, against whose name it was noted in a list of the House prepared for Lord Bute: 'Old Whig', 'by Whiggism attached to Lord Powis as the head of that party in Shropshire, but soliciting very few favours of Government'.[2] And in 1785 his son George, pointing to his own record during 30 years' service as Member for the borough, declared:[3]

> To preserve independence, to support the consequence of Parliament is I conceive the only means of protecting and preserving the rights and liberties of the people, and in order to do that, I will be independent myself whilst in your service.

Most of all, there was the group of Yorkshire Whigs, which hardly finds its counter-part in any other county. There was Cholmley Turner whose 'distinctive characteristic was a dislike of aristocratic domination in the county', and who with the support both of Whig and Tory gentlemen was 'able to show a certain coolness towards some of the greater magnates'. In 1734, and again in 1741, he would not accept nomination from the Whig peers but would await what he called 'the command of the gentlemen' in a county meeting; and 'in 1747, he could not be persuaded to stand again, giving as his reason that there were "so many noblemen" who were "thought to have the interest and direction of the county".[4] A similar attitude was adopted by his nephew: in 1768 when Rockingham wanted to recommend him as Parliamentary candidate for York, Charles Turner was reluctant to join the Rockingham Club (the society

---

[1] See *The Structure of Politics at the Accession of George III*, by L. B. Namier, vol. ii, p. 321.

[2] Add. MS. 38,333, f. 93.

[3] Forester MSS. in the possession of Lord Forester at Willey Park, Salop.

[4] See Cedric Collyer: 'The Rockinghams and Yorkshire Politics 1742–1761', *Thoresby Society Proceedings*, vol. xli, part 4 (1954), no. 99.

of York Whigs) since he did not wish to seem to owe his seat
in Parliament to aristocratic patronage.[1] Further, there were
the two Armytages, the three Lascelles, old William Aislabie,
and young Belasyse. And foremost among these Yorkshire
Whigs was George Savile, a close friend of Rockingham's, who
declined nomination by him either at Higham Ferrers or York,
but would only stand for the county, with the support of its
gentlemen;[2] who neither in 1765 nor in 1782 accepted office
from his friends, and during his many years in Parliament
probably never gave a factious vote; and in the list of the Commons drawn up for Shelburne in August 1782, after Rockingham's death, is placed in the residual column of 'country
gentlemen and persons unconnected'.[3]

Still, these independent country gentlemen were a mere trim-
ming to the Whigs in Administration or in Opposition, just as
a few peers were to the Tory country gentlemen. It is the
gradual identification of Tories with the independent country
gentlemen which empties the party name of specific contents.
There were men whom political managers hardly knew how to
label. Thomas Hill, M.P. for Shrewsbury, was nephew and
heir of Sir Richard Hill, a Tory of the reign of William III;
Thomas, who never held any office, entered Parliament under
the wing of Lord Powis, head of the Shropshire Whigs, and
with the support of Sir John Astley,[4] M.P. for Shropshire, an
arch-Tory; and he still appears as a Tory in Newcastle's list
of 1767[5] although he used to receive Newcastle's 'circular
letter', the eighteenth-century Parliamentary whip. There were
knights of the shire such as Robert Shaftoe in Durham or Lord

---

[1] Rockingham MSS. of Earl Fitzwilliam in the Sheffield Public Library
R1–588 and R78–32.   [2] Collyer, *loc. cit.*

[3] Dundas Papers in the National Library of Scotland.

[4] Sir John Astley to his agent, 28 February 1748/9: 'Jones, Mr. Hill of
tarn who i mett here i find intends to offer himself a candidate for
Shresbury att the next ellection in cace a vacancy happens you must
imeadetly aply to my tennants that are burggeses or any body i have any
interest in and desire the faviour of them to oblige me with their vote
and interest for Mr. Hill att the next ellection, I am your friend Sir
John Astley.' Attingham MSS. at the Salop R.O.

[5] Add. MS. 33001, ff. 357–363.

Downe in Yorkshire, members of Tory families returned 'on Whig principles' with the support of Administration, without losing that of the Tory gentry. In spite of such uncertainties, it is still possible about 1750 or 1760 to compile a list of so-called Tories; but hardly in 1770: and by the 1780s the designation of Tory is completely replaced in Parliament by that of country gentlemen, 'independent and unconnected'—men not owing suit to any political leader.

There is peculiar difficulty even about 1750 in the study of a nation-wide group without a leader or program or deeper coherence; especially as its members were seldom literary men addicted to writing, and very few collections even of their personal papers have survived. Bolingbroke belongs to the age of the 'pre-exile from office' Tories. Even William Wyndham is still a politician of the Queen Anne period (and his papers seem to have been destroyed). Nor have those of Sir Watkin Williams Wynn so far come to light; they are said to have perished in the fire at Wynnstay in 1858. After his death in 1749, the country gentlemen threw up no leader approximating him in stature. Influential among them, and sometimes acting as their spokesmen, were two men of curiously disparate mentality: Sir John Phillips, the Pembrokeshire squire, long suspected of Jacobitism, and Alderman William Beckford, the richest and most prominent of the West Indian planters, and in the 1760s leader of the Chathamite City radicals. Some papers of John Phillips are at the Welsh National Library at Aberystwyth but nothing of political importance; while those of William Beckford seem lost—the papers of his son, the much biographized author of *Vathek*, survive, but not of the father. In fact, I have so far found only one very rich collection of manuscripts of a Tory country gentleman: that of Sir Roger Newdigate of Arbury, Warwickshire, and Harefield, Middlesex.[1] His experience and the range of his activities were wider than that of most of his fellow country gentlemen. In 1742, he was returned for Middlesex in place of William Pulteney, created Earl of Bath; ousted in 1747, he was returned in 1750 for Oxford University, which he

[1] The Newdigate MSS., in the possession of Mr. Humphrey Fitzroy Newdegate, are now deposited at the County Record Office, Warwick.

F

continued to represent till 1784. He had thus a triple connexion within the group: with the metropolitan Tories, with the country gentlemen of his own region, such as the Mordaunts of Warwickshire or the Bagots of Staffordshire, and with the Tories of Oxford University.

The man from whom Newdigate first heard that he was being considered as candidate for Middlesex, and who in fact proposed him 'as a very proper person', was George Cooke, Member for the county from 1750 till his death in 1768, and in the sixties a well-known Chathamite. In April 1747, when Newdigate's colleague, Sir Hugh Smithson, subsequently 1st Duke of Northumberland, proposed to him to stand as joint candidates at the forthcoming election, Newdigate declined, considering it 'want of due deference to propose ourselves without the authority of a general meeting'.[1] It was etiquette among country gentlemen to await an expression of the sense of the county as declared in such a meeting; and even canvassing would be given a tentative form pending such approval. I adduce one example only, remarkable in that it refers to much less than a county: the borough of Cricklade, converted in 1782 (as punishment for 'most notorious bribery and corruption') into a quasi-rural constituency through the inclusion of five adjoining hundreds. In May 1782, Ambrose Goddard, successful candidate of the country gentlemen against a Herbert of Wilton in the Wiltshire election of 1772, wrote to Lord Shelburne:[2]

> The nature of my situation in the county lays me under the necessity of declining to take any active part in the Cricklade election at least 'till the sense of the gentlemen and freeholders is taken at a publick meeting which is appointed for that purpose the 27th inst. at Wooton Bassett, my conduct must depend upon the result of that meeting.

Information about Newdigate's life, both in the country and in London, can be gathered from his pocket diaries. In a minute

---

[1] Newdigate's canvass book of 1747, A. 260.
[2] Shelburne MSS. in the possession of the Marquis of Lansdowne at Bowood.

handwriting he entered each day's activities, visits, and inter-
views, and sometimes even lengthy reports. His social intercourse seems to have been mainly with other Tory country
gentlemen; besides calling on each other, they used to meet at
certain taverns, the Cocoa Tree, the Horn, the St. Albans, etc.;
and in 1755 there are accounts of several meetings convened
at the Horn Tavern to settle the line the 'minority', as he
calls them, should take over a bitterly contested election petition. These meetings are also recorded, in a derogatory manner,
by Walpole in his *Memoirs of the Reign of King George
II.*[1]

The Mitchell election, in which Robert Clive and John
Stephenson, supported by Thomas Scawen and Lord Sandwich,
had been returned against Richard Hussey and Simon Luttrell,
backed by the Edgcumbes and Boscawens, turned into a major
affair—and for once Lord Hardwicke and the Duke of Newcastle were taking opposite sides. 'The Court members being
pretty near equally divided made this election to be of more
than ordinary consequence; great sollicitations were us'd to the
minority', noted Newdigate on 24 February 1755. Lord
Lichfield and George Cooke supported Stephenson,[2] while
another Tory, William Northey, favoured Luttrell, and both
Stephenson and Luttrell, writes Newdigate, professed themselves 'inclin'd towards them [the minority], but were answer'd in general that they would attend if desir'd but would
vote according to the merits'. On the 28th, some 20 Tories,
led by John Phillips, voted with Fox, Sandwich's friend and his
manager in that affair, who thus carried his point against Newcastle. After this Horace Walpole has a story to tell, uncon-
firmed by anything either in the Newdigate or in the Newcastle
papers: Northey is alleged to have offered Newcastle that, if he
would give up the Oxfordshire election[3] and dismiss both Fox
and Pitt, the Tories 'would support him without asking a single
reward'. Northey, on the same side as Newcastle, may have
made approaches to him, but not on behalf of the whole group;

[1] Vol. ii, pp. 12–14.   [2] Add. MS. 35592, f. 162.
[3] Petition against Sir James Dashwood and Lord Wenman, returned
for Oxfordshire on the 'Old [the Tory] Interest'.

nor do the terms seem likely. But Newcastle, writes Walpole, would not pay that price for 'nothing but about a hundred of the silentest and most impotent votes' (as if anyone could have controlled the votes of a hundred independent country gentlemen).

This notable project being evaporated [continues Horace Walpole] the Tories were summoned on the 5th [should be the 4th] of March to the Horn Tavern. Fazakerley informed them that they were to take measures for acting in a body on the Mitchel election: he understood that it was...a contest for power between Newcastle and Fox:...that he for every reason should be for the former. Beckford told him, he did not understand there was any such contest:...were he obliged to name, he would prefer Mr. Fox. The meeting, equally unready at speeches and expedients, broke up in confusion.

And here is Newdigate's account:

A meeting 63 of the minority at the Horn Tavern to consider what measures to follow in regard to the two contending parties for power. About 40 members agreed as Michael[1] election not advanced far enough to judge of the merits to meet again on Friday.

On that day, 7 March, according to Walpole,

62 Tories met again at the Horn, where they agreed to secrecy, though they observed it not; and determined to vote, according to their several engagements, on previous questions, but not on the conclusive question in the Committee.

Similarly in Newdigate's account the meeting resolved

not to vote in the decisive question in the committee of Michael[1] election but to stay for the report.

On the 12th, the last day in Committee, Sandwich won by 158 votes to 141; the Tories, in accordance with their resolution, having almost all left before the division. But eight remained

---

[1] According to Tonkin's MS. Parochial History, compiled between 1700 and 1730 and now at the Royal Institution of Cornwall, the original name of the borough was 'Myshell, Mitchell or Modishole,...and nowhere St. Michael till of late, to which denomination it has no pretence but vulgar error'.

and were equally divided; their names are given in Admiral Boscawen's report to Newcastle[1]—on the Sandwich-Fox side: Curzon, Barrow, Hanger, and Cooke; against: Sir William Meredith, Sir Armine Wodehouse, Grosvenor, and Sturt. Some twelve years later, Meredith and Barrow were Rockinghams, and Cooke a Chathamite; and in 1773 it was Meredith who moved to abolish in the Universities the subscription to the 39 Articles, a motion of which Newdigate as member for Oxford University was one of the strongest opponents.

Next, on 24 March, Walpole writes:

> The morning of the report, the Tories met again at the Horn, and here took the shameless resolution of cancelling all their engagements, in order to defeat Fox. . . .

And he goes on to inveigh against 'the wretched remnant of the Tories' crowning 'their profligacy with breach of promises'.

> Only twelve of them stood to their engagements; the Duke of Newcastle, assisted by the deserters, ejected Lord Sandwich's members, by 207 to 183; the House, by a most unusual proceeding, and indeed by an absurd power, as the merits are only discussed in the Committee, setting aside what in a Committee they had decided.

But here is Newdigate's account:

> At eleven to the Horn Tavern. 68 met. Sir J. Philips propos'd to disappoint both parties by voting against both and making it a void election. Sir Charles Mordaunt, Mr. Northey, Mr. Crowle, R[oger] N[ewdigate], Mr. Bertie, against it. Nothing in the evidence to warrant it. Mr. Beckford for it. Came away without any joint resolution.

In the House, Phillips

> moved to make it a void election by rejecting the petition too. Oppos'd by Northey, R[oger] N[ewdigate], and Sir Robert Long. Question Ays 201. Nos 178. These questions were carried by the bulk of the minority who were clear from engagements to either side and determin'd only upon the merits which were very strong with the petitioners.

[1] Add. MS. 32853, f. 260.

What, then, emerges from these reports? Some Tories were engaged on either side; a few political leaders such as Phillips, Beckford, and Fazakerley, thought of political manœuvres; but the great body of independent country gentlemen deemed it proper to judge the case on its merits. Their behaviour was highly respectable but politically ineffective.

The next meetings of the country gentlemen recounted by Newdigate deal with the projected inquiries into the loss of Minorca and the reverses in America at the beginning of the Seven Years' War. Here is the entry of 14 January 1757:

> Mr. [George] Townsend's met his brother Charles, Lord Pulteney, Mr. Vaughan, Sir J. Phillips, Cornwall, Sir Ch. Mordaunt, Sir A. Wodehouse, Mr. Bagot, Mr. Fazakerley, Mr. Hanger, Moreton, W. Harvey, Mr. Ward, Ad[miral] Vernon, Affleck, Vyner, Beckford, Northey, Sir R. N.[1]
>
> G. Townsend said he had in the H[ouse] declared he would move an enquiry which made him desire the meeting, that Mr. Pitt and the Administration would support and assist with papers, etc., but desired to be excused appearing at this meeting for fear of offence somewhere but heartily desired an enquiry—consulted what method proper, by secret, select or committee of the whole House? Sir J. Phillips was for the last. Ch. Townsend the only placeman there. P. the questions must be divided—that for America to go as far as the Peace of Aix-la-Chapelle and in a select committee because facts must be reported and printed as in that for the Army. But that Minorca would be best in a Committee of the whole House because it lay in smaller compass. Resolved to leave it to the gentlemen in administration to consider what expedient.

And on 1 February:

> Walked to Mr. Townsend's, met many of the same gentlemen as before. Mr. Townsend said he had a commission from Mr Pitt to say that he would support the enquiry in the House. Desired questions might be settled by the gentlemen. A good deal of conversation and that matter but not the questions were settled.

Thus Pitt is seen sending messages to the Tory country gentlemen though excusing himself from appearing personally 'for

[1] Barring the Townshends, Pulteney, and Vaughan, all were Tories.

fear of offence somewhere'—presumably to George II. The
country gentlemen desired to leave the decision 'to the gentlemen in Administration', and Pitt to them. And nothing was
settled.

About the transactions concerning the Qualification Bill,[1]
January–March 1760, we learn from the Newcastle papers only
—Newdigate at that time was serving with the militia. The
Duke wrote to Hardwicke on 26 January 1760:[2]

> I saw Mr. Pitt . . . who told me Sir John Phillips and Alderman
> Beckford had been with him from the *country gentlemen*; and
> tell him they intended to bring in the Bill to oblige every Member
> to swear to his qualification at the table of the House of Commons
> . . . they wish'd the Administration would not oppose it in con-
> sideration of the assistance, which *they* had given to the King's
> measures. Mr. Pitt said he was for it *in opinion*; and should de-
> clare for it.

Thus Phillips and Beckford are seen acting for the country
gentlemen; and the measure demanded was in line with the
perennial motions against placemen—it might have excluded
some hard-working civil servants and humbler politicians, and
a few bankrupt parasites, but rich contractors, equally loathed
by the country gentlemen, could undoubtedly have produced
and maintained their qualification. Attempts further to tighten
up the provisions of the Bill were made, arousing opposition.
Lord Egmont in the debate on 5 March called it a 'wicked
and weak bill' whose principle was wrong and 'leading to an
aristocracy'. It certainly had a class character. All that finally
reached the Statute Book (33 George II c. 20) was that each
Member had to take an oath at the Bar of the House that he
possessed the qualification, and to deliver a schedule of his
property.

On 2 November 1762, Newcastle, preparing for the battle
with Bute and Fox over the Preliminaries of Peace, wrote about
a conversation with the Duke of Cumberland at Windsor
Lodge:[3]

---

[1] By 9 Anne c. 5, county members had to possess landed property worth
£600 p.a., and borough members £300 p.a.
[2] Add. MS. 32901, f. 479.   [3] Add. MS. 32944, ff. 212–3.

The Duke gave me some comfortable accounts of Parliament; that my Lord Grosvenor and his brother had declared for us; ... that Sir Walter Blackett and Mr. Noel had declared for us ... that His Royal Highness had heard that Sir Charles Mordaunt and several of the Tories would not support this Administration ....

Legge had similar news about his Tory friends, 'honest sensible men and by much the best of the corps'. But the Duke of Devonshire remarked on 30 November[1] that he did not think 'it will come to anything'—wherein he was right.

About the same time, Roger Newdigate wrote:[2]

I can't answer your Qu. what my party is? I am only sure it is neither C[um]b[erlan]d nor Pelham, landed men must love peace, men proscribed and abus'd for 50 years together be presented with fools caps if they make ladders for tyrant Whigs to mount by, I like the King and shall be with his Ministers as long as I think an honest man ought and believe it best not to lose the country gentleman in the courtier.

Note: 'landed men must love peace'—presumably because of the Land Tax. Next, expressions of dislike of the Whigs who had proscribed them so long. But did he desire office? He thought 'it best not to lose the country gentleman in the courtier'.

Another Tory meeting, on 24 February 1763, is reported both in Newdigate's diary and in the Newcastle MSS.[3] Newdigate writes in his pocket diary:

Mr. Blackstone and Mr. Ward came to breakfast. Walk'd to the Cocoa Tree—a meeting—walk'd to Sir Francis Dashwood's Chancellor of the Exchequer to hear the estimates read—Sir Charles Mordaunt, Sir J. Phillips and self objected to the mode of 50 instead of 40s[4]—to the House ...

---

[1] Add. MS. 32945, f. 149.

[2] On a scrap of paper which I found slipped into a document of 25 November 1762, Newdigate MS. B.2311.

[3] Add. MS. 32947, ff. 92–3. About that meeting see also *Bedford Correspondence*, vol. iii, pages 210–11, and *Letters from George III to Lord Bute*, ed. by Romney Sedgwick, p. 191, no. 270.

[4] The figures 50 and 40 refer to the strength of infantry companies.

The paper in the Newcastle MSS. reports that the meeting consisted 'of 60 or 70 persons, Tories and others', and quotes Sir Charles Mordaunt as saying that he

> loved the King; had no suspicion relating to him; but the increase of corps was an increase of expence.

Similarly Newdigate, John Phillips, Eliab Harvey, and Dr. Blackstone opposed the larger army establishment.

In my book *England in the Age of the American Revolution* I compiled a list of 'Tories returned to Parliament at the general election of 1761', 105 for English,[1] and nine for Welsh constituencies. Only four were sons of peers: Thomas Harley, Robert Lee, Thomas Howard, and John Ward. The remaining 110 were country gentlemen. During the next few years disintegration set in among them: a few turned courtiers under Bute, some joined the Rockinghams, another batch joined Chatham in 1766. Of the Tories returned in 1761, 31 died before the end of that Parliament, and only half of the original 114 re-entered Parliament in 1768. Many of their successors were no less independent; but the grievance of their exile-from-office period, imaginary in men who did not desire office, was gone. Henceforth their independence was even more obvious, and even more colourless. There was no longer a group—neither meetings nor spokesmen. For Parliamentary divisions after 1766, I therefore take as test of the vote of the country gentlemen the English knights of the shire, subtracting sons of peers, as mostly connected with Court.

For the crucial division on General Warrants, on 18 February 1764, we have the names of 220 Members who voted in the minority, and of 81 absent; and the number, though not the names, of the majority: 234. As there were two vacancies, the names of 20 members, presumably absent, are still lacking to complete the count. Of the original 114 Tories, 104 were still in Parliament. Of these 41 voted with the Opposition, and 14 are known to have been absent. Of the 20 unplaced Members,

[1] pp. 487–90. From that list I would now delete Simeon Stuart, M.P., for Hampshire, and add to it Thomas Noel, M.P. for Rutland: the total remains the same.

at least four have to be added to the absent Tories,[1] which leaves 45 voting with the Administration, a mere majority of four on its side. But three days later, on 21 February, Newdigate notes in his diary: 'Mr. Grenville's levy [levée] where I met most of the country gentlemen by agreement.' There is nothing more about it in the Newdigate papers, nor in those of Grenville, printed or unpublished. Country gentlemen, as a rule, did not attend Ministers' levées. Did perhaps Newdigate merely mean a majority of those he consorted with? So much is certain: that most of those who voted against General Warrants were not in formed opposition to the Grenville Administration, which, bent on peace and economies, gave the country gentlemen reasonably cheap government.

At the next important division, over the Repeal of the Stamp Act, on 21 February 1766, 93 of the original 114 Tories were still in Parliament: 39 voted with the Opposition. We have no lists either of those absent or of the majority; but the total number of absents was 116 which, on a pro rata basis, would yield 20 for the Tories. If so, 34 voted for the Repeal.

For the division of 17 February 1767, on the question of reducing the land tax from four to three shillings, I use the English knights of the shire for my test. The vast majority of the county members voted for the reduction: 52 against 9, while 19 were absent. Of the 9 who voted with the Administration, 5 were sons of peers sitting on an aristocratic interest and not as the choice of the country gentlemen.

Over the expulsion of Wilkes on 3 February 1769, there is an almost equal division among the knights of the shire: 24 voted with the Court, 23 against, while 33 did not vote. But if we abstract the sons of peers, we get 14 voting with the Court and 21 with the Opposition— a 3:2 majority against Administration.

Over the American Revolution, as over the Stamp Act, the feeling of a majority of country gentlemen was probably against the Colonies. Some Members previously inclined to side with the Opposition—for instance Thomas Grosvenor, or even Rocking-

---

[1] 3 or 4 on a pro rata basis, but men who were politically independent are more likely to have been absent without being mentioned as such in the lists of absents on either side.

hams, such as Lord Belasyse and Edwin Lascelles, henceforth tended to vote with the Government.

From the book of cuttings about Members, 1779–81, I pick out six original Tories who voted with the Administration:

Sir William Codrington (Tewkesbury): 'Has much the appearance of being an independent man. He always gives his vote with the Ministry.'[1]

Assheton Curzon (Clitheroe): '. . . a man of Tory principles, votes with Ministry, but sometimes affects to be conscientious, by quitting the House when the Minister's question is not agreeable to him.'

William Drake, snr. (Agmondesham): 'A respectable independent gentleman, a Tory in principle, and a great admirer of Lord North, votes with the Ministry in general, but sometimes in the Minority.'[2]

Thomas Grosvenor (Chester): '. . . a staunch Tory, and votes constantly with Government, and procures places for his constituents.'

Sir Roger Newdigate (Oxford University): 'A rank Tory, with an affectation of honesty and independence.'

Clement Tudway (Wells): 'Appears an independent man, although he votes constantly with the Ministry.'

The writer's sympathies are clearly with the Opposition; yet he does not question the honesty of any one of these Tory Members as he does in many other cases.

And here are five other original Tories:

Richard Wilbraham Bootle (Chester): 'A very honest man, and votes on both sides, according to his opinion, but oftener with Opposition than with the Ministry.'

Richard Milles (Canterbury): 'A man of fair, respectable character. He generally votes with Opposition.'

Thomas Noel (Rutlandshire): 'A very old Member of Parliament, and attends but very seldom. He is an independent man, and inclined to the Minority.'

John Parker (Devonshire): 'Usually known by the name of

---

[1] This statement is not borne out by extant division lists.

[2] Another newspaper describes him as uniformly supporting the measures of Chatham; see above, page 61.

Devonshire Parker, a very honest, sensible, independent, man, and votes in Opposition.'

Humphrey Sturt (Dorsetshire): 'With many peculiarities, is a man of inviolable integrity and a good heart. He supports his character as one of the country members, with great independency and respect, and votes with Opposition.'

In the two most significant divisions of the next two years, the vote of the country gentlemen went heavily against the Government. Dunning's motion of 6 April 1780, 'that the influence of the Crown has increased, is increasing, and ought to be diminished', could not fail to secure their support: although giving old grievances a new turn, it summed up in one striking sentence the country party's inveterate dislike of Government interference in the constituencies, and its objection to placemen and contractors in the House. Of the 80 knights of the shire, 70 voted: 9 with the Court and 61 against. But if we eliminate the sons of peers, the division becomes even more striking: 5 *v.* 55, that is a 11 : 1 against the Court. Similarly when the vote of no confidence in North's government was moved on 15 March 1782, of the country gentlemen representing shires 7 voted with the Government and 51 against: a 7 : 1 majority for the Opposition.

What, then, broadly speaking, was the influence and part of the country gentlemen in Parliament? Their votes being determined by individual convictions, and not by pursuits or manœuvres of party, on ordinary problems they were, as a rule, so much divided as roughly to cancel out each other. But whenever a strong movement of public opinion produced some degree of unity among them, their weight would make itself felt. Faced by the American crisis, they inclined to assert authority and were averse to giving in to rebellion, and their feeling of fairness to themselves told them that the Americans should be made to shoulder part of the burden of taxation. On the other hand, the more far-sighted among them saw that the struggle would be long and expensive and lead nowhere, and these, besides a small group of pro-Americans, were opposed to the war. Saratoga did not convince the anti-Americans; if anything it stiffened their attitude. But Yorktown produced a complete swing over among them, as in public opinion at large, against the American war and the North Administration. The leader of that tiny group of country gentlemen who on 15 March 1782, still voted against the no-confidence motion, Thomas Grosvenor, after the division told North that they could not support him any longer. And this was the end.

During the confusion over the dismissal of the Coalition, at the end of 1783, a body of country gentlemen reconstituted itself in the so-called St. Alban's Tavern group. Their dislike of factious politics combined with the wish to avoid a dissolution and general election. They tried to reconcile Pitt and Fox, and make them unite in a King's Government on a national basis. Lord Sydney, Pitt's Home Secretary, referred to them, in a letter of 17 February 1784, as 'the foolish Committee at the St. Albans'[1]; and Pitt himself wrote that day to the Duke of Rutland: 'The *independents* are indefatigable for coalition, but as ineffectual as ever.'[2] Any experienced political observer could have told them before hand: 'I do not think that it will come to anything.'

---

[1] See *Hist. MSS. Comm.*, Report 14, Appdx. Part I, *Rutland MSS.*, III, 75.

[2] See John Duke of Rutland, *Correspondence between Mr Pitt and Charles Duke of Rutland* (1890), p. 7.

6

THE LONG PARLIAMENT

Mr. Brunton and Mr. Pennington, in their study of the composition of the Long Parliament,[1] have set out to examine what differences in origin, social standing, education or profession can be traced between the Royalists and those who took the side of Parliament; and between the 'original members' of the Long Parliament, that is, those elected before August 1642, the 'Recruiters', elected in or after 1645 to replace 'disabled' Royalists, and members of the 'Rump'. And this is their conclusion:

> We found that the Royalist and Parliamentarian, so far as can be judged from the members of the Long Parliament, were very much the same; and the greater and lesser gentry were not on different sides; that it made no difference whether a member belonged to an 'old' or to a 'new' family; that merchants and lawyers were to be found on both sides ... The only significant difference seems to have been that the Royalists were on average ten years younger, and more often belonged to families with a parliamentary history.

On the other hand, regional differences were marked: and class or economic interest was but one, indirect, and by no means the most important, factor in determining the intellectual 'climate' of 'country' or group.

In 1641–2 the House consisted of 507 Members; and with those returned at by-elections before the outbreak of the Civil War, there were 552 'original' Members. But there was no

[1] *Members of the Long Parliament*, by D. Brunton and D. H. Pennington (Allen and Unwin, 21s.).

sharp division into two parties at the outset—nine-tenths of the House were then united in opposition to the existing régime. Of 538 Members who can be classified in the light of subsequent events, 236 were Royalists and 302 Parliamentarians. The landed interest was dominant in the House (as it was in 1740, and even in 1840); and it was flanked by the lawyers and the merchants, who were regarded as distinct groups, and (as also a century later) 'were added collectively to Committees concerned with their professional interests'. Yet in education, and usually in origin, the lawyers and the country gentlemen were indistinguishable; and also land and trade were closely connected—landowners would engage in trade and speculation, apprentice a younger son to a City firm, and conclude 'City marriages', while merchants invested in land and founded county families.

There was a slight preponderance of Royalists among the sons of peers in the House of 1640–2—due, no doubt, to their closer connexion with the Court. But the number of baronets and knights, and also of practising lawyers, of whom there were 75 among the 'original' Members, was roughly proportionate to the strength of the two sides in the House. It is more difficult to define, and therefore to count, merchants: 'including some small local men but excluding those who, despite interests in trading companies, had no mercantile establishment of their own', the total amounted to 45–50. Among these ten Londoners were, with one single exception, on the Parliamentary side: a regional group which finds its counterpart in the rest of Middlesex, solidly Parliamentarian, and in Essex, with one Royalist among its eight Members. Among the merchants returned by provincial towns in which they traded, there was a considerable majority, but nowhere a solid body, of anti-Royalists; and a closer examination of their political allegiance 'does not suggest that commercial interests were in themselves enough to bring a Member to the Parliamentary side'.

The regional distribution of the two parties is striking: the East (Essex, Herts., Cambs., Hunts., Suffolk, Norfolk, and Lincs.) and the South-East (Hants., Sussex, Middx., Surrey, Kent, and the Cinque Ports) returned 42 Royalists and 125

Parliamentarians, that is, a three-to-one majority for Parliament; the West (Wales, the four Border counties, and Worcs.) and the North (Yorks., Lancs., and three Northern counties—Durham was as yet unrepresented) returned 80 Royalists and 48 Parliamentarians—a five-to-three majority for the King. In the Midlands there was a substantial majority for Parliament, while in the South-West the two parties were almost equally balanced (of its three biggest county representations Cornwall was predominantly Royalist, Wiltshire Parliamentary, and Devon equally divided). To explain that formation, region by region, will be the task of further, much more detailed, research which the authors of this book had necessarily to eschew. As they rightly remark, the greatest obstacle in the historian's work is 'his inability to penetrate men's minds'; and whatever he can attempt in that direction requires very careful study of documents and correspondence which cannot be undertaken by two scholars on a nation-wide scale. Some groups will probably be found to have earlier foundations; some may be due to an outstanding personality in the district; and religion will probably prove the most important single factor. In religion itself a sociological component is almost invariably present, but it counts for far less in times of intense religious feeling than in periods of comparative indifference. It is the tendency to read history back (beside the 'materialistic conception') which has produced neat and untrue class theories about the Puritan revolution. Snobbery or, to use a milder expression, social considerations, and material interests did not determine men's religious allegiance in that era.

The outstanding difference between the two sides noted by the authors concerns age and parliamentary experience, two inter-connected aspects.

> The median ages of the two parties for the whole country have been worked out at 36 and 47 respectively—a very large difference.

I would call it staggering. It takes a lot to produce a difference in the median for groups of two to three hundred. The median of the entire House of 1640 must have been about 42; of the Parliaments of 1761 and 1818 it was above 43; and of that of

1945, 46, that of the Conservatives and Labour being the same (though not the distribution between age groups). In every region the Royalists were younger men than the Parliamentarians. There were 172 Parliamentarians against 92 Royalists among those born before 1600, *i.e.*, an almost two-to-one majority for Parliament among men above 40; a slight Parliamentary preponderance in the next decade; and 72 Royalists against 37 Parliamentarians among those born in 1610 or after, *i.e.*, nearly a two-to-one Royalist majority among those of 30 or below. Here is a fact which, when explained, may throw new light on the period—had an anti-Puritan reaction set in among the young by the time the Long Parliament was meeting? Were they getting sick of their stern, austere parents? But before drawing any such conclusion it would be necessary to ascertain the politics of the sons of the elderly Puritan Members, and of the fathers of the young Royalists—which might, indeed, prove an arduous task.

The age median of the Recruiters is not given, only their distribution between age groups. They were even younger than the Royalists: a new generation on the Puritan side. Pamphleteers at a later date

> developed the idea that the Recruiters were obscure townsmen or upstart colonels. It is true that the number of officers among them was large ... Including militia regiments roughly a quarter of the Recruiters held or had held the rank of colonel or a higher one ... A few obscure townsmen who had won success in the Army were elected for their local boroughs; a few richer townsmen who could in any case have expected election held office in militia regiments. But the majority of the colonels in Parliament were gentry ... and they included many strong opponents of the Army's political domination.

Similarly the 'huge influx of Independents and irreconcilables' was a fear before the event, and a legend after: 'many prominent and extreme Independents were Recruiters', but 'Independency was only just perceptibly stronger among the new members than among the old'. The last few inches make a man abnormally tall or small; and statistical statements based on mere impressions are apt to generalize from marginal facts. It

G

is a great merit of this book that it establishes true perspective in place of subjective impressions.

While a general survey is given of the entire country, the representation of two regions, the East and the South-West, has been analysed in greater detail. The chapter on 'The Eastern Association' is by Mr. Brunton, who died in a road accident on 16 May 1952; it is replete with interesting information which, however, has not undergone the last pruning that only the author can give to his work: and writers of mass biography, not to tax unduly the absorptive capacity of the reader, should eschew giving detail which is irrelevant or distantly related to their theme. One feature brought out by Mr. Brunton, modifying the general contention of the book (p. 7) that 'the most important qualification was . . . to belong to the locality', is the extreme electoral mobility of certain families, especially when backed by Court influence. Thus the Hattons, between 1580 and 1680, sat for fifteen constituencies in twelve counties extending from Lancashire to Wiltshire and Kent; the Jermyns sat for eleven constituencies in nine counties extending from Lancashire to Cornwall and Suffolk; while the Gawdys sat on their own interest for seven constituencies in Norfolk and Suffolk: Norfolk itself, Norwich, King's Lynn, and Thetford, Dunwich, Eye, and Sudbury. Such wanderings would hardly have been possible about 1760; it would have meant encroaching on too many firmly established family preserves, and was attempted by one family only of Irish interlopers.

Mr. Pennington's carefully constructed chapter on the South-West, beside illustrating some of the basic theses of the book, contains much valuable material on the family history of that region. There is remarkable continuity in the Parliamentary history of Cornwall, and most of the leading families of the eighteenth century go back, often in the same houses, to Tudor days, or even to the Middle Ages. To name a few: the Godolphins of Godolphin, the Edgcumbes of Mount Edgcumbe, the Eliots of Port Eliot, or the Rashleighs of Menabilly near Fowey (these last were 'a local ship-owning and trading family which transformed themselves by easy stages into a landed one'). Indeed, Cornwall, with its 21 boroughs and long traditions, would

be an unequalled field for the Parliamentary historian, had not
several of its richest collections of manuscripts suffered destruction. It is only when he tries to reach the sources of Parliamentary history that he realizes how fast his materials are disappear-
ing. Probably not even half remains now of what there was two
or three generations ago.

7

THE NORTH-EAST IN THE EIGHTEENTH CENTURY

FIVE GREAT sources of wealth have gone to build up the English aristocracy and landed gentry: the earliest was agriculture; next, mines and metal, foremost coal and iron, copper, lead, and tin; third, in point of time, came urban rents; in certain periods, fortunes made in the King's service or in the law; and in all periods, City fortunes and 'City marriages'.[1] If the History of Parliament based on its personnel, that is, on a highly representative cross-section of the 'political nation', succeeds in supplying data for even approximate outlines of that growth, we shall have written an important chapter of English social history. But prerequisite to such a survey are hundreds of well-documented monographs about individuals, families, or regions.

Professor Hughes's new book, *North Country Life in the Eighteenth Century*, bearing the sub-title 'The North East, 1700–1750', proves how much can be achieved by a thorough search for local sources and a patient analysis of the materials they yield. His work is based primarily on the manuscripts of a number of Northumbrian and Durham families: Cotesworth and Ellison, Bowes, Liddell, Ridley, etc.; and it shows what

---

[1] Some would name 'sugar'—the West Indian plantations—as a sixth source. I doubt whether it can rank with the others. The West Indians cut a great figure in London society, but I suppose on closer inquiry it will be found that the coal mines, say of Northumberland, Co. Durham, and Yorkshire alone, added greater numbers to Debrett and Burke than all the treasure islands of the Caribbean.

amazingly rich sources can be tapped by breaking away from the traditional concentration on metropolitan politics and life, and on the activities of leading statesmen. Of the families which appear in Professor Hughes's book, some were already country gentry at the opening of the eighteenth century, others were founded by self-made men; but the spectacular rise of them all was bound up with developments which transformed the social and economic character of the North-East.

The sixteenth century found the Border country 'much in poverty and penury', the seventeenth was a period of disasters: the Scottish military occupation, 1639–41, and sequestrations and confiscations by the victorious Roundheads; Royalists and Roman Catholics being specially numerous in the feudal North. By 1715, there was scarcely a Roman Catholic gentleman in Northumberland whose estates were not heavily mortgaged— 'indeed, one begins to suspect,' writes Hughes, 'that the last civil war in England, the Jacobite Fifteen, was due, in no small degree, to the desperate poverty of the northern Catholic gentry,' and that the rising was the occasion rather than the cause of the elimination of many old families. Their estates were bought by new men who had made their money in trade, or by merchant families, like the Liddells, who had already entered the ranks of the gentry; and in wealth both outstripped by far their predecessors. Owing to the greatly retarded social and political development of the North, the rise of the landed gentry, 'the most notable social phenomenon in the making of Modern England', occurred here a century and a half later than in most of the country, while the Industrial Revolution occurred much earlier: Newcastle is 'the centre of what is in all probability the oldest industrial region' of England. Thus the great age of the gentry in those counties was made possible by the profits derived from trade, mainly coal mining and satellite enterprises: which produced 'a greater fusion of landed and merchant interest in these parts than elsewhere.' Yeomen grew into merchants, and merchants into gentry; and throughout the eighteenth century the new northern gentry, the Liddells, Carrs, Ellisons, Ridleys, and Blacketts, for example, continued to intermarry with local merchant families.

The most important single collection of papers used by Professor Hughes is that of William Cotesworth, a name little known hitherto owing to the early failure of the family in the male line. Described by Hughes as the prototype of the new rising men, Cotesworth was a yeoman's son; born *c.* 1670, in Teesdale, he was apprenticed to a mercer and tallow-chandler of Gateshead; formed a partnership with his late master's son; and for more than twenty years the tallow and candle business constituted his main trading interest: he worked for the London wholesale market, and for local consumption, especially in the coal- and lead-mines. 'Some idea of . . . the candle-trade alone may be gained from Cotesworth's accounts with Sir Henry Liddell for a single year, 1716—£237 17s. 1½d. for the collieries, £6 10s. 7d. "for the house".' But by 1705, Cotesworth was engaged in a highly miscellaneous trade, 'exporting grindstones, lead, glass bottles, and later salt to Holland, Hamburg, and the Baltic ports, and importing flax, hemp, madder, and whalebone in return'; and buying indigo, dyestuffs, hops, sugar, and tobacco in the London market: as he put it himself, he traded 'in anything he could gain by'. Next he turned to a form of transport business anticipating railways: in 1705 he

> obtained from the dean and chapter of Durham a lease, jointly with Dean Montague himself, of exclusive way-leave rights for a term of twenty years with leave to build a wagon-way for the carriage of coals and grindstones to Jarrow staith from half a dozen adjoining parishes. He came to specialize in obtaining way-leave rights of this kind, thereby threatening to hold to ransom coal-owners of the neighbouring hinterland.

By 1710 he himself held shares in various collieries; and next started buying up salt-pans: he could use in them small coal unfit for the London market. By 1715 he claimed to be the biggest salt proprietor in the country, paying over £1,000 a year in duties, and holding the contract for supplying the Victualling Office. But even more important became his coal interests. In 1711, he negotiated for his brother-in-law, Alderman Ramsay, the purchase of Gateshead and Whickham, 'once reputed to be the richest coal-bearing manors in the country'; and on

Ramsay's death, in 1716, that estate passed to Cotesworth. Moreover, since 1710 he had been the moving spirit and paid secretary of a powerful coal cartel or 'Regulation'.

The coal-trade is naturally given pride of place in Professor Hughes's book, of which about one-fourth is taken up by the chapter specifically dealing with it. Its story is told in concrete terms: as lived by a representative group of men. First there is the development and technique of coal-mining, and its finance; and next the great problem of marketing the coal. At times it was, in the words of one deeply concerned in it, 'a fighting trade run in a tempestuous shallow stream'. Yet another one wrote:

> There will always be something to fight about in the coal-trade though for all that, there's few that gets into the trade that is willing for to [go?] out, the profit is so great.

And W. B. Bowes, one of the leading Durham coal-owners, wrote in 1720: 'The colliery never made less than £1,500 per annum these last thirty years past, and made me last year £2,500.'

The question of 'way-leaves' was as burning a problem in those early decades of the eighteenth century as that of canals became in its second half: their course often determined what mines could be worked with profit. Next there was the problem of the ports: the great concern of the coal interests on the Tyne was the competition of Sunderland which had virgin seams in its immediate hinterland, had no old privileged bodies to 'oppress' its traders, and was some hours' sailing time nearer the London market. This naturally led to attempts to 'regulate' by agreement the proportions of the rival ports; and the names of those engaged in such negotiations give an idea of the character and standing of the leading men in the trade: Colonel George Liddell (M.P. for Berwick), writing in 1731 to Cotesworth, like himself from the Tyne, mentions as spokesmen of the Wear interests Lord Scarbrough, J. Hedworth (M.P. for Co. Durham, 1713–47) and H. Lambton (M.P. for Durham City, 1733–61). But whatever the differences between the two groups, they were faced by common marketing problems, and had a common battle to fight with the ships' masters, the London lighter-

men, and the London dealers. Each of these groups, in order
to hold its own, had to organize itself—there would have been
anarchy and waste if they had not. Yet such 'combinations'
were 'in restraint of trade', and savoured of a 'monopoly' cal-
culated to raise the price of coal. This would affect the
London consumer, and bring the City and its representatives
into the fray. Prosecutions, Parliamentary inquiries, and legislation to prevent such combinations would follow. And each
party would have M.P.s among its spokesmen: the coal-owners
would be represented by Northumberland and Durham Members (or some of their body sitting for outside constituencies—
for instance, the Wortleys); the ship-masters by Members for
Scarborough, Yarmouth, etc.; and the consumer by men like
Sir John Barnard and Sir William Thompson, Members for the
City of London, or perhaps also by some brewers and distillers
—great consumers of coal—with seats in the House. In 1729,
at a conference at the Guildhall, in which the coal-owners met
the Lord Mayor and aldermen, 'seven distinguished representatives of the Tyne owners, including four M.P.s, were present,
and Mr. Hedworth and Baron Hilton for Wear owners'. So far
insufficient attention has been paid to that aspect of Parliament
and of the activities of its Members: there was as yet no 'welfare
State', but there was a State which looked after production and
had to deal with a multitude of new problems raised by changes
in its methods and in transport; and more patient, honest work
was done in this matter by Members with local knowledge and
local interests, and inspired by the exuberant and creative spirit
of the time, than they and their period are credited with.

'Local issues . . .,' writes Professor Hughes, '—the Wear navi-
gation in 1747 and 1760 [in elections for Durham city], the
threat to the time-honoured grazing rights of Newcastle free-
men on the Town Moor in 1774—were the staple of politics in
the eighteenth century.' Even the subjects on which the Northumberland and Durham Members spoke in the House were
mostly local; and they themselves were, as a rule, of the county
(least at Berwick, a Government borough 'where a combination
of military, ordnance, custom house, and post office tipped the
balance'). There was remarkable continuity in the representa-

tion of Durham city: a Lambton represented it in unbroken succession from 1733 to 1813, and a Tempest from 1742 to 1800, when the male line became extinct. 'There is no case of a local tradesman being returned for the city during the century...'

At Newcastle the picture is rather different. Sir Henry Liddell of Ravensworth was Member from 1700 to 1710 (he still owned a family house in the town); William Wrightson, Member from 1710–1722, had married a local merchant's daughter; while William Carr (1722–34), the Blacketts (1710–77), the Fenwicks (1727–47), and the Ridleys (1747–1836) all had long-established trading connexions in the town... It is significant that the attempts of a powerful 'stranger' like George Bowes of Streatlam to insinuate himself into the borough by getting himself made a freeman were frustrated.

But what about 'Whigs' and 'Tories' in a region where in view of the strength of Catholics and Non-Jurors, and the proximity of Scotland, those divisions had been specially marked and could be expected to survive longer? At a by-election in 1748, a 'Tory' country gentleman, R. Algood, stood for Northumberland against Lord Ossulston (eldest son of Lord Tankerville), the official Whig candidate. H. T. Carr wrote about it to Henry Ellison, his brother-in-law (they were married to the two daughters of William Cotesworth):

I should certainly vote for Lord O. if he had been opposed by any person reasonably suspected of Jacobitism, but considering Mr. Algood's good character and his zealous behaviour in the late Rebellion, I cannot bring myself to vote against him in favour of the son of a man who, though Lord Lieutenant of the County, deserted it so shamefully in the time of danger and who himself seems to have nothing said in his favour but that he is a Whig set up by the Whig Party, who I wish had made choice of a man of more merit, as I think we shall look a little too sour and shew ourselves too irreconcilable to the bare name of a Tory if we can't be so far soften'd and reconciled by Mr. Algood's behaviour as to look upon him almost as one of ourselves, but must to a man oppose him.

And Robert Ellison, a kinsman of Henry's and Collector of Customs at Newcastle, reported though apparently he himself

favoured Ossulston: 'The general bent of the people's inclination
is to Mr. Algood in preference to Lord O.'; and he added that
there was personal resentment against Ossulston: 'he being a
stranger in the country and military gent and son of a peer are
most industriously propagated'—arguments most effective in
eighteenth-century county elections though hardly of a 'party'
character. And Algood, not Ossulston, was returned with the
support even of 'several of the Dissenters, nay some of the
Ministers. . . .'

Even more remarkable was the by-election in Co. Durham
caused in 1760 by the death of George Bowes. The Whig candidate was Sir Thomas Clavering; Lord Ravensworth, one of his
supporters, wrote about him to the Duke of Newcastle: 'His is
a very old family in the county, it has been as true a one for the
Protestant Succession and to the present Royal Family, I may
say, without exception as any in it.' But the Earl of Darlington,
another prominent Whig, head of the powerful Vane family,
and a relative and political associate of the Duke, had forestalled
Ravensworth and secured the Duke's support for Robert Shafto.
Newcastle's embarrassment was increased still further by the
discovery that Shafto's father and family 'were always very
violent Tories', though 'this gentleman I hear is not'. The
Duke had felt certain all along that the Tories would 'take the
side where they can do the most mischief', and now he foresaw
that because of Shafto's family antecedents they would incline
toward him. He therefore appealed for help and mediation to
Trevor, Bishop of Durham, and as such in control of one of
the greatest electoral interests in the county. But Trevor meant
first to feel its pulse at the general meeting: he would not risk
appearing on the weaker side, and would therefore follow, and
not try to force, the bent of the county. He wrote to the Duke
of Newcastle on 7 October 1760, the day before the general
meeting:

> Shafto has been with me to declare his attachment to the Govt.,
> in which I believe him sincere, but the Tories are certainly pleased
> with his standing and glad to join him. The run for him is cer-
> tainly very great and he gets on much faster without expence than
> the other does with it. . . .

And again on the day after the meeting: 'Mr. Shafto in the meeting declared his attachment to the Govt. upon Whig principles. . . .' And so Shafto had the support of the Tories although he stood 'upon Whig principles', and of the Duke of Newcastle, Lord Darlington, and the Bishop of Durham, in spite of his Tory antecedents. Let those who know everything about Whigs and Tories, and confidently operate with those denominations, disentangle such politics in terms of parties.

A new and remarkable intervention on the side of Clavering was a circular addressed by John Wesley to the Methodists on 20 November 1760:

> I earnestly desire all who love me to assist him—to use the utmost of their power: what they do, let them do it with all their might: Let not sloth nor indolence hurt a good cause; only let them not rail at the other candidates. They may act earnestly and yet civilly. Let all your doings be done in charity and at the peril of your souls receive no bribe.

Shafto won the election, and retained the seat until 1768; Clavering held it from 1768 till 1790. And here I add a few facts concerning these two Members for Co. Durham for the benefit (and exercise) of those who continue to attach the labels of 'W' and 'T' to the names of Members in the reign of George III. Shafto, the 'Tory', voted against General Warrants in 1764, and in 1765 received a Secret Service pension from the Rockingham Administration; Clavering, the 'Whig', in his first years in Parliament seems to have voted with the Opposition, but during the American Revolution, though independent and occasionally voting on the popular side, he supported Lord North and adhered to him till the end in March 1782.

8

THE EAST INDIA COMPANY

THE EAST INDIA COMPANY, or, to give it its full name, the
United Company of Merchants of England trading to the East
Indies, was formed in 1709 through a union of the 'Old' and
the 'New' Companies. From the outset it had to encounter
European rivals supported by their own Governments, and to
carry on commerce sword in hand in an India where the power
of the Moguls was crumbling. This need of armed support increased its dependence on the Crown, from whom it anyhow
held its charter and trading monopolies: thus a close association
with the Government was inevitable, which exposed the Company to difficulties and perils in times of political crisis. Happiest for it were therefore the days of Walpole and Henry Pelham: it was then that it became

> the prosperous, respectable, and sound commercial and financial
> corporation which was not only far and away the biggest and
> most complicated trading organization of the country, but was
> (together with the Bank of England and the South Sea Company)
> the centre of the financial market rising in London and of the
> Government's political and financial interest there.[1]

Its management was in a chairman, deputy chairman, and in
24 directors elected annually by the Court of Proprietors, in
which every holder of at least £500 stock had a vote, and one
vote only, however great his holdings. The membership of the
Court of Directors was remarkably permanent in the reign of

[1] Lucy S. Sutherland: *The East India Company in Eighteenth-Century
Politics.*

the first two Georges; the 'House list' submitted by the out-
going executive was carried without much difficulty by the
prestige of its leaders, and by a voting strength built up on
patronage, on merchant shareholders dealing with the Company, the shipping interest, etc. The business organization of
the Company was efficient; the produce of its sales about the
middle of the century was roughly £2m. a year; its shares were
widely held; and a good many of its directors sat in Parliament,
without the Company as such engaging in political controversy.
But about 1746 conditions began to deteriorate: there were war
with France, conflicts with rival Indian rulers, and growing
difficulty in controlling the Company's own servants; and 10
or 12 years later, a permanent crisis supervened in its affairs.

> The new period was to see ... English control spread over the
> neighbouring Indian territories and an expansion of territorial
> power which [was] ... inevitable but which, thanks to ... the
> spectacular exploits of Clive ... came more suddenly than anyone
> could have expected. The Company had long experience of the
> problems of government as well as those of the administration of
> commerce; but now ... those of government ... began to prevail.
> In addition ... the new period brought ... a desperate struggle in
> England for the control of the Company's political machine ...
> between Robert Clive, the Company's greatest soldier, and
> Laurence Sulivan, its ablest ruler since Sir Josia Child ... a
> struggle involving issues vital for the Company and the State,
> but one in which personal hatreds and personal interests played
> the greatest part.... The period was also to see the re-entry of
> East Indian affairs into the sphere of party politics and the inter-
> vention of the State in the affairs of a Company become at once
> so rich and so disordered. There was Chatham's first intervention
> in 1766-7, Lord North's Regulating Act..., Fox's India Bill,
> Pitt's India Act, and, as a sequel, the long-drawn-out agony of
> Warren Hastings' impeachment.

It was the story of 'a company struggling to adapt itself to totally
new responsibilities oversea, hampered at every turn by disorganization arising from too-sudden wealth and the speculation
born of it'; and of shifting Governments and violent Oppositions,
whose component groups found advantage in forming connexions with interests and groups within the distracted Company.

A rich historical literature on East Indian questions during this period has hitherto been focused on a few great figures and their exploits in the field, in administration, or in Parliament. But of the history of the Company itself, its management, negotiations, and internal struggles, and its relations with Government and Parliament, that 'intricate and often unedifying background' to more spectacular activities and scenes, no proper analysis had so far been attempted: hence a fragmentation of that history which rendered it well-nigh impossible to see its disjointed sequence in perspective. And yet Indian affairs impinge all along on British domestic history during the first 25 years of the reign of George III, and deeply affect its course. It was high time that they were elucidated and worked into the pattern of which they are an essential part. This has now been achieved by Miss L. S. Sutherland in her book on *The East India Company in Eighteenth-Century Politics*, a piece of historical research so thorough and comprehensive in its groundwork, and so masterly and lucid in its presentation, that it must rank among the foremost works on the period, a standby and directive for students in cognate fields, and a secure foundation for further research in its own. Miss Sutherland's knowledge of City finance and politics in the eighteenth century, and also the practical experience of administration which she acquired during the last war, have served her well in her study of the East India Company; she has been able fully to appreciate the problems of its day-to-day management, to value the work of a Laurence Sulivan, and to pay well-deserved tribute to the honest and intelligent labours of John Robinson and Charles Jenkinson, forerunners of the modern Civil Service: administrators who laid the foundations for constructive reform in India but, despised by men of fashion in their day and maligned by orators and pamphleteers, continue to appear as sinister or suspect figures in books of a well-known type. Still, while doing justice to these men, and also to Warren Hastings, 'the greatest Company servant of his day', Miss Sutherland takes a lenient, and even generous, view of his persecutor, Burke.

He may have adopted the East Indian question for party and personal reasons; he may have placed his trust in most unworthy witnesses, in his contemptible cousin William ... and the virulent and disappointed Francis ... ; and he showed far more interest in exposing abuses and attacking individuals than in working out a constructive policy of reform. But he was sincere in his savage anger, had mastered a mass of complicated information and ... was undoubtedly one of the formative influences on the development of a government policy for India.

Laurence Sulivan spent more than 20 years in India; owed his advance in the Company's service solely to his competence; returned to England in 1752 a wealthy but not a rich man, and further improved his fortune in the City; was elected a director in 1755, and deputy chairman in 1757, when developments in India called for men with Indian experience; and entered Parliament in 1762. Meantime Clive by his Arcot campaign, the recapture of Calcutta, and the battle of Plassey laid the foundations of British rule in India; but there was a price to pay: his example and victories did a great deal to upset the precarious balance between public and private interest hitherto observed by the Company's servants. Convention allowed senior officials to make fortunes 'through the recognized channels of perquisite, private trade, and money-lending'; but Clive, having replaced Siraj-ud-daula by Mir Jafar, accepted from him more that £200,000 in presents and an annual *jagir* of £27,000: the first of the gainful interventions in conflicts between native rulers. Moreover, as conquerors the Company's servants now freely extended their private trade in the hinterland, making profits and committing abuses; thus enriched they became unmanageable, or if recalled came back acutely hostile to the directors, spreading disorganization to the headquarters in London; lastly, servants of the Company in India would remit their gains to England by bills on it, after having laid out the money on occasions and terms largely of their own making: all this at a time when the administrative responsibilities of the Company were rapidly increasing.

A split among the directors produced a contested election in 1758; Sulivan's side was victorious; he was elected chairman, and retained control for the next six years. In that election he had Clive's support. But a General Letter which Sulivan sent to

Bengal in March 1759, with bitter reproaches for remittances, etc., gave umbrage to Clive, although Sulivan had taken care to dissociate him from the criticism. 'The seeds of the great feud had been thrown.'

Clive returned home in 1760, determined to cut a great figure in the country. The *jagir*, the fee of a purely nominal office under the Mogul, became his dominant concern, overriding every other consideration. 'My future power, my future grandeur,' he wrote to a friend, 'all depend on the receipt of the jaghire money'; and again: 'Believe me there is no other interest in this kingdom but what arises from great possessions'— had he stayed in India and acquired a yet greater fortune, he might have been 'an English Earl with a Blue Ribbon'. But the Company hesitated to recognize his *jagir* by transferring to him a yearly rent for lands near Calcutta payable by the Company to the Nawab, who still owed them reparation for damage suffered from his predecessor. The peace negotiations of 1762–3 increased ill-feeling between Sulivan and Clive—there was no conflict of principle, but Clive, excluded from a share in the intricate discussions, attacked the terms which Sulivan had accepted; and when a formed opposition arose over them in the Company, he announced his adherence to it. 'The great Civil War of the Company had broken out.'

The election of directors in April 1763 was marked by new and ominous features: large-scale organizations were set up for the production of faggot-votes—East India stock was bought and holdings were 'split' to create voting qualifications; the Government, whose Peace Treaty was impugned, intervened in favour of Sulivan (Fox using the resources of the Pay Office); consequently the Parliamentary Opposition aided Clive; and both sides rounded up supporters. Sulivan won; and payment of Clive's *jagir* was stopped by order from India House. He appealed for help to the Opposition, but was told that it was hopeless to raise the matter in Parliament. To save his *jagir* he now swore fealty to the Grenville Administration; still, the compromise which they tried to patch up for him was rejected by the directors. But his chance came when news reached

London of administration chaos and renewed fighting in Bengal; his return to India was urged by anxious stockholders; he, however, refused while Sulivan headed the Direction; and at the ensuing, bitterly contested, election in April 1764, Clive had the support of the Government. The result was a dead-heat; but soon Sulivan's following began to crumble; Clive's demand for recognition of his *jagir* for 10 years was accepted; and he sailed for Bengal, armed with wide discretionary power. The election of 1765 completed his victory over Sulivan—he had won a decisive round. Still, as early as May 1764, Charles Jenkinson wrote:

> The affairs of this Company seem to be become much too big for the management of a body of merchants... these disputes will probably end in a Parliamentary enquiry.

In April 1766 news reached London of Clive having assumed, on behalf of the Company, control of Bengal's finances; he himself estimated the net gain at more than £2m. a year, a view widely accepted in spite of scepticism among the directors. A wild boom in East India stock ensued in London, Amsterdam, and Paris. Rich men, including Clive himself, invested in it, while speculators started large-scale dealings in 'differences'. One such group of prominent men was headed by Lord Verney, M.P., Edmund Burke's patron, and included several other M.P.s; and its affairs were managed by two adventurers, William Burke and Lauchlin Macleane, who now began their long and discreditable connexion with Indian affairs. When the directors would not raise the dividend, the 'bulls' set out to obtain a majority in the General Court; split stock and organized an unprecedented publicity campaign; obtained support from deluded proprietors and from the Clive group (which, besides being engaged on the 'bull' side, hoped in the glow of Company affluence to secure an extension of the *jagir* for a further 10 years). The speculators succeeded: in September 1766, the dividend was raised from 6 to 10 per cent.; and they emerged as a new element in Company politics.

Stock-jobbing was at all times in ill-repute with the nation, and the rich, monopolistic Company with the 'popular' party in the City; dislike of Nabobs forcing their way into Parliament and society was growing among the country gentry; and uneasiness was spreading at the 'rapine and oppression' practised in India. The State was grappling with problems of post-war finance, and the question naturally arose what right a trading company had to the territorial revenues of a province subdued with the help of the King's forces. Chatham, in office since July 1766, denied it, and desired a parliamentary inquiry into the Company's affairs as a prelude to State intervention. But his illness, and divisions in his Government, prevented the attack from being pressed home, and, after long debates, manœuvres, and negotiations (for the first time properly elucidated in Miss Sutherland's book), an agreement was reached for two years: the Company undertook to pay the Treasury £400,000 a year. In the meantime the speculators rashly used their majority in the General Court further to raise the dividend from 10 to 12½ per cent. The Government replied with the first parliamentary intervention of the century in the internal affairs of the Company: by an Act limiting the dividend to 10 per cent., and another against gerrymandering elections—no one was to vote who had not held his qualification for at least six months. And such intervention had to be continued in order to safeguard the financial interests of the Treasury and of the nation, and to replace the short-term agreement of 1767 by a new settlement. Still, this again was for five years only; the contribution of £400,000 per annum was maintained, but if the Company at any time had to reduce its dividend to 6 per cent. the claim would lapse; the maximum dividend was set at 12½ per cent.

The Act against faggot-votes proved ineffective: operations had merely to start half a year earlier. The opposition in India House, led by Sulivan, was gaining strength, and the election of directors in 1769 was most fiercely contested; the Government intervened, while groups of rich men recklessly bought up stock at inflated prices. The result was a draw which brought Sulivan back into office. A month later election-mongers and speculators were caught by a sharp break in price caused by news of fighting in India and rumours of an impending French

attack: Verney and the Burkes, Sulivan, Macleane, and a great
many others were brought to the verge of ruin. But the storm
blew over; an attempt of the Government to interfere in the
Company's territorial affairs by agents sent out to India ended
in failure; and by 1770 a lull supervened in the faction fights
at India House, as also in Parliament; during the next two years
relations between the Company and the Government were
remarkably free of political implications. Meantime information reaching England about Company misrule was producing
genuine dismay both in Parliament and in the country, and
Sulivan made serious attempts at reform from within. But for
this the Company's control over its servants in India had to be
strengthened; and moves in that direction were defeated by
powerful ex-servants with more than doubtful records. Sulivan's
only success was in the remodelling of the Bengal administration, where the man he had chosen, Warren Hastings, laid the
basis for Bengal's prosperity under British rule.

But a new crisis in the Company's affairs was impending.
High dividends and payments to the Government were based
on an illusory surplus from the Bengal territorial revenues. The
truth was masked for some time even from the directors, who
in March 1771 raised the dividend to 12½ per cent. But even
when the situation became clear to them they did not reduce
the dividend (which would have stopped also payments to the
Government) for fear of a catastrophic break in East India
stock, which some of them were heavily 'bulling'. The maximum dividend was continued in August 1771 and March
1772. Then in June a severe financial crisis set in, causing widespread bankruptcies in this country and on the Continent; and
now the financial problem of the Company had to be tackled.
At first it was hoped that an unspectacular way might be found
for the Treasury to help the Company out of its difficulties;
but its commitments proved excessive; on 24 September 1772,
the half-yearly dividend was passed; and the consequent panic
'raised a frenzy of indignation among shareholders, speculators,
and the public at large'. This, on top of the mounting anger
of humanitarian opinion, produced a demand for Parliamentary

action. The North Administration were forced to evolve an
Indian policy.

The view universally held that if the Company were to be
helped this must be in return for radical improvements in its
organization and rule was grounded 'not only in the desire to
obviate financial loss or military danger to the nation but in a
wider sense of obligation for law and order in India'. Some
favoured the assumption by the Government of full responsibility for the administration of India; but the machinery
of government was as yet entirely inadequate for intervention
in that distant and unfamiliar field, and the purpose of the
temporary settlement embodied in Lord North's Regulating
Act of 1773 was 'to leave the Company in control both of trade
and day-to-day administration, while checking its worst excesses
at home and abroad', and 'to prepare the ground for a more
permanent and sweeping reorganization when the Company's
charter came up for renewal in 1780'. A small Parliamentary
committee was set up of Government supporters, with Jenkinson for *rapporteur*, to examine the Company's books and report
on reform. Although its proposals met with considerable opposition, especially in the General Court, the difficulties did not
prove insuperable. The Parliamentary Opposition was disunited
over India and ineffective; while in India House the Government secured in 1773 a compliant directorate. The Government
was ready to help the Company with a loan, and concessions
regarding the export of tea; but in three ways established its
control over the Company: through the right to receive copies
of the Company's accounts and correspondence (henceforth carefully scrutinized by the Secretary of the Treasury, John Robinson); through the nomination of the Governor-General of
Bengal and his Council; and through a Government-controlled
majority in a reorganized Court of Directors.

.... there began ... the first period of indirect control by the
Government over the East India Company. During this period
the 'management' of the Company became one of the regular
activities of the Treasury; the King was kept as regularly informed of East Indian elections and of important votes at East
India House as he was of the proceedings of Parliament, and

there arose to prominence those official experts in Indian affairs of whom Robinson and Jenkinson were the pioneers, and Henry Dundas the most famous.

Here too began the participation of government in the administration of India ... none the worse for basing itself on no particular doctrine of relations of government and Company....

... A step had to be taken that could not be reversed and some of the worst abuses of the Company's rule both in India and at home disappeared for ever....

The Government, 'looking for capacity rather than connexions', appointed Warren Hastings Governor-General, but joined to him three councillors (including the notorious Philip Francis) who within seven days of their arrival launched an attack against him; and from Miss Sutherland's lucid and impartial account of the conflict Hastings comes out much better than his opponents. He was an excellent administrator, absorbed in his work and devoted to duty, and 'widely known among Company servants for his indifference and carelessness about his private fortune'; and though his financial principles hardly 'transcended the conventions of the day, his hands were a good deal cleaner than those of most of his contemporaries': the fortune he amassed was not great by the standards of the time. But the services which he rendered were incalculable: in the circumstances of his last years of office 'it is difficult to think of any other man then concerned in Indian affairs who would have averted disaster.' As for the Parliamentary Opposition, their attitude over those affairs was dictated by personal considerations and the desire to harass the Government. Francis long endeavoured in vain to rouse Burke's concern at the alleged misdeeds of Warren Hastings, and when the Government and the directors decided to recall Hastings, the Rockinghams came out on his side; when Hastings's (ill-chosen) representatives concluded a compromise with the Government, the Rockinghams swung over to the other side; but when Hastings incurred the wrath of the King and the Ministers by refusing to accept that agreement, the Opposition attacks against him stopped abruptly, only to be resumed with increased virulence when he made his peace with the Government.

In the summer of 1778 Robinson started to draft a plan to be followed when in 1780 the renewal of the Company's charter would come up for settlement. While he thought that the Company should resume its contributions to the Exchequer, his experience of the last five years did not make him favour the transfer of the Company's territorial acquisitions to the Government: the change would be dangerous in war-time; the administration of those territories, their commerce, and the remitting of revenue from India were 'greatly connected'; lastly, 'the errors which must be committed in the management of such acquisitions at so great a distance ... had better fall upon the directors of the Company than ... upon the Ministers of the King'. But while the Cabinet was preoccupied with America and the war, and the Government in a weak position, little progress was made with regard to Indian affairs; the Act of 1773 was renewed for one year, and in May, 1780, for another year. It was not till January 1781, after the Gordon Riots and the General Election, that Indian matters came again to the fore; but even then the strength for decisive measures was lacking. The agreement renewing the charter for 10 years was, in Sulivan's words, 'a paltry performance'; further legislation was vaguely promised. News from India, first of serious conflict in the administration, and next, of military danger in the Carnatic, led to the appointment of two important parliamentary committees. When in February 1781 the Opposition demanded a committee of investigation,

> it did not seem necessary for the Government to oppose it. Carelessness and indifference on North's part, however, permitted ... the election of a Committee in which members of the Opposition preponderated both in numbers and quality.... Thus came into existence the famous Select Committee ... the field of Edmund Burke's Indian activities.

And in April a secret committee was set up to investigate the causes of the war in the Carnatic; but this time Robinson took care that it should be controlled by the Government side: Dundas was its chairman, with Jenkinson as his right-hand man.

In the two years between the fall of the North Administration and the rise of Pitt, the Indian question became 'one of the major controversies and problems which claimed the attention of Parliament'. Nothing in the terms of reference of either committee suggested that they were intended to formulate general policies of East Indian reform; but under the short-lived Administrations of 1782–4, the two committees became increasingly important, changing their political status several times: the secret committee was connected with the North, Shelburne, and Pitt Administrations, and the select committee with the Rockinghams and the Rockingham Coalition. The Rockingham Administration took no initiative in Indian affairs, and its record was 'somewhat ignominious'. Shelburne inserted in the King's speech of 5 December 1782, a reference to 'fundamental laws' to be framed for India, and Dundas was preparing a Bill (based on the work of Robinson and Jenkinson), which is 'a landmark in the history of Indian legislation', 'the blue-print of Pitt's East India Act of the next year'. Ignoring 'the dislike of the executive characteristic of eighteenth-century political opinion', it proposed to increase the powers of the Governor-General and the Governors; to settle the claims of the rulers of Tanjore and Arcot, and investigate their notorious debts to Company servants; to prevent the General Court from overriding the directors on political matters; and to strengthen the Government in its dealings with the Company. But brought in after the Shelburne Government had fallen, it seemed still-born.

Now the Rockinghams and Burke had their innings. They had long opposed an increase of the authority of ministers over the Company because of the patronage this would give them, and of that of governors as leading to tyranny. Their Bill, which adhered to those tenets, was 'a product of Burke's intelligence', ingenious and unpractical. It was a most sweeping attack on the independence of the Company; the powers, however, and the patronage taken from it were not to be vested in the Crown but in seven commissioners, nominated in the Act for at least four years: that is, in Fox's party whether or not they were in power. Misrule in India was to be checked by a complete subordination of the Indian administrators to commissioners sitting in England—which shows how little Burke understood of the problems of administration. It was a poor Bill, and although its defeat was due to the action of a few resolute men, these were helped by the 'widespread hostility and dislike' which it aroused 'not only among the threatened Indian interests but among a wide body of opinion throughout the country'.

When Pitt in turn introduced his India Bill it was in an understanding with the Company; after what had threatened them they accepted a measure which under normal conditions would have created an uproar. It was Dundas's Bill, modified to meet objections: some of the powers of the Governor-General were dropped, and the extent of the Government's declared patronage was limited. A board, the future Board of Control, was established for India, and measures were enacted against oppression and abuses by the Company's servants.

> What Pitt and Dundas had set out to do was to give themselves both the sanctions and the machinery for carrying out the methods of government supervision and infiltration which North and Robinson had been seeking to employ ever since the Regulating Act of 1773.

And although much remained which called for improvement in Indian administration,

> the confusion of the past twenty-five years had come to an end and a new era had begun in the Government of India and in the relations of State and Company.

9

BASIC FACTORS IN NINETEENTH-CENTURY EUROPEAN HISTORY

THE TITLE of my lecture seems to call for a closer definition. The basic factors which I have in mind concern the political history of Europe in its international aspects during the period 1815–1919, the nineteenth century of European history. That century and its aftermath witnessed on the Continent the triumph of linguistic nationality, and of democracy in the sense of a levelling of classes rather than of constitutional growth; and it was foremost nationality and the struggles engendered by it that in Central and Eastern Europe defeated the movement toward self-government and liberty. 'The language chart is our Magna Charta', was the slogan of nationalism on the European Continent; and a comparison of the political map of Europe in 1920, and still more in 1945, with that of 1815 shows that, by and large, the program has been realized, though hardly with the results its enthusiasts had anticipated: the operation was successful, but at what cost to the patient? I propose to examine the patterns that can be discerned in the seemingly confused historical process which recast the map of Europe on a linguistic basis. I refrain from inquiring into the sense of the envenomed struggles we have witnessed; for such inquiry would take us into inscrutable depths or into an airy void. Possibly there is no more sense in human history than in the changes of the seasons or the movements of the stars; or if sense there be, it escapes our perception. But the historian, when watching strands interlace and entwine and their patterns intersect, seeks, for the logic of situations and the rhythm of events which invest them at least with a determinist meaning.

The political problems of the European Continent in the nineteenth century were posed by the French Revolution; and the basic change which it ushered in was the transition from dynastic to national sovereignty, and a progressive widening of the 'political nation' from the privileged orders to democracy, till the nation came to comprise, in theory at least, the entire people. The emphasis of dynastic sovereignty, quasi-proprietary in character, was on the territory of the State; the emphasis of national sovereignty was on the human community—which postulated that a true sense of community should weld the population into one people. From the principle of national sovereignty spring constitutional movements and national demands, claims to self-government and to self-determination. In appearance these had cognate aims, a delusion fostered by their having that common source, and a common opponent in autocracy based on dynastic heritage. In practice, however, there is an antithesis between self-government, which means constitutional development within an existing territorial framework, and self-determination for which there is no occasion unless that framework is called in question and territorial changes are demanded; and acute disputes concerning the territorial framework naturally retard, or even preclude, constitutional development.

In linguistically mixed regions delimitation is a thorny problem even where there is mere juxtaposition of national groups. But in Europe intermixture was as a rule the result of past conquests, political and cultural, which had reduced the original national group to a state of social inferiority. Conquests created Ulsters, and over further, wider regions spread the network of an 'ascendancy' primarily based on the landowning classes and the town population, alien to, or alienated from, the peasantry which retained its own language or religion, or both. Self-government meant, in the earlier stages, the rule of the big landowners and their retainers in the countryside, and of the upper middle class and the intelligentsia in the towns; their language or religion determined the national character of the country (Grattan's Parliament, composed of Anglo-Irish Protestants, deemed itself representative of the Irish nation). Hence in the numerous Irelands scattered all over Europe turmoil and strife were bound to result from the rise of the lower classes, and especially of the peasantry, to political consciousness and action. National and religious conflicts interlocked with agrarian movements, envenoming each other: war was waged for both the national and the personal ownership of the land, and either side felt that it was fighting not for private interests only. An educated upper class, for centuries accustomed to consider the country its own, would not easily allow itself to be reduced to the position of alien interlopers, while peasants rooted in the land, as only they can be, fought the long-drawn battle with an obstinacy unsurpassed by any other class. Moreover the dominant minority invariably had the backings of its Ulster and of its homeland: even under democracy. With the progressive widening of the political nation, the unprivileged orders, one by one down the social scale, were taking over the quasi-proprietary claims of dynasties and feudal oligarchies to territorial dominance; they became ideological partners or heirs of their *quondam* rulers, and frequently their actual partners by being settled on the land or in government posts in the disputed territory. Peasant-settlers planted as a garrison to keep down the subject race, school-teachers sent to spread the language of the minority, and a host of petty officials, constituted a master-nation whose rule was much harder to bear, and more galling, than that of a dynasty or of a remote oligarchy. Consider the amount of disturbance which during the nineteenth century was caused in the political life of this country by an Ireland geographically isolated and not subjected to any further encroachments; and you can gauge the effect which two dozen Irelands were bound to have on the life of nineteenth-century Europe as borderlands between contending nations, especially while attempts continued to be made to complete conquest and conversion.

On the European Continent incomplete conquests fell into two patterns. The main stream of migrations, which had overrun Europe from East to West, was reversed about the eighth century: from West to East the French pressed against the Flemings and Germans, the Germans against the Lithuanians and Slavs, the Lithuanians and Poles against the Russians, and the Russians against the Finnish tribes, and ultimately also against the Mongols; each nation was yielding ground in the West, and gaining much more at the expense of its Eastern neighbours: in the East were wide spaces and a reduced capacity for resisting pressure. Similarly the Swedes spread across the Baltic, and the Italians across the Adriatic. The Flemish-Walloon problem in Belgium and the Franco-German problem in Alsace, the numerous problems of Germany's ragged Eastern border, Poland's problems both on her Western and on her Eastern flank, and the conflict between the Yugoslavs and the Italians, all originate in that great West to East shift on the linguistic map of Europe. The other pattern of conquests whose consequences were formative of nineteenth-century European history, goes back to the continued Asiatic incursions, of the Avars, Magyars, and Turks into South-Eastern Europe. The Germans met them at the gate of the Danube, between the Bohemian quadrilateral and the Alps: this is the origin of Austria whose core was the Ostmark round Vienna, with its flanking mountain bastions and its access to the Adriatic. Germans and Magyars in their head-on collision split off the Northern from the Southern Slavs and established their dominion over that middle zone; and next the subjection of the Southern Slavs and the Rumans was completed by the Turkish conquest of the Balkans.

And now compare the political map of Europe in 1815 with the nationality map which forms the approximate basis of the frontiers of 1920 and 1945. Practically all the territorial changes occurred in Central and East-Central Europe. In 1815, the Germans and the Italians, the two most numerous nations in that region, were disunited through dynastic fragmentation. Between them in the West and the Russians in the East, thirteen to nineteen smaller nations inhabit a belt stretching from Petsamo to Candia (their exact number depends on what linguistic divergences or historical differences are deemed to constitute a nation): in 1815 all these smaller nations were engulfed in the

Habsburg and Ottoman Empires, in the Eastern fringe of Prussia, and the Western fringe of Russia. But if in that year anyone had attempted to draw a nationality map of Europe, he would have treated Finland as Swedish; the Baltic provinces, all East Prussia and Upper Silesia, and the Czech and Slovene provinces of Austria as German; Lithuania, Latgalia, White Russia, and the Western Ukraine as Polish; practically all Hungary as Magyar; the Austrian Littoral as Italian; and the Christian populations of Turkey possibly as Greek. Thus between the Gulf of Finland and the Turkish border there were only four nations that counted; and in 1848 an educated Englishman discoursing on the rights of nationality would probably be aware of four problems only and of four programs deserving his sympathy: those of German and Italian unification, of Hungary's independence, and of Poland's resurrection (presumably within the frontiers of 1772). As enemies of these programs he would indict the Habsburgs and the Tsar; and if later in the year he heard that ignorant peasantries were fighting on the side of autocracy against those enlightened nations and their eloquent leaders, this would fill him with regret and disgust.

The nationality problem naturally first came up for solution in terms of the master nations; and the main obstacle to three of their four programs was the Habsburg dynasty with its prescriptive rights and policy: of the Polish Question alone, the origin and gravamen lay outside their sphere. No deeper need or conflict had caused Austria's participation in the dismemberment of Poland—only the indiscriminate passion of the Habsburgs for extending their dynastic possessions; and this in time gave rise to schemes for a reconstitution of Poland under Habsburg dominion. Very different was the position of Prussia and Russia with regard to the Polish Question. Geographical consolidation was Prussia's primary purpose in the Partitions: in West Prussia (the 'Corridor' of the inter-war period) there was a conflict between the unity of the seaboard and that of the Vistula river-basin; and in Posnania Polish territory came within seventy miles of Berlin. The Russo-Polish conflict was over White Russia and the Western Ukraine, territories almost twice the size of ethnic Poland, in which the landowners were Roman

Catholic and Polish (or Polonized) while the peasants belonged to the Eastern Churches and continued to speak Russian dialects: the Poles could claim those territories on grounds of nationality so long as peasant-serfs politically counted for little more than cattle; but the frontier attained by Russia in the Third Partition was in 1919 reproduced in the Curzon Line.

One may well ask how in 1795 the Russians came to draw for themselves a frontier correct in the terms of 1919; and the answer sounds even more paradoxical: because they did not think in terms of nationality, or of the political rights of nations as then constituted. They thought in terms of religion, the only ones in which peasant-serfs counted; and by and large religion and nationality coincided. Thus backward Tsarist Russia jumped the period of the master nations, but without being able to destroy the social and economic foundations of the Polish claims to mastery over the disputed provinces: she could not even emancipate the serfs, still less dispossess the big landowners for their benefit, while serfdom and latifundia were maintained in the rest of Russia; nor could the Poles, in 1848 the General Staff of the *sansculottes* of Europe, raise the peasant masses against the Tsarist régime, or they would have destroyed their own hold on those Eastern borderlands. That incongruity of claims and realities, coupled with the impossibility of adjusting them, gave a unique turn to the Polish Question at a time when elsewhere nationality problems were being solved in terms of the socially and culturally dominant nations.

I pass to the alignment of the European Great Powers and the interplay of their interests and policies. What were in 1815 the leading *dramatis personæ* on the European stage? Great Britain and Russia, Powers flanking Europe, in it but never altogether of it, possessed of growing extra-European interests—the rising World Powers; France and Austria, European Great Powers, whose political ambits covered the entire Continent; and Prussia, the least among the Great Powers in size and resources, with limited regional interests and objectives.

Even in 1815 Great Britain and Russia were conscious of their separation from Europe. Next, England expanded into the Second British Empire, which now seems about to combine

with the Western half of the First Empire into an as yet un-
named and ill-defined working community of English-speaking
nations, centring on Washington rather than on London. A
similar shift away from Europe has transferred Russia's capital
from St. Petersburg to Moscow, a distance not to be measured
in miles only, while the centre of gravity of Russia's population
and production has been moving East, toward the Volga and
the Urals. Between 1815 and 1914 the full weight of these two
Powers was seldom felt in Europe, partly owing to the dispersal
or poor organization of their forces, and partly because they
seldom actively intervened in European conflicts except when
the Ottoman Empire was in question, an Asiatic Power which
in the Eastern Mediterranean held the key position between
three continents; and then they were usually ranged on opposite sides. Similarly in the ideological struggle between constitutional systems and autocratic régimes they were opposed to
each other. But three times in 150 years their forces were joined,
first to defeat the French bid for dominion over Europe, and
next the two German bids; and in these German Wars, the
United States started by supporting, and finished by virtually
replacing Great Britain as the flanking Power in the West.
Now the English-speaking nations and the U.S.S.R., engaged
in a contest of global dimensions, can hardly be said to flank
Europe any longer: they face each other in the very centre of
Europe—indeed, what remains of Europe, of its history and its
politics?

On the Continent the game of power politics, in whatever
terms it was played, normally made a neighbour into an enemy,
and therefore the neighbour's neighbour on the opposite flank
into an ally. Hence the rule of odd and even numbers in international politics: if Germany was France's enemy, then Poland
was France's ally, and consequently Russia the ally of Germany
—numbers one and three against two and four; and even sharp
ideological divisions between Germany and Russia could not
prevent that rule from asserting itself in 1922 and 1939. Yet
during the first half of the nineteenth century there was latent,
or even open, hostility between France and Austria which had
no common frontier, while for a century a frontier of more than

500 miles never gave rise to conflict between Prussia and Russia. The intervening numbers in Germany and Italy, whose pressure against France and Austria would have forced them to recognize their common interest, were latent; whereas Prussia and Russia were acutely conscious of their common interest in Poland, the suppressed intervening number—a frontier across territory whose population is alien and hostile to both neighbours is not apt to produce friction between them.

In 1814–15 the Habsburgs withdrew from Belgium and the Rhine, and deliberately divested themselves of responsibility for the defence of Germany; while Prussia, which before 1789 had been primarily an East European, Baltic Power, was entrusted with the 'Watch on the Rhine', and, stretching from Königsberg to the Saar, now covered the entire length of Germany. This redistribution of territory predetermined the ultimate exclusion of Austria from Germany, and Germany's ultimate inclusion in Prussia. But so long as Prussia made the 'Watch on the Rhine' her foremost duty, and *deutsche Treue* toward Austria her leading principle, she was internationally immobilized, and Germany neutralized; and the struggle between France and Austria was carried on across the power-vacuum of Italy. That struggle, begun when Habsburg possessions flanked France both in the East and the West but discontinued during the last thirty-three years of the *ancien régime*, when the Bourbons and the Habsburgs recognized that Great Britain, Prussia, and Russia had become their real rivals, was renewed by the French Revolution and Napoleon, and continued by their epigoni for half a century after 1815.

Austria's existence and Habsburg hegemony over Germany and Italy rested on the principle of dynastic property in States; the presence of the Habsburgs kept the two countries disunited; their disunion secured French primacy in Europe; here was a basis for Franco-Austrian co-operation. But the French flaunted the principle of national sovereignty at Austria: a fit weapon against the Habsburgs, but not an ideological basis for a continuance of French power politics. French statesmen and diplomats from Talleyrand to Thiers were pro-Austrian, but the current of popular feelings ran against Austria—till July 1866 when the cry of *revanche pour Sadowa* resounded on the Paris boulevards: the intervening numbers had emerged. But soon the basis disappeared for a Franco-Austrian alliance. Between 1815 and 1894 France had no ally on the European Continent, and only one constant friend, the Poles, whose friendship was a liability rather than an asset for her; because the implied threat, though never real, tended to draw Russia closer toward Prussia.

The co-operation between the Courts of St. Petersburg and Berlin was based on a human affinity between them, on a common autocratic ideology, and on the common anti-Polish interest. Berlin, on the very fringe of German-speaking territory, and St. Petersburg built in Finnish land and given a German name by its Russian founder, stood close to the two ends of the Baltic fringe, territory conquered in the thirteenth and fourteenth centuries by the Teutonic Knights, and ruled until quite recently by their descendants, the Prussian Junkers and the Baltic Barons. These Lutheran Germans, makers and servants of the Tsarist régime, and a power under it, were alien to Slav and Greek-Orthodox Russia, and averse to Pan-Slavism or to constitutional developments which would have endangered their own position. They were anti-Polish and friendly to Prussia; elsewhere they worked the power politics of the Russian Empire, with little distinctive colouring of their own.

The European nationality problems raised in 1848 fell almost all within the ambit of the Habsburg Empire which would have suffered disruption had the programs of the four master nations been realized: Western Austria would have been included in a Greater Germany, and the Czechs and Slovenes engulfed in it; Lombardy and Venetia would have gone to Piedmont; Hungary would have achieved independence, and full dominion over its Slovaks, Yugoslavs, Rumans, and Ruthenes (or Little Russians); over these the Poles would have achieved similar dominion in Galicia. The subject races therefore came out on the side of the dynasty against their social and economic rulers: in order to prevent that rule from being reinforced by political dominion. It was all a phantasmagoria. The Tsar and the King of Prussia still stood by the Habsburgs on grounds of dynastic solidarity; revolutionary forces, which

I

alone could in Germany have cut through the dynastic tangle by proclaiming a Republic one and indivisible, were lacking; the Prussian-Polish conflict in Posnania soon put an end to anti-Russian velleities among the Germans; Piedmont and the Magyars were not a match for the Habsburg Monarchy supported by Russia and the subject races. The transformation, if it was to be, had to be attempted in a different manner.

The Crimean War lost Austria Russia's support; Napoleon III opened up the Italian problem; Bismarck by anti-Polish action in 1863 secured Russia's friendship. In 1859–67, the Habsburg problem was solved in accordance with the modified programs of the master races. The Habsburgs were expelled from Lesser Germany and Italy, but retained the German and Italian provinces which were part of their old hereditary dominions (*Erbländer*); Hungary achieved complete constitutional independence while remaining within the military and international framework of the Habsburg Monarchy; and the government of Galicia was handed over to the Poles. The Austrian Empire changed into the Dual Monarchy, rebuilt on a German-Magyar-Polish basis; and the subject races were delivered to their masters (more completely in Hungary than in Western Austria or Galicia).

In one way Francis Joseph built better than he knew. To the Austrian Germans Western Austria was their heritage, to the Magyars all Hungary, and to the Poles Galicia, and each of these three nations was prepared to fight to the last for every square mile of what it considered its own, while the three heritages together covered the entire Monarchy. No such community of interest could have been found between the dynasty and the subject races. On the other hand, the Emperor's conscious calculations miscarried: he concluded the compromise with the Magyars in the hope of gaining their support for future action against Prussia. In 1870 the Austrian Germans were not willing to fight on the side of France against other Germans, while the Magyars did not wish for a victory which would have re-established the dynastic power of the Habsburgs and might have enabled them to go back on the Settlement of 1867. The logic of the situation defeated Francis Joseph's schemings.

If the struggle for supremacy in Germany could not be resumed any more, a German-Austrian alliance was in the logic
of the situation. Austria-Hungary was surrounded by neighbours each of whom saw populations of his own language within its borders. The Habsburg Monarchy reconstructed on a
German-Magyar basis was a fit ally for Germany, while Germany alone had an interest in its survival, and could therefore
accept an alliance in lieu of complete national reunion (in fact,
Bismarck did not want the Austrian Germans in the Reich,
which inclusion would have unfavourably affected the balance
between the Catholic South and the Prussian North). For
Germany Austria-Hungary was a more convenient ally than
Russia, for in such an alliance Austria-Hungary as the weaker
and more exposed of the two was dependent on Germany,
whereas Germany would have been dependent on Russia.
Moreover Germany had to count with the possibility that the
Power whom she did not pick for ally, would become that of
France; and as such Austria would have been more dangerous
because of the appeal she could make to the Roman Catholic
Germans—Bismarck dreaded a Roman Catholic league against
the Second Reich. Still, Bismarck did not mean to tie Germany
to Austria-Hungary, nor to cut the wire to St. Petersburg. But
again the logic of the situation prevailed: even if Bismarck's
successors had been wise and strong men, it seems doubtful
whether the consequences of an Austrian alliance could have
been permanently avoided. In 1877 Bismarck, when asked by the
Russians what his attitude would be in case of a Russian-
Austrian war, replied that much as he would regret such a
war he could see either side win or lose battles, but not suffer
one of them to be knocked out as a Great Power. Obviously he
feared Germany being left as an isolated intervening number
between two Great Powers, France and Russia or France
and Austria. There was no need for Russia to seek a German guarantee for her existence; there was for Austria. But
once Germany had committed herself to upholding Austria-
Hungary's existence, she was moving from the Baltic fringe
into the Danube Valley and the Balkans; and how long could
the common anti-Polish and reactionary interest preserve

Russia's friendship for a Germany which crossed her path in the Balkans?

Here Russia continued her 'historic mission' of freeing the Greek-Orthodox populations. Of the dominant nations the Turks had the weakest social, economic, and administrative hold over their subject races; even so, the process of destroying the Ottoman Empire in Europe took a hundred years, from the rise of Serbia and the liberation of Greece, across the Russo-Turkish War of 1877–8, to the Balkan War of 1912. But in that process Russia suffered surprises and disappointments; she found Hellenes and Rumans where she had merely seen followers of the Greek-Orthodox Church; and the Bulgars, however pro-Russian in sentiment, from hostility to the Serbs twice joined the Germans in accordance with the rule of odd and even numbers. By 1914 the Balkan nations were free, and the problem of the Greek-Orthodox Serbs and Rumans in the Habsburg Monarchy came to the fore: the survival of the Habsburg Monarchy reconstituted in terms of the dominant nations was now at stake. In 1867, at half-time between Vienna and Versailles, the Austrian Empire changed into the Dual Monarchy; at the close, the Dual Monarchy broke up into the Succession States. But the Russian Empire having collapsed a year earlier, its alien Western fringe, too, disintegrated into national States. The end of the First World War saw the middle zone of the small nations resettled on the basis of linguistic nationality.

In three regions only, socially and culturally dominant minorities retained, or even regained, superiority and possession. The Polish-Masurian fringe of East Prussia and about half of Polish Upper Silesia were left to the Germans on the strength of plebiscites which should never have been held: for there is a nationality *in posse* no less than a nationality *in esse*, and in these territories the process of national revival, universal in Europe, had not yet reached its natural term. On the Adriatic the Italians acquired territory with Yugoslav majorities. And the Poles managed, against the decision of the Allied and Associated Powers, to substitute the Riga for the Curzon Line. All these gains were wiped out by the Second World War. The process which formed the essence of European history since the French Revolution has now reached its term.

Looking back, converted though we cannot be to the *ancien régime*, to the 'system Metternich', or to Tsarism, we no longer exult over the age of nationality and democracy and its victories. All past social superiorities have been wiped out behind the Iron Curtain, and most of the cultural values which the educated classes had created. Anti-Socialist, clerical peasant communities may yet arise in States now satellites of Russia. But a reinstatement of the dispossessed upper and middle classes is impossible. And it is even more idle to think of a reconquest of territories once held on the basis of those lost superiorities. Now territories in Europe can only be regained with 'vacant possession': that is, radically cleared of their present inhabitants. The process of transfers or exchanges of population was started in the Balkans and Asia Minor at the end of the First World War. It was applied by Hitler where it suited him to withdraw German, or expel non-German, populations; and it was planned on an infinitely greater scale by the Germans had they won the war. As they lost it, the process was carried through against them. Hence their wrath.

10

DIPLOMACY IN THE
INTER-WAR PERIOD, 1919-1939

THE DECLINE in the position and influence of Foreign Ministers and their staffs at the centre, and of their representatives abroad, is the central theme which runs through the collection of essays on *The Diplomats, 1919-1939.*[1]

In Great Britain 'before 1914', writes Professor Craig, 'the right of the Foreign Secretary and the permanent officials of the Foreign Office to consider themselves as the chief advisers of the Cabinet in matters of foreign policy was never seriously questioned'. But after the First World War, 'Foreign Office advice was frequently ignored', and policies were 'adopted by the Prime Minister which ran counter to those advocated by the Foreign Secretary and his staff': important negotiations were taken over by political leaders and their agents, who lacked the necessary training and experience, and this although 'the British foreign service in 1919 compared favourably with that of any other country in Europe'. 'The precedents had been established. In the 1930's . . .,they were to be improved upon, first by Ramsay MacDonald and later, and more disastrously, by Neville Chamberlain.' Those later developments are only touched upon in a chapter by Professor Gilbert: how Chamberlain (with none of Lloyd George's genius, but even more distrustful of the diplomatic service) would constantly employ emissaries of a very unsuitable kind, and through his confidants maintain 'close relations with the German and Italian Ambas-

[1] Edited by Gordon A. Craig and Felix Gilbert. Princeton University Press.

sadors in London', behind the back of the Foreign Office. At Munich, the chiefs of the other three Governments were accompanied by representatives of their Foreign Offices, but Chamberlain only by Sir Horace Wilson, as unversed as he was himself in international affairs. That nadir of British diplomatic history is not discussed in the book.

'The French Foreign Office', writes Professor Challener, '. . . emerged from the first world war and the Peace Conference with its prestige undimmed'; 'the vast majority of top diplomatic positions in the French foreign service were held by career men'; and during the seven years of Briand's reign at the Quai d'Orsay, 1925–32, there was close collaboration between him and its Secretary-General, Phillippe Berthelot. The fact that the French nation, in its vulnerable and precarious position, at all times paid attention to foreign policy, upholding its basic traditions, and that the Prime Minister himself frequently held the Foreign Office, added to its strength. Yet there is another side to the picture. At the Paris Conference Berthelot was passed over by Clemenceau who 'preferred to run his own show', and for the same reason the post of Secretary General was left vacant during the thirty months of Poincaré's tenure of the Foreign Office. Nor was Berthelot's régime synonymous with that of the service as such: he had not served outside the Quai d'Orsay since the early years of the century, but, with a group of other *fonctionnaires trop sédentaires*, is alleged to have stood between the ministers and their representatives abroad; similarly his successor, Alexis Léger, after a few years in China, spent the rest of his professional life at the Quai d'Orsay. And when the slide toward appeasement started in French policy, Léger, and with him the Quai d'Orsay, were, as is shown by Miss Cameron, short-circuited by their political chiefs: 'he had no idea of the extent of Laval's private concessions to Mussolini'; in London, after the re-militarization of the Rhineland, he was 'locked out of the decisive conversations', while Flandin 'followed the *politique de complaisance*'; and under Bonnet, in March 1939, Léger found himself 'surrounded with reticence'.

German diplomacy during the inter-war period is dealt with in two essays, by Professor Hajo Holborn and Professor Craig.

In the 1920's, writes Holborn, the regular diplomats 'radiated considerable ill-will toward a republican foreign policy and Ebert at first insisted on Germany being 'represented in eminent diplomatic posts by men who had made their career outside of the German bureaucracy'. None was a failure; and most of them, especially the three Socialist ministers, proved 'unusually effective diplomats'. Yet after 1923 'the restoration of the German professional diplomat was fully achieved', and under Stresemann it was the old guard who dealt with the Western Powers. In relations with Eastern Europe the Foreign Office had a competitor, or rather a pacemaker, in the German army: Seeckt started collaboration with the Soviet Government; the Wilhelmstrasse followed suit, and concluded the Rapallo agreement, well-received by German public opinion as a defiant gesture toward the Western Powers. Nor was that attitude changed by Locarno: in the 'first marked sally of Nazi foreign policy', over the disarmament conference, 'the Foreign Office and the Führer were at one'—Neurath and Bülow, representatives of the old diplomatic service, enthusiastically greeted Germany's break with the Geneva system. In fact, Hitler had his forerunners in the diplomats of the Weimar era; but Holborn, while criticizing the German campaign over the 'war-guilt' clause, omits to add how much the German Foreign Office, with its *Schuldreferat*, was behind it, nor does he mention its concern with the *Auslandsdeutsche*. In ultimate aims there was little to choose between the 'good Germans' and the Nazis; the difference was mainly in tactics and boldness (or rashness): the hesitations or apprehensions of the career diplomats, just as those of the professional soldiers, made Hitler turn elsewhere for advice. 'The Foreign Office', writes Craig,

> was entering an era in which its formerly proud position was to be systematically destroyed ... and ... the Wilhelmstrasse was to be degraded to the role of a mere 'technical apparatus', to carry out decisions in the formulation of which its staff had had no share.

In the very first year of the Nazi régime Goebbels 'annexed most of the staff and the duties of the press section of the Foreign Office'. Next, Ribbentrop established his *Büro* in competition to the official Wilhelmstrasse, and as Special Ambassador negotiated the naval agreement with Great Britain. In 1934, von Papen made his acceptance of the Vienna Embassy conditional upon being 'free from the jurisdiction of the Foreign Office but ... responsible to Hitler alone'.[1] Further, Fifth Column operations were entrusted to the *Auslandsorganisation*, which started to make policy on its own. And when Ribbentrop, placed at the head of the Foreign Office, set out to win back for it ground lost to other departments so as to secure its institutional survival, it was 'a survival without meaning', for policy was to be the exclusive concern of Hitler and himself, while the Foreign Office became 'little more than a stenographic bureau': this at least was the line of defence adopted by its officials after the war.

Italian diplomacy during the inter-war period is discussed in two essays by Professors H. Stuart Hughes and Felix Gilbert. There was a conflict between the traditional policy of Italy 'of slow and patient negotiation towards modest goals and the new [Fascist] program of vast ambitions and quick results'. But to begin with the differences were largely 'a matter of vocabulary'. 'Throughout the first decade of Fascist rule, most of the ambassadors continued to be men of the old type, career diplomats and frequently aristocrats.' Even Dino Grandi, 'one of the tough young men of the Fascist movement', when appointed Under-Secretary of the Foreign Office soon came to side with the professional diplomats. Mussolini himself was satisfied with small and cheap triumphs which could be boosted at home: his expansionism was as yet cautious even if his language was

[1] Craig here quotes from Papen's *Memoirs*. But Papen further relates how in 1936 he was saddled with a Counsellor, von Stein, 'an ardent Nazi' who negotiated on his own with the Austrian Nazis and reported direct to the Wilhelmstrasse. Papen refers in particular to one memorandum: 'Its contents have only come to my notice since the war, as part of the collection of German Foreign Office documents published by the Stationery Office in London.' A fine *alibi*—but in fact there is among the German documents a covering note from Papen forwarding that memorandum and commending it as valuable support for a *démarche* of his own. Given due care and caution, German balloons can usually be pricked.

not. When in May 1930, Grandi, now Foreign Minister, pro-
tested against some inflammatory speeches, 'What does it
matter what I say to my crowds?' asked Mussolini. 'Why do
you think I made you Foreign Minister except to be able to talk
here exactly as I please!' But after 1931 revisionism became a
dominant element in Mussolini's foreign policy: in response to
pre-Nazi German revisionism. In 1936 Ciano, who as Minister
of Propaganda had accused the diplomats of pusillanimity and
betrayal of the heroic spirit of the régime, became head of the
Foreign Office; and a year later boasted that it was 'the most
Fascist' Ministry in Italy. Without great changes in personnel,
something had changed in the atmosphere of the Office—'the
clockwork was broken'. The officials no longer knew what was
going on, for all the important work was done in Ciano's
Gabinetto which assumed control over the distribution of in-
coming information. Decisions were now made from above;
'the Ministry existed only to obey', while ambassadors were
poorly informed or briefed. 'Ciano liked to work outside the
regular diplomatic channels. At important embassies he had
confidants'; he also employed special emissaries, and 'cultivated
the method of direct meetings with foreign statesmen'. The
tono fascista in Italian diplomacy pointed to an alliance with
Hitler, and the belief that Mussolini could still be deflected
from it was a fatal delusion fostered in London by the British
Ambassador in Rome, Lord Perth, whom Professor Gilbert
describes as 'one of Britain's most successful and experienced
diplomats'—a statement which hardly does justice to British
diplomacy.

Soviet diplomacy is discussed in two chapters on Chicherin
and Litvinov by Mr. T. H. von Laue and Professor H. L.
Roberts. The Soviet Government started by abolishing diplomacy: they would address themselves to the peoples rather than
negotiate with Governments which they meant to overthrow.
And though in fact things were to develop along very different
lines, the Foreign Office and its representatives never again
attained real weight or any degree of independence. At the
slightest pretext the Politburo would deal with matters within
the jurisdiction of the Foreign Office; Chicherin, who held it

from 1918 till 1939, ranked low in the Communist party and 'could not expect to be heard in the inner councils'; he rarely dared to assert himself—both at home and abroad the Foreign Office suffered from the competition of the Comintern and the secret police, powerfully represented in the Politburo. Litvinov, an old Bolshevik, was introduced into the office to watch over his chief, before replacing him. But 'the post of the People's Commissar for Foreign Affairs did not, in itself, carry a great deal of weight in the Soviet system', and Litvinov himself did not rank high in the Party. 'Indeed, late in his career he is reported as remarking rather sourly: "You know what I am. I merely hand on diplomatic documents".' The Soviet system and its aims are hardly compatible with any degree of diplomatic autonomy.

The chapters on American diplomacy are of special interest to European readers. The subject is treated in Professor Perkins's chapter on 'The Department of State and American Public Opinion', and in sketches of three American Ambassadors: Dodd by F. L. Ford, and Bullit and Kennedy by William W. Kaufmann. Perkins starts by declaring that 'American diplomatic action has been determined by the people', that 'the general sentiment of the people lies at the root of every great issue', and that Presidents 'have been powerless to withstand these deep-seated feelings'. Are things different in Great Britain or France? And had not Hitler or Mussolini popular feeling behind them? More distinctive is the fact, conditioned by the nature of the American constitution, that in the United States the balance of influence 'is always tipping, . . . now to the executive, now to the legislature, and rarely to the professional diplomat'; and that 'no definite and fixed role can be assigned' to the Secretary of State. The uncertainty of harmony between executive and legislature, the power of Congressional Committees, and the non-Parliamentary position of the Secretary of State, account for some basic differences in the conduct of foreign affairs in the United States and in Great Britain; and in the absence of a deeper integration of the governing bodies, the personality of the President or the Secretary of State is apt to count for more than that of Parliamentary Ministers. American diplomacy in the inter-war period was dominated by the dogma of freedom of action—aloof and ineffective, it was as yet unconscious of the responsibilities of power. The account of the reception given to the honestly meant British inquiry concerning the Geneva Protocal, makes curious reading. And here are the three outstanding cases of active American intervention in world politics during that period: the Four Power pact with regard to the Pacific—'somehow or other . . . even in 1922 . . . regarded as innocent' (because it applied to the one region in which the United States took an active interest); the Kellogg Pact (even more naive though less mischievous than the League of Nations with which American idealism had burdened Europe); and the naval agreements of 1930 which lulled the United States 'into false security', and compelled the British, 'in order to propitiate the American Government', to reduce cruiser strength, with serious consequences in the 1940s.

Of the three American Ambassadors discussed in this book not one was a career diplomat. William Dodd, sent to Berlin in July 1933, was an ageing historian, who had studied in Germany and who, as so many sentimental pro-Germans, was harking back to 'a Germany that had once been', or that had never been at all. He believed that 'he was to go to Berlin as a living sermon on democracy', and that such an honest, frank mission could hardly fail of good result (consciously austere, he 'never dissembled the hostility he felt toward most career diplomats and businessmen in the Foreign Service'). He practised 'admonition-by-analogy', and found himself disliked in German official circles; and 'once he discovered that he could not convert the Nazis, his despondency practically incapacitated him as a diplomatic representative'. He was a 'worry' for the State Department, and never a key figure in its formulation of policy. Very different was the position of two men with eminently practical experience, Bullit in Paris and Kennedy in London. Their status in the Democratic party and their relations with President Roosevelt (who 'distrusted foreign service officers as a class') gave them a freedom of action not ordinarily accorded to diplomats, and their reports carried, to begin with, considerable weight in Washington, where 'policy was the product of cables received from abroad rather than of a dynamic conception of American interests'. But they, too, lacked an independent approach to the situation. Bullitt, who had long been convinced of the necessity of an agreement with Moscow, having gone there as Ambassador in 1933, returned disgusted and disillusioned, and was henceforth 'dominated by his distrust of the Soviet Union', 'with Great Britain playing the role of minor villain'. Extremely popular in Paris, especially in Government circles, he echoed their views, and played 'minister without portfolio in the kaleidoscope of French cabinets'. Similarly Kennedy in London became an intimate of Chamberlain and his circle, and an appeaser at any price. In short, both took their cues from the governments to which they were accredited, and their influence in Paris and London merely helped to 'reinforce the views already held by Daladier and Chamberlain'. After Munich Bullitt perceived at last the full extent of the German danger and at the time of the collapse of France played a part which did him credit (though even then he was capable of suspecting Britain of conserving her 'air force and fleet as bargaining counters for future negotiations with Hitler'). Kennedy, on the other hand, remained convinced that the United States must keep out of the conflict whatever may happen, and that England 'will go down fighting' but that it will not do 'the slightest bit of good'. He became 'a prophet of unrelieved gloom' and inaction, and lost all influence with the President. Both failed in their mission; they 'could obtain little or no guidance from the State Department', and gave it as little in return. But could they not find 'a fund of knowledge and experience' with the staffs of professional diplomats by whom they were served? Kaufmann's conclusion is that they could not, and that most of their faults derived 'from the sterility which characterized the thought of the professional diplomat during the inter-war period'. The book closes by registering insufficiency at all levels.

About a hundred years ago Guizot wrote in his *Mémoires*:[1]

The professional diplomats form, within the European community, a society of their own which lives by its own principles,

[1] Vol. ii, pp. 266–7.

customs, lights, and aspirations, and which, amid differences and even conflicts between States, preserves a quiet and permanent unity of its own. Moved by the divergent interests of nations, but not by their prejudices or momentary passions, that small diplomatic world may well recognize the general interest of the great European community with sufficient clearness and feel it with sufficient strength, to make it triumph over differences, and cause men, who have long upheld very different policies without ever quarrelling among themselves, and who have almost always shared the same atmosphere and horizons, to work sincerely for the success of the same policy.

The picture may be somewhat idealized but is not altogether fanciful. That diplomatic community had for its background the great French-speaking 'international' of the European aristocracy, which Guizot, French but not an aristocrat, diplomat but not *de carrière,* beheld with perhaps excessive admiration during years influenced by Princess Lieven. Now it is gone, and nothing can re-create it; and whatever of it had survived into the present century, was apt to rouse the ire, first of 'democrats' prating about 'open diplomacy' and 'diplomacy by conference',[1] and next of the dictators; and besides, the disapproval of a good many who fall into neither category. Distrust of professional diplomats is registered in almost every single chapter of this book.

But were a book attempted on the generals of the period, a similar story would be told. Clemenceau is credited with the

---

[1] Professor Craig touches upon the activities of that egregious group in Great Britain which, in the first quarter of this century, went by the name of Union of Democratic Control, and seems to overrate its importance. As *finale* to its activities he might have quoted the *démarche* undertaken on 29 July 1939, by one of its last survivors, Charles Roden Buxton, who told the Counsellor of the German Embassy that public discussion of how to preserve peace could 'no longer achieve its purpose', and that it was 'necessary to revert to a sort of secret diplomacy', and seek a way out of the difficulties 'by conversations from which the public was totally excluded'. In short all that was left of the *credo* of the U.D.C. was a pathetically naive belief in their own fitness to conduct diplomatic negotiations. (See *Documents and Materials relating to the Eve of the Second World War*, published by the Ministry of Foreign Affairs of the U.S.S.R., vol. ii, *Dirksen Papers*, pp. 106–12).

dictum that the conduct of war is too serious a business to be left to generals; others too, have acted on that principle. The man who bears the supreme responsibility in the State must retain the supreme direction of its most vital business: of home policy in peace time; of diplomacy in times of crisis; and of operations in war. So did monarchs in past ages; and so do modern heads of the Executive. And in this century international affairs so much dominate the life of the nations that the direction of foreign policy cannot be left to experts nor even to departmental chiefs, but must become the attribute of Presidents, Prime Ministers, or dictators: if ill-chosen, the worse for those who place them in positions of supreme power. But outside interference with the work of professionals, however authoritative, is apt to cause friction; and then the man at the top is likely to look for tools of his own: which adds to the difficulties of the situation. Still, in spite of a few outstanding men such as Rumbold, Coulondre, or Schulenburg, the diplomats, especially during the second half of the inter-war period, seem to have been hardly better fitted to deal with the situation than were their chiefs. There was insufficiency at all levels. There may have been in Europe an all-round decline during the inter-war period caused by human losses suffered in the war, and by deep disturbances of the mental and moral atmosphere among the survivors. Or perhaps the complexities of man-created problems now transcend the capacities of man with consequencies rendered even more serious by the steady growth of his technical power.

2

The European situation during the inter-war period turned on the same two pivotal problems with which we are now faced once more: of German nationalism and Russian Bolshevism, and how to contain one without playing into the hands of the other. The capacity of either for military renascence was vastly underrated, and so was their capacity for co-operating despite ideological differences and a cordial mutual dislike. The frontiers of Germany as drawn at Versailles were eminently fair to the Germans: France gave in over the Rhineland and even over the Saar; and plebiscites were held in East Prussia and Upper Silesia where the Polish national revival was advancing without having reached its term. Still, the Germans kept up a spurious agitation over the Corridor and Danzig; while the Sudetens, Pan-Germans in 1848 and forerunners of the Nazis in 1898, could be trusted to reject even a Swiss settlement with the Czechs (a *Verschweizerung* Henlein contemptuously called it in 1937). How then could the national existence of Poland and Czechoslovakia be safeguarded except through a French hegemony in Europe? And how could French hegemony be maintained without restrictions on German sovereignty and armaments? The triple failure of French, Czech, and Polish diplomacy, working on different lines, forms a curious pattern in the book on *The Diplomats*.

Could the policy of Clemenceau and Poincaré toward Germany have been carried through, as that of containing France was after the Treaty of Vienna, Europe might have been spared a new deadly dose of German aggression. It was abandoned by the French themselves: French humanitarian liberalism was averse to indefinitely holding down the Germans; there was the old, deep-rooted pacifism both of the French *haute finance* and of the French labour movement, and a widespread fear and dislike of Russian Bolshevism; a horror at the idea of another war, and a weakening of the French national fibre; hence an exaggerated regard for British and American opinion: a nation which abandons safeguards essential to its own security in deference to foreign opinion ceases indeed to be a Great Power. Whatever the reasons, there was French *défaillance* after 1925: disguised at first, stark in its concluding stages; and the action of French diplomacy toward Germany during those fourteen years was almost invariably softer than its professions.

The French system as planned in 1919 attached considerable importance to the alliances with Poland and Czechoslovakia, 'partners in the job of holding Germany in check'; and Philippe Berthelot, the Secretary General of the Quai d'Orsay, was their 'most consistent artisan'. Yet he was opposed to the Ruhr occupation, being convinced 'that, somehow or other, Germany and France must manage to live together in the same

European system', or the weight of 70 million organized hard-working Germans would ultimately prove too much for 38 million Frenchmen: 'if...we don't try to create a German republic hostile to war, we are doomed'. The fact which neither he nor other advocates of reconciliation with Germany would squarely face was that a free hand toward Poland was Germany's irreducible price for friendship with the West: otherwise she would seek and find her natural ally against the Poles in Russia. Briand's guiding rules for French diplomacy, 'to insure for France...all possible elements of immediate security ...and in rhythm with its development, to seek the broader bases of European peace', sound well so long as no attempt is made to translate them into concrete terms. How could close Anglo-French co-operation and a Franco-German rapprochement be reconciled with Eastern alliances in which Great Britain refused to participate and which the Germans were out to annul? Locarno drew a clear distinction between Germany's Western and her Eastern frontiers; but an attempt was immediately made to obscure it by making Germany conclude arbitration treaties with Poland and Czechoslovakia, which neither reassured the Poles nor were ever taken seriously by the Germans.

The Locarno treaties were well-nigh symbolic of the self-deceiving diplomacy of the League of Nations period. Berthelot, according to his friend Claudel, 'put the Locarno program into effect and between 1925 and 1932 went along with Briand not so much because he believed in the policy but simply because he could envisage no alternatives'. In fact Locarno was an abdication on the part of France: 'the French never again would act alone', writes Challener; 'they had...lost a large part of their nerve....' To the Germans, on the other hand, it was a mere starting point. 'What was so alarming', wrote Alexis Léger, 'was that it seemed impossible to reach finality; each concession, freely granted in the desire to conciliate, was promptly followed by fresh and yet more extravagant demands.'[1] Briand died in

[1] Cf. also Rumbold's despatch of 3 July 1930: 'It is an unattractive feature of the German character to display little gratitude for favours received, but when the receipt of favours is followed up by fresh demands, there are grounds for feeling impatient.'

1932, before the bankruptcy of his policy had become blatantly obvious. Berthelot, unnerved by the impact of failure, 'isolated himself more and more in the accomplishment of his purely routine, administrative tasks'; and a short time before his death, bitterly remarked that the law of gangsters was being imposed everywhere, and that 'brigands have more energy than honest men'.

By 1935 the growing weakness of France was patent, and led to an independent policy on the part of Poland, which in turn still further undermined the French system. There were only two logical lines which French policy could have now pursued: to contain Hitler Germany through an alliance with Soviet Russia, even if this was to estrange Poland still further; or to adopt a policy of *rapprochement* with Germany tacitly sacrificing her Eastern allies. Both these policies were attempted, without ever being fully avowed or carried through to their distasteful end. M. Coulondre, the outstanding French diplomat in the last years of the inter-war period, though under no illusions as to the character and ultimate aims of the Soviet Government, 'clung with dogged consistency to two simple ideas: first, that Germany must be stopped; second, that only a tight military alliance between the Western Powers and the Soviet Union could stop her'. And he clearly realized that Czechoslovakia was 'the only country on which the action of the three great peaceful Powers could be conjoined'. He also saw that, especially in view of Poland's expansion beyond the Curzon Line, no such junction could be expected for her defence, and he did not overestimate, as many did, her military importance. But he was 'The Voice in the Wilderness'—the title of the essay about him which Mr. Ford and Professor Schorske contribute to the book.

A more comprehending reception was given in the Laval-Flandin-Bonnet period to the policy advocated by M. François-Poncet, whose career is sketched in Mr. Ford's essay on 'Three Observers in Berlin'. François-Poncet started as a scholar and teacher; during the war of 1914 turned to applied economics; through his marriage 'acquired substantial holdings in the steel industry'; during the Ruhr occupation was economic adviser to the commanding general; sat in the Chamber of Deputies, 1924–31, 'a skillful opponent of organized labour and one of French industry's cleverest parliamentary spokesmen'; in 1930 was appointed Under-Secretary at the Quai d'Orsay, and next in the Premier's office under Laval; and in 1931, at the age of 46, was sent as Ambassador to Berlin. While inclined to be tough toward Weimar Germany, he always favoured closer industrial ties between Germany and France, and even before he went to Berlin, 'had proposed a complex international cartel plan'. He soon came to doubt the chances of blocking Hitler by frontal resistance, and anyhow would only have attempted it with Mussolini for ally: he openly showed to the Germans his dislike of the Spanish government, 'this last stronghold of the Popular Front', and of the French-Soviet pact of 1935.

The policy for which François-Poncet was agitating, once identified beneath the disavowals that burden his *Souvenirs* . . . was, in fact, the common property of a substantial section of the French Right. Fear of the Russia of Stalin, indifference towards the Czechoslovakia of Beneš, reliance on the Poland of Beck, admiration for the Italy of Mussolini, all were implicit in the ambassador's attitude. . .

'It is time', he said to Neville Henderson in May 1938, 'that Europe revised its opinion of M. Beneš'; and to Sir Eric Phipps, Ambassador in Paris, early in June, 'that the Allies should offer Hitler a deal on the Sudeten question'. Soon he was urging 'the possibility of a Great Power settlement and "evolutionary changes" in existing alliances'; and 'the vital preparatory work' for Munich was carried out by him in a visit which, on orders from Bonnet, he paid to Hitler on the morning of 28 September —but the 'ambassador's memoirs tend to minimize his own importance in this instance, stressing instead the decisive role of British policy throughout the crisis'. And next, he made his 'culminating effort to achieve better relations between Paris and Berlin': during his visit to Berchtesgaden on 18 October, he broached the idea of the Franco-German declaration, signed on 6 December during Ribbentrop's visit to Paris. But by that time François-Poncet had left Berlin 'to take up his duties in

Rome, where he remarked to the German Ambassador that it had been time for him to leave the Reich: "You should stop while it tastes best".' In Rome he declared to Mussolini 'that "he had come to develop the policy of the Munich Agreement" by converting into reality the dream of a four Power system'. He certainly did not relish the crudities of the Nazi régime, yet 'nothing about Nazism so repelled him as to inhibit his efforts to arrange an understanding between the French government and French industry, on the one hand, and Hitler's Reich, on the other'; and in Rome 'he was willing to swallow the insults he received', and still pursue his European plans based on business pacifism.

It was possible, though hardly sensible, to imagine that France could achieve security behind a military and diplomatic Maginot line; but in the case of Czechoslovakia and Poland geographical situation and ethnic composition alike precluded isolation. The basic factor in the national restoration and the national survival of both was their alliance with France: yet even this failed to create any real community between the Czechs and the Poles. On the German front there was a fine but significant difference between them: Austria was the old enemy of the Czechs, but Prussia of the Poles; elsewhere their hostilities and policies diverged still more. Besides, in outlook and traditions, based on widely different social structures, the two nations were unsympathetic to each other; and the conflict over Teschen was merely a symptom of a much deeper cleavage. Both States bore the imprint of their makers, Masaryk and Pilsudski; and the two found their disciples and heirs in Beneš and Beck who, especially after the deaths of their masters, were in complete control of the foreign policies of their States.

'Czechoslovakia: The Diplomacy of Eduard Beneš' is the title of Mr. Paul Zinner's essay. Indeed, during the twenty years of Czechoslovakia's independent existence, her foreign policy was made by Beneš who became 'Foreign Minister by profession'. As such he combined expert knowledge derived from long practice with 'a general disdain for expert advice and a penchant for informal diplomacy' which he practised travelling as 'a roving ambassador of his country' from one European capital to another and to Geneva, in 'an attempt to deal with the responsible European statesmen personally ... ' He 'clearly saw that the welfare of a democratic Czechoslovakia coincided with the maintenance of a stable and peaceful Europe', of the Versailles *status quo* and the effectiveness of the League of Nations system. His foreign policy was a continual search for security, both through bilateral and regional agreements—the French alliance and the Little Entente—and through general schemes of arbitration and pacific settlement of disputes. He tried assiduously to increase the moral and political prestige of the League, and within the League he vindicated the rights of the lesser European Powers: among their representatives he 'perhaps stands out as the one who was most often and most intimately involved in events of European significance'. Truly conciliatory, a believer in Parliament and Assemblies, always keen to explain his thought and to discuss compromises, an enthusiastic supporter of any scheme aiming at collective security, he was listened to with attention in the 1920's, but with growing impatience in the changed international climate of the 1930's: 'his old gifts had little relation to the realities of the new age of power politics'. When the crisis came of Czechoslovakia's existence Beneš's alliances and treaties proved mere scraps of paper, and his League concepts idle dreams; and he was run down, derided, and traduced. 'Diplomacy by conference' used Geneva phraseology in its Munich performance; and Beneš, who had so long employed it, believing or wishing to believe in the shams of the League, was in the end unable to face stark reality and capitulated, rather than take the risk of single-handed action. Even Czechoslovakia's re-establishment after the war could not repair the loss of prestige which he had suffered through his surrender in 1938. It was a contributing factor to his second and final defeat in 1948.

Masaryk was of humble origin, a scholar and thinker with a humanitarian outlook; Pilsudski, of gentry extraction and a revolutionary conspirator and terrorist by early training, was a bold and bitter fighter, contemptuous of other men, and scornful of Parliamentary institutions and public opinion. Beneš and Beck both tried to walk in the paths of their masters; but to fall

short in philosophical elevation is far less pitiable than to flop
as the strong man; and as Mr. Henry Roberts says of Beck,
'this ... rather Mephistophelean figure conveyed an impression
of hardness without depth'. When disaster overwhelmed him,
he received scant sympathy, and is remembered

> as the man who refused to work with the Little Entente or the
> League of Nations, who pursued, in substance, a pro-German
> policy after 1934, who joined in the dismembering of Czecho-
> slovakia, and, finally, as the man whose stubborn refusal to enter
> any combination with the Russians contributed to the failure of
> the Anglo-French-Soviet negotiations of the spring and summer
> of 1939.

Beck's manner of doing things, with a gratuitous display of
arrogance and brutality, and by temperamental reaction rather
than to rational purpose, put an unpleasant complexion even on
policies not lacking deeper justification. Doubts might well
have been entertained concerning the League; still, it was not
for Poland in her precarious situation to try to impair its authority, from sheer resentment at the 'minority treaties' and League
control in Danzig. The Little Entente was directed against the
Magyars, a gentry nation like the Poles and their traditional
friends; and while to the Czechs Russia was their 'big brother',
to Poland, in possession of White Russian and Ukrainian lands,
she was a dangerous enemy. France expected unquestioning
devotion from the Poles, but at Locarno concluded an equivocal
treaty with the Germans, after that attempted an Eastern
Locarno with the Russians, and throughout displayed weakness
toward Nazi Germany. No wonder if the Poles tried to re-
insure themselves in their own fashion. Beck's action towards
Czechoslovakia was mean, brutal, and stupid, but it hardly
became French Munichers to rate him for it. In 1939 the Western
Powers ought perhaps to have sacrificed Poland to Russia;
but the Poles could not be expected to do so themselves. Mr.
Roberts, while admitting certain criticisms of Beck, says that
'in all probability no arrangement by the Eastern European
States could have assured the security of the area, even had their
statesmen been far wiser and more self-restrained'; and Mr.

Zinner, speaking about Czechoslovakia's paper alliances, questions 'whether an alternate course of action by Beneš ... would have been crowned with greater success'. There are situations wherein it is well-nigh impossible for statesmen or diplomats to be justified by results.

11

'HITLER: A STUDY IN TYRANNY'

MUST WE talk of Hitler? We must, however distasteful the subject: for a reckoning there has to be with the forces that made
him, and we shall have to reckon with them also in the future:
and the viler Hitler the man, the more significant is the part
which he was able to play in history. The first thing therefore is
to have the facts about him carefully sifted, soberly stated, and
properly documented: this Mr. Alan Bullock has done in the
730 pages of his book, *Hitler: A Study in Tyranny*. He does not
attempt ingenious explanations, which would unavoidably
result in a one-sided selection and grouping of material: scope
is left to the judgement of the reader. I shall try to delineate
some of the essential features of Mr. Bullock's story.

Adolf Hitler, born in 1889 the son of a petty Austrian official,
refused to follow his father's profession. 'One day it became
clear to me', he writes in *Mein Kampf*, 'that I would be a
painter, I mean an artist. . . .' Note how he guards against
being misunderstood: an artist, not a house-painter. He speaks
of the deep ditch that separated the *petit bourgeois*, 'among
whom I passed my younger days', from the working classes;
'this division,' he says, 'which we may almost call enmity',
springs from fear of reverting to the condition of manual lab-
ourers, or at least of being classed with them; and he himself,
in his passionate refusal to join a trade union, reproduced that
attitude. At the climax of his career Hitler still thought that
he should have been a great painter or architect and not a statesman. But he had neither artistic taste nor ability and, in spite of
training received at an art school in Munich (an episode left

out of *Mein Kampf*), he failed to secure admission to the Vienna Academy of Fine Arts. Unwilling to settle down to regular work, lazy and moody, he became a social nondescript: he slept in doss-houses, did casual jobs, or painted picture post-cards or posters and advertisements for small shops. But all along his passion was reading newspapers and talking politics, which even then he did with uncontrolled violence. 'He gave rein to his hatreds—against the Jews, the priests, the Social Democrats, the Habsburgs. . . . The few people with whom he had been friendly became tired of him, of his strange behaviour and wild talk.' 'During these years', writes Hitler, '. . . a defin-ite outlook on the world took shape in my mind. . . . Since then I have extended that foundation very little, I changed nothing in it . . .'—which was only too true. Mr. Bullock repeatedly adverts to the Austrian strands in Hitler's character and men-tality; he was truly representative of his class and country, and especially of that unadulterated provincial Austria with its surly hostility to Imperial, cosmopolitan Vienna and its Jewish intel-ligentsia. 'It is not by the principles of humanity that man lives', declared Hitler in February 1928, '. . . but solely by means of the most brutal struggle.' This Mr. Bullock describes as 'the natural philosophy of the doss-house'. But there is another, per-haps more significant, side to it: after 1866 and 1870, German nationalists in Austria had come to worship Prussia's strength; of the positive qualities from which it sprang—hard work, mental tidiness, devotion to duty, regularity, and an austere (though very narrow) morality—they had none, least of all Hitler, nor could he have acquired them; what such a sham-Prussian could reproduce on the cheap was brutality.

Hitler left Vienna in 1913, perhaps to evade military service for which he failed to report. In 1914 he joined the German Army: war was to him an escape from frustration and failure. In December 1914 he was awarded the Iron Cross, Second Class, and in August 1918, the Iron Cross, First Class, 'an uncommon decoration for a corporal'. Neither the reason of that award, nor of his remaining a corporal, has been satisfactorily ex-plained. At the end of the war Hitler was in his thirtieth year; he had little prospect of finding a job; in fact, 'he was not interested in work. . . ; he never had been': 'I resolved', he writes, 'that I would take up political work.' What part he played, if any, during the Munich Communist régime of April–May 1919, is uncertain. After its overthrow, Bavaria, under a right-wing government with strong particularist leanings, became the refuge of shady elements from the late Freikorps, bitter enemies of the Weimar régime, and a training school for political murder and terrorism; the Police President of Munich, when asked if he knew that there were political murder gangs in Bavaria, replied: 'Yes, but not enough of them.' Similarly minded, Major-General von Epp of the Munich Army Command, and his Assistant, Major Roehm, gave Hitler in its Political Department the post of educational officer for the troops 'with the task of inoculating the men against contagion by socialist, pacifist or democratic ideas'. Into the German Workers' Party which Hitler was building up, Roehm pushed ex-Freikorps men and ex-servicemen; and the first 'strong arm squads' were formed under an ex-convict, the nucleus of the S.A. Hitler was now able to prove his powers of agitator and mob orator, and under protection from the Army Command to form and practise with impunity his methods of incitement, violence, and intimidation.

In a speech of 30 January 1941, Hitler claimed: 'No human being has declared or recorded what he wanted more often than I'—nor his methods: few politicians have made known with equal frankness their views about the masses and how to appeal to them. Their receptive powers 'are very restricted', Hitler wrote in *Mein Kampf*, 'and their understanding is feeble . . . all effective propaganda must be confined to a few bare necessities and . . . expressed in a few stereotyped formulas'. 'The broad masses of the nation . . . more readily fall victims to the big lie than to the small lie, since they themselves often tell small lies in little matters, but would be ashamed to resort to large-scale falsehoods.' 'The masses feel very little shame at being terrorized intellectually and are scarcely conscious of the fact that their freedom as human beings is impudently abused.' 'The very first condition . . . in every kind of propaganda is a systematically one-sided attitude towards every problem that has to be dealt with. . . . When they see an un-compromising onslaught against an adversary, the people have at all times taken this as proof that right is on the side of the active aggressor . . .' 'The art of leadership consists of consoli-dating the attention of the people against a single adversary. . . . The leader of genius must have the ability to make different opponents appear as if they belonged to one category.' Here then were in a nutshell the precepts of the supreme political gangster with an insight bordering on genius into the psyche of his own nation: the crass immorality of his tenets and methods shocked few among the Germans who have long relished an ostentatiously cynical attitude in politics; and whatever was offensive in his pronouncements, each would only apply to the others.

Hitler had no use or respect for truth, hardly any conception of it. The mental processes of criticism and analysis jarred on him, and his hostility to 'freedom of thought or discussion represented a personal dislike quite as much as a political ex-pedient'. He talked incessantly, and with a blend of fanaticism and calculation would talk himself into conviction or 'whip himself into a passion which enabled him to bear down all opposition, and provided him with the motive power to enforce his will on others'. 'The most obvious instance of this', writes Mr. Bullock, 'is the synthetic fury, which he could assume or discard at will, over the treatment of German minorities abroad.' He would not listen to the Germans in the South Tyrol and helped to uproot them in the Baltic States, but worked himself into a frenzy of indignation over imaginary persecut-tions in Czechoslovakia or Poland when he wished London or Paris to soften up for him the victim he was about to attack. 'Hitler in a rage appeared to lose all control of himself. His face became mottled and swollen with fury, he screamed at the top of his voice, spitting out a stream of abuse, waving his arms wildly and drumming on the table or the wall with his fists. As suddenly as he had begun he would stop, smooth down his hair, straighten his collar and resume a more normal voice.' There was 'skilful and deliberate exploitation of his own tem-perament.'

He hit, according to Mr. Bullock, on a psychological fact
(certainly true of the Germans): 'that violence and terror have
their own propaganda value, and that the display of physical
force attracts as many as it repels'. In using violence Hitler
would give it the widest possible publicity. 'The reputation of
our hall-guard squads', he wrote in *Mein Kampf*, 'stamped us
as a political fighting force and not as a debating society.' In
his speeches he stressed and repeated such words as 'smash',
'force', 'ruthless', or 'hatred'; and his shortcoming as an orator
'mattered little beside the extraordinary impression of force,
the immediacy of passion, the intensity of hatred, fury, and
menace conveyed by the sound of the voice alone without regard to what he said'. 'With an almost inexhaustible fund of
resentment in his own character to draw from', he made the
appeal to nationalist resentment an essential part of his stock-
in-trade, and offered the Germans 'a series of objects on which
to lavish the blame for their misfortunes'. 'Lashing himself to
a pitch of near-hysteria, he would scream and spit out his
resentment', evoking a hysterical response in his audience. Otto
Strasser, one of his bitterest critics, wrote:

> Adolf Hitler enters a hall. He sniffs the air. For a minute he
> gropes, feels his way, senses the atmosphere. Suddenly he bursts
> forth. His words go like an arrow to their target, he touches each
> private wound on the raw, liberating the mass unconscious, ex-
> pressing its innermost aspirations, telling it what it most wants
> to hear.

And Hitler himself says about the orator: 'He will always
follow the lead of the great mass in such a way that from the
living emotion of his hearers the apt word which he needs will
be suggested to him and in its turn this will go straight to the
hearts of his hearers.' There is a Jewish legend that the burning
bush, from which the voice of the Lord spoke to Moses, was
the nation of Israel gathered at the foot of Mount Sinai. The
wording of the *Declaration of the Rights of Man and Citizen*,
over which the most distinguished draftsmen had floundered
in the seclusion of their studies, came to them, lapidary and
noble, as they were facing the crowded Assembly. And it was

again on the masses that Hitler drew: what was worst in the Germans, their hatreds and resentments, their envy and cruelty, their brutality and adoration of force, he focused and radiated back on them. A master in the realm of psyche but debarred from that of the spirit, he was the Prophet of the possessed; and interchange there was between him and them, unknown between any other political leader and his followers. This is the outstanding fact about Hitler and the Third Reich.

Hitler made also a tactical discovery: that it was possible in Germany to create a mass-organization comprising hundreds of thousands of armed men, to extol its 'indomitable aggressive spirit' and its determination brutally to enforce its will, and yet play safe. The S.A., says Mr. Bullock, was for street brawls only, 'the shock troops of a revolution that was never to be made': Hitler was determined to obtain power 'without a head-on collision with the forces of the State, above all with the Army'. On May Day 1923, 20,000 armed Stormtroopers were gathered in a field near Munich for an attack against the Socialist procession; but when a thin cordon of troops was thrown round them, Hitler, though urged by some of his lieutenants to use his superior numbers to overpower the troops, capitulated. That no further action was taken against him by the Bavarian Government and the Army 'suggested that, in more favourable circumstances, another attempt to force the hand of the authorities might succeed'. It was indeed with their help that, half a year later, he hoped to pull off his *Putsch*. But he bungled the affair, and would have withdrawn once more had not Ludendorff forced him to act. They marched the next morning, were met by a line of police, and were fired at; Ludendorff and his A.D.C. pushed through the line, but the Nazi leaders, who had all the time 'appealed openly to violence, crumpled up and fled', Hitler first. 'His revolution—even in 1923—had been designed', writes Mr. Bullock, 'as a "revolution by permission of the Herr President"'; and proposals to have him deported—he was still an alien—were shelved by indulgent protectors in high places.

Never again was he to risk a collision with the armed forces of the State: when in 1925 he was forbidden for a time to speak in public, he obeyed; and when in April 1932, the dissolution was ordered of the S.A., by then 400,000 strong, and Roehm thought of resisting, Hitler insisted that the S.A. must obey. Revolutionary action as he understood it, that is violence on a grand scale, had to be postponed till he was invested with the power of the State and in control of its machinery (but when five Nazis in the Silesian village of Potempa kicked to death a Communist in front of his mother, he addressed them as 'My comrades', and told them that their liberation was 'a question of our honour'). In Parliamentary and Presidential elections he engaged under protest: 'For us Parliament is not an end in it-self, but merely a means to an end . . . we are a Parliamentary party by compulsion . . . democracy must be defeated with the weapons of democracy.' But once he was able to do so constitu-tionally, he would form the State in the manner he thought right; and then, he added, 'heads will roll': a prospect which was apparently cheering rather than repellent to the ever-growing throng of his followers.

Within the Party, the Führer insisted on unquestioning sub-mission to his will and commands: disobedience was the only 'moral turpitude' punished with expulsion from the Party. Discipline heightened in individual members the feeling of aggregate strength; and the Party program was declared un-alterable, and was never allowed to become a subject of discus-sion. 'But the attitude of the leaders towards the program', writes Mr. Bullock, 'was entirely opportunist. For them . . . the real object was to get their hands on the State. They were . . . the gutter *élite*, avid for power, position, and wealth. . . .' Hitler would adjust his program to suit his audience. 'The Com-munists deliberately limited their appeal to one class, while Hitler aimed to unite the discontented of all classes.' Much of his following still adhered to anti-capitalist tenets, but he was building up the movement on large subsidies from the political funds of the heavy industry and big business. Conservative politicians and the generals had control of the State and the Army, and the bankers and business men had the money; but Hitler had the masses. While they carried on government by Presidential decrees and with dwindling popular and Parliamentary support, he, in the Reichstag elections of July 1932, secured nearly 14 million votes, 37·3 of the total cast. The question was when the two sides would join hands, and on what terms. In the end Hitler attained power not through a clear electoral majority, nor through an irresistible revolutionary or national movement: 'he was jobbed into office by a backstairs intrigue', writes Mr. Bullock, 'by a shoddy deal with the "Old Gang".' Yet his power 'was founded on popular support to a degree few people cared, or still care, to admit', and he made a genuine appeal, especially to the younger generation. Moreover millions of non-Nazis showed no moral repugnance to him and his methods; and, what mattered most, he was favoured by the Army and its leaders.

The Conservative politicians who had placed him in office and joined him in it, believed that he could be held in check and tamed. They were soon left gasping for breath. He was free of all restraint or inhibitions in using the formidable power placed in his hands, 'a man without roots, with neither home nor family', writes Mr. Bullock, '. . . who admitted no loyalties, was bound by no traditions, and felt respect neither for God nor man.' Conscience was to him 'a Jewish invention, a blemish like circumcision', and Providence was invoked only as a foil to his own person. He boasted. 'We have no scruples, no bourgeois hesitations'; he combined considerable intellectual powers and a political virtuosity; and he was now ruler of a nation which, like himself before he had attained power, would duly submit to any decree of those placed in authority over it. Step by step he achieved arbitrary power, more absolute even than that of Mussolini. All political landmarks were eliminated in the German scene; the Federal States, the political parties, the Trade Unions, were annihilated in the process of *Gleichschaltung*. The Civil Service and the police were purged; the spoils of office went to the Nazis. 'The street gangs', writes Mr. Bullock, 'had seized control of the resources of a great modern State'. From the first the Jews were delivered to merciless persecution, and violence and cruelty were encouraged against previous opponents. There was a breakdown of law and order with the connivance of the State. 'Men were arrested, beaten and murdered for no more substantial reason than to satisfy a private grudge, to secure a man's job or his apartment, and to gratify a taste for sadism.' This was the revolution of the S.A. in power; but when Roehm came into conflict with the Army leadership, the S.A. was broken in the purge of 30 June 1934, in which Hitler murdered some of his oldest friends, and in exchange secured, a month later, the succession to Hindenburg from the Army very well satisfied with the events of that June weekend. There is no denying the ability with which he got the better of all his domestic opponents, and next of the statesmen on the international scene. They were feeble; they would not believe that anyone could act as Hitler did, time after time; and he had luck—his methods suited the circumstances. Still, the fact remains that under Hitler the German nation won victories and attained an extension of power not seen in Europe since the days of Napoleon, and far surpassing what it had achieved in the First World War; and that in so far as the leadership was concerned, diplomatic and military, the merit was mainly with Hitler himself. He and his story pose the insoluble enigma of success.

Hitler's mind was uncreative and unoriginal, and he 'seems to have been genuinely unaware of the extent of his unoriginality'. His appearance was unimpressive, 'plebeian through and through, with none of the physical characteristics of the racial superiority he was always invoking'; while in his coarse and curiously undistinguished face, the eyes alone attracted attention. His imagination, soaked in German neo-romanticism, produced a travesty of Wagner, Nietzsche, and Schopenhauer. Originality he achieved solely 'in the terrifying literal way in which he set to work to translate fantasy into reality', war and conquest having removed all restraint on him. 'The S.S. extermination squads,' writes Mr. Bullock, 'the *Einsatzkommandos*, with their gas-vans and death camps; the planned elimination of the Jewish race; the treatment of the Poles and Russians, the Slav *Untermenschen*—these...were fruits of Hitler's imagination.' No generous ideas inspired the Nazi revolution whose only themes were domination and destruction. 'It is this emptiness, this lack of anything to justify the suffering he caused . . . which makes Hitler both so repellent and so barren a figure.'

In the end megalomania wrought Hitler's own destruction. Suspicion of the expert, class-resentment against the Officer Corps, and a firm belief that he himself was endowed with more than ordinary gifts, made him assume the direction of war, even in detail. His 'unbounded confidence' in himself, of which he boasted, destroyed self-criticism and cut him off from reality. More and more, he shut himself up and 'lived in a private world of his own, from which the ugly facts of Germany's situation were excluded'. Finally he could no longer be persuaded to make a speech in public: he said he was waiting for a military success; Mr. Bullock suspects a deeper reason: 'Hitler's gifts as an orator had always depended on his flair for sensing what was in the minds of his audience. He no longer wanted to know what was in the minds of the German people.' And then, when his power had vanished and the enemy was closing in on him, nothing remained but a snarling, raving maniac, who in his quieter hours bored his companions with a monotonous repetition of reminiscences from his youth, and with 'anecdotes about his dog and his diet, interspersed with complaints about the stupidity and wickedness of the world'. At fifty-five he was an old man with ashen complexion and shuffling gait. 'It was no longer simply his left hand, but the whole left side of his body that trembled . . .' writes General Guderian. 'He walked awkwardly, stooped more than ever, and his gestures were both jerky and slow. He had to have a chair pushed under him when he wished to sit down.' And another witness at a conference in Hitler's bunker, in February 1945: 'His head was slightly wobbling. . . . There was an indescribable flickering glow in his eyes, creating a fearsome and unnatural effect. His face and the parts around his eyes gave the impression of total exhaustion.' Yet at this, and at other conferences, he would shout at his Service chiefs his impossible demands and arbitrary decisions, treating them as pygmies who failed to rise to the level of his genius and vision, or cursing them for their cowardice, treachery, and incompetence: in the increasing vulgarity of his language, the Hitler

L

of the Vienna days was once more to the force. Amid the sufferings and defeat he had brought on Germany, he thought of himself as betrayed, by a people unworthy of their Führer. On 19 March 1945, he said to Speer, his Minister for Armaments and Munitions:

> If the war is to be lost, the nation also will perish. . . . There is no need to consider the basis even of a most primitive existence any longer. On the contrary, it is better to destroy even that, and to destroy it ourselves.

A crude fantasy of a Wagnerian 'Night of the Gods', farcical and ludicrous like all his fancies and ideas when he had no longer the power to inflict them as tragedy on millions of men. Yet his ghost and figure may work still further havoc. The relation of the Germans to him and what he stands for in their history, will deeply affect its further course.

12

'THE NEMESIS OF POWER'

THE PART played by the German Army in the politics of the Weimar Republic and of the Third Reich forms the central theme of Mr. John Wheeler-Bennett's new book *The Nemesis of Power*. It is the paradoxical story of maximum ascendancy attained by the army leaders under the Parliamentary Republic, and of gradual decline in status under Hitler; of the way in which they who despised the parliamentary régime and patronized the Nazis brought about their own downfall and humiliation.

The book links up with Mr. Wheeler-Bennett's previous three major works on contemporary history, *Hindenburg, Brest-Litovsk*, and *Munich*, and is his crowning achievement in that field: in it the *genre* which he has created appears in a matured and highly perfected form. Writers of contemporary history are usually either men who had a direct share in its making, or who had watched the scene from a distance: which gives their work an egocentric or an academic character. Mr. Wheeler-Bennett has intimately known many of the actors in the drama, and watched them at work, but without playing an active part of his own; and next he settled down to years of study of documentary evidence concerning the events he had witnessed, in a manner worthy of a master historian, keeping at the same time in close touch with men who from their own experience could help to elucidate and supplement such evidence. Impersonal in his work and yet supremely interested in his subject, alert and a good listener, he has the gift of eliciting information and critically incorporating it into his story. There is in him a touch of Boswell, and more than a touch of Horace Walpole who moved among the leading politicians but seldom had a political task to perform, and thus became the observer *par excellence.* Diplomacy or politics would have been for Mr. Wheeler-Bennett his obvious choice of a career; ill-health in his earlier years debarred him from either; and so he, too, settled down as an observer, where in the regular course he might have been a doer, with the limitations which action imposes. Circumstances determine our lives, but we shape our lives by what we make of circumstances.

The theme of Mr. Wheeler-Bennett's new book is crucial to the history of our time. When, on 7 May 1945, a representative of the German High Command signed the instrument of Unconditional Surrender, it was hoped that the German era in European history, so replete with disaster, had reached its term, and that the foremost aim of the Allies, repeatedly emphasized by their leaders, would be realized; Prussian militarism was to be destroyed along with the iniquities of National Socialism. The Prussian Army had enabled the Hohenzollerns and their servants to forge the bonds of German unity, the basis of German predominance in Europe. During the first world war the German High Command, under Hindenburg and Ludendorff, established its supremacy over the civilian government, and even over its own nominal Supreme Commander, the Emperor. When military defeat put an end to monarchical rule, the Army re-emerged under the Republic as the guardian of order and of national unity. Never was its independence and political power more pronounced than under the Weimar Republic; and it was even greater during the six years of the Socialist President Ebert than during the next eight years, when Hindenburg, premier soldier of the Reich, overshadowed the Army Command. The fear of Bolshevism at home, and the desire to see Germany's might re-established abroad, made the Army leaders into recognized arbiters of the internal affairs of the Reich and, to a great extent, of its foreign policy also.

In October 1918 Ludendorff hysterically cried out for an armistice and, to placate President Wilson, helped to stage a democratic transformation. The moderate Socialists, while making revolutionary gestures, frantically tried to shore up the imperial régime; they feared responsibility and they hated communism. Hoisted into power, Ebert, on the first night in the Chancellor's office, made a well-nigh symbolic discovery: on the table stood a telephone connecting him by a private and secret line with Army Headquarters. It rang: General Gröner, Ludendorff's successor, was speaking. Was the Government willing to protect Germany from anarchy and to restore order, he asked. Yes, it was. 'Then the High Command will maintain discipline in the Army and bring it peacefully home.' In a few sentences a pact was concluded between a defeated army and a tottering semi-revolutionary régime; and the Weimar Republic was doomed at birth. The Socialist Government helped to restore the authority of the Officer Corps; and when the troops, like victors, marched through the Brandenburger Tor with standards and music and arms, they were greeted by Ebert with the words: 'I salute you, who return unvanquished from the field of battle'. So saying, he unwittingly absolved the General Staff and indicted the revolution. The legend of the 'stab-in-the-back' was born.

Soon the General Staff was dictating to the Socialist Government. Ebert, bourgeois at heart and patriotic German, retained a deep respect for a Prussian Field-Marshal; Noske, Socialist Minister of Defence, purred when flattered by army officers. Polish incursions and Communist risings were apprehended; and with the Army practically disbanded, the High Command started raising from its wreckage Free Corps of 'politically reliable' adventurers and gangsters, the nuclei of future Nazi formations. Legalized by the Socialist Government, they crushed the Berlin Communists; and the National Assembly met to draft a constitution and conclude peace.

'In 1919, as in 1945', writes Mr. Wheeler-Bennett, 'no collective sense of war-guilt was evident among the German people', and the peace terms, however just, came as a shock to them. Ebert, inclining to rejection, consulted the military on the possibility of armed resistance. Their soundings yielded most discouraging results: the people were war-weary; the extreme left would rise, the Allies march in; the Officer Corps would be destroyed, and the name of Germany disappear from the map. The reply of the Army Command left no choice to Government and parliament; yet formally the decision to sign was made by the parliamentary ministers, henceforth the target of Nationalist hatred, abuse, and bullets.

The Kapp *Putsch* of March 1920, an attempt of the extreme Right and of rebel generals to seize power, was defeated by a general strike, while the Reichswehr under General von Seeckt remained neutral. And yet, once the *Putsch* was over, Ebert, to avoid chaos, had to renew with Seeckt the pact of November 1918; and when workers, armed during the *Putsch*, refused to disarm, they were ruthlessly put down by the Free Corps. Again, when during and after the Ruhr occupation revolutionary and separatist movements broke out in various parts of Germany, the government of the Reich was entrusted to Seeckt and the Reichswehr, the artificers and guardians of the German unitary state.

What mattered to Seeckt was the restoration of German power. Political strife being detrimental to discipline, he made the Reichswehr eschew sterile ambitions and adventures: aristocratic in character, ideologically linked up with the old Army, under him it kept aloof from current politics. Technically he made it a military microcosm capable of unlimited expansion. With an intake of a mere 8,000 a year, he could insist on high standards of physical and intellectual fitness. At one time there were 40,000 N.C.O.s among its statutory 96,000 'other ranks': this was to be an army not of mercenaries but of leaders. Seeckt envisaged the future war as one of movement, to be waged by comparatively small armies of high quality. The necessary equipment, denied to Germany by the peace treaty, he would obtain from Soviet Russia; for him and the Reichswehr she was the natural ally, France an implacable enemy, and Poland's very existence was intolerable: the Russo-German frontier of 1914 was to be restored. Close contact was secretly maintained with the Red General Staff; aircraft, motors, etc., were to be manufactured in Russia; tank and flying schools were established with German participation. New types of weapons were studied, and ordnance works in neutral countries were brought under German control; in December 1925, the month of the Locarno Agreements, Krupp acquired a controlling interest in the great Bofors works in Sweden, to manufacture there the latest patterns of heavy guns, anti-aircraft guns, and tanks.

Stresemann wished to conciliate the Western Powers in order to expedite the end of Allied military occupation. His aim was the same as Seeckt's: the restoration of the German *Machtstaat*. From a study of the available evidence, Mr. Wheeler-Bennett and the eminent American historian, Professor Sontag, have reached the conclusion that Stresemann, holder of the Nobel Peace Prize, was well-informed of Seeckt's policy and fully aware of Germany's illegal rearmament, first in Russia and later in Germany. A renewal of Germany's aggressive force was well and truly secured, and had these men been able to complete their work, Germany's frontiers and dominance would have been re-established and extended by a different version either of Munich or of the Ribbentrop-Molotov treaty.

Ebert died in February 1925, and Hindenburg, in his seventy-ninth year, became his successor. The President was now actual Supreme Commander of the armed forces and his military entourage started dabbling in politics—foremost, Kurt von Schleicher, a brilliant staff officer with a passion for intrigue. Seeckt resigned in October 1926. His period, writes Mr. Wheeler-Bennett, 'had seen the German Army established as the strongest single political factor within the State, the recognized guardian of the Reich; the Schleicher period saw the descent of the Army into the arena of political intrigue, with a consequent besmirching of its reputation and the ultimate destruction of its authority'.

Schleicher is to Mr. Wheeler-Bennett 'the evil genius of the later Weimar Period'. In time of parliamentary decay and political confusion a clever intriguer in the entourage of Hindenburg, that senile *faux bon homme*, could indeed do infinite harm. Yet so far as the Reichswehr is concerned, can the blame be squarely placed on his shoulders? Was Seeckt's political aloofness ever sincere? Did not his attitude to revolt vary with the quarter from which it came? By 1930, as Mr. Wheeler-Bennett points out, both officers and the rank and file of the

Reichswehr were infected with Nazism. When, by order of Gröner, then Minister of Defence, three subalterns were prosecuted for Nazi propaganda, their Colonel, the later General Beck, leader of the conspiracy of 20 July 1944, defended them: 'The Reichswehr', he said, 'is told daily that it is an army of leaders. What is a young officer to understand by that?' A year later Seeckt himself appeared on Hitler's platform at the Harzburg Rally. And when, in April 1932, Gröner, the man with the cleanest record in that sordid period, tried to suppress the S.A. and the S.S., he was told by Schleicher that he 'no longer enjoyed the confidence of the Army'. They were dreaming 'of a martial state in which the masses, galvanized and inspired by modified National Socialism, would be directed and disciplined by the Army'.

In the early days of the Third Reich, the Army was a petted favourite, deferred to in all things; they, in turn, preserved impervious equanimity toward the ever-increasing horrors of Nazi terror and the moral record of the S.A. But within a year a situation was developing of supreme danger for the Army: while its guardian, Hindenburg, was rapidly declining, Röhm, at the head of 2,500,000 disgruntled Storm Troopers, demanded that the army should be merged with the Nazi para-military formations. Then a compact was concluded between Hitler and Blomberg, and unanimously accepted by the senior officers: the Army was to support Hitler for the presidency, and in return he undertook to put an end to the military claims of Röhm and the S.A. Hitler's part of the bargain was fulfilled in the Blood Purge of 30 June; but other disputes also were settled that day by murder. The upper ranks of the military hierarchy had been well aware of what was coming, and by permitting the butchery which rid them of rivals accepted the moral standards of the Third Reich. On 25 July followed the murder of Dollfuss. And when Hindenburg died on 1 August, and Hitler proclaimed himself Führer and Reich Chancellor, Blomberg, Fritsch, and Raeder, followed by all the armed forces, took an oath of personal fealty to him. They became Hitler's Army.

In March 1935 Hitler announced Germany's rearmament and introduced conscription, which filled the ranks with young

Nazis. A year later, against opposition from the military, he took what seemed a mad risk by marching into the Rhineland, and scored a victory over his hesitant generals: now the last remnant of respect vanished from his attitude towards them. Even within the Reich they ceased to be a serious political factor. They had been great while Socialist ministers reverently deferred to their judgement; they grew puny when roughly handled by Nazi toughs. On 5 November 1937, Hitler expounded to them his plans with regard to Austria and Czechoslovakia. Once more they were appalled at the risks he proposed to take. Still, it was not over basic issues but over Blomberg's marriage and the Fritsch scandal that, in January 1938, an acute crisis broke out among the top ranks of the German Army. For the first time they rose against the iniquities of the Gestapo because one of their own body was the victim. Even so their action was ill-concerted and ineffective; and interest in that disgusting and farcical story vanished when Hitler successfully invaded Austria.

Pastor Dietrich Bonhöffer, executed by the Nazis in April 1945, said in 1940, at the peak of Nazi successes: 'If we claim to be Christians, there is no room for expediency. Hitler is antiChrist. Therefore we must go on with our work and eliminate him whether he be successful or not'. And Bonhöffer prayed for the defeat of Germany, for, said he, 'only in defeat can we atone for the terrible crimes we have committed against Europe and the world'. There were Germans who opposed Hitler on moral grounds, and honour must be done to their memory. But, writes Mr. Wheeler-Bennett, their number was 'small beyond belief in a nation of 80,000,000'. The opposition in the summer of 1938 was not against war but against the horrifying prospect of a war which Germany might not win. Accurate knowledge of Germany's weakness and an inaccurate evaluation of the strength and courage of the Powers opposed to her roused resistance to Hitler in military circles. Was there a serious plot against him, baulked by Chamberlain's journeys to Berchtesgaden and Munich? Mr. Wheeler-Bennett's examination of 'that carefully organized uprising which withered at the first touch of reality' discloses ineptitude in planning and fatal hesitancy in execution, and the rapidity with which the conspirators seized an excuse for their inaction is, he writes, 'at least an indication of their unreadiness'.

On that conspiracy, much publicized at the Nuremberg trials, followed a long, almost unbroken period of plotting, of amateurish efforts, of quasi-plans, and fanciful academic discussion: till at long last the approaching national disaster forced on the *coup* of 20 July 1944, again remarkable for ineptitude and hesitancy in execution. Mr. Wheeler-Bennett's analysis of the available mass of evidence enables the reader to see those conspiracies as one whole, and as part of the history of the German Officer Corps, or rather of its top-ranking circles. For while a majority of these, at one time or another, participated in conspiratorial talks, or at least were cognizant of them, nothing is known of a revolutionary ferment among junior officers or among the rank and file. Similarly support from the masses never entered into the calculations of plotters against Hitler. When in October 1939 the so-called 'X-report', alleging that the British Government were ready to conclude peace with a non-Nazi Government on terms favourable to Germany, was shown by General Thomas to Brauchitsch, then Commander-in-Chief of the German Army, he took no action against the conspirators nor against Hitler either.

> I could have had Hitler arrested easily (he said to one of the conspirators after the war)... But... why should I have taken such action? It would have been action against the German people... The German people were all for Hitler. And they had good reason to be, particularly the working man. Nobody had ever done so much to raise their standards of living as Hitler.

There was a revolt of starving working men in Eastern Germany in June 1953, but when well fed by Hitler, at other people's expense, they had no thought of rising. Apparently revolutionaries, at least in Germany, march like armies on their stomachs, except that theirs have to be empty.

Who then were these German resisters to Hitler? Foremost generals, diplomats, and high civil servants opposed to him on technical and professional grounds: they agreed with the aims of his foreign policy, and at each stage wished to consolidate the gains secured by him, but feared that his methods would engulf Germany in fresh disaster. Hence the spirit of resistance in them rose or dropped in accordance with the dangers he incurred or the successes he achieved. Moral disapproval was at best a contributory factor, usually weak, or it was altogether absent: before Hitler plunged into foreign adventures most of these men had readily served him, undeterred by his crimes. In November 1939, one of the military chiefs thus defined his attitude toward revolt against Hitler: 'The military situation of Germany', he said, 'particularly on account of the pact of non-aggression with Russia, is such that a breach of my oath to the Führer could not possibly be justified.' Conscience determined by fine calculations makes neither effective rebels nor heroes.

In fact these conspiracies were mostly of the 'palace revolution' type, and leading plotters at times considered replacing Hitler by Göring, or even by Himmler. When in 1943 Field-Marshal von Bock, whose Headquarters in Russia were the operational centre of conspiracy, declared that he would not join any plot unless Himmler was in it, an attempt was made to gain Himmler's co-operation. Popitz, Prussian Minister of Finance, conveyed to him some of the aims of the plotters, and claimed to have found him not averse in principle: a common friend was allowed to meet Allied Intelligence officers in Switzerland, and only when a relevant message from an Allied agency was decoded by German rivals of Himmler, did he disavow and intern that friend. That such talks should have been possible illustrates conditions in both German camps and the *Realpolitik* of the German 'resistance' movement. But foresight in men without backbone, unsupported as it is by moral convictions or passion, cannot engender determined revolutionary action. Hence the ineffectiveness of the one big plot, that of 20 July 1944.

As the Russian armies were pressing on and German cities were reduced to rubble by Anglo-American bombing, a sense of urgency arose among the plotters. Once rid of Hitler they counted on being able to negotiate, and perhaps to start a bidding-match between the Anglo-Saxon Powers and Soviet Russia. Still, the only way to eliminate Hitler satisfactorily was to kill him. Many generals claimed to be bound by their oath of allegiance to obey Hitler, though apparently not to protect him from murder: was this an involution of the German conscience unfathomable to non-Germans, or disguised fear of the living Hitler? Either way it proved decisive on 20 July. But why did the many plots against his life all fail? Why did a conspiracy of unequalled dimensions, with exceptional facilities and means, fail to achieve in seven years what in other countries is often done by groups of insignificant conspirators? Because most of the would-be German assassins called off at the last moment; while two attempts which were carried through mark a new technique in tyrannicide: murder by indirect fire, *in absentia*. Had Count Stauffenburg, instead of leaving behind a time bomb, handled it himself, he would have died twelve hours earlier than he did, but Hitler would have died with him. There is cogency in the argument of Erich Kordt, who himself claims to have planned in 1939 Hitler's assassination, but admits to having dropped the idea 'with suspicious speed'. 'Few', he writes, 'are prepared to strive for an end and renounce seeing it accomplished'; and 'all watchfulness . . . can protect a tyrant only against those who mean to witness the sequel. . .'. The plotters of 20 July were to witness the horrible sequel of an attempt that failed.

Time after time before the war Hitler had proved right and his generals had proved wrong; but over questions of policy and not of strategy. During the war even in these his judgement repeatedly triumphed over theirs: they refused to operate the occupation of Denmark and Norway, being convinced that it would fail; and they did not believe that a break-through in France was possible. Their prestige and authority consequently dwindled, while the disdainful insolence and ruthless brutality with which Hitler treated them grew beyond bounds. After 20 July 1944, he could give vent to long suppressed feelings: he had the aristocratic military caste in the hollow of his hand. 'You dirty old man', shouted the Nazi judge Freisler at an ex-Field-Marshal; 'You are a filthy rascal', at another officer.

They, for their part, made 'pitiable attempts to excuse themselves', and 'not one of them', writes Mr. Wheeler-Bennett,
'could muster up the strength of will to interrupt the flow of
Freisler's obscene rhetoric and to make it clear . . . why they
stood in the dock and why they would shortly die'. 'It is my
wish that they be hanged like cattle', decreed Hitler; and they
were hanged on meat hooks screwed into the ceiling.

And those not directly implicated in the plot? The failure of
a few 'to carry out what all had known to be necessary' left the
Officer Corps fawning and frightened. They were ordered to
give in future the Hitler salute, and to declare their adherence
to National Socialism. 'None resigned, none resisted'. 'The
Nemesis of Power' had overtaken the once-proud Officer Corps.